You'll never get enough of these cowboys!

Talented Harlequin Blaze author Debbi Rawlins makes all your cowboy dreams come true with her popular miniseries

Made in Montana.

The little town of Blackfoot Falls isn't so sleepy anymore...

In fact, it seems everyone's staying up late!

Get your hands on a hot cowboy with

#837 *Anywhere with You*

(March 2015)

#849 *Come On Over*

(June 2015)

#861 *This Kiss*

(September 2015)

And remember, the sexiest cowboys are Made in Montana!

Dear Reader,

I think I'm starting to have a thing for rodeo cowboys. In *This Kiss* you'll meet Ethan Styles, a champion bull rider and the third rodeo hero I've written for the Made in Montana series.

During late spring and throughout the summer, there are a number of rodeos that take place close to my home. I like most of the events—not so much others, which I'll refrain from naming though you'll probably be able to guess from reading this book. But something occurred to me while doing some research, and by that I mean I begin "skimming" one of my rodeo books and forget to put it down. It seems my growing fondness for this true American sport has a lot to do with the cowboys, for whom rodeo is not just a sport or a job but a way of life. These men are a different breed. So much passion and dedication. What's not to love?

The heroine, Sophie, is a bit younger than most of my heroines, but she is so perfect for Ethan, I couldn't resist.

I hope everyone is enjoying their summer!

All my best,

Debbi Rawlins

Debbi Rawlins

This Kiss

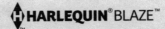

HARLEQUIN® BLAZE™

Recycling programs for this product may not exist in your area.

ISBN-13: 978-0-373-79865-0

This Kiss

Copyright © 2015 by Debbi Quattrone

The publisher acknowledges the copyright holder of the additional work:

Hard Knocks

Copyright © 2014 by Lori Foster

This edition published by arrangement with Harlequin Books S.A.

For questions and comments about the quality of this book, please contact us at CustomerService@Harlequin.com.

Printed in U.S.A.

CONTENTS

Debbi Rawlins grew up in the country and loved Western movies and books. Her first crush was on a cowboy—okay, he was an actor in the role of a cowboy, but she was only eleven, so it counts. It was in Houston, Texas, where she first started writing for Harlequin, and now she has her own ranch...of sorts. Instead of horses, she has four dogs, four cats, a trio of goats and free-range cattle on a few acres in gorgeous rural Utah.

Books by Debbi Rawlins

HARLEQUIN BLAZE

Made in Montana

Barefoot Blue Jean Night
Own the Night
On a Snowy Christmas Night
You're Still the One
No One Needs to Know
From This Moment On
Alone with You
Need You Now
Behind Closed Doors
Anywhere with You
Come On Over

To get the inside scoop on Harlequin Blaze and its talented writers, be sure to check out BlazeAuthors.com.

All backlist available in ebook format.

Visit the Author Profile page at Harlequin.com for more titles.

THIS KISS

Debbi Rawlins

1

"GOTCHA!" SOPHIE MICHAELS grinned when she saw the motel's address on the computer screen. After a quick sip of morning coffee, she sent the file to her partner, Lola, who was sitting in the next office.

The rush from *getting her man* lasted barely a minute. Sophie sank back in her chair and sighed. Lately, the thrill of success was fleeting and not all that sweet.

Locating the deadbeat dad was rewarding because, well…he had three kids to support. But if he was going to jump bail anyway, couldn't he have done a better job of covering his tracks? For God's sake, a fourth grader could've found him.

After four years the job was finally getting to her. Too much sitting at the computer. Too much of the same old thing every day. Skip traces, lame excuses, shaken or re-signed parents putting up collateral for their wayward children or, almost as frequently, the roles being reversed. Here in Wattsville, Wyoming, nothing much exciting happened. Oh, they had bank robberies occasionally and liquor store holdups, but those types of criminals tended to be really stupid and that made her job boring.

Sophie sighed. Working in the bail bond business

wouldn't be forever. Mostly she'd signed on to help Lola get the company off the ground. Sophie looked on her cousin more like a sister. And Lola didn't mind that Sophie was sticking around only until she'd figured out what to do with her life.

Rolling her chair away from her dinged-up metal desk, Sophie dropped her chin to her chest and stretched her neck to the side. Feeling the strain of muscles that had been worked too hard earlier at the gym, she tried not to whimper. At least not loud enough for Lola to hear.

The front door to the reception area squeaked open and she glanced at the clock. "Oh, come on," she muttered. How could it be only eight-fifteen? It felt like noon.

They were expecting Mandy, the third member of their team, to return from Jackson Hole sometime this morning. But in case it was a potential client, Sophie got up. When she heard Hawk's voice, she promptly sat back down. And wished her door was closed. Hawk was Lola's sleazy boyfriend of three months. Sophie didn't like him, but so far she'd kept her mouth shut.

Lola hadn't had much luck with men in the past, but two people had never been less suited to each other. Hawk wasn't very bright, was sometimes crude and was under the delusion that riding a Harley and wearing black leather made him a badass.

He was a poser, no doubt in Sophie's mind. She knew something about desperately pretending to be someone you weren't just to fit in. A tiny bit of sympathy for him stopped her from telling Lola that his real name was Floyd and he was a high school dropout.

Sophie smiled. The idiot didn't get that she was really, really good with computers. And she knew a whole lot more about him than she'd let on.

Which she'd keep to herself. Unless Floyd kept pissing

her off. She wasn't the quiet, naive young girl she used to be in high school. Unlike Floyd aka Hawk, she had put a great deal of effort into transforming herself.

"Hey, Shorty," Hawk said, lounging against her office door frame. "Missed you at the gym this morning."

She hated the nickname, which he knew. Anyway, five-four wasn't that short. She gave his tall, lanky body a once-over. "Like you've ever seen the inside of a gym."

He laughed. "Gotta admit, you're looking pretty buff," he said, pushing back his straggly hair and eyeing her legs.

"Lola's in her office."

"I know. She's busy."

"So am I." Resisting the urge to tug down the hem of her bike shorts, Sophie swiveled in her chair so that her legs were under the desk, her gaze on the monitor.

"You guys working on something big?"

She noticed that line 2 was lit. Lola was on the phone. "Why are you still here?"

"Chillax, Shorty. Just making conversation while I wait for the old lady."

The front door opened again and Hawk glanced over his shoulder. His look of dread made Sophie smile. It had to be Mandy. She'd been working as a bounty hunter in Colorado before Lola hired her two years ago, and she could be intimidating at times. Plus, she didn't like Hawk any more than Sophie did. Only, Mandy wasn't as circumspect.

A whoop came from Lola's office. "Okay, ladies, we've got a live one. Mandy, are you here?"

Sophie leaped out of her chair and barreled past Hawk, who had enough smarts to get out of her way. "Somebody jumped bail?"

"Oh yeah." Lola walked out of her office waving a piece of paper. "You'll never guess who."

The waiting area was small, with two chairs, a ficus that

was alive only because Lola remembered to water it and a rack of magazines, where Mandy stood, tall, beefed-up and calm as could be. She wasn't the excitable type. "Ethan Styles," she said, and dropped her duffel bag.

Lola shoved back her long red hair and sighed. "How did you know?"

"Ethan Styles," Sophie murmured under her breath. She must've heard wrong. If his name was on the list of bonds they'd posted, she would've noticed. She knew him...sort of... "Who did you say?"

Lola's concerned gaze found Sophie. "I'm pretty sure you remember Ethan."

"The rodeo guy, right?" Hawk moved to the circle and sidled up to Lola when Sophie and Mandy gave him butt-out glares. "He's that hotshot bull rider."

Lola nodded and looked at Mandy. "You just get back from Jackson Hole?"

"An hour ago," Mandy said with a curious glance at Sophie. "I turned Jergens over to Deputy Martin."

Sophie couldn't seem to slow down her brain. Too many memories of Ethan revolved like a slide show on speed. She hadn't seen him up close since high school. She'd gone to a few rodeos just to see him, but only from the bleachers and it had been a while. Sometimes she watched him on TV, but not often. She wasn't a kid anymore and there was only so much daydreaming a woman could do without feeling like a dope.

"You get any sleep yet?" Lola asked Mandy, who just smiled.

"I hate to send you out again, but I got a tip that Styles might be headed for northwest Montana. A town called Blackfoot Falls."

"No shit. Pretty boy has an outstanding warrant?" Hawk

laughed. "What did he get locked up for? Screwing some-body's wife?"

The expression on Lola's face hinted that Hawk might not be far off the mark.

It wouldn't surprise Sophie if he was in trouble because of a woman. Half the girls in school had had the hots for him. Even now he left female fans across the country pant-ing, but so what? Lola was mistaken if she thought Ethan's reputation with the ladies bothered Sophie. He didn't faze her. Not anymore.

"Why didn't he pay his own bail? Between his winnings and endorsement deals, he has to have money," Sophie said, mostly thinking out loud.

Lola shrugged. "He wouldn't be the first pro athlete to blow his cash on stupid things," she said. "We have the pink slip for his motor coach as collateral, so I had no prob-lem with posting. I have to say, though, I'm surprised he skipped. He's not due in court until Monday, but he wasn't supposed to leave the state."

"I'll do it." Sophie squared her shoulders when they all stared at her. "I'll go after him."

Lola shook her head. "Not a good idea, Soph."

"You've never worked in the field." Mandy's quiet re-minder somehow felt like a betrayal.

Even though Sophie had started kickboxing and tae kwon do back in college, it was Mandy who'd inspired her to go all out, work her body to its full potential. So-phie was in the best physical shape of her life and Mandy knew it. Anyway, Ethan might not come along willingly, but he wasn't the type to get rough.

"I told you guys I wanted to be more involved." She glared first at Lola, and then Mandy. "I know Ethan. I can bring him back with the least amount of fuss."

Hawk snorted. "No way. You don't know Styles."

"Shut up," Mandy said without looking at him. Her gaze stayed on Sophie. "You think you're ready?"

"I know I am." She glanced at Lola, who'd just given Hawk an impatient look. So maybe all wasn't peachy keen with the lovebirds. Good. Her cousin deserved better.

Lola met her gaze. "No, not Ethan. You can have the next one."

"I'm not asking for permission. I own half this company." Flexing her tense shoulders, Sophie ignored the looks of surprise. She and Lola never argued. Not over business, or their personal lives. "Text me the details. I'll go home, grab a few things and leave within the hour."

"Come on, Soph." Lola pinched the bridge of her nose. "Let's talk privately. Please."

"What she says makes sense." Hawk cut Lola short, earning him a warning look, which he obviously didn't like judging by his creepy scowl. "Why not let her go after him?"

"Excuse me—" Sophie stopped. Hawk was defending her? Okay, now, that was weird. She didn't need his help, but hey, bonus points for trying. "This isn't up for discussion," she said. "All we're doing is wasting time."

"Knowing him might not be an advantage," Mandy said. "Surprise is your best weapon. He sees you, he could run."

"Ethan won't remember me." Sophie avoided Lola's gaze. "Even if he does, he won't associate me with Lola's Bail Bonds."

Lola followed Sophie into her office. "We need to talk, kiddo," she said, closing the door behind her.

"You're not changing my mind." Sophie sifted through her cluttered drawer and found her wallet. Now, where were her keys?

She crouched to check under her desk and found them

next to a protein bar she'd misplaced yesterday. Grabbing them both, she pushed to her feet.

"Will you at least hear me out?" Her cousin's dark eyes weren't just worried but annoyed.

"Go ahead." Sophie unwrapped the bar and stuck half of it in her mouth, since she wouldn't have time to eat anything else. She had to get on the road fast. No telling how much of a head start Ethan had… "When did he leave for Montana, do you know?"

"Are you going to listen to me at all?"

"Probably not."

"Goddammit, Sophie." Lola paused and lowered her voice. "We can't afford for you to get all goo-goo-eyed over him. He'll sweet-talk you into letting him go and we'll be screwed."

Sophie chewed a bit, then said, "Wow, your faith in me is really touching."

"It's not that. The money's important, but I hate to think of you getting all twisted up over him again."

"Oh, for God's sake, I was never twisted up."

"Yes, you were." Lola smiled. "Don't forget, I was there. Anyway, that was high school, so you were allowed."

"Exactly. It was high school. I was fifteen. We had a fleeting encounter. Don't make a big deal out of it."

"He was your hero," Lola said, her voice softening.

Sophie turned away to pick up her gym bag. "You're only twenty-eight. I'm sure you still remember what it was like to be fifteen."

At the beginning of her freshman year, Sophie and her mom had moved to Wyoming. Lola had been a junior and the only person Sophie knew in her new school. They hadn't become friends quickly. Her cousin had had her own clique, and back then, Sophie had entered a nerdy phase, trying to balance her high IQ and an awkward social life.

That alone hadn't made her the target of bullies. Having had the audacity to wear the *wrong* dress was the line she'd crossed. She found out later that the most popular girl in school had worn the same sundress the week before Sophie even started at Wattsville High. The whole thing was ridiculous, considering that Ashley had huge boobs and Sophie had little more than two mosquito bites. So of course Ashley had looked so much better in the spaghetti-strap dress.

God, Sophie still remembered what it had felt like to have those girls come after her with scissors. They'd cut her dress to ribbons before Ethan had stopped them and put his jacket over her shoulders.

Turned out Ashley was Ethan's girlfriend. But he'd been furious when he stepped in and warned them off. After that, the girls still gave her evil looks, but they kept their distance.

Damn straight he'd been her hero.

"Are you still following his career?" Lola asked.

"No." Sophie set the gym bag on her chair and shut down her laptop, refusing to look up. "I know you saw me at my worst, sneaking around, following him, trying to stay on his radar. Frankly it embarrasses me to even think about it." All while he'd acted as if she hadn't existed. That part she left out, and met Lola's gaze. "Did you and Hawk have a fight?"

Lola's brows went up. "Why?"

"I saw the look you gave him."

"No, it's just…" Lola waved dismissively. "I'd already told him he shouldn't be hanging around here."

Sophie tucked her tablet under her arm. "Look, the thing with Ethan happened a long time ago. I was a kid." She smiled. "I can do this."

Lola studied her for a moment. "Okay," she said with a resigned sigh. "I just don't understand why you'd want to."

"I know," Sophie said softly. She didn't quite get it herself. It wasn't as if she needed closure, but in a weird way, that was exactly how it felt. She stopped halfway to the door. "Don't you think it's odd he jumped bail? Ethan has a reputation for being a stand-up guy."

"I don't know what he's thinking. He certainly doesn't have a low profile."

"Nope. The National Finals Rodeo in Las Vegas starts in about a week. He's going for his second championship title—" She saw the concern in Lola's eyes. "I read something about it online the other day," she murmured. "Try not to worry, okay? I've got this."

She hoped.

THE WATERING HOLE was noisy, crowded with cowboys drinking beer and gorgeous accommodating women dressed to kill. Ethan Styles had frequented hundreds of bars just like this one in the nine years since he turned pro. He knew what it was like the night before a rodeo, especially in a small town like Blackfoot Falls. So why in the hell had he suggested meeting his friend Matt here?

Somehow Ethan had gotten the dumb idea that this rodeo would be different. No prize money was involved or qualifying points. The event was a fund-raiser for Safe Haven, a large animal sanctuary, so all the ticket and concession money went directly to them. But he should've known better. Rodeo fans were a loyal bunch, and having to travel to this remote Montana town obviously hadn't bothered them.

Normally he was up for signing autographs and getting hit on by hot women. But with the finals a week away he'd been on edge since he hit Montana late this morning.

After that bogus arrest in Wyoming and then hearing how fellow bull rider Tommy Lunt had busted his knee, foreboding had prickled the back of his neck.

He'd missed the finals himself because of injuries. Twice. Last year broken ribs and a punctured lung had sidelined him. Two seasons before that, it had been an elbow injury. So he had cause to be jumpy.

"Hey, Styles, 'bout time you showed up." Kenny Horton stood at the bar with another bronc rider and three women, who all turned to eyeball Ethan.

He shook his head when Kenny motioned for him to join them. "Maybe later. I'm meeting someone."

"Right behind you."

At the sound of Matt Gunderson's voice, Ethan grinned and turned around to shake his hand. "Glad to see you, buddy."

"Same here. What's it been…a year?"

"About that." Ethan moved aside for a short, curvy blonde who'd just entered the bar. Their gazes met briefly, surprise flickering in her brown eyes. But then she brushed past him. "So, how's retirement?" he asked Matt and shifted so he could watch the blonde walk up to the bar.

The seats were all taken. A cowboy jumped to his feet and offered her his stool. Shaking her head, she dug into her pocket. Her tight jeans didn't leave room for much, but she managed to pull out a cell phone. She wasn't wearing a wedding ring. He always checked, though it hadn't done him any good last week.

Wendy hadn't been wearing one when he met her at the Ponderosa Saloon last Saturday, or when she invited him to her ranch that night. That hadn't made her any less married, and to a mean, rich son of a bitch on top of everything.

"Retirement? Shit, I work twice as hard for half the money," Matt said with a laugh. "But yeah, it was time."

That part Ethan didn't understand. Matt had been the one to beat. Yet out of the blue he'd just quit competing. Talk around the tour was that his new wife might've had something to do with it. "So, no regrets?"

"Not a one." Matt frowned. "You can't be thinking of getting out—"

"Hell no. Now that you're off the circuit, maybe I can finally win another title."

"Right." Matt laughed. "I seem to remember you leaving me in the dust more than a few times."

"Never when it counted."

"Man, you've had some bad luck right before the finals. I should've convinced you to drop out when we changed the date. You're the main draw this weekend. A lot of people are coming to see you ride Twister, but I should've thought this through."

"Come on, you probably figured I wouldn't make it to the finals."

Matt reared his head back, eyes narrowed. "What the hell's the matter with you, Styles?"

Ethan grinned. "Just joking." No way he'd admit that he had considered bailing because he couldn't risk injury. But then he'd only be superstitious about bad karma or some other bullshit. "It's a worthy cause. I'm glad to do it."

Just before Ethan turned to check on the blonde, he caught his friend's sympathetic look. Most rodeo cowboys started young and came from families of die-hard fans. Matt had been a casual fan who'd climbed onto his first bull at a late age, and yet he understood the pressure coming at Ethan from all sides. Winning another gold buckle wasn't just about ego or satisfying a lifelong dream. He came from rodeo royalty. Both his parents held multiple world champion titles. Most of their fans were also his fans. A lot of expectations drove him to succeed.

The woman was still standing at the bar, guys on either side of her vying for her attention, but she didn't seem interested. She slowly sipped a drink, checked her phone and then leaned over the bar to talk to the older woman filling pitchers of beer.

Ethan smirked to himself. Bending over like that sure wouldn't discourage guys from hitting on her. She knew how to wear a pair of plain faded jeans. Her boots were brown, low-heeled, scuffed. And the long-sleeve blue T-shirt was nothing fancy. No, she sure wasn't dressed to be noticed like the other women circling the room. Maybe she lived on a nearby ranch and had just quit work.

Damn, she was hot.

And familiar. Yeah, women were plentiful for a bull rider, and he was no saint. He also wasn't the type to forget a name or face. It sure felt as though he'd run into her before. More than that, he felt this odd pull… The kind of pull that could get him into trouble. Which he did not need, especially not now.

Someone called out to Matt and he waved in acknowledgment. "We're not gonna find a table or a place at the bar. Maybe we should head over to the diner. Unless you're looking to hook up with that blonde."

"What blonde?" Ethan asked, and Matt smiled. "That describes half the women in here."

"I'm talking about the one at the bar you've been eyeing."

"Nah, I'm not looking for company. I'm keeping my nose clean until the finals."

"A whole week? You'll never make it."

"Probably not." Ethan laughed and glanced back at the bar. "Is she local?"

Matt studied her for a moment. "I don't think so."

"Well, I'll be damned if it isn't the twins," a voice boomed from the back room.

Ethan and Matt exchanged glances. They both knew it was Tex, a bronc rider from Dallas. Though he wasn't the only one who called them *the twins*. They'd joined the pro tour within months of each other, and in the beginning they'd often been mistaken for brothers. Ethan figured it wasn't so much because they shared similar builds, or even because they both had light brown hair and blue eyes. It was their height. Six feet was tall for a bull rider.

"What are you boys doing standing there talking like two old women?" Tex yelled, a pool stick in one hand, an empty mug in the other. "Grab yourselves a pitcher and get on back here."

"Guess he's had a few," Ethan said. Tex was quiet by nature. But after a couple of beers…

"He'd better be able to ride tomorrow," Matt muttered, then turned when someone else shouted his name.

More people had poured into the bar. Ethan was willing to bet the place had reached capacity before the last ten customers had squeezed inside. And now that big-mouthed Tex had called attention to them, fans were approaching him and Matt for autographs.

They each accepted a pen and began scrawling their names. "You check in at The Boarding House yet?" Matt asked under his breath.

"An hour ago."

"It's not too late. You can stay out at the Lone Wolf. We've got a big house, trailer hookups. The inn's overbooked, so the owner won't have any trouble renting out your room. And my wife's dying to meet you."

"Hey, that's right. You're a married man now. Sorry I missed your wedding."

"No problem. I warned Rachel there'd be conflicts no matter which weekend she chose."

Ethan smiled as he passed the Safe Haven flyer he'd just signed to a middle-aged woman wearing a promotional Professional Bull Riders T-shirt from the 2010 finals, the year he wanted wiped from his memory forever. To be kept from the finals because of an injury was one thing, but to make it that far and then get hurt in the third round? Talk about fate landing a sucker punch.

This year nothing was going to keep him from the finals. Or from winning another gold buckle.

Nothing. Period.

2

SOPHIE SURE WISHED she'd known he was here in Blackfoot Falls for a rodeo before she'd left Wyoming. The event was a fund-raiser, so of course it wasn't listed on the PBR tour. The whole town, which wasn't saying much, since it was so small they had no traffic lights, was busting at the seams with rodeo fans. There was only one inn, a dude ranch twenty minutes away and a number of impromptu bed-and-breakfasts scattered around the area, all of which were booked. So was the large trailer park over thirty minutes away, not that a vacancy there would do her any good.

Somehow she had to get him alone. No clue how she was going to do it with so many fans clamoring for his attention. Those crazy people would string her up if they knew she planned to drag their favorite bull rider back to Wyoming.

The buckle bunnies worried her most. Turning completely around so that her back was against the bar, she sipped her tonic water and watched the women practically line up, just waiting their turns to hit on Ethan.

She didn't care one bit. If he had enough stamina to screw every last one of them, then God bless him. She was twenty-six, not a silly teenager anymore, and he no longer haunted her dreams. Though if he took one of those eager young ladies back to his room for the night, Sophie could have a problem.

It might mean she'd have to wait till morning to bag him. That left her a very narrow window before the rodeo started at noon.

Maybe she'd have to seduce him herself.

The thought sent a bolt of heat zinging through her body. A hurried sip of tonic water barely made it down her throat. He was still hot as hell. She'd be fooling herself if she couldn't admit that much. Tall and lean with the perfect proportion of muscle, and those dreamy blue eyes... Good Lord.

Bumping into him when she first entered the bar had thrown her. She hadn't been prepared at all. But the wig had done its job. Even up close he hadn't recognized her, and now she was ready for him.

In the middle of signing an autograph, he swung a look at her and she shifted her weight to her other foot. Okay, maybe his gaze hadn't landed on her but vaguely in her direction. Unfortunately her female parts couldn't tell the difference.

Seducing him? That might have to take a few steps back to plan Z.

"Now, why are you sittin' here drinkin' alone, darlin'?" The same husky and very tipsy cowboy who'd offered her a beer earlier wove too close, nearly unseating the guy on her left.

She steadied Romeo with a brief hand on his shoulder. Boy, she sure didn't need either of the men making a scene. "Are you here for the rodeo tomorrow?" she asked.

"You bet."

"Fan or rider?"

He frowned, clearly affronted.

Sophie smiled, despite the wave of beer breath that reached her. "Better go easy on the booze if you're competing."

The younger cowboy sitting on the stool twisted around and grinned. "Yeah, Brady, you don't wanna give those calves a leg up."

Ah, they knew each other. Made sense, since they were both probably here for the rodeo. Sophie relaxed a bit, and while the two men traded barbs, she slid a glance at Ethan, who was still surrounded by women.

Oddly he didn't seem all that interested in any of them. Not even the blondes. According to the articles and blogs she'd read earlier, his past three girlfriends had been blondes. Although it seemed he hadn't stayed with any of them for more than a few months. Probably thought he was too hot for any one woman to handle. Or decided it was his duty to spread the hotness around.

The cowboy, whose name was apparently Brady and who continued to stand too close, said something she didn't catch. Shifting her attention to him, she wondered if a well-placed knee could seem accidental. "Excuse me?"

He turned his head to look at Ethan. "Okay, now I see why you're being so uppity. You've already got your sights set on Styles. Figures." Lifting his beer, he mumbled, "Damn bull riders," before taking a gulp.

Oh, crap. Was she being that obvious? "Who's Styles?"

Brady frowned. "Are you kiddin'?"

She shook her head, the picture of innocence.

"See, Brady?" Grinning, the other cowboy elbowed him. "She's not snubbing you 'cause you're a calf roper. I bet she's got a whole lot more reasons than that."

Sophie ignored the troublemaker. "A calf roper?"

"That's right, darlin'. You're lookin' at a two-time champ."

"So you're one of those guys who chases the poor little calves and then ties them up?"

Brady's boastful grin slipped. "It's all for sport, darlin', don't you understand?"

"No, I don't. Not at all." She faked a shudder. "I always feel so sorry for the calves."

Even the guy sitting on the stool had shut up and swiveled around to face the other way. Brady just stared at her, then shook his head and walked off.

Sophie hid a smile behind a sip of tonic and turned back to Ethan. He was watching her. This time there was nothing vague about it. He gave her a slow smile and a small nod. She had no idea what that was supposed to mean. Other than she might need something stronger than tonic water.

Her nipples had tightened, and thank God the room was dim, because her entire body blushed. He couldn't have overheard her taunting Brady, not from over twenty feet away and with all the noisy laughter competing with the jukebox. And no way did Ethan recognize her.

He'd been a senior the year she started at Wattsville High, so he hadn't seen her in eleven years. She doubted he'd recognized her even once since the day he rescued her. How many times had she taken great pains to be in the perfect spot, like the cafeteria or near the boys' locker room so he couldn't miss her? Yet he did, and with unflattering consistency.

A fan stuck a piece of paper in his face and only then did he look away from her. Her heart hadn't stopped pounding.

"Sophie?"

She jumped so hard she nearly knocked over the waitress's loaded tray.

The woman moved back. "Sorry, didn't mean to startle you. Sophie, right?"

What the hell? No one here knew her. She nodded.

"Sadie asked me to give you this," she said, inclining

her head at the bartender and passing Sophie a piece of paper. "It's a name and phone number. She said you're looking for a place to stay tonight?"

Ah. Sophie smiled. "Yes," she said, accepting the paper. "Thank you."

"It's a long shot. The Meyers have probably rented out their spare rooms by now. But Kalispell is only a forty-five-minute drive from here." The waitress was already pushing through the crowd. "Good luck."

Sophie sighed. She thought she was so smart, but she stank at this covert stuff. Using her real name had been a stupid rookie move. No matter how doubtful it was that Ethan remembered her.

She studied the scribbled phone number, then glanced at Ethan. Fortunately he was too busy being mobbed to pay her any more attention. Both he and the man with him gave her the impression they'd bolt as soon as possible. She'd be a fool to let Ethan out of her sight, but it was too noisy to make a call in the bar. She'd have to step outside and just stay close to the door.

If she were to find a room, she'd be shocked. But she had to at least try in case she was forced to stay till morning. Or, God forbid, until after the rodeo was over in two days.

It would be so much easier to grab him tonight and leave Blackfoot Falls pronto. She didn't need his buddies interfering, because if they did, what could she do, really? And returning to Wyoming empty-handed wasn't an option.

She thought back to her earlier idea. Coaxing him to ask her to his room might be her best bet. But not if she couldn't get the damn jitters under control. Who was she kidding, anyway? There were several gorgeous women waiting for him to say the word. The only guy she'd attracted was one who roped and tied baby cows.

Hoping her half-full glass of tonic would hold her spot at the bar, she squeezed her way toward the door. The standing crowd was truly ridiculous, oblivious of anyone trying to pass, and forcing her in Ethan's direction.

"Boy howdy, was I shocked to hear you'd be riding this weekend, Ethan! Aren't you afraid of getting injured and missing the finals again?"

Sophie stopped. She turned and saw Ethan tighten his jaw. The people closest to him grew quiet and watchful.

The stout, ruddy-faced fan who'd asked the moronic question continued heedlessly. "I told the wife I figured you'd be too superstitious to take the chance, especially for no prize money."

"It's for a good cause," Ethan said quietly.

"Don't get me wrong, son. I'm glad you're here. I'm looking forward to seeing you ride tomorrow." The man rubbed his palms together, ignoring the blushing woman tugging at his arm. "I understand Matt Gunderson has raised some hard-bucking bulls."

"Yep. I heard the same thing." Ethan's jaw clenched again, then he smiled and moved back a little. "I sure hope all you folks are generous to Safe Haven. They take in a lot of animals who otherwise wouldn't have a chance of surviving. Any donation you'd like to add to the price of the ticket would be appreciated."

Unable to listen anymore, she shouldered her way to the door. No, she told herself. *Uh-uh.* She could not, and would not, feel sympathy for Ethan. As he'd said, Safe Haven was a good cause. He'd volunteered to ride. Great. Good for him. He wasn't letting superstition spook him. That didn't mean she wouldn't drag his ass back to Wyoming. He'd broken the condition of his bail by taking off. And clearly he didn't care at all about screwing her and Lola out of the money they'd posted for his bond. Sure, they had his motor coach as collateral. But until they could sell it, they were on the hook for a lot of cash.

Finally she made it outside. The biting cold November air nipped at her heated cheeks. She drew in a deep breath and immediately started coughing from all the cigarette smoke.

She turned to go the other way. Great. Smokers overran the sidewalk. She refused to stray too far from the door in case Ethan left, so she ducked behind a silver truck. No doubt he was anxious to get away from the stupid questions. And who could blame him?

The lighting was poor. She dug out her phone but could barely make out the number on the crumpled paper. Using the Bic app on her cell to see, she memorized the seven digits, then called. And promptly got the no she'd expected. Disconnecting, she sighed.

"No luck, huh?"

Sophie knew that voice. She slanted a look at Ethan, who stood on the sidewalk, his hands stuffed in his jeans pockets.

He wore a tan Western-style shirt, no jacket. His broad shoulders were hunched slightly, against the cold, she imagined.

"You must have me mixed up with someone else," she said, reminding herself to breathe. "I don't believe we've met."

"No?" He studied her a beat longer than she could manage to keep still. Thankfully he stepped back when she slipped between him and the truck to return to the sidewalk. "I thought maybe we had," he said, shrugging.

She shook her head, held her breath. "Nope."

Jeez. Of course he didn't recognize her. Or really think they'd met before. It was a pickup line guys used all the time.

"You're looking for a place to stay tonight," he said. "Aren't you?"

That stopped her again. "How do you know that?"

"The waitress." His intense stare wasn't helping her nerves, so she moved into the shadows. "I asked her."

Sophie huffed a laugh. "And of course she told you, because..." She closed her mouth. Because of that damn sexy smile of his, that was why, but this was what Sophie wanted, to get him alone, so she'd better lose the attitude.

"Because she's my buddy Matt's sister-in-law," he said, and glanced over his shoulder when the door opened and raucous laughter spilled out into the moonlit night. "Hey, how about we go someplace else? Get away from the bar."

"Sure." She tried not to seem too eager. Or irritated. Picking up a woman was this easy for a guy like Ethan. Just a look, a smile, and he was all set. She moved closer to him. The Boarding House Inn, where she knew he was staying, was within walking distance. "What did you have in mind?"

He looked both ways down Main Street. "How about the diner? Shouldn't be too crowded."

"The diner?"

"Is that all right? We can cross after this next truck."

"Um, sure. I guess."

Glancing at her, he asked, "You have somewhere else in mind?"

A diner? Okay, she was officially insulted. "I was thinking someplace more private," she whispered, linking arms with him.

Surprise flashed across his face. His eyes found hers, then he lowered his gaze to her lips. "I'm Ethan."

"I know who you are."

"And you're Sophie?"

So stupid. She nodded, promising herself that after this,

she'd stick to her desk job. At least her name hadn't triggered his memory. If he were to remember anything, it would probably be the pesky twerp who'd kept popping up in the weirdest places half his senior year.

The door to the bar opened again and they both turned. A tall brunette and her blonde sidekick walked out, scanning the groups of smokers.

The moment their gazes lit on Ethan, he tensed. "Let's go," he said, and draped his arm across the back of her shoulders. "Mind walking? It's not far."

"Fine." She huddled close, soaking in the warmth of his body and trying to decide if it would be too much to slide her arm around his waist.

He walked at a fast clip, and with her shorter legs she had some trouble keeping up. "Sorry," he said. "I'll slow down."

She saw her green Jeep parked at the curb just ahead, and two things flashed through her mind. She needed the handcuffs she'd left in her glove compartment, but she couldn't stop for them because of her Wyoming plates. If he knew the Jeep was hers, he could easily put two and two together.

"Cold?" he asked, pulling her closer.

"What?" She realized she'd tensed. "A little." Checking random plates, she saw a variety of out-of-state vehicles from Colorado, Utah, even an SUV from Wyoming. It was worth taking the chance. She really, really needed the cuffs. "Could we stop a minute?"

Ethan frowned and glanced back at the Watering Hole. "Am I still walking too fast?"

"No. We just passed my car and I wanted to grab my jacket."

He started to follow her, but she shook her head while inching backward and digging for the key in her pocket.

"It's kind of a mess," she said, relieved that he only smiled and stayed put.

She unlocked the driver's door. And kept an eye on him while she quickly transferred the handcuffs from the glove box to a deep pocket in the puffy down jacket she'd left on the passenger seat. Pausing, she considered scooping up her purse hidden on the floorboard.

Couldn't hurt. She probably could use some lip gloss about now. Jeez. *This is not a date.*

The door was closed and locked, her purse in hand before she considered the incriminating ID and *bail piece* authorizing her to arrest him inside her bag. It didn't matter, since she was going to do this thing quickly. Preferably the minute they were inside his room.

Instead of continuing to walk when she rejoined him, he studied her car. "I've always liked Jeeps. Looks new. Have you had it long?"

"I bought it last year." She drew in a breath. He was staring at her plates.

"You from Wyoming?"

"Not originally, but I've lived there for a few years now."

"What part?"

"Sheridan," she lied, purposely choosing the farthest town from Wattsville that she could think of.

"I'm from outside Casper myself." Either he was a very good actor or the Wyoming coincidence didn't bother him.

"Really? We're not exactly neighbors, but still…"

"Here, let me help you with your jacket."

Sophie thought she heard the handcuffs clink and clutched the jacket to her chest. Giving him a come-hither smile, she said, "I'd rather have your arm around me."

"Always happy to oblige a beautiful woman." Ethan took her free hand and drew her close. The jacket served as an unwanted buffer. "You aren't a rodeo fan, are you, Sophie?"

"Um, a little…"

He smiled. "It's okay. My ego isn't that fragile."

"I know who you are. That should count for something."

His puzzled frown sent up a warning flag. It lasted only a moment before the smile returned, and he started them walking again. "So you aren't here for the rodeo."

"No." Wrong answer. She wasn't sure why, but it felt wrong. She was missing something. "Well, yes, sort of. Does it matter?"

"I suppose not." He checked for traffic and guided her across the street, his arm tightening around her shoulders.

The Boarding House Inn was just up ahead. They had another half a block to go and she hoped the men standing on the porch steps deep in conversation would hurry up and leave. If she did her job well, by tomorrow morning it would appear that Ethan Styles had disappeared into thin air. And she preferred not to be identified as the last person seen with him.

That was where the wig came in handy. As a blonde, she barely recognized herself.

Luckily the porch cleared just as they approached. The silence that had fallen between her and Ethan was beginning to feel awkward. She slanted him a glance and caught him watching her. The porch light shone in both of their faces and he stopped, right there, several feet from the steps. Turning to face her, he nudged up her chin and studied her mouth.

She held her breath, certain he was about to kiss her.

"I have one question," he said. "Are you a reporter?"

"What? No."

Something in her expression must have made him doubt

her. His gaze narrowed, he seemed to be trying hard to remember...

"Why on earth would you think I'm a reporter?" It hit her then that everything would have been so much easier if she'd just pretended to be one of his buckle bunny fans. The wariness in his face convinced her to fix that situation right now.

"Okay, I lied," she blurted, the words rushing out of her mouth before she could think. "I'm a huge rodeo fan. The biggest. I go to rodeos all the time. I'm a buckle bunny. I didn't want to admit it and I—" She cleared her throat. "I wanted to stand out to get your attention, and that's why I lied. About not being a fan." She held in a sigh. "Does that make sense?"

Ethan looked as if he was going to laugh.

So she threw her arms around his neck and pulled him down into a blazing kiss.

3

ETHAN RECOVERED FROM her sudden burst of enthusiasm, thankful he hadn't landed on his ass. Sophie was small but strong, too. Strong enough that she'd forced him back a step. He put his arms around her and slowed down the kiss, taking the time to explore and sample the sweet taste of her mouth.

They were standing on the porch, under the light, in full view of Main Street where anyone passing the inn could see them. That didn't bother him. He just couldn't figure out what had caused her unexpected display of passion.

Way before he was finished with the kiss she stepped back, only to stare up at him with dazed eyes, and was that regret? Probably not. He wasn't seeing so clearly himself.

Damn, he should've moved them to his room before now. "How about we go inside where it's warm?" he asked.

She jerked a nod, clutched the jacket to her chest and inched farther away from him, as if she was afraid he was going to grab her.

Wondering if she'd ever picked up a guy before, Ethan was careful to give her some space. More practiced women who followed the circuit had a completely different air about them. He opened the door and motioned for her to go inside. The lobby was tiny, furnished with a desk and two wing chairs, a small oak table on which rolls and coffee would be set out in the morning, or so he'd been told.

"Turn right," he said, and she did so without a word or a backward glance. "I'm near the end."

He watched her as she led the way, admiring the view. Sophie claimed they'd never met, but he wasn't so sure that was true. Once he'd seen her up close, he was even more convinced they'd met before. The shape of her pouty lips had given him the first inkling that he knew her from somewhere. Even now, watching the slight sway of her hips tugged at his memory. It wasn't a particularly distinctive walk, so he didn't get it.

Hell, he could've seen her in the crowd at a rodeo. She'd admitted she was a fan. But that didn't feel right, either. If it turned out she'd lied and really was a reporter, man, he was going to be pissed. So far he'd been lucky. The public didn't know about his arrest. But one more media question about the black cloud that seemed to follow him to the finals every year and he'd shut them all out. No more interviews. No more sound bites. Screw 'em.

Sophie stopped to examine the baseboards and then looked up at the ceiling. "I think this place really was a boardinghouse at one time."

"Yep," Ethan said, glad she seemed more relaxed. "It was built around the 1920s. The new owner bought the place last year and kept the renovations as close to the original structure as possible. She even tried to replicate the detail in the moldings."

Sophie grinned at him. "I like that you know all that stuff."

With a laugh, he pulled the key out of his pocket. "It was on the website."

"The halls are awfully narrow. Men couldn't have had

very broad shoulders back in the twenties…" Her voice trailed off, her gaze flickering away from his chest.

"Two doors down," he said, staying right where he was, waiting for her to start walking again so he wouldn't crowd her.

He had to decide what to tell her. That kiss kind of ruined his plan. He hadn't actually been hitting on her. Blackfoot Falls was small, and with all the fans in town, he'd been rethinking Matt's offer to stay at his ranch. Ethan knew some of the guys had parked their motor coaches there instead of at the RV park outside of Kalispell.

Still, it would be quiet out there. He could help Sophie out by giving her his room. And staying at Matt's meant less chance for Ethan to get in any trouble.

He stuck the key in the lock and glanced at Sophie. With those soft brown eyes and that generous mouth, she looked like big trouble to him, tasted like it, too.

Who was he kidding? If he'd really wanted to just give her his room, he would have said something when they were outside. By her Jeep. Now, though, it would be awkward as hell to pack up and leave. He pushed the door open and she went right on inside.

After glancing around at the antique chair and the old armoire, she focused on the queen-size four-poster bed that took up most of the small room. She moved closer to it, stopping a moment to check out the patchwork quilt, and then ran her hand down the oak post close to the wall.

His cock pulsed.

When she wrapped her fingers around the smooth wood and stroked up, Ethan had to turn away. Yeah, he needed to erase that image real fast.

Between her obvious interest in the bed and his dick's growing interest in her, he decided it was time to offer the room as he'd intended, even if it would make him look like an ass.

"It's nice," she said, smiling, walking close enough he could inhale her sweet scent. "Quaint. Too bad the furniture is so small. I bet you can't even sit on the chair."

She laid her jacket over the back of it, sat on the edge and pulled off a boot.

And there went his last good intention. Ethan sighed. If even her red-striped sock turned him on, he wasn't going anywhere. She was already here. He was here. They were consenting adults. So he couldn't see a reason to deny himself a little recreation before heading to the Lone Wolf. Matt had left the invitation open.

"Need help with your boots?" she asked, mesmerizing him with those eyes the color of melted chocolate.

He pulled both his boots off before she'd finished removing her second one. "Tell me you're over twenty-one," he said, straightening and pausing at the first snap on his shirt.

Sophie laughed. "Are you serious? I don't look that young."

"I just like to be sure."

"Well, you can relax. I'm twenty-six. Anyway, I think the age of consent is sixteen in Montana."

The same as in Wyoming, not that he paid it any mind. Twenty-one was his personal cutoff.

Getting to her feet, she pulled her shirt from her jeans, then stopped and frowned. "Is something wrong?"

His snaps were still intact. "I have one last question."

"Okay," she said, taking a step closer, her sultry smile designed to scramble his brain.

"Are you married?"

Her eyebrows arched and her lips parted. She looked startled, and maybe confused. "No. Of course not." She shook her head, her eyebrows lowering into a delicate frown. "No, I'm not married, nor have I ever been married." She drew in a breath, seemed to calm herself and took over unsnapping his shirt. "Would it really matter?"

"If you have to ask, damn good thing you're still single." He could see he'd irritated her. Too bad. He wasn't about to get into another scrape like the mess he'd narrowly escaped in Wyoming. After discovering Wendy was married, he'd refused to sleep with her. To get back at him, she'd filed a false charge that he'd stolen some jewelry.

Sophie looked torn for a moment and then unfastened his next snap.

He caught her hand and inspected her ring finger. No mark, not even a faded one. "Sorry, but I'm touchy about the issue," he said, staring into her wary eyes and lifting her hand to his lips for a brief kiss before releasing her. "It's nothing personal."

Without another word, she finished unsnapping him, her eyes cast downward, until she parted the front of his shirt and pushed it off his shoulders. Her preoccupation with his bare chest was flattering but somewhat awkward. He finished shrugging out of the shirt, impatient to see what was under hers.

Uncertainty betrayed itself in the soft, hesitant palms she skimmed over his ribs and then his pecs. Her touch was almost reverent, her expression dreamlike. A few buckle bunnies he'd been with had tried to use their phones to sneak pictures of him shirtless, and even buck naked. But this was different. This seemed more...personal.

Jesus, he hoped it didn't turn out she was one of those crazy stalkers.

He captured her hands and gently lowered them from his chest. When he tried to draw up her T-shirt, she tensed, angling in a way that cut him off.

He took half a step back. "You change your mind?" he asked, keeping his tone low and even, letting her know it was all good. She was allowed.

"No," she said, shaking her head. "I haven't."

He tipped her chin up so he could see her face. "It's okay if you have. Tell me to stop and I will."

Sighing, she pulled off her own shirt and tossed it somewhere over her shoulder. He was too busy taking in the pink bra and creamy skin to see where it landed. Her breasts were the perfect size. They'd fit nicely in his hands. Her arms and shoulders were well toned, and her abs…a woman didn't get that kind of definition from casual exercise. Sophie took her workouts seriously. But she hadn't gone overboard, either, which he greatly appreciated.

He drew his thumb across the silky skin mounding above her bra. She had no freckles, just the faint remnant of a summer tan.

Damned if he wasn't the one staring now.

She shivered and shrank back.

"You're beautiful," he said, and looked up to meet eyes filled with disbelief. "I'm sure you get that line a lot, but I mean it."

She let out a short laugh and went for his belt buckle. He wished she wasn't so nervous. But if he brought it up, it would probably spook her into leaving.

Would that be the right thing to do?

Her frenzied movements confused him. It was as if she was racing the clock. Or…maybe she had someplace else she needed to be. Dammit, he couldn't figure her out. Although once they were in bed, he could slow things down. Make her feel real good.

"Hey."

When she looked up, he caught her chin and kissed her, taking his time, enjoying the velvety texture of her lips, trying to show her he was in no hurry. Although his dick wanted to argue.

She opened up for him and he slid his tongue inside, where it found its mate. The funny little tango that followed made them both smile. He'd always liked kissing best when tongues were involved, but simply moving his lips over hers felt more than satisfying. They found their rhythm and he deepened the kiss while pulling her tighter against him.

Sophie made a startled little sound in the back of her throat and stiffened. But she had to know she was making him hard. Thank God she didn't pull away. She pressed even closer, until her breasts pillowed his chest.

He reached behind to unfasten her bra, anxious to see her bare breasts, to watch her nipples harden and beg for his mouth. With his free hand he cupped her nape, slid his fingers into her hair. A sexy moan filled the inside of his mouth with her warm breath.

All of a sudden she froze.

She let out a squeak and wiggled out of his arms, her hand shooting to the top of her head.

"What happened?" Staying on the safe side, he kept his hands in plain sight. "Did I hurt you?"

They just stared at each other.

She didn't strike him as a woman who'd care if a man mussed up her hair. So what the hell?

"Sorry," she said, her cheeks pink. "Really sorry. I'm not freaking out or anything. About being here…you know…in the room with you. I promise I'm not."

Could've fooled him. "Look, we don't have to—"

"Let's get in bed, okay? I'll feel more relaxed then."

After a quick look at her parted lips, he watched the alarm fade from her eyes. "You don't like leaving the light on?" Ethan asked, worried he was missing something that would come back to bite him. "Is that it?"

"I don't care about the light." She smoothed back her hair and smiled as if nothing had happened.

Now that his body had cooled off some, he needed to think before she took another step toward him. This year he faced more pressure than ever to claim another championship title, partly because of his age, and also because of his kid sister. Mostly, though, it was about his left shoulder. It didn't hurt all the time, but he knew his rodeo days were numbered.

Sophie came up flush against him and looped her arms around his neck. Her pink lips parted slightly as she tilted her head back. She was still wearing the damn bra, not that it seemed to matter, since his mind went blank.

He put his hands on her waist, waiting, hoping he wasn't in for another surprise squeal. Her skin was soft and warm above the jeans waistband. The satiny texture made him itch to explore the rest of her. He settled for rubbing the small of her back, then moved his hands over the curve of her firm backside. Squeezing through denim was better than nothing, he supposed.

Screw that.

The jeans and bra both had to come off.

His request was preempted by an urgent tug. Sophie pulled his head down while she lifted herself up to meet his lips. When she leaned into him, moving her hips against his born-again erection, his whole body tightened. He slid his tongue inside her mouth and touched the tip of hers before circling and sampling the sweetness of her.

"Bed," she whispered.

He lifted her in his arms. With a soft gasp, she hung on tight even after he'd laid her down against the pillows. She resumed the kiss, refusing to let go of his neck, even

as he followed her down. The fierce way she was cling-
ing to him made things tricky. He stretched out alongside
her, keeping his weight off her and on his braced elbow.

He dragged his mouth away from hers and trailed his
lips along her jaw to her ear, wondering where she might
be sensitive. After a few nips at her earlobe, he cupped a
breast and murmured, "How about we get rid of this bra?"

She vaguely nodded, then stiffened. "Wait."

"For?"

She sat up and sighed. "I forgot something."

Ethan fell onto his back. She just wasn't going to make
it easy, was she? "What did you forget?" he asked as she
crawled over him and got off the bed.

"Just one sec," she said, raising one finger before she
headed for the chair with her jacket draped over the back.

Ethan watched her rifle through the pockets and found
it in his heart to forgive her for the interruption. Only because she had one helluva nice ass. Which he hoped to see
in the flesh, preferably before the next full moon.

Okay. He finally understood the problem. "I have a condom," he said, rolling to the side and reaching into his back
pocket. "It's right here. You can stop looking."

She murmured something he couldn't make out, yet
managed to give him the impression she hadn't heard him.

"Sophie?"

She turned to face him, holding the jacket against her
front. Fortunately not so her breasts were hidden. Yeah,
except the bra took care of that. Shit. Not being able to see
and touch was driving him crazy.

He took the packet out of his wallet and tossed both on
the nightstand. "Did you hear me?" Why the hell was she
bringing the jacket with her? "I have a condom."

"What? Oh." She stopped by the side of the bed. "No,
we don't need one."

"Uh, yeah, we do." He never broke that rule.

"I changed my mind about the light." She smiled and leaned down to give him a quick kiss and quite a view. "I think I want it off."

Ethan had never met a woman who ran so hot and cold, and at the speed of sound on top of that. He'd ridden a hundred ornery bulls that had given him less trouble. *Trouble* being the keyword here. Maybe this—Sophie—was an omen he needed to take more seriously.

She kissed him again, lingering this time, using her tongue, while trailing her fingers down his chest. She traced a circle around his navel and then rested her hand on his buckle. "I'll be right back."

Jesus. "What now?"

"The light."

Something else that was confusing. He knew she wasn't shy, and she had a killer body. "How about we leave the one in the bathroom on with the door closed partway?"

She straightened, thought for a moment and then nodded. "I think that might work better, actually."

Yep. She was a strange one, all right. But that nice round bottom of hers wasn't easily dismissed. He watched her walk to the bathroom, flip on the light and angle the door just so.

"I doubt you'll need the jacket," he said.

She only smiled and moved to the wall switch that controlled the two lamps.

"Why don't you get rid of those jeans while you're up?" He'd take care of the bra, no problem.

"Okay. Good idea." The room dimmed. "You take off yours, too."

Ethan watched her approach while he unbuckled and unzipped. It was a little too dark for his taste. Once he fi-

close, her hard nipples grazing his chest…the feel of cold metal…

The hard band closing around his wrist jerked him from his haze. He heard a click. Confusion still messed with his brain. Sophie drew back, staring down at him, breathing hard.

He looked at his wrist handcuffed to the bedpost.

Sophie was into that kind of stuff? He wasn't, but he didn't mind accommodating her.

4

"YOU COULD'VE JUST told me." Ethan smiled. "This isn't my thing, but I'll play for a while," he said, and touched her breast.

"Oh, brother." She slapped his hand away, jerking back. For God's sake, she'd forgotten she had no top on. "This isn't a game, you idiot." She climbed off, glanced around the room for her shirt. Finding it near the chair, she pulled the tee over her head.

"What the hell is going on?"

The wig got caught and shifted. Boy, was she glad to get rid of that stupid thing. No one had warned her it would itch like crazy. She grabbed a handful of the fake blond locks and yanked it off her head.

"Jesus. What the—"

Pulling pins from her own hair, she shook it loose from the tight bun and glanced at Ethan, lying against the cream-colored sheets, his muscled chest smooth, bare and tanned. A light smattering of dark hair swirled just below his belly button and disappeared into the waistband of his boxer briefs.

Oh no. No looking there for her.

"I know you," he said, narrowing his gaze.

The light from the bathroom washed over his face, the tanned skin bringing out the blue of his eyes, as he studied her with an intensity that made her turn away. Did seeing her as a brunette trigger a memory? Doubtful. He'd barely noticed her after his grand gesture outside the cafeteria right in the middle of lunch period.

She walked into the bathroom and groaned at her image in the mirror. Well, of course her hair was plastered to her head and looking as unattractive as possible. He hadn't been staring because he remembered her. She could've just stepped off the set of some horror movie.

Rubbing her itchy scalp, she bent at the waist and fluffed out her hair. She straightened to look in the mirror again, not expecting much. And that was exactly what she got.

"Are you gonna get out here and explain what the hell is going on?" Ethan sounded angry.

"You jumped bail," she said, strolling back into the room and picking up her phone. Mostly so she didn't have to look at him. "Without giving a thought to the large bond that was posted on your behalf."

"No, I didn't. Jump bail, I mean. The charges were dropped."

"When?" If that was true, Lola would've told her by now. But he sounded so certain she had to look at him. "When?" she repeated.

"I'm not sure."

A lock of sun-streaked brown hair had fallen across his forehead. His face was lean and spare like the rest of him. Same square jaw she remembered, except for the dark stubble. And that perfect straight nose. He was even hotter now than he'd been back in high school.

Some friggin' nerve.

"So, you weren't sure if you had to show up in court or not and decided to take off anyway. Brilliant move."

"No, it's not like that." He jerked his wrist, clanging the handcuffs against the wooden post. "Is this necessary?"

Well, that had to be rhetorical. She checked for texts or voice mails. "If the charges were dropped, my partner would've notified me. So guess you're out of luck."

"Okay, look, my friend Arnie... Can we turn on more lights?"

"No." She sat on the chair and faced him. "Continue."

Ethan's normal, easygoing expression had vanished, replaced by a piercing frown that made her tense. "Who are you?"

"Sophie's my real name."

"You know what I'm asking."

"I'm a fugitive retrieval agent—"

"Fugitive?"

"You asked."

He cut loose a pithy four-letter word. "What's that, a fancy name for a bounty hunter?"

"Yep."

"And that gives you the right to slap handcuffs on me?"

"It sure does. Didn't you read the bail bond contract?" By signing the document, he'd given her and Lola more authority to arrest him than even the police.

She watched him scrub at his face with his free hand and waited out his mumbled curses. Leaving him with an unrestricted hand wasn't a smart move. The bedpost was made from solid wood and plenty sturdy...she'd checked first thing. But Ethan was agile and strong.

The memory of his hands on her body made her shudder.

Dammit, she should've brought two pairs of cuffs. Mandy preferred using zip ties and had given Sophie a few. But they were sitting in the Jeep.

"So that's why you're in such great shape," he murmured.

"Excuse me?"

"I thought maybe you were a personal trainer or something, but that didn't make sense, either," he said, letting his gaze wander over her.

"What are you talking about?"

"Look, if you just let me make a phone call, I can straighten this out in no time."

"I have a better idea. You can do it in person when I take you back to Wyoming."

"Bullshit."

Sophie smiled. "It's late. No sense driving tonight. We'll leave first thing in the morning."

He jerked hard on the cuffs. The whole bed seemed to shake. "You know I won't let you do that."

"Oh?" She rose. "What are you going to do? Scream?"

Wow, that sure pissed him off. His face reddened, and his eyes turned positively frosty. He looked as if he wanted to put his hands around her neck and strangle the life out of her.

It gave her a new respect for what Mandy had to do all the time. Face down criminals who might actually want to hurt her. Ethan was angry, and he'd try to get away if he could, but Sophie wasn't afraid of him. She knew he would never do her harm.

She walked to the window and parted the drapes, just enough so she could take a peek down the street. The Watering Hole wasn't visible from here. Neither was her Jeep. Lots of people were still milling around, though. Another reason she wouldn't try forcing Ethan into her car tonight.

Damn, she wished she'd grabbed her bag along with the jacket. She needed her toothbrush, face cream, a change of clothes, all that stuff… And she hated leaving Ethan alone while she ran to the Jeep. She turned and caught him staring at her butt.

He gave her a lazy smile.

Oh, so he was pulling out the charm again.

"Aren't you gonna ask if I did it?"

"What's the point?" Sophie said. "Unless you have proof, your answer means nothing. And if you had proof, I wouldn't be here."

His face darkened. "I didn't steal a goddamn thing. Wendy lied."

"Hmm, well, that's what you get for sleeping with a married woman."

"You mean, for *not* sleeping with her." Ethan shook his head, briefly closing his eyes. "Wendy lied about that, too. When I found out she was married, I left. She was pissed. I knew that… I just didn't know how bad."

Sophie thought back to earlier when he'd asked if she was married. He'd even inspected her ring finger. Maybe he was telling the truth, or maybe he'd learned an expensive lesson. The thing was, she didn't believe that he'd stolen anything. It made no sense. Even if he did need money, she'd seen the teenage Ethan's moral center, and age didn't change a person that much. But what she believed didn't matter.

"If I'm supposed to have a hundred grand in stolen jewelry, why would I need someone to post my bond?"

"You didn't have enough time to sell it?"

"Get real. I earned a lot more than that in endorsements alone this year. Plus my winnings."

"Okay, so…" What was she doing? Sophie knew better than to get involved. Her job was to take him back to Wyoming, period. "Why not use your own money to post bond?"

"I don't have that kind of cash lying around. My money's invested. I start withdrawing funds and I get questions. The media are already all over my ass about the finals in a week."

"Why?" She hadn't realized that she'd walked closer to him until she bumped her knee on a corner of the bed.

"Because of my track record. Every year I—" He plowed his fingers through his hair, the action drawing attention to the muscles in his arms and shoulders. "It doesn't matter."

"What?" She snapped her gaze back to his face. "I'm sorry, I missed that last bit."

He was staring at her again, with the same intensity as earlier. Trying to decide if she was the girl from school? Maybe. "My friend Arnie, he was supposed to take care of it. He knows the charge is bogus and said it would never make it to court."

"Is he an attorney?"

Ethan sighed. "He dropped out of law school."

She remembered an Arnie, a dopey junior who used to tag along behind Ethan. If this was the same guy, she sure wouldn't have trusted him with anything important. "Hope he didn't quit before he learned the part that would keep you from getting locked up."

Ethan blew out a breath. It seemed clear he'd had the same thought. "How about we call him? Can I at least do that?"

Sophie wandered toward the window while she tried to think. Talking to Arnie wouldn't help. Only Lola could tell her if Ethan was in the clear and the bond reimbursed. And for some reason Sophie wasn't anxious to admit she'd found him already. Why, she didn't know. She should be ecstatic and gloating.

"Tomorrow's the Safe Haven Benefit Rodeo," Ethan said. "They could really use the money. Since I'm the main attraction, it would be a shame if I missed—"

"Shut up." She glared at him. "I know about the rodeo. And guess what, genius…trying to make me feel bad isn't helping your cause. It's just pissing me off. I didn't create this problem. You did."

He glared back. "You're gonna deny me a goddamn lousy phone call?"

"Where's your cell?"

Frowning, he glanced at the nightstand. "My shirt... where is it?"

"What am I, your maid?" she grumbled, and spotted it on the floor by the chair. She picked up the shirt and then noticed his phone sitting on the armoire. Tempted to toss the cell to him, she moved close enough to drop it on the mattress barely within his reach.

With the most irritating grin, he strained toward the cell and grabbed it. "What are you afraid of? Huh? What did you think I was going to do to you? I've got one wrist cuffed to this post," he said in a taunting tone of voice. "What are you doing to my shirt?"

"What?" She looked down at the garment she was hugging to her chest. "Nothing."

"Were you sniffing it?"

"No. Ew." She flung the shirt toward the chair. *Oh God, oh God, oh God.* Heat stung her cheeks. She kept her face averted, knowing it must be red, and pulled out her own phone.

If he was laughing at her...

If?

Did she really have any doubt?

One word. Just one wrong word out of his mouth, and she'd drag him to her car in front of the whole damn town. Announce to everyone he was a fugitive from justice.

Her sigh ended in a shudder. She hadn't even been aware of smelling his shirt.

He was awfully quiet.

"Arnie?"

Sophie let out a breath and slowly turned to see Ethan holding the cell to his ear and glaring at the ceiling.

"Don't pull that you're-breaking-up bullshit on me," Ethan said, his voice furious. "What the hell, dude? I thought you were taking care of the charges."

Sophie perched on the edge of the chair to send a quick text to Lola.

"That's good, right?" Ethan stacked two pillows behind his back. "If she insists on lying, her husband will know she's been cruising bars and picking up men while he's out of town." He listened for a few seconds. "And I had to call you to find all this out?"

Before hitting Send, she glanced up again.

Ethan looked worried. His chest rose and fell on a sigh. "Jesus, Arnie, you've got to find out by tomorrow. The finals are in a week. You know this year could be it for me…"

The despair in his voice made her stomach clench. Thank God she had her phone to occupy her, because she couldn't stand to look at him right now. This year could be it for him? Why?

"Maybe I should call my agent," he said, his eyes meeting hers when she looked up. "Brian's going to find out anyway. They think I jumped bail. I've got a damn bounty hunter staring at me right now."

"Fugitive retrieval agent," she muttered.

"She's got me cuffed to the friggin' bed. Plans on dragging me back to Wyoming tomorrow." He paused. "Shut the fu—" He glanced at her. "Just make the damn call and get back to me first thing tomorrow. And, Arnie, this is your last chance." Ethan disconnected and threw the cell down. Hard.

No point in pretending she hadn't been listening. Anyway, the second he'd left her and Lola holding the bond, so to speak, he forfeited his right to privacy. And no, she absolutely would not feel sorry for him. He'd done this to himself.

She watched him inspect the handcuffs and flex his hand. Then he stared up at the ceiling, thumping his head back against the wooden bed rail, working the muscle at his jaw.

"I wouldn't trust Arnie if I were you," Sophie said. "At this point you really do need an attorney."

Ethan brought his chin down, a faint smile tugging at the corners of his mouth. "You know Arnie?"

Oh, crap. This was what she got for being nice. "No, but it sounded like you don't have confidence in him. So I'm saying, you should go with your instinct." She shrugged, carefully keeping her gaze level with his. "Didn't you mention something about calling your agent?"

His eyes continued to bore into hers. He hadn't so much as blinked. All she could think to do was stare back. She doubted that little slip about Arnie had been the thing that convinced Ethan of her identity. Just because she looked familiar didn't mean he remembered they'd gone to the same high school together for seven months, one week and two days.

Yeah, okay, so she'd counted. Down to the minute, actually, but when she'd been... Fifteen. *Jeez.*

"What did he say, anyway?"

"Arnie?"

"Yes, Arnie." Her phone signaled a new text. She glanced at the brief message. No surprise there. "I texted a friend who works in the sheriff's office to check on whether the charges were dropped. It seems you alread. know the answer."

He tightened his mouth. "Can you recommend a attorney?"

"Not really. I know a few, but I couldn't say if they're any good." Except for Craig, but she tried to stay clear of him. "What about your agent? Bet he knows one."

"Brian lives in Dallas. I can't call him this late. But yeah, he knows everybody. I trust he'll steer me right."

"You should've called him before you jumped bail."

Ethan sighed. "I didn't realize I'd jumped bail," he said with forced patience. "The charges were supposed to have been dropped."

"What about your parents? I would think they either have someone they use or know of someone."

"It's clear you're not a rodeo fan, yet you know who they are?"

She shrugged. "I think everyone in Beatrice County knows the name Styles. They own that big ranch and rodeo camp near Otter Lake. And didn't your dad win something like five championship titles for calf roping, and a few more for something else?"

Ethan nodded. "All-around cowboy three years in a row."

"Even your mom has four gold buckles for barrel racing, right?"

"You get all that from doing homework on me? Or did you already know this stuff?"

"Half and half."

"So you probably read about my kid sister." His tone stayed noncommittal and his expression blank.

Nevertheless, she'd bet there were a lot of emotions bubbling under the surface. She'd definitely seen pride in his eyes, but she wondered if there might be some jealousy in the mix.

"Last December Cara won her first championship title on her twenty-first birthday," he said. "She'll be competing for her second title next week. She'll be headed to Vegas with me. Assuming I get to go." He jerked on the cuffs so hard the post shook.

"Ah." Sophie nodded.

"Ah?"

"Sibling rivalry. I get it." She didn't have any siblings, but she could imagine the pressure Ethan was feeling. And a kid sister besting him? Ouch. "Well, I know barrel racing is a woman's event, so I'm guessing that's what she won?"

He nodded.

"Your dad won first place for tying up poor little calves—"

Ethan stared as though she'd just grown fangs.

"And your mom and sister got prizes for riding a horse around a few barrels without knocking them over."

Ethan started laughing.

"I'm not finished," she said. "And you're a bull rider. Correct me if I'm wrong, but don't you compete in the hardest, most dangerous event in rodeo?"

"Look," he said, his laughter ending with a sigh, "I don't know what your point is. I just need to make it to the finals." His mood had soured again. "So, what's it gonna take, Sophie? Tell me."

"You have to return to Wyoming and face the judge."

"I can't ride the next two days here, then go back to Wyoming and the unknown, and trust that I can still make it to Vegas for the finals."

She sucked in a deep breath. He wasn't thinking it through. "It's not as if you have a low profile," she reminded him. "If you fail to appear in court on Monday, the judge will issue a warrant and someone will be waiting in Vegas to arrest you."

"No. No, that can't happen. How can they come after me? I didn't do it. Dammit."

She bit down to keep from stating the obvious. Besides, Ethan had to know the legal system was far from perfect. Or maybe his charmed existence had spared him life's injustices. "Look, I know you don't want the publicity, but your folks live in the next county, along with lots of rodeo fans who adore them. You're probably the most popular bull rider in the country. Who do you think people are going to believe? You or what's her name?"

"Wendy." Ethan's mouth curved in a derisive smile. "Wendy Fullerton."

Fullerton? "Any relation to Broderick Fullerton?"

"His wife."

"Oh, shit."

"Exactly what I said." Ethan's sigh sounded a lot like defeat.

"How could you not know who she was?" Fullerton owned half the county. People generally feared him more than they liked him. But the fact remained, he provided over 60 percent of the jobs and his bank owned a ton of mortgages and notes. Including Sophie and Lola's business loan.

"Wendy is wife number four. They've been married for eight months." He shrugged. "How the hell would I know, anyway? I don't read the society pages and I'm rarely home. Jesus. Here I've been keeping my head down. Staying healthy. Staying out of trouble…"

"You picked up a strange woman in a bar," she muttered, really hating this whole mess. No room for sympathy now. Everything had to go by the book. "And instead of learning your lesson you came here and did it again."

"When?"

Sophie got to her feet so she could pace, hoping to

loosen up. Maybe she should be more concerned with toughening up. She'd started to soften toward Ethan, wondering how she could help him out. But anything she did would reflect on Lola, too. Their business loan wasn't in jeopardy. They'd been late with their payment only once in four years. It was silly to worry.

Ethan's response from a moment ago finally sank in and she faced him. "*When?* Is that a joke?"

"Do you see me laughing?" he said, his stare unflinching. "Did you forget how I ended up here with you?"

"Nope. But you obviously did."

She pushed her fingers through her tangled hair. This was good, him being an ass. Made it easier to shove sympathy aside, be more objective. "Okay, I'll bite. Go ahead."

"Nothing. It's just that you hit on me."

She gaped at him. "Are you nuts?" It took a few more seconds to find her voice again. "You're crazy, you know that. You brought me to your room."

"Actually I was going to give it to you."

"What the hell are you talking about?"

"My friend Matt invited me to stay at his ranch. So when I heard you needed a room, I'd decided to give you this one and I would move over to the Lone Wolf," he said slowly, and with exaggerated patience. "Then you hit on me, and I…I went with the flow." He smiled. "I was only trying to be a gentleman."

"Oh, that's right. I forgot. You like to play hero and then move on." She held her breath. She couldn't believe she'd actually said *play hero*.

With a single lifted eyebrow, he held her gaze until she turned away. He didn't seem surprised or curious about what she'd meant, just faintly amused. So he'd probably remembered…

Swallowing, she stalked to the window, shoved the drapes aside and stared at nothing.

The stupid bastard had recognized her from school and hadn't said a word.

5

FINE. SO WHAT if he remembered? It didn't really matter. Sophie stayed at the window, though nothing happening outside was of particular interest. She simply knew better than to look at Ethan while she planned her next move. The inn sat directly on Main Street. And Blackfoot Falls was crawling with out-of-town fans. The only chance for an uneventful exit would be if they left in the middle of the night. Not her first choice, but...

The more she thought about it, the more she liked the idea. Once the Watering Hole closed, there wouldn't be anything for these people to do. They'd return to the trailer parks and dude ranches, or wherever they were staying. She could pull her Jeep up close to the porch and stuff him into the backseat. She'd gag him if she had to. But she doubted that would be necessary. He wouldn't want to call attention to himself.

Later, once they were on the open road, he'd try to make a move. Plenty of lonely stretches of highway between here and Wyoming for him to give it his all. But that was okay because she'd be ready for him. Sure, he could easily overpower her if he somehow broke free of his restraints. That was why she'd brought pepper spray.

Despite wanting to smack him, she hoped he was considering what she'd said about finding an attorney. With his high profile he'd be arrested sooner rather than later, and she really didn't want that to happen.

"I have a question," Ethan said.

Good for him. She had a million. Like whether he'd honestly intended to give her the room. And when exactly had he recognized her. He might've thought she seemed familiar and figured he'd met her in another bar, another town. Until she'd made the *hero* crack.

None of those things mattered, really. Her job was to take him back to Wyoming. And that was exactly what she was going to do. As long as she stayed focused, avoided looking at him whenever possible. Because she had enough wits about her to know he was dangerous to her self-control, to her ability to reason. If she wasn't careful, she'd revert to that same smitten fifteen-year-old girl who'd finished her freshman year with a bunch of newly awakened hormones and a broken heart.

Even now, ten feet away, she swore she could smell him. His rugged masculine scent drifted over to her, distracting her. Tempting her to forget she had a job to do.

"Why the blond wig?" he asked after she'd refused to so much as glance at him. "You're much prettier with dark hair."

"Oh, please." Sophie rubbed her eyes. This sucked. She was too tired to drive tonight. And she had to get him back as quickly as possible. For her own peace of mind, if nothing else.

"I'm not trying to butter you up. It's the truth. Were you worried I'd recognize you?"

She knew he was playing her. Or maybe he was still fuzzy about her identity and was looking for confirmation.

She wasn't about to fill in the blanks for him. "You like blondes, that's why."

"Who told you that?"

"Every one of your girlfriends has been blonde. Think that might've given me a hint?"

"It's been three years since I've had a steady girlfriend. And she was a brunette…who happened to dye her hair blond."

Sophie snorted a laugh. "Do you ever hear yourself?" Without thinking, she spun around…and let out a squeal. "What are you doing?"

The bastard was using something to pick the lock.

"No. Oh no, you don't."

She dove onto the mattress and crawled over to him. She leaned across his chest, trying to pry his free hand away from the handcuffs. Her right breast smooshed his face, startling him. Her, too. But it was probably the only thing that saved her, since she had barely reached his hand in time.

Unable to get a good grip of his wrist, she threw a leg over him. Straddling him hadn't been the objective, but there she was. She didn't know which was worse, sitting on his junk and squeezing his hips with her thighs or having her boob in his face. But she couldn't back down now.

Pulling on his arm was like trying to move a boulder. "Damn you, Styles. Don't you get it? You're going back to Wyoming one way or another. Why are you making this so hard?"

He grinned.

Okay, unfortunate word choice. He didn't have to be a child about it. She ignored him, other than to use all her might to pull his hand away…

He went completely still. Relaxed his arm. Dropped the small pocketknife.

"Would you stop that?" he growled. "I know you're a lunatic, but my dick doesn't, okay? So ease up. Damn."

"What did you say?"

"Stop wiggling."

"Oh." She stayed right where she was but tried not to move. *Holy shit.* There was a bulge under her left butt cheek. "Then stop trying to pick the lock."

"And how am I supposed to go to the bathroom, huh? Answer me that."

"Is that what this is about? You could've said—"

"No. I don't need to go now. But the point is, you can't keep me prisoner like this. You know damn well it isn't practical..." He trailed off and quietly exhaled, his eyes, wary and watchful, meeting hers dead-on.

Sophie couldn't tell if she was breathing or not. Heat coursed slowly through her body as she fought the urge to touch his muscled shoulders and chest.

They just stared at each other. His pupils were so big and dark she hardly saw any blue. She hated to think what she looked like with her wild tangled hair. Though the bulge under her fanny hadn't subsided, so she couldn't be the utter mess she imagined.

She finally shifted her gaze to his hand, still secured to the bedpost, and she picked up the pocketknife. She had no reason to be sitting on him. Or staring at his bare chest.

She gave the cuffs a reassuring tug, mostly for show, then lifted herself off him. Very carefully. No peeking, no unnecessary touching.

One thing was for certain. She didn't want to be tempted by his bare chest all night, so she'd have to figure a way for him to put his shirt on. As for his lower half, the sheet draped over his lap would have to do for now. It sure wasn't lying flat, though.

"So, how do you plan to deal with bathroom trips? Are you going in with me to be my…handler, so to speak?"

Luckily it took very little for him to annoy the hell out of her. "You're despicable."

Ethan laughed. "I'll make a deal with you."

Sophie rolled to the side of the bed and jumped off. "You have nothing I want."

"You sure about that?"

She glanced back at him. "When you get thrown off a bull, you must land on your head a lot."

"Ah, rodeo humor. Not very good, though. Hey, don't lose my pocketknife."

She shoved it deep into her jeans pocket. "Oh, so now I have everything you want, and you have nothing of interest to me." She swept a pointed gaze over his body. "So, as for making a deal…" She shrugged. "Too bad."

"I'm being serious."

"You should be. You're in a lot of trouble, Ethan." If he made her regret this, she'd save the court time and money and just shoot him. "What is it you want?"

He started to smirk, then gave up the smug act. "Let me ride for Safe Haven," he said, steadily meeting her eyes. "And you have my word I won't run."

"What about the finals?"

"I'll make it to Vegas."

Sophie was on the verge of a colossal headache. He hadn't been a stupid boy in school, and she assumed he hadn't lost any IQ points since then. "I doubt you can do both and still meet your legal obligation."

"Watch me."

"How am I supposed to believe you won't take off on me?"

"Because I gave you my word."

"Right." She rubbed her left temple.

"Just like I gave Matt Gunderson my word I'd ride for Safe Haven." He sure seemed intent on making a mess of his career. His life. "They haven't done one of these benefits before. If it goes well, it'll become an annual event. What do you think will happen if their headliner scratches at the last minute?"

She sighed. Her job would be a lot easier if he was only pretending to be noble. But this wasn't an act. Even back in high school Ethan had had a reputation for stepping in for the underdog, and not just her.

With a small shake of her head, she reached into her pocket for the key. "What time do you ride?"

"I think I'm last."

"Of course you are," she muttered. "So, after that we leave, right?"

"I'm on the lineup for Sunday, too."

"What if you get thrown on your ass before the eight seconds tomorrow?"

With a deadpan expression, he said, "This isn't about qualifying, so it doesn't matter."

Boy, did she hope she'd packed aspirin. "We'll split the difference. You ride tomorrow and then Sunday we drive straight to Wyoming. That way you can—"

He was already shaking his head. "People paid a lot of money for tickets."

"I bet they pay even more for the finals."

"Let me worry about that."

"Oh yeah? Hmm." She frowned at the key, and then at the lock. Anything to avoid those hypnotic eyes. "That should take care of everything."

"Sarcasm? Sure, that helps."

She glared at him then. "Your main problem is that you're not concerned enough."

He had the most annoying habit of looking like the boy

next door one minute, and sex wearing a Stetson the next. It had to stop. Being in the same room with him was nerve-racking enough. But this close?

Just as she was about to free him, someone knocked on the door.

"Oh, Ethan... Ethan Styles?" It was a woman's sing-song voice. "Are you in there, sugar?"

Sophie stepped back. "You expecting company?"

He shook his head, staring mutely at her.

"Obviously you gave out your room number."

"Nope," he said, keeping his voice low.

Was she being a total idiot? Once Sophie released him, that was it. She could barely stand this close to him without her skin feeling flushed.

There was another knock. At someone else's door.

Sophie strained to hear.

"Oh, Ethan..." Same woman, same question. Trying every door? That was sick.

Kind of like her back in school. Sophie cringed at the memory of hiding under the bleachers to watch him run track. Begging for a transfer to auto shop, of all the dumb things, just so she could be in the same class as Ethan.

Teenagers did lots of crazy stuff. She couldn't let it get to her. And anyway, she'd bet the woman in the hall was a lot older than fifteen.

She held the key poised at the lock. "Wait," she said, and started when he put a shushing finger to her lips.

It was unnecessary. No one in the hall could've heard her low pitch. And she'd bet he knew that. Yet she simply stood there, staring into the vivid blue of his eyes, while he lightly skimmed the pad of his thumb across her bottom lip before lowering his hand. The move was so subtle, she'd be a fool to make anything of it.

Her cousin was right. Lola had worried Sophie would

have trouble dealing with Ethan. But she'd honestly thought he no longer had any effect on her. She was wrong. She would just be more cautious, that was all. Ultimately she trusted he'd keep his word.

"We haven't come to terms on Sunday yet," she said, voice low and firm.

Their eyes dueled a moment.

"We'll renegotiate tomorrow," he said with a sexy smile that could get a ninety-year-old woman in trouble. "After the rodeo."

She laughed. "Oh, hell no." Sophie jabbed a finger at him. "You will stick to me like glue until I tell you otherwise. I want your word on *that*."

He grinned as if he was enjoying this. "You've got it."

"And shut up when I tell you to shut up."

"Yes, ma'am."

"Without the smirk," she murmured as she inserted the small key, narrowing her attention to the task as she gathered her courage. "You think you know me. From where?"

"Wattsville High."

Her heartbeat went bonkers, and heat flooded her face, but she refused to look at him. "Because I used my real name?"

"No. I didn't remember that."

Okay, at least that was settled. The second the lock sprang, she thought of something else. "Dammit."

"What?" He was quick to pull his wrist free.

It was too late but she should've considered leaving him cuffed until she brought the Jeep closer and got her bag. She glanced at the cuffs still clamped to the bedpost. Maybe she'd leave it there for now.

"Don't worry. I'm staying right here," Ethan said. "I'm not even going for that beer I'd wanted at the Watering Hole."

"You're right about that."

He put a hand on her hip, and a soft gasp slipped past her lips.

"Hands off," she warned, as much with a glare as with words.

"Mind moving so I can get up?"

She ignored the subtle undertone of amusement in his voice and headed back to the window. After she saw him grab his jeans, she looked out through the parted drapes, aware of him moving behind her. The bathroom door closed and she sighed with relief.

Her swirling thoughts would drive her insane if she didn't get a handle on what to tell Lola. Sophie had had no business making any kind of deal with him. Would Mandy ever negotiate with a bail jumper? Not in a million years.

The minute the rodeo started tomorrow, anyone who cared would know exactly where Ethan Styles was, so she had to tell Lola something.

The smartest story to tell was mostly true. Ethan had unknowingly violated the terms of his bail and he was willing to cooperate. Which saved Sophie from having to fight off hordes of fans. Yes, some gray area existed, since she had Ethan in her clutches at this very moment, but no one had to know...

It didn't feel good lying to Lola like that. In fact, Sophie couldn't recall having ever lied to her cousin, not about anything important, anyway. And here she was doing it now because of Ethan?

God, he was like a drug. And she felt like a junkie. A cocky junkie telling herself she'd clocked in enough sobriety. She could resist him. Easy. Might as well have had *denial* tattooed across her forehead. She'd tempted fate, and fate had kicked her right in the butt.

Her phone buzzed. It was Lola's ringtone. Sophie hesitated, briefly before deciding it was better to talk now, while she had privacy.

Just as she accepted the call, Ethan opened the door.

With his damp hair slicked back, it looked darker, more like the dusting of hair visible above the waistband of his jeans. Which she could swear now rode even lower on his hips than before.

"Sophie? You there?"

"Yeah. What's up?" She started to turn, then decided she'd rather keep an eye on him. He really needed to put his shirt on.

"I thought I'd hear from you by now," Lola said. "Where are you?"

"Blackfoot Falls. I texted you when I arrived."

"Yeah, two hours ago. Have you seen him yet?"

"Yes." She watched him open the closet and pull out a duffel bag. He appeared to be ignoring her, but she wasn't stupid. He was listening, hoping to hear something he could use to his advantage. Fine. As long as he stayed quiet.

"And?" Lola's impatience came through.

"I'll have to call you later."

"Got it. Just tell me this," Lola said. "Will you be able to pick him up tonight?"

She swallowed. "No."

Ethan turned in time to see her wince. Or maybe her voice had given away her guilt over the lie. He studied her a moment before swinging his bag onto the bed and sorting through his clothes.

Lola was still there—Sophie could hear the police scanner her cousin liked to keep on low volume in the background—but she hadn't said boo.

"Okay." Sophie swallowed. "Give me an hour."

"Hey, kiddo." Lola's voice had softened. "This turning out harder than you thought it would?"

Sophie sighed. Her head hurt, as did every lying bone in her body. "Yes," she admitted. "But I can do this." She realized what she'd said and spun to face the window. It was too late. Ethan had heard. "Gotta go."

She disconnected, then stared out at Main Street until she was satisfied no telltale blush stained her cheeks.

Ethan was watching her when she turned to him. He gave her a small crooked smile that didn't help at all.

"I have to move my car and get my bag," she said with deliberate gruffness. "You going to be here when I get back?"

"I gave you my word."

"Okay." She glanced around, pretending to search for the keys she knew were sitting under her jacket. "Guess I'll just have to hope that means something to you."

"I expect so," he said, his tone making it clear he didn't like his integrity questioned. "Mind picking up a six-pack? There's a market at the other end of Main." He dug deep in his pocket, pushing the jeans down another inch before producing a twenty.

It occurred to her that he was trying to buy time by sending her to the store. Not likely. She believed his word did matter to him. And even if she was wrong, he knew he'd be a sitting duck tomorrow, so why bother disappearing now?

She grabbed her jacket and keys. "What kind?"

"Your choice."

Sophie laughed. "You're not getting me drunk."

"Sharing a six-pack? I didn't think so."

Funny, she didn't remember him having such an intense stare. It made her jumpy. She spotted the room key and scooped it up as she passed him.

He caught her arm. "You forgot this," he said, trying to give her the money.

"My treat." She pulled away. His touch had given her goose bumps she didn't want him to see. "A condemned man always gets a last meal."

Ethan's slow smile wasn't altogether pleasant. "I was going to be a gentleman and sleep on the floor. Not anymore. We're sharing the bed."

"I wouldn't have it any other way," she said with a toss of her hair, and then fled the room before she hyperventilated.

6

FUZZY WITH SLEEP, Ethan opened his eyes to slits, just enough to see if the room was dark or if morning was trying to sneak in. He wasn't a big believer in alarm clocks and only used them if he had to.

Still black as night. Good.

Yawning, he changed positions and tried to get comfortable. The mattress wasn't bad, but not great, either. He lifted his lids again, trying to remember where he was...

Not Sioux City. That was last month.

Ah, Blackfoot Falls.

That's right...the Safe Haven Rodeo.

The shock of seeing the steel handcuffs dangling from the bedpost jerked him awake. Memories of a dark-haired beauty teased him. Not just any beauty, but the girl he remembered from Wattsville High.

He looked over his shoulder at Sophie. Her long brown hair was everywhere, and so was the rest of her. One arm was thrown out clear to his pillow while she slept partially on her side, her body slightly curled away from him. Her left leg was straight, but her right leg bent at the knee, bringing her foot up near his ass.

How could someone her size take up most of the bed?

No wonder he felt cramped and achy. He needed more room to stretch out.

He rolled over to give her a gentle nudge but stopped. His eyes had adjusted to the darkness, but he couldn't see much with her other arm plopped over her face. Her chin was visible, and so were those damn pouty lips that had distracted him as a teenager and were doing a number on him now.

Ethan had a feeling she underestimated how sexy she was. More so now that she was in her twenties and had filled out. He smiled at the oversize U of Wyoming T-shirt and men's plaid pajama pants that couldn't hide her curvy body. Sophie had insisted on sleeping on top of the covers while he stayed cozy under the sheet and blanket. As if that would've stopped them from doing anything if the mood had struck.

Hell, the mood had struck plenty. At least for him. He just refused to do anything about it.

Sophie was the sort of trouble he needed to avoid. Not because she wanted to drag him back to Wyoming, although the phony accusation bullshit was something he had to straighten out. Sophie herself was the problem. That nice toned body and gorgeous face would turn any man's head, so, yeah, the packaging didn't hurt, but half the women following the tour fit that description.

But he couldn't think of a single one who had Sophie's keen curious brown eyes. The kind a man could stare into and know he was in for a real interesting ride. Hell, he knew he'd get thrown before it was all over, maybe even stomped on. But for as long as he managed to stay in the saddle, he sure wouldn't be bored.

He liked that she wore her hair longer now, past her shoulders and kind of messy. What he liked most was that she didn't seem to give a shit how it looked. Which had been pretty bad when she pulled the wig off. Any other woman he knew, including his grandmother, would've fixed it until it was just so. But not Sophie, and when she tossed back all that long hair, it was with impatience. She sure wasn't flirting.

Another thing that struck him as sexy was the way she walked. Slow and easy. And with that almost-smile teasing her lips. That was why he'd noticed her in the bar. He hadn't recognized her then. But it was the same understated sexiness that had gotten her bullied in school.

Unfortunately Ethan might've had something to do with the bullying, too.

She shifted in her sleep, making a soft throaty sound that got his cock's attention.

God, he wanted to touch her.

The thought had barely flickered when she pulled her arm from his pillow, effectively removing his best excuse. And then she turned completely over on her side, her body curling away from him so that he couldn't see her face.

Well, shit.

No, he was better off staying away. This close to the finals he needed her cooperation more than he needed anything else she could offer. Because he still wasn't convinced that he shouldn't head straight to Vegas while his agent figured things out.

Statistically the odds were against him winning another championship title. At twenty-nine he was getting too old. He had to compete against younger riders. The guys who made it to the top ten were mostly in their mid-twenties. Very few guys close to his age had claimed the title in the past fifteen years. And lately, each time he strained his left shoulder, it took longer to heal.

Damn, he wanted that second title. He wished he could say winning was strictly about funding the rodeo camp he was eager to build. But his pride was equally invested in getting that buckle for the family trophy case. His sister had a good chance of claiming another title this year. The little shit wouldn't let him forget that she'd shown him up. He knew Cara didn't really mean anything with all the jabs. In their family, competitiveness was a sport unto itself.

He stared at the back of Sophie's head, then followed the line of her body, the dip at her waist, the narrow strip of exposed skin where her shirt had ridden up, the curve of her hip.

Her hair had spread to his pillow and he picked up a lock. Rubbed the silkiness between his thumb and forefinger. He hadn't expected it to be this soft. Or to smell faintly of roses. He figured she'd be into something more edgy, spicier. But the floral scent was nice, too.

This wasn't doing him any favors. His heart started pumping faster. He should be trying to go back to sleep, not letting himself get worked up. Had to be close to sunrise. Turning his head, he searched for the time. The small bedside clock reflected the old boardinghouse feel. It was useless in the dark.

He could flip on the lamp. Instead he rolled back to face Sophie. She hadn't moved. He didn't think she was faking sleep, either. She would've tugged down her shirt and covered herself.

Hell. She was just too tempting.

Ethan inched closer. He listened to her steady even breathing before sliding in to spoon her. She didn't move, not one tiny muscle. He'd half expected a startled jerk, or an elbow to his ribs. Was she used to sleeping with someone? Maybe she had a boyfriend. Yeah, probably. Why wouldn't she?

Now, why did that idea rub him the wrong way? He

hadn't seen her in over ten years. And he'd barely known her then. What did he care if she was involved with someone?

He waited a moment and then carefully put an arm around her waist. She'd stubbornly refused to take the blanket, and now her skin was cool. A lit candle would do a better job than the overtaxed heater.

Sophie moved suddenly. Just when he thought he was about to get busted, she wiggled back until they were touching from knees to chest. Her body was instinctively seeking warmth, and he was fine with that. But if she were to wake up right now, she'd blame him for where she'd stuck her sweet round bottom. And slap him into next year.

It would be worth it.

Tightening his arm, he buried his face in her hair and closed his eyes. She was soft and sweet. They fit together real well. It felt so nice having her in his arms that maybe he could get a couple more hours of sleep. He settled in and she pressed her backside closer. His damn boner would be the thing that woke her.

"What time is it?" she murmured, her voice husky.

Ethan braced himself. "Go back to sleep," he whispered, waiting for her to go all out ninja on him.

Slipping her small hand in his, she let out a soft contented sigh.

The moment passed. Her breathing returned to steady and even. Ethan closed his eyes again, hoping for sleep. So he'd quit wondering whom Sophie thought was snuggled against her.

SOPHIE SQUINTED INTO the sunlight that managed to creep in between the drapes and hit her in the face. Morning was always her favorite time of the day. She took pride in being one of those annoyingly energetic people who jumped out of bed ready to conquer the world.

Today she felt sluggish. No, that wasn't right. The feeling was more pleasant. Warm. Comfy. Safe. Was she coming out of a dream? Smiling, she closed her eyes again and snuggled down under the weight of a—

Her eyes popped open.

She pushed the arm off and shot up from the bed.

"What the—" Ethan lifted a hand to block the sun now shining in his face. He rolled onto his back, rubbing his shoulder and frowning at her. "Christ, you damn near took my arm off."

"Don't put it where it doesn't belong." Sophie tugged down her T-shirt, then remembered she wasn't wearing a bra.

"Huh?" His expression dazed, he seemed to be having trouble focusing on her. He was still under the blanket, his lower half, anyway. Okay, so he must've been sleeping and hadn't pressed against her on purpose.

She could see how that might happen. He was probably used to having a different woman in his bed every night. Arms folded across her chest, she headed for the bathroom.

It was too cool in the room. She vaguely remembered trying to adjust the thermostat last night, for all the good it had done. Since the inn had been recently renovated, she would've expected a better heater. Tonight she was using the blanket. Ethan could just—

No. Tonight they'd be long gone. Headed back to Wyoming. No more negotiating. Someday Ethan would realize she was doing him a favor. His best shot at making the finals was to show up in court Monday.

After taking care of more urgent business, she turned on the shower. The water didn't have to be hot, just warm. That was all she asked. And since she'd stupidly forgotten her bag, if it were to suddenly appear, that would be great, too. Fresh out of magic wishes, she sighed and opened the bathroom door, then made a dash for the leather carry-on she'd left by the closet.

Ethan didn't say a word and she risked a look at him. He was lying on his stomach, arms around his bunched pillow, his face buried. No shirt. She paused just inside the bathroom to admire his well-defined shoulders and back. He had to keep himself in good shape to ride bulls. But she was glad he didn't go overboard like so many guys she knew at the gym.

His elbow moved and she hurriedly closed the door. First, she tested the water. A bit warmer would've been more to her liking, but she wasn't complaining. She stripped off her clothes and got under the spray.

Damn, she shouldn't have been so hasty to leap out of bed. Of course she'd had no way of knowing he was asleep. But if she'd lain still a few seconds to find out, it would've been nice to feel his arm around her. To bask in his heat, maybe touch him and pretend…

Oh, brother. Did she want him to carry her books and save her a seat at lunch, too? She was almost twenty-seven, had pretty much taken care of her mom and herself after her father left on Sophie's fourteenth birthday, and she had a master's degree in computer science. So how was it that she could stay stuck at fifteen when it came to Ethan?

She finished showering, dried off and got dressed without once letting her mind stray from the day ahead. The rodeo started at two. Whether he liked it or not, she was waking his ass up right now. She wanted him packed, their bags stowed in her Jeep and both of them ready to go the minute his event was finished.

Breathing in deeply, she reminded herself she was a warrior, not a silly schoolgirl. She grabbed her bag and flung the door open. Ready for whatever he—

The bed was empty.

Sophie blinked. Panic rushed through her. "Son of a bitch."

"Looking for me?"

She turned toward the sound of his voice. He stood to her left pulling a shirt out of the closet with a look of amusement. "The bathroom's all yours," she muttered, and set her bag on the bed so she could rummage through it.

Somewhere in the mishmash of clothes and toiletries was a Ziploc bag with a tube of mascara, an eyeliner pencil and lip gloss. She found it and saw a couple of blush samples the saleswoman at the makeup counter had given her some months back, maybe a year. Sophie wondered if they were still good.

She felt him watching her and looked up. "Need something?"

He shook his head, his gaze narrowed. "You didn't have to rush. If you still need time in there," he said with a nod at the bathroom. "No problem."

"Nope. Go for it."

"Okay." He drawled out the word, but it was his faint smile that made her think she should be worried. He pulled out jeans and socks from his duffel. "I'll be quick so we'll have time to grab some breakfast."

"Fine. I'll run to the Food Mart now while you—"

"We're going to the diner," he said, walking over to her and forcing her chin up. "So you'll probably want to fix your face."

Sophie gasped. She reared back and shoved his hand away. "Forgive me for not meeting your standards."

He looked confused. "That's not what I meant," he said, and had the nerve to sound frustrated.

"Go. Take your shower." She turned back to her bag, trying to hide her disappointment and hurt.

The second he closed the bathroom door, she sank onto

the edge of the bed. Screw him. The stupid insensitive jerk. She pushed her fingers through her damp hair, working past the tangles and wincing at each tug on her scalp.

She eyed the bag beside her. She doubted she had a mirror, and even if she did she'd hate herself for caring enough to look. He thought she should fix her face? Asshole.

Gee, she wondered if she looked sufficiently presentable to pick up breakfast at the Food Mart. He could forget about the diner.

All of a sudden she felt totally drained. The kind of bone-deep exhaustion that followed an adrenaline high. Great. So much for getting a good start for Wyoming tonight.

How could Ethan have said something so hurtful?

She fell back on the mattress and rubbed her eyes. After a pot of coffee and some protein, she'd feel better. She wouldn't let the remark bother her.

She had to stay sharp, remember her objective. Pulling herself into a sitting position, she glanced at the clock.

No way. It couldn't be almost noon.

She yanked her phone from the charger and stared at the numbers. This wasn't possible. She'd never slept so late in her life. Never. Last night she drank one beer. Read for an hour while Ethan watched TV. The moment he'd fallen asleep, she got into bed and conked out herself around midnight.

Huh.

She noticed something black on her fingertips. She checked the phone, but it was fine, so she set it down. Her other hand was also smudged. Glancing down at her red shirt, she saw that it was clean. And her jeans, well, who could tell…they were brand-new and still dark blue.

The dye maybe?

A thought struck her.

She grabbed her bag and turned it upside down on the bed, not sure whether or not she wanted to be right about the cause of the mysterious smudges. After checking every inside pocket, she dumped the meager contents of the purse she hated carrying but kept on hand.

God bless Lola and her makeup addiction. And for giving Sophie some of her castoffs. The blush compact was small, the mirror tiny. But it did the job.

Sophie stared at her raccoon eyes and laughed. She wasn't used to wearing the epic amount of makeup she'd put on with the wig and obviously had done a poor job of removing all of it.

She found some tissue and went to work fixing her face, relieved she'd misunderstood Ethan. Though she had the feeling she would've been better off thinking he was a jerk.

7

"ARE YOU SURE this is a private ranch?" Sophie asked as they pulled into the Lone Wolf in Ethan's truck. They'd argued over who would drive and ended up flipping a coin.

"Yeah, I'm sure. It's been in the Gunderson family for several generations. Matt owns it now. Keep an eye out for a place to park."

Sophie recognized his friend from the bar last night. "Look, isn't that Matt motioning for you?"

"Yep. He must've saved us a spot."

Sophie glanced around at the rows of parked cars close to the gravel drive, the trailers and motor homes lined up to the right of the beautiful two-story ranch house with green shutters. The two barns were easy to identify, and so was the large stable, but she had no idea about all the other smaller buildings.

"That must be the new arena he built," Ethan said as he pulled up to Matt and lowered his window.

Sophie saw the large structure standing north of the corrals. Behind it were acres of sloping pastureland.

"Were you expecting this kind of turnout?" Ethan asked his friend.

Matt's sigh ended with a mild curse. "We've got some

kinks to work out, that's for sure." He looked at Sophie, nodded and then did a double take.

"Long story," Ethan muttered. "I'll explain later."

"Should be good. See that kid with the yellow flag?" Matt pointed. "He's holding a place for you. I'll catch up with you in a few minutes." He smacked the side of the truck and stepped back.

They were shown to a parking spot next to the arena. The huge building was definitely new with a green roof and rust-colored wooden siding. She couldn't imagine what it was used for besides hosting a rodeo, and she wouldn't find out anytime soon judging by the mob about to converge on them.

Or rather on Ethan.

The crowd barely let the poor guy climb out of the truck before they swarmed him. Two reporters pushed their way to the front. The thirtysomething man wore credentials around his neck, and the woman had a cameraman with her. A cowboy Sophie had seen at the bar last night stood to the side, grinning and watching fans shove pens and pictures in Ethan's face.

He accepted the attention better than she would have. He smiled politely, greeted a few people by name and pretty much ignored the pair of blondes wearing skintight jeans and showing off their boob jobs.

Sophie took a discreet glance at herself. Okay, so she had no room to talk. Her jeans could've been sprayed on. The boobs were all hers, though. She pulled her shoulders back. It helped some.

A heavyset man wearing a diamond pinkie ring the size of her Jeep, and who'd been talking with Ethan, turned and gave her a friendly smile. "Now, who do we have here?"

Sophie had purposely stayed back and hadn't expected

any interaction. She cleared her throat. "Sophie," she said, and stuck out her hand.

He seemed surprised but broadened his grin and shook hands with her. "You're here with Ethan?"

They should've discussed this in case someone asked. For God's sake, why hadn't they? She smiled, nodded, managed a quiet "Yes." And hoped the man would leave it at that.

"Sorry, Hal," Ethan said, appearing at her side. "I should've introduced you two right off." He slid an arm around her shoulders and smiled at her, his eyes asking her to go with it. "Sophie's my girlfriend."

"You don't say." The man seemed delighted. "Good for you, Styles. Though you best watch yourself. Your young lady has quite a grip," he said, chuckling and flexing his hand.

"Um, sorry." She'd been told that many times.

"No need to apologize," he said, winking at her. "This boy needs a firm hand." Hal was mostly bald, had no facial hair, but for some reason he reminded her of an overly friendly Santa Claus. "I'll leave you to finish signing autographs, son. I'm sure we'll meet again, Sophie." He gave her a nod and then wandered toward the arena entrance.

"Hal's a good guy," Ethan said, intently watching the older man stop and shake hands with a young cowboy. "I didn't expect to see him here."

She wondered if Ethan realized his arm was still around her shoulders. "Who is he?"

"Hal and his brother own Southern Saddles." He glanced at the sponsor patch he was wearing on his sleeve, then returned his watchful gaze to Hal and the young man. "Probably checking out the new talent. Danny just joined the pro tour this year, but he's kicking ass."

"What does he do?"

"Bull rider." Ethan finally lowered his arm from her shoulders but then resettled it around her waist.

"You're not worried about being replaced, are you? Companies sponsor more than one athlete all the time."

He shrugged. "If I miss the finals again, yeah, I'd expect they might replace me. That's what I'd do if I were in their shoes."

"That's not fair," she said, and noted his small tolerant smile. "I understand it's just business, of course I do. But if you miss the finals, for whatever reason, yeah, it'll totally suck, but the fact remains that out of hundreds you qualified to ride in the first place. That has to count for something."

He just kept staring at her and smiling. "How about a kiss?"

With a laugh, Sophie leaned away from him. "People are waiting for autographs."

"How long does a kiss take?"

She moved back in close, brushed her lips across his ear and whispered, "Depends how slow and deep you go."

Ethan promptly released her and started laughing. "Yeah, thanks, I need to ride a nineteen-hundred-pound bull while I'm distracted by a hard-on."

"Go sign autographs. That should cool you off."

He kissed her right on the mouth before she could stop him. "Remember, anybody asks, you're my girlfriend."

"I could've just as easily been your cousin," she grumbled, which she knew he'd heard as he walked back toward his waiting fans.

Ethan Styles's girlfriend for the day, she thought, and actually caught herself stupidly twirling her hair around her finger.

How pathetic.

ANOTHER THIRTY MINUTES and the rodeo would officially start. Sophie sure hoped Ethan wouldn't give her a hard time about getting on the road right after his event.

Damn, the man knew everyone. Rabid fans, casual fans, the volunteers from Safe Haven who'd helped organize the fund-raiser...

Sophie couldn't keep track of all the people she'd met. But she'd taken an instant liking to Matt and his wife, Rachel. She was friendly and outgoing and treated Ethan and Sophie as though she'd known them forever.

The four of them stood near the stable, the only open area where cars weren't parked bumper to bumper.

"If we do this again next year," Matt said, eyeing the swelling crowd with unease, "we're setting up a table for autographs. Off to the side, maybe near the east barn."

"Oh, trust me, we'll be doing this again." Rachel scanned the list on her clipboard. "Here you go, Ethan," she said, and passed him a number to wear.

Ethan removed the protective sheet to expose the sticky back and slapped it on the front of his shirt.

"This should've been a one-day event," Matt muttered, too preoccupied with what was going on around them to keep up with the conversation. Poor guy. He did seem tense.

"I wondered about that," Ethan said.

Matt strained to look beyond them and nodded to someone.

"My fault." Rachel sighed. "You warned me, and I was stubborn and wanted to help, but..."

"It's okay." Matt caught her hand and pulled her close. Looking into her eyes, he smiled before kissing her. Someone yelled for him, but he was completely focused on his wife. "Ethan and I have to go. Call me if you need anything." Matt gave her another quick kiss before pulling back and winking. "Everything will be just fine."

Rachel nodded. "Thank you," she whispered.

Busy being a voyeur, Sophie hadn't noticed Ethan moving closer. She felt his hand at her waist and with a start turned to him. "What?"

So much for a tender moment à la Matt and Rachel. Sophie had barked like an old harridan.

Ethan grinned. "I'm waiting for my kiss."

She knew Rachel was watching, so Sophie leaned in to plant a peck at the corner of his mouth.

He slid his hand behind her neck, preventing a retreat. "I know you can do better," he murmured near her ear. "Kiss me like you did last night."

She was about to warn him not to push it, but he slipped his tongue inside her mouth and didn't pull back until her heart almost thumped out of her chest.

"Come on, Styles," Matt yelled. "She's not going anywhere."

"He's right about that," Sophie whispered with a gentle shove to his chest.

Ethan stared at her a moment, his smile so faint it barely qualified. "You had to ruin it."

Her breath caught. She had no idea what he meant. Or how to respond. Somehow he seemed disappointed and it bothered her.

And dammit, that bothered her, too. Why should she care?

He glanced at Rachel, touched the brim of his hat, then turned and jogged toward Matt.

"Did you mess up his ritual?"

Sophie dragged her gaze from him and looked at Rachel. "Excuse me?"

"I know a lot of rodeo cowboys are superstitious, especially right before they ride. At least that's what Matt told me. I wasn't around when he was part of the tour."

"Did you meet him after he quit?"

"No. I've known Matt most of my life. We both grew up here in Blackfoot Falls. Although we had a ten-year interruption." Rachel waved an acknowledgment to someone motioning for her. "Mind walking with me?"

"Not at all. If you have something for me to do, put me to work."

"I probably will," Rachel said, grinning at first, and then she glanced back toward the guys and sighed. "Poor Matt. I don't know how he puts up with me. I had no idea this thing would be such a headache. He's right. One day would've been enough, but everyone in town got so excited about the business the rodeo was bringing and I just figured, why not add a day?"

"You want to help your community. That's nice." Sophie smiled, starting to feel better. She liked Rachel and really hoped there was a way to help. "I have a feeling Matt isn't too upset with you."

"Oh, I'm sure he'll think of some way for me to make it up to him," she said, her green eyes sparkling even as she blushed.

"How long have you guys been married?"

"Almost eight months."

"Wow. Not that long. You mentioned a ten-year interruption?"

"Matt's four years older and he left town at nineteen. I had a stupid crush on him and was completely convinced my life was over. Oh, but please don't tell anyone. God forbid the other half of the town should find out." Rachel rolled her eyes, making Sophie laugh. "A few years later I went off to college. After graduate school I came home—it was only supposed to be for the summer." She shrugged. "I stayed to help with my family's ranch and never left again."

They reached the frazzled woman who'd waved for

Rachel. How to handle the collected entry tickets was briefly discussed and then Rachel and Sophie headed for the concessions.

"What do you do here at the Lone Wolf?"

"Not much. Most of the hired men have been here forever, so they take care of the cattle. Matt's more interested in raising rodeo stock. The horses and bulls they're using today are his. In fact, that's why he built that monstrosity," she said, glancing at the building that housed the arena. "He wanted a year-round place for demonstrations and such."

"Is he riding today?"

"Oh, God no. I'd be a nervous wreck." Rachel pressed her lips together. "Sorry, I shouldn't have—"

"No, it's fine." Sophie shrugged. "Frankly I'm not a fan. But I try not to say much."

"Yes." They exchanged looks of mutual understanding, and then Rachel said, "Okay, I want to hear all about you and Ethan."

"It's not what you think." Sophie saw they were approaching the hot dog booth and hoped a mini crisis would distract Rachel. Nothing big or awful. Just a little something—

"Oh? How long have you two been together?"

"We're not, really. When he calls me his girlfriend, it's not like— We knew each other in high school." Sophie was a horrible liar. "And honestly we hadn't been in touch for years until…well, recently."

"Huh. How weird. Kind of like Matt and me."

Sophie sniffed the chilly air. "I think the hot dogs might be burning."

"Oh, great." Rachel glanced over her shoulder. "We'll talk later. At the barbecue." She was already backing toward the booth. "There won't be too many people staying."

"Barbecue?"

"Yes, at the house. Ethan said you two could make it. Didn't he tell you?"

A woman passing out programs intercepted Rachel. Sophie thought about reiterating her offer to help, but she figured she'd mostly be in the way. She also was anxious to go inside and find a seat, though not thrilled about having to sit through so many other events before it was Ethan's turn.

Dammit, she was nervous for him.

Bull riding was dangerous enough without Ethan's eerie penchant for having one thing or another go wrong just before the finals. So how could he not be distracted? Which only upped the chances of something bad happening.

Sophie felt her stomach knot. A stiff breeze coming off the mountains made her shiver. The Lone Wolf was a beautiful spread carved into the foothills. Thousands of pines made up for the barren trees. Up this far north and at this altitude, the leaves had fallen weeks ago.

She looked up at the overcast sky and wondered if snow was expected.

Her Jeep was okay in snow. Though she had yet to put it to a real test, since the county where she lived kept the roads plowed. Out here, driving could get tricky. They could take Ethan's truck and get to Wyoming in time, but not if he insisted on being pigheaded.

A barbecue?

Right.

Under different circumstances it might've been fun, Sophie thought as she finally entered the new arena. The place was huge and, according to some people in line, had only been completed last week. There were rows of bleachers on two sides, wooden picnic benches and folding chairs directly across. Metal pens and chutes for the animals finished the makeshift rectangular arena. The floor was a combination of concrete and dirt, and whiffs of sweat and manure had already taken Sophie by surprise. She tried not to inhale too deeply. No wonder the food concessions had been set up outside.

She studied the ticket Rachel had given her earlier. Her seat was supposed to be close to the action. She sure hoped it wasn't in the row of folding chairs. Yes, there was a steel barrier separating spectators from the bucking animals. And yes, she was confident Matt knew what he was doing. But no way in hell was Sophie going to sit that close.

Volunteers from Safe Haven, identified by orange vests, were running around, answering questions, directing people to seats and, in general, looking harried.

Wow, there were a lot of people. Families with kids dressed as little cowboys were just too adorable. Herds of teenage boys crowded the barricaded pens, dividing their attention between the horses and the lists of names printed on the white poster boards hanging on the wall. An older gentleman climbed a metal ladder and, with a fat felt-tipped marker, added another name. *Mayhem.*

Horse or bull? Sophie wondered. Then decided she didn't want to know.

Of course the buckle bunnies had turned out in considerable numbers. The women stood close to the chutes, mostly in pairs, and some of them were really gorgeous. Sophie wished she'd put a bit more effort into her makeup.

When her phone rang, she saw it was Lola and quickly picked up. "Sorry. I meant to call you earlier."

"Everything okay?"

"Yes." Sophie pressed a finger to her free ear to buffer the noise and walked as far away from the crowd as possible.

"Sounds like you're at the rodeo," Lola said.

"I am, but it hasn't started yet. And unfortunately Ethan rides last."

"A lot of people show up?"

"I'm guessing over four hundred."

"Whoa. He'll get mobbed when it's over."

"I know. He's already been overrun with kids wanting autographs." She saw Rachel walk in, and the first thing that popped into Sophie's mind was the barbecue. "Oh, did I mention it might snow?"

Lola responded with silence. And then, "Is that pertinent?"

"No. Not at all." Sophie gritted her teeth.

"So what's the plan?"

Luckily an announcement that the rodeo would begin in three minutes bounced off the walls at an ear-shattering volume. The crowd responded proportionately.

"Lola? It's crazy in here. I can't hear you very well. I'll have to call you later."

The noise level was settling down and Sophie could've finished their conversation. Instead she disconnected and turned off her phone.

8

AFTER SITTING THROUGH three hours of calf roping, team calf roping, steer wrestling, saddle bronc riding and having to listen to the pair next to her, Sophie figured her penance for blowing off Lola was paid in full.

The two middle-aged men had opinions about every damn thing in the whole universe. They certainly were entitled to express themselves. Sophie didn't have to listen. Now, the tobacco chewing? That was getting to her.

She was mentally rehearsing what she could politely say to get them to keep their tobacco juice to themselves when the announcer mentioned Ethan's name. She straightened and concentrated on what the commentator was saying. His slight twang wasn't always easy to understand.

"Think he'll wear a helmet?"

"Shh." Sophie scowled at the bearded man next to her. Then she processed what he'd said. "Who?"

The man gave her a long look, then nodded toward the area behind the chutes. "Ethan Styles."

Sophie panned the faces of three cowboys. "I don't see him."

"He's not riding yet. Danny Young is up next. Then Cody Clark. Weren't you listening?"

Sophie sucked it up and just smiled. Okay, now she remembered. There were supposed to be three bull riders today.

Danny Young was announced and she leaned forward, watching him secure a protective blue helmet, then lower himself onto the back of a bull already bucking to get out of the chute.

So far all the other cowboys had worn Stetsons or another brand of cowboy hat. But then their events weren't as dangerous as bull riding. She couldn't recall seeing a helmet in Ethan's truck. She knew not all bull riders liked wearing a helmet...

After wrapping a short bull rope around his left hand, the rider gave the nod. The chute gate swung open and the black bull charged out bucking and whirling and twisting. Dirt flew from the animal's hooves. With his free hand held up high, the rider clung to the rope with his other gloved hand. The crowd shouted and cheered.

A buzzer sounded and more cheering as the crowd leaped to their feet. The rider pulled the rope free and bailed to the right, landing on his feet while two cowboys distracted the bull. As the announcer sang his praises, Danny Young jogged to safety and then pulled off the helmet and grinned at the crowd.

"I bet the kid makes it to the finals next year," the bearded man said. "He finished the season ranked forty-ninth. Damn good for this being only his second tour."

"I'd sure like to see how he does on a fiercer bucker," said his friend with the weathered face.

Sophie turned and stared at him. "Are you saying that bull wasn't scary as hell?"

The other guy laughed and leaned back. "Hey, Lenny, she's talking to you."

"What?"

Sophie sighed. "That bull looked pretty intimidating to me."

"Is this your first rodeo, honey?" Lenny asked, his craggy features softened by a kind smile.

"No, but…" She breathed in deeply and glanced toward the chute. She wished she could see Ethan. Wearing a helmet. "Bull riding is nerve-racking."

"Then you might want to sit out the last ride."

"The last— You mean Ethan Styles," she said, a sickening wave of dread swelling inside her. "Why?"

"Matt Gunderson's new to the stock contracting business. But he's raising some good rodeo bulls. I heard Twister is one mean son of a—" Lenny gave her a sheepish grin, then shifted his gaze to the arena.

She realized the next rider—Cody something or other—was being announced, so she kept quiet and let the two men enjoy the event. Although how they could voluntarily watch a bloodthirsty bull try to pulverize someone, she'd never comprehend.

Yes, she understood some rodeo basics. For instance, the bulls were scored on their performance, just as the riders were. The scores were then combined for a potential of one hundred points. So clearly the more difficult the bull was to ride, the more points the rider received overall. But points didn't matter here. Ethan had told her so last night. Matt was supposed to be his friend. So why give Ethan a son of a bitch to ride?

No, it hadn't been Matt who'd made that call. It had been Ethan. She'd bet anything he'd insisted on riding the toughest bull. Stupid, reckless idiot.

She stared down at her aching hands. And only stopped wringing them to drag her damp palms down her jeans. The crowd's collective gasp made her look up.

The rider had been thrown over the bull's massive head.

He landed face-first in the dirt and then crawled until he could finally stand. When he staggered, it was Matt who jumped into the arena and helped the cowboy to the side. The bull continued to furiously buck, trampling the man's tan Stetson. Why wasn't he wearing a helmet?

He lifted a hand to let everyone know he was all right.

The crowd responded with deafening applause. Sophie squeezed her eyes shut. Ethan was next.

Please, please, please be wearing a helmet.

"All right, folks, you all know who's up next... Having finished the season at number two, Ethan Styles is arguably the hottest rider on tour," the announcer said, which inspired a few catcalls. "Whose agility and athleticism has won him the respect of his fans. And once again a trip to the finals in Las Vegas—"

Applause and cheering nearly drowned the man out. Handmade signs had popped up in the crowd. Some clever, some incredibly corny. One sign read Marry me, Ethan.

"Settle down, folks. It might be another minute or two. Looks like he might be having some trouble with Twister, who I've been told is a savage bucker. Like the other two bulls we've seen today, Twister belongs to Matt Gunderson. No stranger to you all, but new to the world of raising bulls. He assured me we won't be disappointed with Twister, says he's a real killer. I guess we'll all find out soon enough..."

The announcer continued talking, but Sophie had stopped listening. She rose from her seat, trying to catch a glimpse of Ethan. She could see his sun-streaked hair as the bull rocked him against the metal railing. No helmet. Damn him.

"Miss? You mind sitting down? We can't see from back here."

Sophie heard the voice behind her, but not until someone touched her arm did it register the man was speaking to her. With an apology she sank back onto her seat. Maybe it was a blessing that she couldn't see. Her nerves were already frayed. Why wouldn't he wear a helmet? It was just plain foolish.

"Styles is nuts," Lenny said. "I can't figure out why he's riding this weekend. With his track record you'd think he'd be holed up somewhere with the door double-locked."

The bearded man spat into a cup. "That's what I would do. He gets injured today, he won't never forgive himself. Sure would be a shame if he missed the finals again."

"You get a chance to see him ride Bad Company at the season opener?" Lenny asked his friend. "Reminds me of this bull. Thrashing and lunging against the gate like that, he ain't about to let Styles get comfortable. What was it that happened last year before the finals? Was it his elbow—"

"Please stop saying those things." Sophie turned to the two men. "Riders are superstitious enough. Ethan doesn't need to be reminded of what's happened in the past. So, please…"

Lenny frowned at her. "It ain't like we're saying it so he can hear."

"But you're still putting it out there in the universe."

The men glanced at each other and laughed. "Ma'am, you might wanna find another sport that's easier on your blood pressure," Lenny said.

Sophie hadn't been looking for a clear shot of Ethan. But that was what she got between a pair of Stetson-wearing cowboys sitting two rows in front of her. He was still tying his rope.

"What's he doing?" Lenny mumbled. "He can't be using a suicide wrap."

"He'd be a dang fool, since he's not looking to qualify."

"A what?" Sophie asked, but the men ignored her. A suicide wrap? Okay, maybe it was better she didn't know.

Gripping the edge of her seat, she leaned forward, her heart racing. "Damn you, Ethan," she muttered under her breath, her attention glued to him. "Put on the goddamn helmet."

"You know Styles personally?" Lenny asked, frowning at her.

"Yes," she said, swallowing when she saw him give the nod. "I'm his girlfriend."

AFTER WHAT FELT like an hour inside a blender, Ethan heard the buzzer. Another two seconds and he ripped free of the bull rope and jumped off Twister. He managed to land on his feet while a bullfighter lured the bull in the other direction. Pulling off his Stetson, Ethan waved it at the cheering crowd.

Good for Gunderson. He had a winner with Twister. That son of a bitch could buck and change direction with the best of them. When he'd burst out of the chute and cut to the left, Ethan almost let go.

Sophie wasn't in her seat.

What the hell?

He'd known exactly where she was sitting. He'd spotted her after watching Kenny get an ass-whooping by one of Matt's broncs.

People were on their feet, still applauding, so Ethan waved again before he exited the arena. Once he made it to the reserved area behind the pens, he stopped to dust off his hat and the front of his shirt. Matt was waiting for him with a mile-wide grin.

Ethan laughed. "You trying to kill me, Gunderson?"

"What did I tell you?"

"I didn't think the bastard was gonna let me outta the

chute." Ethan wiped his face with the back of his sleeve. "You ride him yet?"

"Nope." Matt handed him a clean rag. "If Twister didn't kill me, Rachel would."

"Smart woman."

Ethan recognized the irritated voice even before he turned around.

Sophie had slipped behind the fence, ignoring the man who tried to stop her.

"It's okay," Matt told the cowboy, and the man backed off.

It didn't appear Sophie was aware of anything going on around her. She was focused solely on Ethan, and she looked pissed.

She stopped a foot away and glared up at him. "Styles, there is something very wrong with you."

"Okay." He grinned and put on his hat. Her cheeks were pink, her dark eyes flashing. He couldn't imagine what this was about, but he didn't like that her lower lip had quivered. "Are you gonna tell me why?"

"We'll talk later," Matt said, nodding at Sophie as he passed her.

She gave him an apologetic smile. When she met Ethan's eyes again, she didn't look angry but afraid. "Why didn't you wear a helmet?" Her voice was so soft he barely heard her. "I know you don't owe me an answer," she said. "I do. But God, Ethan, you're a smart man. Bull riding is dangerous. And I'm just trying to understand—"

He touched her hand, and she threw her arms around his neck. She'd looked so sad and small standing there he wasn't sure what to do or say. Except to hold her close until she stopped trembling. He just rubbed her back and waited for her pounding heart to slow.

"I'm sorry if I'm embarrassing you," she murmured,

her face buried against his chest. "Just give me a minute, okay?"

"Hell, you're not embarrassing me." He almost made a joke, but the words seemed to stick in his throat. "A beautiful woman cares about whether I wear a helmet or not, and I should be embarrassed?"

Keeping her face down, she bumped him with her knee.

"Ethan?" The soft voice belonged to a Safe Haven volunteer. "Sorry to interrupt, but folks are waiting for autographs."

Sophie tried to pull away, but he held her tight.

"Tell them it'll be a few more minutes," he told the older woman standing at the fence. "Please."

"Will do." With a smile she turned and left.

"No, Ethan." Sophie pushed at his chest. "Go. I'm fine."

"Twister couldn't buck me off. You think I can't hold on to a little thing like you?"

"Oh, brother." She sniffed. "Watch it. I kickbox," she said, and slowly lifted her chin. Her eyes were bright, but no tears. "Don't make those people wait."

"Why not? They get bored and hit the concessions, that's more money for Safe Haven."

Sophie laughed. "And here I thought you were just a pretty face."

"See how wrong you can be?" He smiled at her mock glare and wondered what had set her off. He doubted it was just about him not wearing a helmet. But he couldn't get into it now. "How about you come with me?"

"Oh, for heaven's sake, I'm fine. Embarrassed as hell," she said. "Though not fatally. I'm sure I'll live to embarrass myself another day. So go." She tugged at his arm. "Good grief, I think your muscles have muscles."

Ethan caught her chin and tipped her face up so he could look into her eyes. "I usually do wear a helmet. But I left

Wyoming in a rush to get here and forgot it." He brushed a kiss across her mouth. "That's no excuse. It was dumb to forget something so important."

Her bottom lip quivered again. Not from fear this time. How was he supposed to go shake hands and sign autographs when all he could think about was tasting every inch of her? He trailed a finger down her throat, then traced the ridge of her collarbone. The satiny texture of her skin drove him nuts. So smooth and soft everywhere he touched. What must the skin of her inner thighs feel like?

"We can pick one up tomorrow," she whispered, pressing into him and making it damn near impossible for him to think straight.

"Pick what up?"

"A helmet." Her eyes started to drift closed, but then she widened them. "Oh no. We leave tonight."

"I'm not going to do that, Sophie."

"Ethan…"

He kissed her lips, silencing her. And tormenting himself. All he wanted was for them to be someplace far away, alone, without distractions. Someplace where he could explore her body with his hands and mouth. Listen to her soft breathless moans when their kissing got hot and heavy. He wondered what sound she would make when he sank deep inside her.

Her stubborn lips finally yielded, letting him slip his tongue between them.

He jerked a little when her fingers dug into his bum shoulder.

"Can people see us?" she asked, slightly breathless.

"Probably."

"An awful lot of kids are out there."

"Yeah." Ethan straightened and released her. "Let's get this over with," he said, taking her hand.

She pulled it back. "I'll wait in the truck."

"Come on…" Wasn't this just great? They were gonna end up arguing. So be it, but they weren't leaving tonight. "Matt and Rachel are barbecuing."

"I heard," she said, staying a step ahead of him.

"There won't be a lot of people, mostly the riders who are staying here in their trailers." He watched her squeeze between the fence post and the wall. No way he'd fit so he just moved the whole damn temporary fence. "Did you hear me?"

"Yes, I heard you, and you already know what I have to say to that."

"My agent called," he said, and that stopped her. "He's in the middle of something with a football client. We're talking later."

"Did you not tell him how important this is?"

"I will."

She shook her head. Then without so much as a glance, she walked in the direction of the truck, leaving him to face a dozen squealing kids and a pack of buckle bunnies.

9

SOPHIE WAS IN TROUBLE. She slumped down in the truck's passenger seat, grateful for the tinted windows, and checked her texts. Two from Lola, one from Mandy and a voice mail from her mom. Since she could set a clock by her mom's Saturday phone calls, she'd listen to the message later.

But Lola was getting impatient, and Sophie could hardly blame her.

She thumped her head back on the leather headrest. It was far too comfortable to knock any real sense into her thick skull.

God, she was being stupid. Not just stupid. She'd risen to the level of too-stupid-to-live. When had she become the kind of ridiculous airhead she and Mandy liked to make fun of in bars?

Well, payback was a bitch. She was allowing Ethan to make a complete fool out of her. He probably knew she'd gotten all giddy inside when he'd announced she was his girlfriend. He was only using her to buy time and to keep the buckle bunnies at bay.

And yet, a part of her refused to believe that he'd be so heartless. Something other than ego was driving him to go after that second championship. Maybe that something was more important than her ending up as collateral damage.

She really hadn't expected to like Ethan. He was nothing like the self-centered man she'd imagined. But he was being naive. Clearly he hadn't explained the gravity of his situation to his agent. If he had, Brian wouldn't be shelving the problem for later.

Sitting up straighter, she adjusted the rearview mirror, hoping she could see how the fan schmoozing was going. She recognized a young saddle bronc rider dividing his attention between a blonde and signing a kid's T-shirt. The crowd had thinned, but her view was still limited. She couldn't see Ethan and assumed he was around the corner of the building.

A volunteer picked up trash while two more were closing down the hot dog concession. Hopefully the fans would clear out soon. The sun had gone down, and so had the temperature. She should probably offer to help. But there was a call she should make first.

Ethan needed a lawyer. And Craig Langley was an excellent defense attorney. Every deputy and assistant DA she knew couldn't stand the man, which spoke to his success at getting his clients off. The reason she didn't care for him was more personal. For months he'd been asking her out with the same dogged persistence he used to wear down prosecutors. But he was too smooth in his thousand-dollar suits and not at all her type.

She stared at her phone, well aware that if she asked Craig for help, she'd owe him. Just the thought of having dinner with him gave her the creeps. And if any of the deputies found out, she'd be the laughingstock of the whole county.

"Damn you, Ethan." She sucked in a breath and checked old incoming calls. Yep, there was his number.

Craig answered on the second ring. "Sophie?"

"Hey." She forced a smile, hoping it helped make her sound less as though she'd rather be eating worms. "Got a minute?"

"Well, now, honey, for you I've got all night."

"I need a favor," she said on an exhale, and then summed up the problem, leaving out names for now.

"Hmm, you know I always have a full caseload…" he drawled.

She held back a sigh. Fine. She'd figured he would milk the situation. "I know you're busy, Craig," she said shamelessly using that husky tone men liked. "That's why I hated to even ask, but it's a time-sensitive matter. And frankly there's no one I could trust more with this little problem."

"You were absolutely right to call me. How about we meet for dinner to discuss the details?"

"I'd love that. I really would, except I'm out of town at the moment. In Montana, actually."

"Montana? When will you be back?"

"Monday, I hope."

"All right, that's the day after tomorrow. How about I make dinner reservations at La Maison? Would you like that?"

Cringing, Sophie shoved a hand through her hair. "See, this little problem my friend has, it really can't wait that long," she said, then tensed at his silence. "But dinner at La Maison sounds—"

She hadn't realized Ethan had opened the driver's door until she saw him standing there.

"That sounds great," she said in a rush, and saw Ethan frown. "But I need to go right now."

"We don't have to eat at La Maison," Craig said, sounding confused. "I know this little bistro—"

"I'll call you later, okay?"

"Sophie?"

She hung up on him. "All done?" she asked Ethan.

He frowned. "Am I interrupting?"

"Nope. Let's go."

He slid behind the wheel and closed the door. "Did you have to cancel a date?"

"No." She noticed he didn't have his keys out.

"The food's good at La Maison."

"You've been there?"

"A few times."

"Don't they require a jacket and tie?"

Ethan cocked an eyebrow. "I happen to have both."

"Huh. I can't picture you in a tie," she said, and failed to see why he seemed to find that objectionable. "Come on, why aren't we moving?"

"Because I'm not ready to move." He turned most of his body toward her. "Do you have a boyfriend?"

"No." He had some nerve. So why did she want so badly to help him stay out of jail? Might as well change her forehead tattoo from *denial* to *stupid*.

"Well, somebody sure wants to impress you."

She glared at him. "And if he does?"

"Nothing." Ethan took his hat off and tossed it into the backseat. "I'm sorry I screwed up your date. If you want to go to La Maison, I'll take you there myself."

Sophie snorted a laugh. Good to know it wasn't just her who was acting like a ridiculous child.

"What?"

"You like the food at La Maison? How about I bring you a takeout while you're sitting in jail?"

It was Ethan's turn to glare. "You're picking a fight so we don't go to the barbecue."

"You're unbelievable," she said. "You really are." She laid her head back and rubbed her eyes, careful not to streak her mascara. Out of her peripheral vision she saw him take out his phone.

"Arnie? Tell me something good." Ethan stared out the windshield while he listened. His mouth tightened. "Arnie." He drawled the name into a warning, then waited, listening, the muscle in his jaw working double time. "You dumb fuck, you slept with her, didn't you?"

Sophie lifted her head and stared outright.

He dropped the phone into his lap and hit the steering wheel with the heel of his hand.

Cursed.

Hit the wheel again.

"Tell me," she said, the tension in her chest beginning to hurt.

"Wendy isn't going to admit she lied. She can't change her story now."

"But her husband…"

"Fullerton already knows. His ranch foreman doesn't like Wendy, so he told the old man he saw me leaving around midnight. That's why she made up a story about turning me down at the bar and me following her home."

"But as far as Fullerton knows, you could've just been giving her a ride home or dropping something off…"

Ethan smiled.

"It's possible," Sophie said, annoyed that he thought she was the one being naive. "So, why did Arnie sleep with her? And anyway, doesn't that just prove she's a serial cheater?"

"She played him. Wendy found the perfect way to keep the dumb ass from telling her husband the truth. Claiming I'd ripped her off was overkill. She must've regretted it as soon as she realized she'd have to get rid of the jewelry and deal with an insurance investigation. So when Arnie showed up in front of a bunch of witnesses she jumped at the chance to tell everyone he'd brought the jewelry back to get her to drop the charges. He made it real easy for her to keep her jewelry and stick to the lie."

"That's crazy."

"Crazy or not, I don't need that kind of publicity dogging me at the finals."

"Yeah, but who'd believe you would do something like that?"

"Probably no one but her husband, if only to keep the marriage intact and save face."

"Men and their damn egos." She saw his eyebrows go up. "Yes, I'm talking about you, too." She huffed out a breath. Something had been bothering her... "What's a suicide wrap?"

His eyes narrowed. "Where did you hear that?"

"Some guys sitting next to me on the bleachers."

Shaking his head, he sighed. "We wrap the hand we use to hold on to the leather strap. Weaving the rope between the ring finger and pinkie makes it harder for the bull to pull it out of your hand," he said. "It also makes it harder for a rider to let go."

"And he can get hung up on a thrashing bull."

"Yes, sometimes that happens."

She tried to control a shudder. "Did you use one of those wraps today?"

"No."

"Do you ever?"

"Yes," he said, his gaze steady. "But I'm not reckless, Sophie."

"Uh, do you even know what the word *suicide* means?"

"Sorry we can't all be as smart as you," he said, his expression stony. "That doesn't mean I'm stupid."

Sophie briefly closed her eyes. "I'm sorry. I know I'm snide sometimes—of course I wasn't saying you're stupid." This was another reason kids had picked on her. She just didn't know when to keep her mouth shut. "If anyone's stupid, it's me. I'm supposed to be taking you back, not trying to find a way to— You don't even care what happens. Why should I?"

He caught her waving hands and held them both in one of his. "I care," he said, and looked directly into her eyes. "I thought Arnie would come through. Brian will, but probably not in time to avoid court, so we'll head to Wyoming tomorrow."

"In the morning?" she asked hopefully.

"No. After my ride."

"That's cutting it close."

He shrugged. "I got here in twelve hours with one stop. What about you?"

"The same."

"I'll talk to Matt about switching the schedule. We should be able to leave by midafternoon. Stop at a motel halfway and get a few hours' sleep." Ethan leaned over the console to brush a kiss across her lips. "How's that?"

She nodded, happy she could call Lola and not have to lie. Happy she was sitting here in Ethan's truck, feeling his warm breath on her face. "You might still need an attorney."

"I guess it'll depend on how far Wendy pushes her story."

"I bet she wants this to go away as much as you do."

"Sure hope so." He cupped the side of her face and studied her lips, his mouth curving in a slow smile.

"Wait. Let me say this before we get crazy and I forget."

A low chuckle rumbled in his throat. "Make it quick."

"Uh-huh." She touched his jaw, intrigued by the stubble that hadn't been there this morning. The rasp against her fingertips was oddly arousing. Imagining how amazing it would feel pressed to her breasts had her holding her breath.

"Last chance," he said, sliding his fingers into her hair.

Whatever she'd been about to say was already in the wind. She hoped it wasn't important. It didn't matter. She was more interested in what Ethan was doing to her scalp. His touch was sheer heaven. The soothing massage turned into a slight tug. She realized she'd closed her eyes.

Apparently he wanted them open. Watching her face, he held her still as he lowered his mouth. Their lips barely touched and lightning shot through her. His tongue didn't politely wait for an invitation. He demanded entrance, coaxing and teasing his way inside, stoking the fire that had ignited low in her belly.

She clutched his arm, digging her fingers into hard muscle, and met each stroke of his tongue. The console was in their way. She wished they could push it to the floor. Or what if they climbed into the backseat?

A light came on somewhere behind him, closer to the house. She didn't care. Her existence had narrowed to the urgency of Ethan's touch, his greedy mouth, the feel of his warm hard body and the longing about to burst out of her chest. Her young girlish fantasies hadn't prepared her for this, not for Ethan in the flesh.

He moved his shoulder to block the light from hitting her face. But he kept kissing her, touching her jaw, the side of her chin, testing how their mouths fit together from different angles. He traced her ear with his thumb, then followed the curve of her neck, and dipped his fingers under the neckline of her top. He thrust his tongue deeper into her mouth and still she couldn't get enough of him. Finally, gasping for air, they pulled apart.

Trying to catch her breath, she looked around. When

had it gotten so dark? Where was everyone? Low-voltage security lights from the stable and barns provided a soft glow. A couple of ranch hands stood outside the well-lit bunkhouse. Lots of activity happening where the fifth-wheelers and motor coaches were parked. But it was the porch light from the house that had shone in her face. No one was close enough to see them, though.

The fog had lifted from her brain and she looked at Ethan, who was staring at her.

She smiled at him.

He smiled back.

A wave of distant laughter came from the direction of the house.

"The barbecue," they said at the same time.

"Bet they won't miss us," Ethan said, reaching for her again.

Who cared if they did? she thought, and bumped his nose in her haste to get to his mouth. He murmured an "Ouch" and she started giggling.

"I barely touched you, Mr. Big-Tough-Bull-Rider."

"I never said I was tough. I get a paper cut and I cry like a baby." He ran a palm down her arm, then worked his thumb underneath the sleeve, stretching the fabric as far as it would go so he could probe her muscles. "You're the one who feels pretty tough. Work out much?"

She knew the question was rhetorical. "Every chance I get," she said anyway, and punctuated it with a quick teasing kiss.

"Remind me not to mess with you."

"I tried to warn—" She gasped at the feel of his hand sliding under her shirt.

"Nice abs." He smiled against her mouth, then brushed his tongue over hers. His hand skimmed her right breast, proving the bra an ineffective barrier.

Her nipples tightened immediately. He dipped his fingers inside the satin cup and grazed the puckered flesh. His touch sparked a surge of liquid heat that spread throughout her body, seeking release. Seeking more…

"We're making out in your truck," she whispered.

"I noticed," he murmured, his breath coming quick and short.

"People are inside…" She tried to swallow, but her mouth was parched. "The barbecue. We have to—"

"No, we don't."

"We can't stay here—"

"Right." He caught her earlobe between his teeth and tugged lightly. His fingers pushed deeper, plucking at her nipple, while his lips trailed the side of her neck. "I don't know where my keys are."

"They aren't in my bra." She felt his smile against her flushed skin.

"You sure? I should check."

"In high school you might've found tissue, no keys, though."

Pulling back to look at her, he laughed.

Sophie sighed. Not something she would've shared had she not been so fuzzy-headed. "That was a joke."

"I figured," he said, still laughing.

She cupped the bulge straining his jeans, and that shut him up. Holy cow, he was hard. Yeah, they definitely had to go someplace private. And the second she got her thoughts and mouth in working order, she'd tell him just that.

And after he stopped hissing.

And she supposed she'd also have to move her hand. Eventually. She shifted in her seat, causing the light to shine in her eyes again.

She lifted her hand to blot the brightness.

Ethan leaned way back against the seat, and it took

her a moment to realize he was having trouble sliding his hand into his pocket.

"We have to go inside," she said.

"No, we don't. Matt doesn't care."

"You have to talk to him about changing the schedule. So we can leave early tomorrow."

With a grunt, Ethan finally withdrew the keys. "I'll call him in the morning."

"It's better to give him a lot of notice. So you won't put him in a tight spot. Otherwise you'll give in and we'll be delayed." She watched his jaw clench and understood why he was resisting. She wanted to get back to the inn, herself. "Please. I really don't want to have to go out with Craig," she murmured.

"Who's Craig?"

"What?" Oh, crap. That thought wasn't supposed to have left her brain. "Craig who?"

"That was my question."

Dammit. If they were both naked already, they wouldn't be talking. "He's an attorney. From Casper. A very good attorney, and if you need him, then…" She waved a hand, wishing he'd just go inside already. "I can probably make that happen…" She trailed off as she turned her head to stare at the darkness outside her window.

Finally he opened the door, which triggered the interior light. Something she could've done without. "We won't need your friend Craig," Ethan said, and got out of the truck.

"He's not my friend. I don't even like him." She opened her door and slid off the seat. By the time she met him on the driver's side something had occurred to her. "There's really no reason for me to—"

Ethan cut her off by backing her against the truck. He had a good eight inches on her, and with his shoulders broad as they were she couldn't see the porch or even the house. But she heard a door open and close. Heard voices and laughter.

And then Ethan's big, rough hand touched her face. The fingers from his other hand were tangled in her hair. Aware that he had pinned her with a thigh partially nudged between hers, she stood in shock for a moment, feeling the truck's cold metal against her back.

"Ethan?"

"They can't see you," he whispered, and kissed her. "You don't know them."

"But—"

His openmouthed kiss silenced her. She heard the cat-calls, so of course he did, too. And when a man with a heckling tone called Ethan's name, one hand briefly disappeared followed by rowdy laughter, so she was pretty sure Ethan had flipped him off. But even then Ethan didn't miss a beat. He slanted his mouth across hers, hungry and demanding, deepening the kiss until he'd left her breathless.

She gulped in air. "What are you doing?"

"Come on," he murmured, not breathing so easily, either. "Let's go."

She eyed the hand circling her arm and realized he meant they should leave the Lone Wolf. "But you were going to talk to Matt."

"I can't go in there. I'll call him."

A funny feeling slithered down her spine. Since she couldn't bodily force him inside the house, she rounded the hood and climbed back into the truck. He already had the keys in the ignition. "You've changed your mind about going back tomorrow, haven't you?"

He frowned at her, then reversed the truck. "No, I have not." Once he'd steered them toward the driveway, he said, "This has nothing to do with tomorrow. And everything to do with a certain physical condition that is completely your fault."

Sophie smiled when he stopped to kiss her hand. She just wished she believed him.

10

BAD VIBES WERE coming off Sophie in waves. They were halfway to town and Ethan still couldn't figure out what had caused the shift in her. It had started right after he told her he wouldn't be going inside to talk to Matt. Whether Ethan called him to change tomorrow's schedule or asked in person made no difference. And she was well aware of the damn hard-on that wouldn't quit. He couldn't have walked into the house like that.

"Did I embarrass you?" he asked after a long silence.

"When?"

"Just before we left. When I kissed you in front of Travis and those other folks."

"No. You said I didn't know them." She finally turned and looked at him. "But why *did* you kiss me like that in front of those people?"

"Travis Mills. I heard his voice and I did the first thing I could think of to avoid him." Saying it out loud made him sound like an ass. "That was rude. I'm sorry." He tugged at his snug jeans. "I got paid back, though. This hard-on is never gonna ease up."

"You could do a commercial for one of those pharmaceutical companies. I bet they'd give you a nice endorsement contract."

Ethan choked out a laugh. Nice to hear the smile back in her voice. "Yeah, I think I'll pass on that." He saw a turnout and pulled off the highway. He had a feeling he knew what could be bothering her. Might as well put her uncertainty to rest.

"What are you doing?" She twisted around to peer at the dark road behind them.

"Don't worry, I won't jump you. Not yet, anyway." He got out his phone. "I'm calling Matt."

"We'll be in town in ten minutes."

"Like you said, better to give him as much notice as possible." He listened to the rings, aware that the tension in the cab was easing. So she hadn't believed that he was serious about returning to Wyoming. It irritated him, since he'd given his word, but then he hung around with a dumb ass like Arnie, so what was she supposed to think?

Arnie didn't know it yet, but this time Ethan had had it with him. Back in school the jocks had picked on Arnie; so had the geeks, which was really pathetic. Ethan used to think he was one of those kids who just couldn't catch a break and he'd gone out of his way to befriend him. Once Ethan had turned pro he hired Arnie to do odd jobs and help him manage his schedule and social media. But the bastard hadn't only screwed Wendy; he'd screwed Ethan. And it hurt.

No surprise he was sent to voice mail, what with Matt having a houseful and all, but he hated leaving a message. For Sophie's sake, he left one anyway. It was short, to the point, and judging by her smile, it did the trick. He was glad she seemed relieved.

"I'm going to call Lola—she's my partner—oh, and my cousin. She was a year behind you in school."

He watched her pull out her phone. She was about to hit speed dial when her words sank in. "Your partner?"

She looked up, her expression wary. "We own Lola's Bail Bonds together. I'm good with computers. And Lola..." Sophie shrugged. "She's better with just about everything else."

"Why isn't your name in there?"

"I nixed it. The business is more Lola's gig. I wanted to help her get started. She knows I don't to do this forever."

"Yeah, I'm thinking you're a little better than good with computers." He sat back and left the truck idling. "When I first thought I recognized you, I figured I had to be wrong. I mean, why would someone like you be working as a bounty hunter?"

"Fugitive retrieval agent," she muttered. "Scratch that. I like bounty hunter. Sounds pretty cool."

Was she acting flighty on purpose? Sophie was crazy smart. It wouldn't surprise him if she'd skipped her senior year and had gone on to college early. "Is this something you don't like to talk about?"

"I don't understand why you would think I'm such a computer whiz or why the bail bond business wouldn't be for me."

"Because you're too smart, that's why. Jesus. You were a freshman taking junior and senior classes and you were still bored."

She stared at him, her mouth open. "How would you know that?"

Shrugging, he put the truck in gear and eased them back on the highway. "You don't think I noticed you, but I did." He smiled at a memory of her hiding under the bleachers, nearly choking to death on her first and only cigarette. "You used to wear that ugly, oversize blue coat. Remember that? It could be a hundred degrees outside, the sun hotter than hell, and you'd be wearing that damn thing."

She was still staring at him. "After that day you saved me outside the locker room, you never said a word or even looked at me…"

Oh, he'd looked plenty, before and after. Only, he'd learned to be more sly about it after the friggin' incident over the dress. "I *saved* you? When did you get so dramatic?"

She turned away and fixed her gaze on the road ahead, arms crossed in front of her. "You did save me," she said softly. "You were my hero."

Grinding his teeth, he stepped on the accelerator. Kept his attention on the road, wishing like hell he hadn't brought up the coat or the past. He'd been such an asshole.

"You were popular. Everyone liked you. You don't understand what it's like to be different from everyone else and be thrown into a new environment with no friends or…or anybody who's willing to give you a chance." Sophie sighed. "Or pull you aside and explain why everyone thinks you're nothing but a dork."

The sadness in her voice made his gut clench. "I promise you those girls didn't think you were a dork," he said, reliving the anger and shame.

He should've broken up with Ashley that very day. She and her spiteful followers had been mean to Sophie, and who knew how many other girls. All because he'd looked one second too long and Ashley had felt threatened. But he'd put up with her random cruelty because she gave great head. Yeah, some hero.

Sophie surprised him with a laugh. "You don't have to say that, Ethan. It was a long time ago. I'm over it. If anyone calls me a dork now, I'd just put them in a body cast."

He looked over and saw her flexing her left biceps. He relaxed enough to smile. "I'll keep that in mind."

"Excellent idea." She slumped back and blew out a breath. "Okay, I have to say it… You can't claim to have noticed me now, not when you basically treated me as if I were invisible back then. Why didn't you ever talk to me after that day?"

"Well, for one thing, I had a girlfriend."

"Um, yeah. Ashley. I know. Anyway, I said *talk* to me, not ask me out on a date."

"That's the other thing. You were a lot younger than me."

"Guess what? The math hasn't changed."

Ethan shook his head. "Okay, I'll say this…being sarcastic doesn't do you any favors."

"Yes, I've heard that before," she murmured sheepishly. "I'll try to remember."

How was it that he could feel this comfortable with her? She said what she wanted without holding back. And he said whatever he said, and they just moved on, no sweat. Go figure. "You were fifteen. I was eighteen. At those ages it mattered."

"I see your point."

He opened and closed his mouth. Hell, he needed to think about what he was willing to admit. Or whether telling her anything would make her feel worse.

"Just so you know…" She pulled her legs up and hugged her knees. "I thought you deserved better than Ashley. She was a total bitch. But I respect your loyalty and that you didn't mess around with other girls."

"Look, Ashley was…" How should he put this?

"Hot. I get it. You were probably thinking with your dick," she said, and Ethan had to laugh. "How long after graduation were you guys together?"

"We broke up that night."

"No way." Sophie lowered her feet to the floorboard. "There was that big party at what's his name's house."

"Justin."

She'd turned in her seat so she was facing him. "What happened with Ashley?"

"She had one of her tantrums because I complimented her friend Shannon."

"Huh. I always thought they were BFFs."

"So did everyone else, including Shannon."

"Ashley didn't break it off, though. She was too crazy about you." It wasn't a question, but Sophie was obviously waiting for an answer.

He stretched his neck to the side to loosen a kink. "I couldn't take it anymore. She was a little drunk at the party and tried to use it as an excuse, but I knew that was bullshit. Like you said, I was thinking with the wrong body part."

"Wow. See? I was so far out of the loop I hadn't even heard about it. Had to be pretty big news."

"I don't know. I was so glad to be done with school I stayed out of the loop myself."

"Why? You must've had decent grades, since you weren't on the need-a-tutor list like most of the jocks."

"I never really considered myself a jock."

"Yeah, you kind of were. You and the quarterback were the two hottest guys in school."

"Says you."

"Said a whole locker room full of girls every friggin' day. It got pretty annoying."

"Glad I didn't know." He was straight-up serious. It would've been embarrassing. "Some of the guys I hung with thought you were hot."

She stayed quiet a long time, and then she turned back to face the windshield.

He swung his attention between her and the road. "What?"

"I don't understand why you feel the need to lie. I mean, yeah, if I think about those days too much, I can get cranky. But I'm good with my life."

"Do you know why Ashley and her posse destroyed your dress?"

"Because she'd worn the same one a week before I started at Wattsville. So?"

"That was enough to piss her off," he said. "But there was more to it. She overheard me telling the guys that you looked better in the dress. And two of them agreed."

"Why would you say something like that?"

"It was true." He saw lights up ahead and hoped it was Blackfoot Falls.

"You actually said that I looked better?"

"Swear to God."

Her laugh was nervous. "That's crazy. Ashley had the biggest boobs in school."

"Not all guys like big breasts, Sophie."

"You sure?"

Ethan smiled. "Yep, pretty sure I know what I'm talking about."

She stared at him in silence for almost a minute. Who knew what was going on in that head of hers? But it gave him time to recall last night, her standing there braless in a T-shirt while he'd been handcuffed to the bedpost. Sophie fell into the perfect category. He'd had a sample feel less than an hour ago and he was itching for more. His foot automatically pressed down on the gas.

They were getting closer to the lights.

Lord, please let this be Blackfoot Falls.

"I think I like you even more now," she said finally.

Considering that he hadn't gotten to know her in school, and it had been years since he'd laid eyes on her, it was odd how she already wasn't surprising him much. It was that comfort level and familiarity he'd been feeling with her. She wasn't flirty, and she didn't try to dress sexy, which was kind of sexy in itself.

"I had fantasies about you," she said. "When I was a kid."

"Uh, do I want to hear this?"

She adjusted the seat and leaned back. "After you rescued me, I felt really special. I mean, you even loaned me your jacket and told those girls to back off. And they did. Ashley and Shannon gave me the stink-eye, but that was it. Then I heard that you'd stepped in before. For other kids who'd been bullied. Like Arnie. So I knew I wasn't so special after all."

"I'd never gotten in between girls before."

"Really?"

"Nope. The rest of the guys thought I was nuts."

"You were brave. And noble."

More than the words themselves, the conviction in her voice made him feel like crap. "I hate bullies just about more than anything, but what I did had nothing to do with being noble." Guilt had played a big part. "Can we leave it alone?" he slipped in quickly when he saw by her body language she was ready to beat the issue to death.

"Okay." Sophie smiled. "Remember this moment. So you know I can be reasonable."

Ethan held in a laugh. "We're about two minutes from the inn. Have you eaten since breakfast?"

"No. You?"

He shook his head. "I guess we should get something in our bellies." Now that he thought about it, he was hungry. He just hadn't wanted to waste time eating. After they turned onto Main Street, he reached for her hand. "We can hit the diner, or pick up something to eat in the room."

"I vote for the second option," she said, lacing their fingers together.

"Sounds good. I want to shower first, though."

"I can pick up the food. And we should make it an early night, since we might have a lot of driving to do—"

He brought her hand up and kissed the back. "I think we can forget the early night."

"You're probably right," she said, her voice a husky whisper.

"I know I am." He resented having to release her because he needed both hands on the wheel. After he pulled up to the curb, he slid an arm behind her shoulders. He leaned in just as she turned her head.

"This is the diner," she said, and then turned back to him. "I thought—" She blinked, her confused expression fading as she realized he'd been about to kiss her.

He brushed his lips across hers. "What did you think?"

"That you would shower while I got takeout."

"Or…" He zeroed in on that sweet spot at the pulse in her neck. "We could shower together," he whispered.

Her throaty moan hit him low in the belly. "Who needs food?" she murmured, turning to meet his lips.

Ethan felt her tongue slip into his mouth. She practically climbed over the console, which he was seriously tempted to rip out. People strolled down the sidewalk past the truck. Half of them probably rodeo fans, trying to peer through the darkened windows. What the hell was wrong with him? He should've driven them straight to the inn.

He promised himself he'd do just that, in a minute, probably two. Sophie tasted like heaven with a scoop of sin. Her heat filled the cab and fogged the windows. He wanted her so damn bad it was messing with his head.

From her pouty lips to her untamed hair and curvy body, they all did it for him. Those soft brown eyes, though, they got to him the most.

It had taken him months to blot out the image of her the day he'd slipped his jacket over her shoulders. She'd looked so small, her dress in tatters, but she hadn't cried or uttered a single mean word. She'd just looked up at him with so much trust and gratitude that he hadn't deserved. Afterward he'd nearly busted a hand punching his metal locker. Fixing the big dent he'd left had come out of his own pocket.

After that he'd avoided her as much as possible. Arnie had retrieved the jacket from her the next day. Once Ethan left for college the memory had started to fade and eventually disappeared.

When he realized his hand had slipped down to her breast, he tried to cool down the X-rated kiss. Sophie wasn't interested in complying, so he forced himself to pull back.

"What's wrong?" she asked, then jerked a look at the center console under her left knee. She sank back into her seat, ducked her head and swept a gaze down the sidewalk.

"Yep. Too many people around."

"Oh, jeez. Well, they don't know me, but most of them probably recognize you. Sorry."

"I'm not." He drew the pad of his thumb across her lips. They were puffier than usual. From the kissing. He wanted more of that. Leaning forward got him a firm hand to the front of his shoulder.

"We should go," she said, laughing. "As in right now. Before we get carried away again."

"Honey, we haven't even gotten warmed up yet." He turned the key. The engine made a god-awful grinding noise.

Heads turned. They both cringed.

Fine way to learn the truck had been idling all along. He shook his head, and Sophie laughed.

The drive to the inn would take three minutes tops. He doubted he could make it.

11

SOPHIE GRABBED THE room key from him and unlocked the door. She laughed when she felt his hand mold to her backside, then quickly sobered and huffed. "What did I tell you? No touching until we're…"

He gave her ass a light squeeze and smiled.

Oh Lord. He wasn't listening, so why had she bothered? She practically shoved him inside the room before their neighbors from down the hall caught up with them.

"Wait. Okay? Just wait."

"Why?"

She turned away from him because she couldn't think straight while staring into his darkened blue eyes. But Ethan put his arms around her and pulled her back against his chest. There was no missing his very insistent erection. So avoiding his gaze wasn't working at all. She was beginning to think nothing would.

He kissed the side of her neck and then trailed his lips to the slope of her shoulder. She closed her eyes, wondering if he knew what he could do to her with only a look, a smile, a brush of his lips.

It was humbling to accept that she was defenseless when it came to Ethan. In the past five years she'd made progress. She could honestly say she hadn't thought about him much. She'd stopped monitoring his standing with the tour. If a rodeo was televised, she'd sometimes watched him. But she hadn't gone out of her way.

But after only twenty-four hours in his company, she could no longer deny the cold, hard truth. Once an addict, always an addict. And when this was all over, and she and Ethan again went their separate ways... Well, God help her. The road to recovery was going to be infinitely harder this time.

With a sigh, she pushed aside the silly notion that she could save herself some pain by walking away now. No chance of that happening.

She turned around in his arms and pulled on the front of his Western-cut shirt. The snaps came apart easily. He yanked her top up and over her head. Her peach-colored bra distracted him while she pushed his shirt open, exposing well-developed pecs.

He slipped the bra strap off her shoulder, then bent his head to kiss the narrow strip of skin he'd uncovered. The light touch of his lips on flesh that had never been sensitive before almost sent her through the roof.

She went for his belt buckle and he reached behind to unclasp her bra, which he seemed determined to get rid of. Except she was equally interested in unzipping his jeans. Their arms momentarily tangled. Then it became a free-for-all with shirts, boots and socks flying everywhere.

Sophie couldn't contain her laughter, intensified by Ethan's impatient battle with her snug jeans. He was still wearing his Wranglers and wouldn't let her near the zipper while he struggled to get her jeans down, making it only as far as her hips.

"Peel, don't pull," she said, then yelped when he picked her up and dumped her on the bed.

His piercing gaze took her in, starting with her hair and eyes, before locking on her breasts. "You're perfect," he whispered, the gravel in his voice a turn-on all by itself.

"Take off your jeans," she said, her eyes feasting on his strong chest and muscled shoulders, on the flexing and release of his pecs. His skin was still tanned, no sleeve lines, nothing along his low-riding waistband, which made her wonder about a whole bunch of things. Like what she was going to find under those jeans. "Please."

He leaned over and touched his tongue to her left nipple. The light contact sent warm pleasure flowing through her body. His mouth was hot, and so was the hand he used to cup her other breast. So she didn't understand why she was shivering. Or why she couldn't seem to stop.

Ethan took the hard tip into his mouth and gently sucked while he eased the jeans down to her thighs. She put a hand on his shoulder, and with the other she strained to reach his zipper. He intercepted her, using less effort than it took to swat a fly.

But he got the message to hurry it up. In seconds he'd pulled off her jeans, leaving her in skimpy peach panties that seemed to fascinate him. She sat up, but he gently forced her back down and put his mouth on the tiny triangle of silk. His warm breath breached the material and sparked a fire inside her.

"Dammit, you're killing me," she murmured, afraid she was going to have the quickest orgasm in history.

He lifted his head. "I didn't want to rush you," he said, and slipped a finger under the material. With a sharp intake of breath, he pushed his finger intimately between her lips. "Jesus, you're wet."

His patience evaporated, replaced by a fevered haste. He stripped off her panties, dropped them right there on the floor and scooped her into his arms.

Startled, she hung on to his neck. "Where are—"

They reached the bathroom. The very small bathroom with its tiny shower. He set her on her feet and turned on the water.

"I don't know about this," she said. "It's going to be a tight squeeze."

"Luckily I'm very good at that."

Sophie looked at him and laughed. He held a hand under the spray, the other one rested on the curve of her butt and in his eyes, amusement and pure want warred for dominance.

He slipped his arm around her waist, pulled her against him and kissed her. "The water's warm," he murmured against her lips.

"Are you planning to shower with your jeans on?"

"Nope." His kiss was slow and thorough, and with her breasts pushing against his bare chest, she was never going to stop shivering. He broke the kiss. "You're going to get under this warm spray while I take off my jeans."

"Hurry, or I'll use up all the hot water." She stepped inside the narrow stall. It was almost too small for two people. They'd have to be careful—

Sophie found the soap and turned to see if Ethan was getting out of his jeans. He'd unzipped them but was just standing there watching her. It was startling. She'd never been watched like this before, and her first instinct was to yank the shower curtain closed all the way. But it was made of clear plastic, and this was Ethan. It was kind of hot knowing those hooded eyes were focused completely on her.

She rubbed the soap between her breasts and tipped her head back as she slid the bar up to her throat, taking her time and working up a lather. With her free hand she followed the suds sliding down her body, then cupped the white foam and brought it to her breast. She lingered on her nipples, plucking at the stiff peaks with her thumb and forefinger, before soaping around them.

It was easy to sneak a look at him. He sure wasn't staring at her eyes. Never in her life had she been happier that she took working out seriously. Her body was by no means perfect, but she was in good shape, especially considering her weakness for dark chocolate.

Ethan had pushed down the Wranglers, but he'd made it only to his hips. She knew the brand was one of his sponsors, and oh Lord, if they advertised with a picture of him right now, the company would sell out of jeans into the next millennium.

Their problem, not hers. She needed to give him a reason to speed things along. Slowly she turned around and used both hands to soap her butt and the back of her thighs before "dropping" the bar of soap.

Oops.

She bent all the way over until she could flatten her palms on the shower floor, knowing exactly what she was putting on display for him. Before she had a chance to straighten she heard the curtain being yanked across the rod.

Dammit. She'd wanted to get a good look at him before he—

His large hands settled on the curve of her hips. His erection slid up against her butt as he bent forward to kiss the middle of her back.

"You're driving me crazy," he practically growled the words, and removed his hand only to aim the intrusive shower spray toward the wall.

As she rose he banded an arm around her lower ribs, pulling her against him and kneading her left breast, tugging gently at her nipple. She felt his hot breath at the side of her neck, and then the slightly rough texture of his tongue, the scrape of his teeth on her skin.

She reached behind, trying in vain to touch him. But he held her body so tight to his she doubted a breeze could sneak in between them. Turned out the stall had room to spare.

"Do you even know how much I want you, Sophie?" he whispered hoarsely. "I've thought about this all day."

She hoped he'd pinch her soon. Just so she'd know this was real. That she wasn't having one of her adolescent fantasies.

No, she couldn't have come up with this scenario as a teenager.

When she tried to turn around, he wouldn't cooperate. His mouth went from her neck to her shoulder and his hand switched to kneading her other breast. But when she forced the issue, he loosened his hold. She whirled around to face him. And made herself dizzy. She laughed and swayed against him.

Holy crap, he was hard.

She had to look.

He seemed to know what she wanted and even took a step back for her. But he didn't release her arms. Good thing. If he hadn't been holding her up, she would've gone straight down to her knees.

God, he was beautiful. His tan ended about three inches below his belly button. She put her hand out to touch him.

Ethan dropped to a crouch. Apparently he had something else in mind. She gasped at the first intimate brush of his tongue. He parted her sensitive flesh and she slapped a palm against the tile for support. His tongue was sure and pointed, using just the right amount of pressure, circling the spot where she wanted it most. He dipped in for a quick second, just long enough to convince her that dying of bliss wouldn't be so terrible.

His leisurely and confusing retreat turned her thoughts to *his* possible demise instead.

And then he was kissing and licking the soft skin of her inner thigh and he was somewhat forgiven.

He slipped two fingers deep inside her, and she clenched her inner muscles for all she was worth. Her stranglehold on his fingers had him moaning and cursing under his breath.

As soon as she released him he pushed to his feet. "Jesus, Sophie," he murmured, the rasp in his voice making her skin tingle.

He took her face in his hands and claimed her mouth. Thrusting his tongue between her lips, he probed deep inside, stroking her tongue, circling it and keeping her off balance with the heady dance.

He lowered his palms to her breasts. They'd been aching, waiting for his touch, though she hadn't known it until he closed his hands over them. Her head and body swam with so many shimmering sensations that she almost missed her chance.

Finally the path was clear. She curled trembling fingers around his hard, pulsing erection. The smooth taut skin was hot to the touch.

His breath caught in her mouth. His whole body tensed. She fully expected him to shove her hand aside, and damned if she would let that happen. She stroked upward, adjusting her grip in harmony with the urgency of his moans.

He didn't try to stop her. His hips moved in a slight thrust against her palm before he went still. She slid her hand to the base of his cock, hoping to break through the tight control he was struggling to maintain. Not very nice of her, considering that she was fighting the same battle herself. They were both dangerously close to the edge.

And she wanted to push him over first.

"We should switch to cold water," he said, partly laughing, mostly groaning.

"Don't you dare." She shivered just thinking about it.

"I'll keep you warm, honey," Ethan whispered close to her ear, and released her breasts. His hands slipped around and over her bottom and firmly pulled her against him.

She lost her grip, the damn sneak. "Hey, no fair cutting short my playtime."

"Tough," he murmured, his lips and teeth doing amazing things to the curve of her neck.

Somehow he'd managed to take the soap from her. Or maybe she'd dropped it. Things were starting to blur. With a wicked smile, he slid the soap between her breasts, then over her ribs, down to her belly. She snatched the small bar from him. His hand just kept heading south until it slipped between her thighs.

"You're a devil."

His gaze locked on her face, Ethan wiggled his fingers.

Sophie bit her lip, moved a little to the left and gasped. "If I have heart failure, it's your fault."

"I'll take full responsibility." He leaned back to look down at her breasts, the tips flushed to a deep rose. Lowering his chin, he tried to catch a nipple with his mouth, but there wasn't enough room to maneuver. He sighed. "I hate this shower."

"I know." She smiled at his grouchy expression, then got up on her toes and kissed him. It wasn't a long kiss or especially sexy, but his attitude quickly shifted to enthusiastic. She dragged her mouth from his and reached behind him to give his rock-hard backside a light smack. "Turn around so I can get your back."

Wrapping her in his arms, he lifted her off the shower floor.

"Hey," she said with a muffled giggle. "What are you doing?"

"Hang on." He redistributed her weight and lifted her higher. A little nudge from him and she locked her legs around his waist. Her arms circled his neck. "You should be able to reach my back from there," he murmured, his stubbled chin lightly scraping the tender skin above her breasts.

Even if she stretched she'd only be able to reach his shoulder blades. "Um, pretty sure there's an easier way." As good as his trailing lips felt, she was kind of anxious to trade the cramped shower for the queen-size bed…

She gasped at the unexpected brush against her clit.

Oh hell, the bed would still be there.

Another fleeting touch and her body jerked, then quickly settled, hoping…no, begging for more. Begging for Ethan. She tightened her thighs around him and the pressure increased.

It was his thumb. Right? Had to be his thumb, she thought, her speeding pulse in obvious disagreement.

With each tiny movement she felt more pressure build. Heat swept off his body in great waves. Calloused fingertips dug into her butt while his palms supported her, shifting her higher when she started to sag…

Oh God, it wasn't his thumb.

She dropped the soap and clutched his shoulders.

"Don't worry," he whispered. "I won't enter you without a condom."

She just nodded, barely managing to do that. The weak shower spray glanced off the tile and hit her hair and the side of her face. She'd put herself there by moving her hips, seeking his touch. And now her hair was completely wet, yet her mouth was so dry she had to moisten her lips.

He watched the swipe of her tongue, his eyes black with desire and torment, but he kept moving, rubbing the swollen head of his penis over her clit. He was doing this for her. And she loved the hot feel of him. But God, how she wished she could sink down, let him fill her to the brink. This was torture. Mostly for him, she imagined.

"Put me down, Ethan," she said, her hand sliding off his shoulder and pausing at his bulging biceps.

"Am I not hitting you right?" he asked, repositioning both of them and rocking her against his erection. The friction made her breath catch. "Is this better?"

"The only thing better would be you inside me." She kissed him. Hard and fast. Before they got distracted again.

His lids lowered to half-mast as he lifted a hand to her face. The arm still anchored around her waist kept her suspended while he exacted a more satisfying kiss.

She wasn't that light, either. She pulled back. "Jesus, you're going to hurt yourself."

He smiled. "I bet you aren't even a hundred pounds."

"That would be a horrible bet."

Somehow he'd found another way to rub her clit, the pressure lasting until her feet hit the floor. She raised her eyebrows at him. "One for the road," she said, and then blushed like crazy. She didn't even know why.

She tried to laugh it off and would've escaped him if she hadn't tangled with the stupid shower curtain. One thing she both loved and hated about Ethan was that penetrating gaze of his. He seemed to be constantly watching her, mostly in a good way. Like when they were making out, it was nice to know he was fully engaged. But if she was being sneaky or wanted to slide something by him, forget it.

Turned out she needn't have worried. Ethan finished

washing up while she dried herself and blotted some of the moisture from her hair. She thought about turning down the covers but she wanted that perfect view of him that she'd been cheated out of earlier.

With her damp towel wrapped around her, she waited for him to turn off the water and push back the shower curtain. He shook back his wet hair and smiled at the dry towel she held up for him. The light hit him just right. Drops of water glistened on his bronzed skin. His erection had gone down some. Such a pity. Although there was still enough heft there to make her happy.

"Where did you get the tan, cowboy?"

"Mending fences."

"You lie."

"What? You think all I do is ride bulls and pimp products? I have a ranch to take care of."

"Really?" Why didn't she know about that?

"Yes, ma'am, I do. You gonna bring me that towel?"

"Nope. Come and get it."

"All right," he said, stepping out of the stall. "But you can bet that sweet little bottom of yours I'm coming for more than that."

"Bring it."

A second later it was *her* towel wrapped around *his* hips, a smug grin curving his mouth. He used the other towel to dry his hair and chest while he gave her a leisurely once-over.

Well, duh. He had lightning reflexes. Terribly stupid thing for her to forget.

She felt like an idiot standing there naked and trying to hide the goods with her hands over her breasts, her bent leg angled over the other thigh barely covering the short landing strip from her last waxing. Ridiculous, considering that she'd given him a show through the shower curtain. She probably looked like a damn cartoon character.

Ethan wasn't laughing, though. The feral intensity of his eyes had her on the move.

"Watch it," she said, backing out of the bathroom. "The handcuffs are ready and waiting…"

Sophie froze.

Oh, shit.

She looked at him, her eyes wide.

He stopped in the doorway, staring back at her, realizing the same thing.

They both turned and looked at the gleaming metal cuffs dangling from the bedpost. The bed had been made. The whole room had been picked up.

"Oh God," Sophie groaned.

Ethan choked out a laugh.

"I'm glad my name isn't on the register," she muttered.

"Yeah, thanks." He caught her hand. "How about you make it up to me?" The towel fell from his hips before he pulled her close, chest to chest, thighs to thighs, skin to breathtaking skin.

12

ETHAN SKIMMED A HAND down Sophie's back and she pressed her body closer to his, as if they hadn't already melded together. She liked touching him. Not in just a sexual way. It was the smooth, firm texture of his skin that felt so good under her fingertips, the ridges of lean muscle absent of bulk that allowed him to move with grace. He truly was a gorgeous man.

"What's that smile for?" Without waiting for an answer he kissed her.

He didn't rush, even as his arousal grew harder and thicker. His lips moved over hers at a leisurely pace. How many times had they kissed already? And yet he was nibbling and tasting as though he were learning her mouth for the first time. Her breasts were tight and beginning to ache. He might've sensed her waning patience, or lost some of his own. Sliding his hands to her hips, he moved her back toward the bed.

She crawled in between the sheets first, and Ethan, his hand on her ass, slid in right behind her.

"We used the same soap," he said, cupping her breasts and squeezing gently. "Why do you smell so good?"

"You do, too."

"Not the same." He rolled his tongue over her nipple, pulled back to study it, then plucked at it with his lips. At the same time he rubbed his thumb across the other one, over and over, until she was ready to scream.

"What are you doing?"

He lifted his head and did a quick check. "Watching them darken," he said with a self-satisfied smile.

Before she could even blink he'd spread her legs and wedged himself between them. Propping himself on both elbows, he got into a position that put his mouth over her chest. He kissed each nipple, then cupped the sides of her breasts, pushing them together and sucking both nipples at the same time.

She wasn't quite busty enough to make the task easy. But he managed to send her back into an arch as she clawed at his arm.

"Your nipples are hypersensitive," he murmured, looking at her face and kissing one tip very gently. "Am I sucking too hard?"

"No. They usually aren't this sensitive. But what you were doing— It's perfect. All of it."

He used his tongue to swirl and soothe, and then reached over her, putting his chest just above her nose. She surged up and licked his flat brown nipple. He jerked, managed to grab the pillow he was after and tucked it next to her hip.

"For that," he said, dropping back down to his elbows and shifting so that his mouth was closer to her belly, "I will show no mercy."

With her legs still spread, she couldn't be in a more vulnerable position. Or be more excited about what was sure to come. Well, besides her.

Ethan moved down a few more inches and kissed inside each thigh before lifting his head. "What? No 'bring it'?"

Sophie frowned. She had no idea what he was talking—

Oh, right. "Yes," she murmured, already out of breath, her brain misfiring. "Do that."

He smiled, but courteously didn't laugh. He tapped her hip so she'd lift her butt, and he slid the pillow underneath her. Reaching behind her head, she centered and plumped the pillow supporting her neck. She wanted to watch.

Their gazes met.

Ethan dipped his chin. She felt the long, flat swipe of his moist tongue against the seam of her lips. Her insides clenched, and her lids drooped.

"Open your eyes, Sophie," he said softly, and took another long, slow lick.

She tried not to whimper. Even when he parted her and slid his tongue along her sex. But then he used his fingers, too, and the steamy blend of sensations elicited a moan from her that could've been made by an animal in the wild.

She clutched at his shoulder, at the sheets, and finally caught a handful of his hair. His answer was to slip his hands beneath her butt and pull her more firmly against his mouth. His fingers went right back to work, plunging in so deep she couldn't breathe. And he refused to stop.

"Ethan?" She tugged on his hair. "Condom. Now."

He lightly sucked her clit.

Sophie exploded.

Her orgasm rocked the bed, shook the entire room. Maybe the whole building. Closing her eyes, opening them, it didn't matter. She couldn't see. Cold one second, and hot the next. Trying to drag air into her lungs, she wiggled and squirmed and whimpered. She pulled Ethan's hair and shoved at his shoulder until he finally eased up.

"Shh," he whispered close to her ear. He was lying beside her, propped on one elbow and petting her hair.

"What?" she mumbled. When had he moved up? "Was I loud?"

He smiled and kissed her mouth.

Able to taste herself on his lips, she shuddered.

Coming from the hall outside the room she heard receding laughter.

Reality heralded its rude reentry. "Oh God." She was never loud. Or this breathless. Or still this warm and tingly. "On a scale of one to ten?" she asked, cringing. "Ten meaning I didn't need a mic."

Ethan didn't answer, but the grin he was trying to hold back told her a lot.

"Okay," she said, wrapping her hand around his erection. "Let's see you top that."

Two strokes and his head fell back.

She took the smooth, velvety head in her mouth, and his groan filled the room. She licked and sucked the crown and stroked the rest of him with her hand until his breathing grew ragged. His long fingers circled her wrist and he gently tugged her hand away. He already had a condom out. Wow, she really had missed a lot.

Ethan tore open the foil packet and sheathed himself. Slowly. Very slowly, his tortured expression hot as hell. He'd been ready for her a long time and close to climaxing himself. Yet he'd been patient and generous, making sure he'd taken care of her first. She hoped she didn't disappoint him. She wouldn't orgasm just with him inside her. Long ago she'd given up on the elusive G-spot. The damn thing was a myth, and no one could convince her otherwise.

She pressed her lips to his shoulder. He seemed surprised when she swung a leg over his hips to straddle him. Surprised, but not displeased. He stacked a second pillow behind his head and then held on to her hips as she sank onto him.

Every millimeter sent new waves of bliss shooting

straight to her pleasure centers. She slowed down, just until she could inhale once more before she died.

Before she knew it, he pulled her up, then flipped her over, sliding his knee between hers and settling in with a kiss that was so hot it left her breathless.

"What was that?" she asked. "Are you okay?"

He smiled as he nodded. "I didn't want to come too fast."

"Oh. Well, I was kind of hoping this part of the evening would include you. Inside me."

"Ah, so you didn't want to just chat, hmm?"

"I—" She closed her mouth, tilted her head and said, "No. In fact, if you don't do something right now, I'll—"

"You'll what?"

"Ethan. I swear to God…"

He raised his right eyebrow as he lifted both of her knees to his shoulders.

She waited, watched as he pressed a kiss on each nipple. Then, with the control of a man who rode bulls for a living, he entered her. In one swift, sure move.

"Holy mother of—" Sophie put her arms over her head and braced herself on the headboard.

"Okay?"

"Quit talking. And don't hold back."

With a feral growl he thrust again. Only this time he changed the angle just a bit. She moaned, and when he started to pull back, Sophie squeezed his cock.

"Sorry," she said, when it sounded as though she'd hurt him. "Are you all right?"

"On a tightrope here. Real tight."

"Wouldn't hurt you to fall," she said, touching his hair with one hand.

"Not yet." He shifted his angle once more. Higher than she was used to, and when he pushed in again, she cried out.

This was different. She had to rethink the whole G-spot issue. Damn, Ethan had found it.

He thrust again. And she let out a scream.

Again.

Another scream.

God, they were so going to get kicked out. But she didn't want him to stop. It was the sweetest torture she'd ever endured. She'd given up trying to keep her eyes open.

One more thrust and then...

Her whole back arched and she came so hard things turned a little gray, shifted upside down, started spinning. They both hit their final shudders within seconds of each other. She'd always known Ethan was a drug, and he'd just proven it.

It took a while to catch her breath, and Ethan, too, but he still managed to lower her legs. When her heart rate slowed to about a hundred beats per minute, she shifted and he tossed himself to the left side of the bed. Good thing he had a lot of practice on his dismounts.

Thinking how loud she'd been, she pressed a hand to her warm cheek. "I can never come back to this town, can I?"

"Nope," he said, and they both laughed.

ETHAN ROLLED ONTO his back and tucked her against his hard, languid body. They sure hadn't needed the heater tonight. His skin was warm from exertion and downright hot in some places. Places that happened to be some of Sophie's favorites. In fact, she was pretty toasty herself.

She barely had the energy to glance at the clock. It was two-thirty and they'd just finished making love for the second time. They'd managed to sleep for a couple of hours before that, but then Ethan had gotten frisky again and she'd been more than happy to oblige him.

And the thing with Ethan—a very admirable, wonderful thing—there was no rushing him when it came to sex. He liked taking his time, trying different angles, milking every last drop of pleasure out of her. Now that she knew she could orgasm without manual stimulation, she wanted to do it every time. She really had to give him props for being the most patient lover ever. Although she'd been with only three other guys and they'd been just okay.

Drowsy and sated, her cheek pressed to his chest, she traced a circle around his belly button, wondering if he'd been like this as a teenager. Probably not. But if he had, good thing she hadn't slept with him. A bar set that high first time around...she would've been destined for disappointment.

"Sleepy?" he asked, idly rubbing her back.

"Why?"

Ethan laughed. "Don't worry. I'm not going to ravish you again so soon."

"Ravish? Is that what you said?"

"Too many syllables for you?"

"Ha." She stifled a yawn. "Probably." Not just sleepy, but exhausted. Yet she was unwilling to give up a single minute with him. Tomorrow they'd have twelve hours together on the drive back to Wyoming, if one or the other wasn't snoozing. "Tell me about your ranch."

"Ah yes. The ranch," he said with a quiet chuckle. "I wondered when you'd bring it up."

"Meaning?"

"I'm busted."

"What?" She brought her head up. "You lied?"

"Technically, no. I own five hundred acres over in Carver County. Including a dilapidated barn and a two-room cabin that were on the property when I bought it."

"You live there?"

"Hell no. I'm a cowboy through and through, but I like

my modern comforts. And describing the place as rustic is putting it way too nicely." He shrugged. "Someday I'll build a house. I don't know—maybe next year."

She hated that he'd tensed, though she didn't know why. He'd been living on the road most of his adult life. Maybe the idea of putting down roots made him nervous. "So, would you raise cattle? Breed horses?"

"Don't ever cut your hair." He pushed his fingers through the thick wavy mass, stopping at a tangle and working some magic that quickly loosened it.

"I hate my hair. I always have." She'd made peace and given up on it. "At least with it long I can pull it back."

"How can you hate this?" he asked, fisting a handful and holding it up before slowly letting the locks fall over her shoulder and onto his chest.

"It's frizzy and wavy and yuck."

He shook his head. "Soft and sweet—" he tugged on a curl and smiling at it "—and very sexy."

"Too many concussions," she murmured, not knowing what else to say. Joking was her go-to when she was embarrassed. Or she'd escape through sarcasm, but she was working on that particular shortcoming.

"You know Matt's arena?"

Sophie nodded, curious and confused. He was still preoccupied with her hair, but his tone had changed.

"After I build the house, I'm going to put up something similar. Probably not quite as big, but I'll leave room to expand. And I'll have to do something about the barn. Hell, it may have to be torn down and built from scratch. Then there's the stable, and after that the corrals, more fencing. I've got a lot of work ahead of me."

"Are you going to do most of it yourself?"

"If I wanted to live in a lean-to, sure." He laughed. "I can handle the corrals and fences, but that's about it."

"Okay." She was still processing the information. "Building an arena means you're going to have rodeos?"

"Not the kind you're thinking of." He stretched his back and neck, but his jaw was clamped tight as he stared up at the ceiling. "I want to open a kids' rodeo camp."

"Oh, like your parents have."

"That's not what they do. For one thing, they cater to adults and it's strictly for profit." He glanced at her. "Nothing wrong with that. It's a business. And mine will be, too. I'll charge a fee. But I won't turn away a deserving kid just because his parents don't have the money or he's not athletic. The goal is to help the kids with self-esteem. Let them come into themselves at their own pace."

"Wow, Ethan." She pushed up to look at him full on. "That's terrific."

"Yeah?" Some of the tension seemed to melt from his jaw and shoulders. "You think so?"

"Are you kidding? That is so awesome." She meant it with all her heart. For a guy like Ethan, who had money, good looks and skills that most men could only dream about, it was amazing that he understood not everyone was handed a life wrapped with a pretty bow. "I'm so excited for you."

"I can tell." He was grinning when he leaned over to kiss her. "Somehow I knew you'd understand."

"Well, of course I do. I was the one who got picked on, remember?" She placed a palm on his chest, right over his big wonderful heart.

"You weren't bullied a lot, were you? You seemed like a pretty confident kid."

"If I kept to myself, then no, I wasn't bothered much. But basically, a smart kid thrown into a new school isn't generally well liked."

"I'm sorry, Sophie." He covered the hand she'd put on his chest and squeezed before he kissed her fingertips.

"Okay, what you just did?" She snuggled against him. "Made it all worth it."

"I'm serious," he said quietly.

"Me, too." She shrugged. "I spent a lot of time in my own head. Only-child syndrome, I guess. Plus, before my dad left my mom and me, he hadn't been around all that much."

"What do you mean by *left*? He just walked out on you?"

"He worked in construction and jumped around for different jobs while my mom and I stayed in Idaho. And then he met a woman—a waitress working at a diner, I think. Anyway, he came home to pick up his things and that was that."

"Jesus, what an ass."

"Oh, I had a much stronger word for him," she said with a wry grin. "Once Mom and I moved to Wattsville to be near my aunt and her family, things were better." Sophie sat up to look into his eyes. "If there's ever a single-parent kid who wants to go to your camp but doesn't have the money, you have to take him or her in, okay? Promise me."

He tucked a lock of her hair behind her ear and smiled. "I promise."

She nodded, satisfied that he'd keep his word. "Are you thinking of a day camp, or more like a summer thing where you board the kids?"

"I haven't decided for sure, but I imagine it'll end up being both. I'd prefer to have the kids for six weeks at a time, but that means we'd open only for the summer."

"That's kind of too bad." Sophie thought for a moment. "You know, lots of schools are open year-round now. I'd have to check, but I think that means they have three weeks off between sessions."

"I hadn't thought of that. Three weeks at a time isn't bad." His brow furrowed in thought, he stared off and absently rubbed her arm. "So maybe I could offer different programs for three weeks or six weeks and put something together in the afternoons for the local kids."

Her hand still rested on his chest and she liked feeling his heartbeat accelerate with his excitement. "Anyway, you have a lot of time to mull over all your options."

He looked at her, his mouth curving in a peculiar smile. "Between you and me, I've already hired a contractor. He's drawing up plans for me to look at after the finals."

"Ethan! That's so terrific."

"You can't say anything. No one else knows."

"Not even your parents?"

"Especially not them." He sighed, looking as if he regretted the remark. "It's nothing. Just another story in itself."

"Want to hear something I've never told anyone?" She lowered her hand to his belly. Not on purpose, but now it seemed he might be interested in something other than what she wanted to share.

"What's that?" he asked, moving her hand up a few inches.

"It's kind of weird, but I've thought about doing something with kids, too. Not on such a grand scale as what you have in mind. I don't have that kind of money, but just a small no-frills martial arts studio. I didn't take up kickboxing and tae kwon do until my first year of college but getting physical and learning discipline made a big difference in my life. I know a couple of qualified people who would volunteer to help teach the kids."

Ethan was silent for a few moments. "I can see how that changed things for you," he said, his slight frown confusing her. "And don't get me wrong, I think it's great you want to give back. But I still don't get why you're not doing something more challenging. I mean, now that I know you're not even from the area, I can't figure out why you'd stick around."

"You sound like my cousin." Sophie sighed. "I told you about my dad, who I don't see and don't care to see ever again. And my mom is a perfectly nice woman who also happens to be clueless. If I were to tell her I was leaving for the moon tomorrow, she would say what she always does, 'That's nice, dear.'" Sophie saw his left eyebrow shoot up. "Seriously. I like being around family. My aunt and uncle, my cousins…we all do stuff on holidays, and if somebody's car is in the shop, we help out.

"I know, it sounds corny. Whatever." She leaned into him while her hand reclaimed those few inches of warm belly. "Who knows? Now that I've gotten you out of my system, maybe I can move on to bigger things."

She felt him tense. Not just his chest and stomach but his whole body seemed to tighten. He should be relieved that she had no expectations beyond this weekend, but instead he looked annoyed.

"We have a long drive tomorrow. You should get some more sleep," she said, and pulled her hand away.

He caught it and peeled open her fingers. "Later," he said, and put her hand back on his lower belly.

13

SOPHIE CRANED HER NECK to see inside the arena. Now that she finally had some time alone, she'd phoned Lola. This was supposed to have been a quick call, but her cousin kept placing her on hold. "Is something wrong?"

"What do you mean?" Lola was rarely this curt. With others, yes, but usually not with Sophie. And here she'd called with good news. Lola sighed. "Sorry. It's that fight I had with Hawk. I think I told you about it—well, now he's being a goddamn baby and not taking my calls."

"Let him stew," Sophie suggested when she really wanted to say good riddance. "Stop calling him and he'll get worried and call you."

"Yeah, you're probably right. So, tell me again. You're at the rodeo now, but you think you'll be leaving in an hour?"

"Basically, yes. Ethan had hoped to be moved up on the schedule sooner, but there was a mix-up. We're still leaving earlier than we originally thought." Sophie waited. "You're quiet."

"Are you a hundred percent sure he isn't playing you?"

"Two hundred percent." A nasty remark about not mistaking Ethan for Hawk sat on the tip of Sophie's tongue. It was mean, so she pressed her lips together. "Do you want me to call you once we're on the road?"

"Are you driving straight through?"

"I don't know. It depends. We're both really tired." The last word had barely tripped off her tongue and she wanted to shoot herself. Eventually she'd tell Lola about Ethan, but not yet.

"Damn," Lola muttered, half to herself. "Hold on, would you?"

"I'll call you later," Sophie slipped in. Then she disconnected without knowing if Lola had heard. She wasn't about to wait around on hold for the umpteenth time and miss Ethan's ride.

She reentered the building, but instead of returning to her seat, she stood by the privacy fence close to the arena. A few buckle bunnies had made camp near the gate used by the riders and volunteers. In the looks department the women ranged from gorgeous to holy shit. And Sophie had overheard enough earlier to know that half the buckle bunnies here had come because of Ethan.

It made her smile to imagine their reaction over him choosing plain Jane her over any of them. There had been a time when she would've been beside herself with jealousy, crippled by self-doubt and mired in suspicion over his motives.

The suspicion part, that wasn't something to be ignored in her line of work. So yeah, she'd been wary at first, wondering if he was playing her. But the 200 percent she'd quoted Lola, that was real. Ethan was one of the good guys. Who just happened to be hot.

On the other hand, maybe she'd idealized him for so long she was being selective about what she wanted to see. He certainly was no monk, not that she expected him to be, but she wondered how difficult it was going to be for him to give up being a rodeo star. Being the guy all the women wanted. Having a slew of companies eager to give him money to endorse their products. Some of that would carry over into his post rodeo career. And it seemed as if his head was on straight enough he could separate his ego from all the nonsense.

But, again, was that what she wanted to see? And heaven help her, she couldn't discount last night. The most incredible, stupendous, holy-crap-I've-died-and-gone-to-heaven night of her entire life. Past and future. And screw anyone who said otherwise.

Ethan wanted to open a camp for kids to help with their self-esteem. Oh, for God's sake, he was just a little too perfect. Maybe she was being punked. Maybe a tiny camera had been hidden in the room. She'd see herself on some stupid reality show in two weeks. Lying next to him in bed, staring at him with big goo-goo eyes. And then she'd have to move to outer Mongolia. Sadly, last night would still have been worth it.

Sophie sighed so loudly the woman next to her turned to eye her. She hoped she wasn't going to be this same idiotic person for the rest of her twenties. So this was what happened after only three hours' sleep.

And in a few minutes Ethan, who'd had the same amount of sleep, would climb on top a two-thousand-pound bull that wanted to annihilate him.

Okay, now she was feeling nauseated.

She pressed a hand to her tummy and watched a young woman with long blond hair, tight jeans and killer boots walk up to the fence. The other buckle bunnies who'd staked their claim an hour ago turned to give her a sizing-up. She ignored them and called out to some of the bronc riders, who acknowledged her with waves. Popular girl.

The team roping event finally ended, and bull riding

was up next. Murmurs rose from the crowd. Fans were used to the bull riders being last. Sophie just wanted the whole thing to be over, period.

Her phone signaled an incoming text. It was from Peggy, Sophie's contact at the sheriff's office. Nothing had changed as far as the charges against Ethan went. And Sophie owed Peggy lunch at her favorite barbecue joint.

Sophie liked the older woman, so hanging out with her was always fun. Now, dinner with Craig, that she dreaded as much as a pap smear. She stared at her phone, trying to decide if it was time to suck it up and call him back.

Ethan's name being announced stole her attention. The signs held by fans shot up in the bleachers. She recognized a few from yesterday. The blonde newcomer let out an ear-piercing whistle, stomped one of her pricy boots and yelled, "Go get 'em, Styles."

His other female fans cast her looks of disdain. She either hadn't noticed or didn't care. Sophie ignored everyone and moved to a spot where she could see Ethan getting ready to be let out of the chute. Again without a helmet, since there hadn't been time to drive to Kalispell and back to buy one.

Today he was riding another bull and not Twister, so she was thankful for that. Although she'd missed the name of the brown bull that was giving him a fit. If Matt had found reason to call him something like the Devil's Spawn, she didn't want to know.

She saw Ethan give the nod for the gate, and then everything happened quickly. The instant the bull lunged from the chute and the clock started, Sophie began counting the seconds.

One thousand one, one thousand two...

The furious animal reared and bucked and did everything in its power to throw Ethan off its back.

One thousand five, one thousand six...

The bull whirled, then changed directions.

She closed her eyes. The crowd's roar had them popping back open.

Ethan was on the ground scrambling away from the monstrous animal. He made it clear of the dangerous hooves coming down like spiked sledgehammers and waved to the fans. The buzzer had gone off at seven and a half seconds. The announcer said something about the heartbreak score and lucky this wasn't the finals.

Sophie wasn't a violent person, but she really wanted to smack the man. He was safe from her. She couldn't move. Not until she was certain Ethan wasn't limping or holding his arm funny. He seemed fine as he left the arena, dusting off his hat and himself. Finally able to breathe again, she headed off to meet him in the back.

She recognized the husky Lone Wolf ranch hand who was acting as security guard and smiled at him when he opened the gate for her. She'd made it a few steps in when the blonde with the cute boots came barreling past her. The poor ranch hand tried to stop her, but the determined woman was too fast.

At the burst of commotion Ethan turned. With a shriek, the blonde jumped at him. He caught her, but unprepared, he staggered back.

"What the hell are you doing here?" Ethan set her down and gestured to the cowboy that it was okay.

Sophie wasn't quite sure what to do. Ethan's gaze had swept over her, so she knew he'd seen her. But his attention was directed at the other woman.

"I bet you're pissed. Damn. Half a second." The blonde shrugged. "At least it didn't count." She jerked a look toward the pen where another bull waited, cupped her hands around her mouth and yelled, "Hey, Matt, the place looks awesome."

Matt flashed her a smile, then went back to doing whatever he and another guy were doing to ready a scary-looking bull for the next rider.

Ethan scrubbed at his face and motioned for Sophie to join them. Nope, he wasn't a happy camper.

"So I was on my way to Vegas, and I thought what the hell…?" The woman paused when she noticed Sophie standing there. Her gaze swept from Sophie's hair to her boots. With a dismissive frown, the blonde turned back to Ethan. "I figured I'd zip up here and see how you were doing. Make sure you weren't laid up in the local hospital in traction or anything."

"Yeah, thanks." Ethan sighed.

Sophie wasn't feeling quite as charitable. The woman was much younger than Sophie initially thought, but that didn't excuse her stupidity.

Blondie grinned, then turned abruptly back to Sophie, staring at her as if she were an intruder. "Who are you?"

"If you'd shut up long enough," Ethan said, "I'd introduce you."

Something in his expression or tone spurred a sudden realization. "You must be Ethan's sister," Sophie said, noting a faint resemblance around the mouth and eyes. "Cara?"

She nodded and shook Sophie's outstretched hand.

"I'm Sophie," she said, and because Cara had the decency to look embarrassed, Sophie liked her better. "A friend of Ethan's."

"Sure, go ahead, introduce yourselves. You don't need me," he said, and Sophie gave him a private look that said otherwise.

She wanted more than anything to put her arms around

him, make sure nothing hurt and kiss him into tomorrow. But not with his sister watching.

Cara barely spared him a glance. "Sorry about before," she said, staring at Sophie with open curiosity. "Some of the buckle bunnies get too pushy and I try to run interference. The ladies seem to just loooove my brother. I don't get it." She gave him a cheeky grin. "They don't know you like I do."

He was still grumpy. Probably overtired. And here they were supposed to hit the road right away.

Damn. It occurred to her that Cara showing up out of the blue could complicate things.

Sophie studied his face, the weariness around his eyes, the smudge at his left temple, the streak of grime on his chin. Everything else fell away. Nothing mattered as long as he was okay. She promised herself she would never let him stay up so late the night before a rodeo again.

That is, assuming she'd be in a position to carry out the promise.

He was staring back at her with those intense blue eyes, the corners of his mouth quirking up a bit.

"How are you?" she asked softly. "Everything in working order?"

His smile took over. "Come check for yourself."

Sophie hesitated. Silence doubled the awkwardness that fueled her uncertainty.

Cara must've felt it, too. She glanced around, then looked from Sophie to Ethan. "How do you guys know each other?"

"From high school," he said as he wiped the remaining dust from his face and moved to stand next to Sophie. "I want to have a few words with Matt…" He trailed off, leaving words unsaid, his gaze steady with hers. "Okay with you?"

"Of course." She knew he meant before they left, but he was reluctant to talk in front of Cara. That proved they had a problem.

When he moved in to kiss her, Sophie gave him her cheek. Clearly he didn't care for that one bit. He caught her chin and forced her to face him before he pressed his lips to hers.

"Okay, then," Cara muttered, glancing around again. "I'm gonna grab a hot dog. You guys want anything?"

Ethan might've responded in some way. Sophie hadn't said a word, but she saw that Cara was already headed for the gate.

Sophie raised her eyebrows at him.

"Look, before you rip me a new one, I kissed you because you looked as though you didn't know what to do in front of my sister." He shrugged and touched her arm. "And I figured it might get rid of Cara for a few minutes." He sighed. "Goddammit, I kissed you because I wanted to. Is that a problem?"

"No," she said. "Are you done?"

Ethan frowned. "Kissing you?"

A short laugh escaped her. "You know what? No more late nights." Sophie rolled her eyes at his instant grin. "I mean it. You could've gotten hurt today."

"Oh hell, I'm pumped so full of adrenaline before a ride I could go all night." His eyes lit and he ducked in to steal another kiss. "We should test that out."

Sophie laughed and pushed him away. "We kind of did last night."

"Let's go for two out of three."

"Come on, we have to get serious," she said, glancing over her shoulder and ignoring his murmured assurance that he was extremely serious. "I'm assuming Cara doesn't know about your little legal problem."

Send For
2 FREE BOOKS
Today!

I accept your offer!

Please send me two
free novels and two mystery
gifts (gifts worth about $10).
I understand that these books
are completely free—even
the shipping and handling will
be paid—and I am under no
obligation to purchase anything,
ever, as explained on the back
of this card.

150/350 HDL GJAQ

Please Print

FIRST NAME

LAST NAME

ADDRESS

APT.#   CITY

STATE/PROV.   ZIP/POSTAL CODE

Visit us online at
www.ReaderService.com

© 2015 HARLEQUIN ENTERPRISES LIMITED. ® and ™ are trademarks owned and used by the trademark owner and/or its licensee. Printed in the U.S.A.

◀ Detach card and mail today. No stamp needed ◀

Send For
2 FREE BOOKS
Today!

I accept your offer!

Please send me two
free novels and two mystery
gifts (gifts worth about $10).
I understand that these books
are completely free—even
the shipping and handling will
be paid—and I am under no
obligation to purchase anything,
ever, as explained on the back
of this card.

150/350 HDL GJAQ

Please Print

FIRST NAME

LAST NAME

ADDRESS

APT.#   CITY

STATE/PROV.   ZIP/POSTAL CODE

Visit us online at
www.ReaderService.com

"No." That sobered him. "Definitely not and it's gonna stay that way."

"Okay, so—any idea why she's really here?"

"She has a friend who lives in Great Falls, maybe that's part of the reason." Ethan looked out toward the crowd, frowning. "It won't be easy getting out of here without kids wanting autographs."

Sophie groaned. "You couldn't have thought of that yesterday?"

"Did you?"

"Sorry. Guess I'm tired, too." She sniffed. "One of us didn't have that extra adrenaline boost."

He barked out a laugh. "You did okay without it."

Sophie tried to think of something clever, but settled for "Oh." And then of course she had to blush.

Ethan's gaze darkened. "Come on, baby," he murmured near her ear. "Don't make me hard. Not here."

Indignant, she drew back and stared. At his face. Nothing lower. "I didn't do anything."

His quiet groan sounded so damn sexy it vibrated all the way down her spine and pooled in the most inconvenient place. And then he had the nerve to look deep into her eyes and smile as if he knew exactly what he'd just done.

Wow, she'd have to figure out what had set him off. She'd definitely do it again. Later, though. She checked her watch. Right now they had to get out of Blackfoot Falls as soon as possible.

"Go sign a few autographs," she said. "You know you'll feel bad if you don't. And if you need to talk to Matt, just please be quick?"

Ethan shook his head. "I realized the timing is wrong. He's got too much on his plate until the rodeo is over. I'll call him tomorrow."

She saw him discreetly adjust the front of his jeans and she tried not to smile. "What about Cara?"

"I don't know. But she's headed back this way."

To make room for the other riders leaving the arena, Ethan and Sophie met Cara closer to the gate. Going beyond that would put them at the mercy of insistent fans. Sophie had really had no idea how much fan and media activity surrounded the riders. A minute ago she'd seen Cara get stopped for her autograph by two excited kids dressed like cowgirls.

"I just talked to Dad," Cara said after chewing a bite of hot dog. "I told him you're still in one piece. Nothing broken that I could see. He's still pissed at you, by the way."

Ethan shrugged. It seemed he couldn't care less about his father's disposition. Except Sophie saw his jaw clench long enough to tell a different tale.

"Mom and I just think you're crazy." She grinned, her eyes sparkling with mischief. "If I were you, bro, I'd be sitting in an isolation chamber until five minutes before the finals started."

"If you were me," Ethan said, "you'd have the good sense to keep your mouth shut." He turned to watch a rider lower himself onto a restless bull thrashing against the metal chute. "Matt has himself a good contender there with Tornado Alley. That sucker's gonna be a high scorer."

"I like Matt," Cara said, ignoring her brother's dismissal. "I always have, you know that. But I think it was shitty of him to ask you to ride this close to the finals."

"The benefit was planned for September. Something got screwed up. When he told me it got pushed back, I could've dropped out. So don't blame Matt."

"Well, that just makes you even more stupid." Cara tossed back her hair. "You get hurt between now and next weekend, and you'll regret it. I'm taking home my second buckle from Vegas this year. You know I will," she said with a nasty gleam in her eye. "And won't your little corner of the family trophy case look lonely?"

Sophie fumed. She pressed her lips together to keep from saying something sarcastic to the little twit. How could she treat her brother like that?

"Too bad you drove all this way to tell me something I already know, runt." Ethan ruffled her hair, which she obviously didn't like. "Why are you here?"

Cara smoothed back her hair. "I told you, to make sure you're in one piece and haven't done anything stupid. Well, stupider than this," she said, gesturing to nothing in particular. "Miss the finals again and you'll feel like a big loser."

"Wow." Sophie couldn't keep quiet a second longer. "I used to wonder what it would be like to have a brother or sister. If this is any example—" she shook her head "—I'm glad I don't have any siblings."

Cara glared at her, a deep red creeping up from her chest to her face.

Sophie tried not to glare back. She figured she'd said enough when Ethan put an arm around her and sighed.

"Cara didn't mean anything," he said. "Our family is competitive. And sometimes we egg each other on."

"Would you ever call Cara stupid and a loser? You can't tell me that doesn't hurt, Ethan." Sophie's voice cracked at the end. Ethan visibly swallowed, and she knew she'd struck a nerve. She lowered her lashes, thoroughly ashamed of her outburst. "I'm sorry. I shouldn't have said anything." She forced herself to look at Cara. "I really am sorry."

The woman's stricken expression made Sophie feel worse. "I wouldn't hurt my brother," Cara said, reverting to her bratty temperament with a contemptuous glare. The next second she deflated into a look of dismay. "Did I, Ethan? Did I hurt you?"

He left Sophie's side to ruffle Cara's hair again. "Hell, runt, you have to do a lot better than that to get under my skin."

He was lying, of course. And Sophie for one was glad he'd done so. For now, it was better that the tension eased.

"Quit messing up my hair," Cara said through gritted teeth. She made a show of smoothing back the long blond locks. Mostly, Sophie guessed, to hide the sheen of tears in her blue eyes. Sophie was right behind her in that department.

She glanced helplessly at Ethan.

He smiled and to Cara he said, "You still haven't told me why you're really here."

Cara dumped the rest of her hot dog in the trash can behind her. "I thought we could drive to Vegas together. But you already have company, so no problem."

"I'm going back to Wyoming first. I have some business to take care of in Casper tomorrow morning."

"Are you serious?" Her eyes widened. "You have to be in Vegas in four days."

"I know."

"Ethan…" She darted a look at Sophie, who wasn't about to say a word. "Can't your business wait? I mean, you don't want to cut it too close."

"No." Ethan inhaled deeply. "No, I don't. But I'll get to Vegas in time. No matter what it takes."

"I hope so," Cara said with a concerned frown.

Jitters flared in Sophie's tummy. She hoped so, too.

14

SOPHIE WASN'T THRILLED about leaving her Jeep behind, but it would be safe in Blackfoot Falls. The main thing worrying her as they drove toward Wyoming was Ethan's uncertain future. It was possible he'd have to fly to Vegas to get there in time. And it was also possible that he wouldn't make it to the finals at all. The thought made Sophie's stomach turn.

If that crazy Wendy Fullerton refused to drop the charges and Ethan ended up spending time in jail, not having a car would be the least of Sophie's worries.

Sophie adjusted the truck's air vents for the hundredth time. They were only five miles outside town. Maybe they should turn around and get the Jeep. The sensible thing was to follow Ethan to Wyoming. No, they were both too tired to drive separately.

"What's wrong?" Ethan took her hand. "You've been quiet and edgy. Are you still upset about Cara?"

"I'm mad at myself for butting in," Sophie admitted. "And I hope your sister doesn't hate me forever, but I'm okay. Just tired." She liked that he had twined their fingers together. "So are you. Don't forget I can take over driving anytime."

"Cara doesn't hate you. And she's really not a bad kid."

"I doubt she'd like being referred to as a kid," Sophie said. "She's only four years younger than me."

Ethan frowned. "Really? Only four years?"

"Technically, four and a half. But we women of a certain age have let that half thing go."

He smiled. "Cara can be a spoiled brat at times. That's for damn sure. And sometimes her teasing can get out of hand, but you have to understand, we were raised in a competitive environment."

"You mean, like riding in junior rodeos and stuff?"

"No. Well, yeah, we did some of that later on. But I'm talking about our parents and how they viewed childrearing. Always pushing us to succeed, to be the best. They can be fairly intense at times. I don't know that I agree with their method. I think using more praise would've been better, but I wanted to explain where Cara's coming from."

Sophie didn't dare say a word. She wouldn't dream of bad-mouthing his parents. But they sounded like bullies and they might've turned Cara into one. Lucky for Ethan, he'd taken the opposite path. No wonder as a teenager he'd championed the underdogs and misfits who'd been picked on. He'd understood what it was like to be bullied, though she doubted he saw it that way.

Her chest hurt suddenly. So much made sense now. His need to win that second title. Even the kids' camp he wanted to build. More than taking the opposite path, Ethan had turned out to be a really good man. Did his family value him for *that*? He did the right thing, and not the easy thing. Like riding for the Safe Haven Benefit even if it ended up costing him a trip to the finals.

"Did you fall asleep on me?" he asked, lightly squeezing her hand.

"No." She managed a small laugh. "I'm just thinking."

"Uh-oh. That doesn't always turn out so well."

"You got that right," she muttered, her brain beginning to speed ahead. "I have an idea." She forced herself to slow down. "First, may I totally butt into your life again?"

"So, now you're asking?"

"I'm being serious here," she said, looking at him.

He gave her a sober nod before turning back to the road and putting both hands on the wheel.

"I know you said your agent would find you an attorney, but it won't be quick enough." Sophie had done a brief search on the man. He was good, had an A-1 client list. Big sports names who made a lot of money. Like the football star he was currently tied up with. If push came to shove, Ethan wouldn't be the agent's priority. Not that she'd tell Ethan any of that. "I should call Craig."

"The La Maison guy?"

"Yes, but I promise that's not important. He's local and good. If there's a way to nip this thing, he'll figure it out. Next, Wendy Fullerton needs a wake-up call. She has to know, or at least believe, that you're willing to let the media have a field day with her accusation and the arrest, everything. Her husband may pull a lot of weight in Beatrice County, but you have fans across the country and a lot of other parts of the world."

"Jesus. I'm trying to keep it out of the media."

"She doesn't have to know that. And anyway, if the charge messes up your chance to go to the finals, you won't have any choice about what's reported." She saw his lips thin and she touched his arm. "I'm sorry, but that's the truth. And honestly I'm thinking it won't go that far. Even if it's a matter of getting a continuance."

Ethan gave a grudging nod.

Sophie took a deep breath. "Hell, if Wendy still refuses

to tell the truth, I can always tell the judge you were with me that night. I'll say you came over after you left the bar."

He slowly turned to her. "Forget it. I won't have you perjuring yourself for me."

"I know it's wrong, but so is what's happening to you. I'd just be canceling out Wendy's lie. Hey, what are you doing?"

He pulled the truck off the road, only there was no exit or turnout. And not all that much of a shoulder for anything other than an emergency.

Ethan left the engine idling and turned to her.

She twisted around to see if any cars were coming.

"We're fine," he said with a quick glance in the rearview mirror. "I want you to know I understand how much it took for you to make that offer. And how much I appreciate your belief in me. But I would sit in jail for a year before I'd let you do that."

Sophie sighed.

He kissed her. "Thank you." He stroked her cheek and looked into her eyes for as long as he dared considering where they were parked. "I mean it, you're a special woman, Sophie."

She dropped her chin, embarrassed and a little sad. Feeling helpless wasn't one of her strengths. "Yeah, let's go before I end up a special pancake in the middle of the highway."

"I've been watching. You think I'd let anything happen to you?" he said as he got them back on the highway.

Oddly she truly believed that if it was within his power, he would do anything to keep her safe. Just as he'd done eleven years ago.

Somebody really needed to call Wendy and ask the lying cheat if she was prepared for a media circus. Not only would Wendy and Broderick Fullerton's names be dragged through the mud, but who knew how many guys might come out of the woodwork willing to tell the world Wendy had picked them up in bars, as well? Sounded like a good job for Ethan's agent.

Sophie was suddenly exhausted. All she wanted to do was stop thinking. About the past. About his sister's taunts. About how his parents had failed to appreciate what a terrific son they'd raised in spite of themselves. She needed to turn off her brain. Maybe take a nap. At least they were on their way back to Wyoming.

She'd laid her head back as soon as they were on the highway again, but the shutting-down-her-brain thing? It wasn't going to happen. She kept thinking over and over how this whole situation was so unfair on every level.

What if she was leading him back to the slaughter? He needed a top-notch lawyer, someone local who understood Fullerton's reach. With enough pull in the DA's office, Fullerton could be petty and have Ethan locked up long enough to miss the finals. Craig might be his best hope. "Ethan?" she said, and smiled at the hand he'd placed on hers. "We should get off at the next exit."

"Sure." He didn't ask why.

"We need to talk," she said, and stifled a yawn. Screw Wendy, screw his family, screw the unfairness of it all. "About turning around and going to Las Vegas. It's your call. Whatever you decide, I'm with you a hundred percent."

ETHAN LET HER SLEEP. It was already dark. They'd been driving for three hours and he knew she was exhausted. So was he, but not so much that he'd come up with the crazy idea to drive to Vegas.

Maybe he should've argued with her more. Or simply turned the truck around and headed back toward Wyoming after she'd fallen asleep. Hell, she'd made it clear that it was his career, his life, his decision.

It was weird because all along she'd been adamant about him showing up in court tomorrow, but now she seemed to think they could handle things— No, not they—he had to stop thinking of her as a partner in this nightmare. Not only was this his problem, but Sophie could get burned if things went sideways.

She had a lot of faith in this Craig guy, not him personally, but his legal skills. And she seemed confident that through him Ethan could take care of everything long-distance. Damn, he wished he knew what the favor would cost her. Beyond dinner at La Maison.

Ethan snorted. Like hell. He'd pay the hotshot attorney twice his fee before he'd let Sophie go on a date with Mr. Slick. What kind of man coerced a woman into going out with him by doing her a favor? For that reason alone, Ethan didn't like the guy. But Sophie had convinced him to get over himself, that his situation was too serious for him to be a dumb ass. Her exact words. They made him smile.

Sophie made him smile. A lot.

He saw their exit coming up. He hoped the motel he'd found on his iPhone was decent. In rural places like this part of Montana, you couldn't be too choosy. But if they continued on to Vegas as planned, they didn't have to rush. So no sense driving more than they had to tonight.

Once they arrived in Vegas, Sophie was going to be real happy with the suite he already had booked. He could almost hear her squeals when she saw the huge jetted tub. On second thought maybe he should find something off the strip. Damn, she could get loud when she came.

Almost on cue, she brought her head up and yawned just as he parked near the motel's ugly stucco office. He surveyed the row of mud-brown rooms. Damn place looked nothing like the website pictures.

"Where are we?" she asked after a second yawn.

"Some motel I found online. They exaggerated by a lot. We don't have to stay here."

She blinked at him. "Have you slept?"

Ethan laughed. "Not that I'm aware."

"Oh, right. You were driving." She gave him a sweet drowsy smile. "Neither of us should be driving, so this is fine. We're just going to sleep here."

"I hope not," he said, and opened his door.

She made a face at the overhead light.

"Stay here while I register." He quickly got out and closed the door so the light turned off.

The owner seemed keen on making small talk, but Ethan took care of business quickly and drove them to the room at the end. He found out their closest neighbor was two doors down. Just in case.

"It's not so bad," Sophie said, glancing around at the queen bed with a green-and-tan floral comforter that matched the curtains.

Ethan put their two bags in the closet. "Brace yourself, they even have a luggage rack."

"Oh my. Very fancy." She seemed to be waking up. "I want to see the bathroom. The size of the shower is the true test."

"Why?" He followed her inside and put his arms around her from behind. "What do you have in mind?"

"I don't even know what to call that color," she said, leaning back against him as they studied the ugly tile walls.

"Well," he said, deeply inhaling her sweet scent until he felt as if he'd had one beer too many. "The bathroom is bigger than the one at The Boarding House, and so is the shower."

"And everything is very clean."

"No bugs."

"Oh." Her gaze darted across the floor and she shifted her feet. "Why did you have to say that?"

He laughed. "Don't worry. I'll protect you."

"Yes, you will. I don't do bugs or mice."

He kept the straightest face he could. "Now, if the bed isn't lumpy or too soft—"

"And doesn't squeak."

He turned her to face him. "And since I have the most beautiful woman in all of Montana in my arms…"

"Right," she drawled with a mocking sigh, and glanced at the ceiling.

"Hey, you're talking about someone I happen to like very much. So knock it off."

Sophie blinked and blushed.

Ethan smiled and kissed her nose. Man, he liked it when she blushed. He didn't know why, but it got to him every time. "I'm thinking shower. Sex. Nap. More sex."

She was smiling up at him, her hands flat on his chest, her brown eyes sparkling. "Individual showers." He started to object and she pressed a silencing finger to his lips. "Only to save time."

He sucked her finger into his mouth.

She pressed closer. "This isn't working."

He released her finger. "Pardon me, ma'am. Please continue."

"Then sex."

"Now we're talking."

"Then sleep for as long as we can. If there's time when we wake up, then maybe…"

This wasn't what he'd expected at all. "You're serious?" He leaned back and searched her face. "This is, what…our third date and you're already cutting me off."

Sophie laughed. "Oh, sweetie, you think we've been dating?"

"Ah, that's right. You're just getting me out of your system." The remark had pissed him off and apparently he was still getting over it. Now wasn't the time to talk about it, though. He released her. "I'll take a shower first if you don't mind."

Staring at him, she nodded. She stepped around him to leave the bathroom, then looked back. "I was just teasing about the dating thing. I mean, I did handcuff you."

"I know." He smiled. "If you change your mind, you can shower with me."

"Actually I have to make a couple of calls."

He nodded, closed the door and turned the water on in the shower, but he didn't get in yet.

Looking in the mirror at the dark stubble shadowing his jaw, he thought about the past three days since he'd met up with Sophie again. Two days, three nights if he counted tonight. Jesus. Not long, but it felt like it. She was easy to be around, even when they disagreed. Or when things got prickly. His sister showing up, for instance.

He knew Sophie had gotten the wrong impression of his family. His parents weren't self-centered ogres. They did what they thought was best. But since when did he give a shit whether a woman he was involved with liked his family? That right there was the problem. He was feeling things that he probably shouldn't.

He pulled off his boots and unsnapped his shirt. Normally he'd wait and shave in the morning, but he wouldn't do that to Sophie. He opened the door and saw her sitting on the bed, talking on her cell.

She looked up in surprise but then smiled at him, her gaze slowly lowering to his open shirt. The way she moistened her lips was so damn sexy he had to force himself to keep moving to the closet. His shaving kit sat on top of his bag.

"I heard you," she said into the phone. "Call me tomorrow as soon as you find out, okay? The earlier the better. Yes, I do."

Just as he was about to close the bathroom door, he heard her say, "Thanks, Craig. I owe you."

15

"I HAVE A QUESTION," Sophie said after she'd had her shower and was crawling into bed with Ethan.

"Why do you have clothes on?"

"It's just a T-shirt."

Ethan was sitting up, pillow behind his back, the sheets at his waist, showing off a chest of the gods while looking at her with the frown of a ten-year-old. "It hides everything."

"Well, duh." She laughed until he pointed the remote at the TV and turned it off. "Okay," she said, and pulled the shirt over her head.

His hands were covering her breasts before she could even ditch the tee.

"Impatient, aren't we?" Already she was shivering from his touch. So much for them having a talk first.

"Damn right." He dragged his gaze away from the nipple he was circling with his thumb and looked at her mouth. "Kiss me now," he said in a dramatically low voice.

"Oh no, were you watching cartoons again?"

Before she knew it, he'd pulled her against his chest and claimed her mouth. She readily opened for him. He tasted minty and achingly familiar. Which was such a crazy thought she could hardly stand it. No, this wasn't a young girl's fantasy, but it wasn't her real life, either. They were two people attracted to each other and using sex to deal with a stressful situation.

His hand moved to her face and he stroked her cheek with the back of his fingers. She liked the smooth feel of his jaw against her chin and cheeks. But she also liked it when he had a day or two's worth of stubble. His tongue stroked hers, gently, seductively, taking nothing for granted. She might be a sure thing, but Ethan wanted her to be present, eager to take this journey with him because she was helpless to do anything but.

If she slid the hand she had pressed to his chest lower, she'd find him hard and ready. It would be easy to get lost in the many ways he could make her feel so good, so content, put her in a state of temporary euphoria. She was an addict, after all.

Oh yes, she had no doubt he could make her forget the things she had to tell him. The difficult question she had to ask, if only to ease her own mind. And hopefully his.

His mouth moved to her throat, leaving a trail of kisses and light nips down to her collarbone. She quickly drew in air and then leaned back, breaking contact with his mouth.

He looked up with a lazy smile. "Where do you think you're going?" he murmured, and wrapped an arm around her.

Constantly amazed at the gentleness of his large hands and strong arms, she tried to remain firm and not give in to his seeking mouth. "I'm not going anywhere," she said. "Actually I wanted to talk." She saw his expression fall, and with a laugh she cupped his jaw. "It's nothing horrible." She lowered her hand. "At least I hope not."

He sat back against the pillow and leveled his intense gaze with her eyes. She took a moment to arrange her own pillow, quickly compose herself and pull the sheet up to her breasts. He very obviously didn't care for that.

"When I said—" She cleared her throat. "The other night, when I made a crack about getting you out of my system…I swear I didn't mean anything by it."

Ethan snorted, shrugged a shoulder. "I know that."

She shook her head. "I hurt you. And I'm so sorry."

"You think you hurt me?" He lifted his eyebrows and gave her a look that bordered on patronizing.

Sophie didn't just think, she knew. She'd seen the same wounded expression in his eyes with Cara. Fleeting but unmistakable.

"All right, I mentioned it earlier, so I get why you think it upset me, but you're wrong. So don't worry about it."

"It was a thoughtless line directed more at myself than at you." She sighed at his stony reaction. "I had a huge crush on you after that day in school. It was so bad I couldn't even concentrate on studying."

His features softened. "Huh. For what it's worth, I couldn't tell. And I'd checked you out plenty."

"Liar."

"I did," he said with an odd laugh that told her he might be telling the truth. "But I was a lot more careful so Ashley wouldn't go nuts again."

"Wow, high school really sucked."

"Yes, in many ways it did." He reached for her hand. "Is that it? That's what you wanted to tell me?"

She held his gaze. "You haven't asked me about what the lawyer I hired on your behalf had to say."

"Craig?"

"Yes, Craig Langley."

"Okay." He released her hand. "I'm listening."

Oh, brother. It wasn't as if she'd done something behind his back. Ethan knew she was going to contact Craig. And yet the same brooding expression was on his face from a minute ago. "He's contacting the sheriff's office for a copy of the arrest report and Wendy's statement. Then he'll get back to us tomorrow first thing. He understands this is time-sensitive." She absolutely had no idea what Ethan was thinking. He'd closed her off. "I know you don't like talking about this, but—"

"I don't like that you feel you owe the guy. Certainly not on my behalf. Hell, it's not as if we're asking him to represent me for free."

Sophie relaxed a bit. "He's super busy, so yeah, I do owe him. And I don't care even a tiny bit. I've said it before, and I'll say it again. Craig is your best shot at making this all go away."

Ethan stared back a moment too long. "Why are you here, Sophie? Helping me like this. Do you feel you owe me?"

It was a fair question, she supposed. The answer, though, wasn't an easy one. Not if she wanted to be truthful. She swallowed around the lump forming in her throat. "No," she said. "I don't feel like I do, which is kind of odd, actually." She forced herself to keep her eyes even with his. "That stupid crush I told you about…I might still have a tiny itty-bitty piece of it left."

Ethan's mouth curved in a heart-stopping smile. "Good," he said, gathering her in his arms. "I might have a crush on you, too."

Before she could respond, he began kissing and biting her neck. She let out a shriek of laughter, then promptly covered her loud mouth.

"It's okay," he murmured, taking another nip. "The next two rooms are vacant."

She shoved him away to look at him. "And you know this because…?"

"Yes, honey," he said without apology, "I asked."

Sophie gasped, embarrassed, flustered… And then she just laughed.

Mostly because he was tickling behind her ear with his tongue. His hands were busy rubbing a nipple and cupping her butt. She loved having the freedom to skim her palm over his pecs while watching his shoulder muscles ripple. He was so damn beautiful it almost wasn't fair.

"Have you ever modeled for your sponsors?" she asked, and when he didn't answer, she rephrased it. "Like for a magazine ad?"

He kissed her collarbone, paused. "Once. When I was younger," he said, and continued blazing a path to her breast.

"Shirtless?"

When he didn't answer, she grinned. How had she not found the ad in one of her many searches back in her obsessive years?

He flicked his tongue over a very hard, sensitive nipple. Just as she thought she couldn't stand another second, he sucked it into his mouth and she arched slightly. The moment she relaxed he slid a hand between her thighs, then surprised her by going in the direction she hadn't expected.

He cradled the back of her calf in his palm, lightly caressing the muscle as he moved toward her ankle. His mouth moved to her other nipple, lightly biting the tight bud, then licking and sucking it until fire had spread through her veins.

Sophie reached under the sheets and found her prize. He hissed at her touch. Groaned when she wrapped her hand tighter and stroked him to the base of his erection. She took her time learning his shape, the smooth texture of his fever-hot flesh. She wanted to feel everything before she got lost in all the sexy things he did to her.

Ethan murmured some indistinct words—it might've been a mild curse—and then he pulled the sheet back and stared down at her hand wrapped around him, stroking upward. She paused at the rim of the crown and kissed him there.

"Sophie," he whispered, his breathless rasp so hot she felt it all the way to her swollen center.

He'd abandoned her leg, and she was sorry she interrupted him before seeing where he was going with that. But then he urged her thighs apart and slid a finger along the seam of her lips, and her mind went blank. Unconsciously she squeezed him tighter, and he dipped two fingertips inside her. Not far, just enough to tease her. To make her whimper.

He leaned forward at a slight angle so he could kiss her mouth. He kept his fingertips inside her and she hadn't given up her hold on his erection.

"I want to try something," he murmured against her mouth before leaning back to look at her.

"Okay," she said, and released him. It briefly occurred to her she should probably be wary. Or at least ask what he had in mind, but gazing into his blue eyes, she knew he wouldn't harm her.

He brought their faces close together and rested his forehead against hers. "It's nothing kinky or weird," he said. "I promise."

"I didn't think it would be."

Ethan smiled as he drew back. His fingers were still inside her. He pushed in a little deeper, his nostrils flaring, his expression strained, as if he might be rethinking his plan. Finally he pulled out.

He threw the covers to the foot of the bed. Grabbed a condom off the nightstand. Pushed the pillows out of the way so there was a clear spot in the middle of the mattress.

He shifted until he was sitting close to the center, his legs crossed loosely at the ankles.

She tried not to stare at his erection, but that was asking too much of herself. She figured out what he wanted to do, and her heart was already racing toward the finish line.

"I want you to sit on me," he said as he rolled on the condom. "As if you were going to wrap your legs around my waist. You'll be sort of sitting on my thighs at first. We'll find a fit to accommodate our height difference."

She nodded, and Ethan put his hands on her waist to help guide her as she climbed on board.

"Making the adjustments should be fun," she said.

Ethan's laugh turned into a groan as she sank down on him.

Maybe that was why he didn't notice that it was still an awkward arrangement. If her legs were a tad longer, it would be easier. She wiggled into a better position and ignored his tormented groans.

He reached behind and cupped her butt with both hands. He lifted her a tiny bit to the right and an inch closer against him. The angle of his erection covered a lot of territory...

Her breath caught at the base of her throat. No air was going in or out. He lifted his hips in the slightest thrust and he filled her utterly and completely to the max. A small cry escaped her lips when she felt her body stretch for him. How could he keep filling her?

She hoped this was good for him.

For her it was like hitting the jackpot.

One hand stayed on her butt, and the other slipped between them and found her clit. His thumb circled and rubbed with varying pressure.

Sensations bombarded her from both sides. They came down from the top and up from the bottom. Everywhere.

They shimmered around her, ruled over her. Awareness of her surroundings slipped in and out. She knew she was with Ethan, though. He was doing all of these miraculous things to her.

His body was warm and solid. Her hands rested on his shoulders, her fingers curling into his flesh and muscle.

"Open your eyes, Sophie," he whispered softly. "Come on, look at me."

She forced them open.

He was right there, his face inches from her face. His darkened eyes looking deeply into hers. And his smile... God, his smile melted anything that might've been left of her.

Holding his gaze, she rocked gently against him. He was still rubbing her, but she moved his hand away. It felt amazing, but she wanted to wait. She wanted to stay in this moment with him for as long as they could bear it.

Each of their movements was so tiny, so overwhelming. Neither of them had blinked. She was too afraid of missing something in his gorgeous blue eyes. He was trembling, his whole body straining to hold back. Sophie couldn't decide if that was what she really wanted.

Freezing this particular snapshot in time was amazing, but watching this incredible man shatter...for her... She had a feeling that would keep her heart warm forever.

She moved her face closer to his, wanting to kiss him without losing eye contact.

It didn't work.

Ethan's smile widened a little. He knew what she was doing. "Guess you have to make a choice," he said, his voice sounding weak from the strain of his tight control.

"Why?" She barely got the word out.

"Can't have both." He ran his fingers through her hair and it felt so great she almost closed her eyes.

"I think I might die," she said. "Right here. In whatever town this is. Cause of death…sensation overload."

"Then I'd better hurry up and come."

She laughed and the forward motion had him hissing through his teeth. It affected her, too. She could've sworn he'd rubbed her, but he didn't have a hand down there.

"I made a decision," she said.

"Good." His eyes were completely black. "I don't think I'm gonna last."

Sophie smiled. "Ready to rock and roll?"

In answer Ethan lifted his hips and her.

"Dammit. You made me blink."

Still watching her face, he smiled. And thrust again, only deeper.

She had to hang on to him.

He used both hands to anchor her hips, holding her steady to receive his thrusts. Semi-controlled at first, consistent, precise, but then that disappeared along with the eye contact.

She wound her arms tightly around his neck, her breasts cradled by his chest, the friction caused by his thrusts driving her crazy. Their whimpers and moans permeated the room.

Again, the pressure began building inside her, expanding and stretching, accelerating beyond her limit. And the heat. God, the heat rolled over them in shimmering waves of otherworldly pleasure, seducing them into the fire, fooling them into thinking they were warm and safe. Suspended here in the eye of the storm.

Ethan's strangled groan penetrated the sensual fog. His arms shook. Sweat beaded on his skin. His hands slipped from her hips. One landed on her thigh. She hadn't let go of his neck. Her own body hadn't stopped quaking. The spasms quivering inside her left her breathless and as weak as a newborn kitten.

She knew she should climb off. She couldn't move.

Ethan kissed the corner of her mouth. He lifted her up and laid her back on the mattress carefully, so her head landed on the pillow. Letting out a big whoosh of breath, he collapsed at her side.

"I think I know what it feels like to ride a bull," she murmured between gulps of air.

His laugh barely made it out. "You stayed on for more than eight seconds."

"I expect a buckle," she said, and then just breathed for a while. "That position really was ridiculously amazing. We have to do it again."

"Not right now."

"Wuss."

Chuckling, he rolled toward her. "We will. Do it again. And again."

"Many times."

He kissed the side of her neck. "Many times," he agreed, the warmth in his voice bringing a tightness to her chest.

She snuggled up against him.

He drew away for a moment, but just to pull the covers over them. And then he wrapped an arm around her, bringing her close.

Many times.

Repeating the words in her head made her smile. Though it was easy to say glib things now when she was here with Ethan, quite literally the man of her dreams.

But there was only one thing she knew for certain.

Ethan Styles was impossible. Impossible to understand. And impossible to resist...

16

Sophie was sitting on a picnic bench near a snack bar about two hours from the motel where they'd stayed last night. No one else was sitting outside. The air was warm for November, but that wasn't saying much. The sun felt good, though, and she wanted to get the dreaded conversation with Lola over with—if she'd ever call back.

If Craig called soon, that would make her exceedingly happy, but she wasn't expecting to hear from him for another hour. He would've only received the paperwork this morning.

Lola was beginning to worry her. She hadn't been answering her texts or calls. Which wasn't like her at all. She couldn't be *that* busy just because Sophie was gone. Anyway, Lola had been anxious to keep in close touch, and since she was expecting Sophie and Ethan to be arriving in Wattsville this morning, it seemed very odd she wouldn't answer her phone.

Sophie sure hoped this weird behavior didn't have anything to do with Hawk. When Sophie checked him out early on, she hadn't found anything significant or violent in his past. She would've definitely alerted Lola.

Just to make herself feel better, she texted Mandy to

see if she knew what was happening at the office. Talking to her would be better, but Sophie wanted to be the one to tell Lola about the last-minute decision to go to Las Vegas. Yes, she could've left a heads-up on a voice mail, but she hadn't felt right doing that. She wanted to explain everything, even let Lola yell and scream at her if she wanted.

Best-case scenario, everything with Lola was fine— just the regular Monday madness keeping her busy. And Sophie would hear from Craig telling her the charges had been dropped, and Lola and Sophie wouldn't be on the hook for the full hundred-thousand-dollar bond.

If only she lived in a perfect world…

She looked up from her phone to take the cup of coffee Ethan had brought her. He bent to kiss her and even before their lips touched, she got that giddy feeling in her tummy that had been hanging around since they left Blackfoot Falls yesterday.

"They didn't have lattes or anything fancy. You should've seen the look I got when I asked for your part-skim, caramel-drizzled whatever."

"Well, if you didn't know what to ask for, how do you know if they have it or not?"

"Trust me, the second I mentioned the word *latte*, the old guy stopped listening. He was too busy mumbling something about yuppies ruining the world."

She eyed the Danish he'd brought for himself. "We just had breakfast."

"So?" He took a big bite, chewed, then sipped his coffee. "Do you know how many meals I've missed since I hooked up with you?"

"Is it my fault you think sex is a meal replacement?"

Ethan touched the brim of his hat and smiled at some phantom person behind her. "Mornin', ma'am."

"Yeah, like I'm going to fall for that," Sophie said,

and heard a tsking sound. She refused to turn all the way around, but managed to catch sight of the little white-haired woman walking toward the snack counter.

She looked at Ethan and they both laughed.

"You're the one who wanted to sit out here in the sun for a while," he said.

"Yes, and now I want a bite of that Danish."

"Then you'd better ask nicer." His next bite demolished half the pastry.

Her phone buzzed and she completely forgot about everything but the fact that she had a confession to make to Lola. And she sure didn't want to do it in front of Ethan.

As if he'd read her mind, he got to his feet. "I'll go pick up more Danish," he said.

"Hey, Lola, you were starting to worry me," Sophie said, watching Ethan stroll toward the snack bar.

"Where are you?" Lola asked. She sounded as if she'd been crying.

"Are you okay?"

"No. Not really."

"Are you at the office?"

"I was, but I'm at home now."

Sophie's chest hurt. Lola practically lived at the office. "Does this have anything to do with Hawk?"

Lola burst out crying. She tried to talk but couldn't seem to catch her breath.

"Can you tell me if Hawk is there with you now? Just say yes or no."

"No," Lola managed to choke out.

Sophie swallowed, feeling helpless and close to tears herself. "Did he hurt you?"

"No. Yes." Her voice broke, but the sobs were easing. "Not like you think."

"Okay, don't rush. I'll be right here when you can talk."

Sophie caught herself rocking back and forth, an arm wrapped across her stomach. She quickly glanced around. No sign of Ethan. She didn't want him to see her like this. He'd want an explanation she might not be comfortable giving. "Lola? I just wanted you to know I'm still here."

"I'm okay," she said. "Or getting there. Where are you? Are you close by?"

"No, I'm not." Sophie bit her lip. "I'm sorry. Is Mandy there?"

Lola sniffed. "No. I have to call her, though. She needs to help me find that goddamn, lying son of a bitch. I could kill that bastard."

Sighing with relief, Sophie listened to her cousin throw in a few more curses. Lola was sounding more like herself. Anger would serve her better than hurt right now.

Sophie's cell signaled an incoming call. She saw that it was Craig and winced. He'd have to leave a message. "Lola? Can you tell me what happened?"

A sob broke. "I'm sorry, Soph. Please don't hate me. I was such a fool. My God, I can't believe I'm that woman."

"I'm not going to hate you, Lola. Just tell me what happened."

Silence turned to quiet sobbing before Lola finally spoke. "He ripped us off," she said. "Hawk stole everything."

Sophie tried to quickly process the information. They really didn't have much for him to steal. "What exactly did Hawk take?"

"I really do mean everything, Soph," Lola said softly, then paused, trying to control her breathing. "He got into the safe."

Sophie felt the blood drain from her face. A violent shiver surged through her body. "How did—" She wouldn't ask. It didn't matter. Staying calm, keeping Lola calm, those were her priorities. Not dropping her phone would be good, too. Her hands were beginning to shake. "Since you guys had a fight maybe he's just trying to get your attention."

"No, I think he might've been planning this for a while. I'm gonna kill him. I am. God, I'm so stupid. This is all my fault."

"Don't go there, Lola. We need to stay focused. Okay?" Hell, Sophie was one to talk. She'd made her own mess. "How long ago could he have done this?"

"Last night, I think. Late. After we talked around midnight."

It was eleven-forty now. That gave the prick a head start. Sophie had to get to the research she'd done on him a few months ago. With any luck, there would be a clue as to where he'd gone. First, she'd get a hold of Mandy. And she had to talk to Craig. Jesus. Ethan was supposed to be in court in two hours. Hopefully Craig had worked his magic and it was a moot point by now. But she couldn't count on it.

"You're awfully calm," Lola said. "Do you understand what I'm telling you? He took *everything*." Her voice had risen and she sounded close to losing it again.

"I know. I'm just trying to think about our next step."

They'd always disagreed about how much cash to keep in the office. But after business had picked up, Lola had stubbornly insisted on having a minimum of twenty thousand dollars they could get their hands on quickly. "Okay... so, I'm going to call Mandy first, but she'll still want you to fill in the details, and then I'm going to see if I can track him electronically. We both know Hawk is too stupid to hide his trail."

"Yeah," Lola said with a small laugh. "There is that."

"So..." Sophie had to ask. "Just so I know what we're

dealing with, can you narrow down what you mean by *everything*?"

Lola let out a sob. "Thirty-five thousand cash," she said, and Sophie wanted to faint. "And two pieces of jewelry we were holding as collateral."

Sophie held her breath. How could she have forgotten about the collateral items? "Do you mean the antique brooch Mrs. Sellars gave us for her son's bond?"

"Yes," Lola choked out. "And the signed Mohammad Ali glove from Mr. Polinski."

Sophie held in a whimper. Mrs. Sellar's ruby-and-diamond brooch alone was worth about sixty thousand. So Lola's Bail Bonds was pretty much ruined financially. "Anything else?"

"I don't know how you can be this calm. I really don't."

Guilt, probably, because Sophie had created her own mess. She turned and saw Ethan approaching. He looked worried, so she tried to clean up her body language. "I don't know. Maybe I'm still in shock," Sophie said. "But let's use it to our advantage. Let's hang up and I'll contact Mandy, then get online."

"You have to call me soon, or you know I'll go nuts," Lola said. "I think I'll go to the bar and ask around. Hawk might've shot off his mouth."

"Mandy should probably do that."

"Everyone there knows me." Lola sighed. "They probably all think I'm a dumb ass, too, so what the hell?"

"For the record, I didn't say you were a dumb ass, nor do I think you are a dumb ass. We all have our blind spots," Sophie said, watching Ethan advance on her. "I'll call you soon."

"Wait. You have Styles, right? He'll make it to court?"

"Let's worry about Hawk for now."

"We really don't need to fork out money for Styles."

"I know that," she snapped, adding another layer of guilt to the growing pile. "Sorry."

"Nope. You have every right. Call me." Lola disconnected.

Sophie wanted to lay her head down and sob her heart out. She found a smile for Ethan when he set the paper bag on the table in front of her.

"Problem?" he asked, his eyes narrowed.

"Nothing I can't handle. Duty calls, though, and I have to get my tablet out of my bag." She glanced around, mostly because she was having trouble with that intense gaze of his. She couldn't explain anything now. She'd lose it and be tempted to hide in the comfort of his arms. He'd feel guilty they hadn't returned to Wyoming and she didn't want that. He had the finals to worry about.

THERE WAS ANOTHER ISSUE. She needed privacy and good Wi-Fi. "How about we find someplace where you can get some rest while I do a little work? Would that be okay?" she asked lightly. "I don't care if we go back to the same motel for a while."

Ethan's eyebrows went up. He looked as though he had a hundred questions. "Whatever you want."

"I have to make a quick call first, okay? To Mandy. She works in our office," Sophie said, trying like hell to sound normal. "Oh, and Craig called while I was talking to Lola. I had to let him go to voice mail, but I'll get back to him. Fingers crossed that he has good news."

Ethan stood there stone-faced, just watching her. She wasn't fooling him at all. He stepped back so she could get up, then offered her a hand. His skin was warm, his grip solid and sure. She felt safe with him. Alive. Happy. Whole. Which made her feel all the more a fool. This bubble in which they'd existed for the past three days was only a blip in time. A page torn from their normal lives and soon to be discarded. Yet she'd been willing to give up so much of herself, jeopardize the reputation of the business she'd built with Lola.

But Sophie couldn't afford self-pity or to let her shame interfere with finding Hawk. There would be plenty of time for all that later.

They were halfway to the truck when a sudden flash of memory stopped her cold. That day in the office when she'd announced she was going after Ethan... Hawk had sided with her. Lola had already been annoyed with him, yet he'd spoken out against her, taking Sophie's side. It made sense now. Lola was right. The bastard had been planning the theft for a while. Hawk knew Sophie didn't like him and he'd wanted her out of the way. But even worse, he'd used Lola.

Sophie was going to find that asshole. She would, because she was smarter than him and she knew so much more about him than he could imagine. And when she finally got her hands on him...

"Sophie? Please." Ethan put his arms around her. She'd never seen him look this worried, not even about his own problem. "Is it me? Am I causing you this grief?"

This wasn't fair to him. And anyway, she couldn't avoid his gaze forever. "We have a problem at the office. It's—" She cleared her throat. "My cousin Lola's boyfriend... We were robbed. The office safe was cleaned out."

"Jesus." Ethan touched her cheek. "I'm sorry. Did he get away with a lot?"

Despite trying to be stoic, she let out a whimper. "It's bad. He stole a lot of cash, some expensive jewelry we were holding as collateral, a piece of valuable sports memorabilia that might be irreplaceable."

When Ethan touched her cheek again, she realized he'd

been wiping tears. She jerked away, embarrassed and twice as furious with Hawk.

"Obviously we have to do something," Ethan said, easily staying abreast of her on the brisk walk to his truck. "I'm sure you have an idea."

"*You* will do nothing. Except whatever it is you do to get ready for the finals." She checked her cheeks for moisture. "I'm calling Mandy, a bounty hunter who works with us. She's the real deal. Totally badass. She'll help me find the stupid prick. Hawk really is stupid, probably left electronic footprints all over the country. I'll work on that while Mandy does her thing. Oh, we will find him, and when we do…"

They got to the truck and Ethan opened the passenger door for her.

"Look," she said, keeping her gaze lowered, "I feel horrible for Lola because she's blaming herself, and she shouldn't. This has nothing to do with you." As soon as Sophie was seated, she glanced at Ethan. He'd been so quiet.

His expression grim, he closed the door. She watched him round the hood. He looked angry.

She understood. She'd been incensed with Wendy Fullerton on his behalf, so she got it. Of course Ethan would be upset for her. And then she thought of something else. Damn. She couldn't afford to lose it now. Craig. She had to return his call. God, she really, really hoped the news was good. She wasn't about to leave Ethan twisting in the wind. Maybe he was angry because he thought she'd dropped the ball on him.

After he slid behind the wheel, she laid a hand on his arm. "I haven't forgotten you. I'm calling Craig now."

"You think I'm pissed about that?" His eyes were blazing mad when he turned to her. "You're a smart, capable woman, Sophie, I'll give you that. But obviously you're in trouble. Do you honestly think I could stand by and not help? Is that the kind of man you think I am?"

"No, of course not, but—"

"Frankly I don't give a shit what you have to say about it. I'm going to help you any way I'm able."

She'd never seen him this angry. Maybe that day back in high school. "Okay."

Looking straight ahead, he turned the key and started the truck. His lips were a thin line, his jaw clenched. Leaving the engine idling, he reached over the console, grabbed her upper arms and pulled her toward him.

"Damn independent little cuss," he muttered, and then kissed her hard on the mouth. He released her, took a deep breath and asked, "Now where the hell are we going?"

17

AFTER CONTACTING MANDY and receiving the bad news from Craig, Sophie worked from her tablet at the small table in the dinky motel they'd found three miles down from the snack bar. The room sucked, but the Wi-Fi was good.

Ethan had stepped outside so he wouldn't disturb her while he called his agent. Brian would probably come in person to strangle Sophie. If they'd gone straight to Wyoming last night as they'd planned, Ethan wouldn't be missing his court date in—she looked at the time and felt a little sick—five minutes.

There was still a possibility that everything would work out for him. Mandy was on the case, and Sophie had a great deal more faith in the bounty hunter than she had in herself at the moment. Sophie was pretty damn close to blowing everything.

Craig was furious that she hadn't warned him about Wendy being Broderick Fullerton's wife. Apparently Craig was on retainer with two of Fullerton's subsidiaries. They'd exchanged a few choice words, and Sophie might've called Craig a yellow-bellied chickenshit. It was actually one of the nicer names that had come to mind after discovering he'd called Lola and told her everything. So now her poor cousin was a complete basket case, worrying that Fullerton would have his bank call in their loan and kill their line of credit.

Sophie had only herself to blame.

Sighing, she rubbed her eyes. The screen blurred. She was tired from stress and lack of sleep, and staring at Hawk's—no, Floyd's—background file was frustrating. She was missing something, but she couldn't seem to pinpoint it. For the third time, she searched through his late teenage years, the job-hopping, being nailed for shoplifting cigarettes, petty stuff. Mostly his past was uneventful.

Her cell buzzed. She picked it up and read the text from Lola. A warrant had just been issued for Ethan's arrest. Sophie briefly closed her eyes. She wanted to call Mandy, but there was no point. If she had news, she would've called.

Sophie stared at the text, wanting so very much to curl up into a ball. Oh God, what had she done? He could've made it to court. They had been on their way to Wyoming. Did she have to pick then to rail against life's injustices? Did she need any more proof that she was hopeless when it came to Ethan? She had no judgment, no ability to reason, and now two people she deeply cared about had been caught in her well-intentioned but destructive wake.

She wondered if she should call Lola. And say what? Sorry I wasn't there for you? Sorry I was too busy chasing a childish dream? Sorry I didn't warn you about Hawk? Sophie could go on forever about the ways in which she'd failed. And she hadn't even gotten to Ethan yet.

Speaking of which… She heard the door being unlocked. She looked up as Ethan walked into the room. He looked grim but gave her a smile. She tried to return it. Had he been keeping track of the time? Was he expecting to hear about the warrant? She had to say something.

She moistened her lips. "A warrant has—"

"I know."

"I'm sorry, Ethan."

"Why? You tried to warn me." He slipped behind her chair and massaged her cramped shoulders.

His strong, gentle hands felt so good, but she didn't deserve his kindness. Or his forgiveness. She didn't deserve him. "I'm also the person who encouraged you to drive to Vegas instead. I was so sure Craig would come through, or that Wendy would finally—"

"Shh, it doesn't matter."

"Of course it does." She stopped when her voice shook.

"Aren't you going to check that?" he asked.

"What?" She realized she'd gotten an alert and looked at the corner of the screen. Floyd had used his credit card to buy gas—he was in Reno, Nevada.

Ethan took the other chair. "This is good. You've located him, right?"

"For now." Something clicked in the back of her mind that made sense about him being in Reno. "I have to check something before I call Mandy," she said, knowing Mandy would head for the airport as soon as she heard the news. So if she hadn't made progress solving Ethan's problem... Well, that was that.

"You should be happy," he said, frowning.

"I am." She paused. "Ethan? Why do you think this might be your last chance to go to the finals?"

His face darkened. "I never told you that."

"I overheard you mention something to Arnie."

He shrugged. "It's nothing." He glanced at her tablet. "Shouldn't you be moving on this information?"

"Please tell me." She begged with her eyes even though she wouldn't blame him for never trusting her with anything again.

He stared back, then sighed. "You ride long enough your

body's bound to suffer some wear and tear. I've had some trouble with my shoulder. Nothing serious, but I'm going to quit before I blow my future. That's all."

"Really?"

"Really. I'm being sensible. Imagine that."

Sophie smiled. She wanted to kiss him. It would be a stupid move. She'd already proven she couldn't think straight when she was around him. She glanced at the file on her screen just when her phone rang. It was Mandy. Sophie told herself not to get excited yet. "Tell me something good."

"Something good," Mandy said in her usual calm voice.

Sophie's heart lurched. "How good?"

"Mrs. Fullerton turned out to be extremely cooperative once I explained all the possible ramifications of making a false charge against a popular rodeo celebrity. She agreed it would be best to explain she'd misplaced her jewelry and drop the charges. Done deal. I just left the sheriff's office."

Sophie looked at Ethan. "What about the husband?"

"He's out of town again," Mandy said. "But hell, that's her problem. Have you got anything yet?"

"I think I might. Call you in ten?"

"Yep."

The moment they disconnected, Sophie hugged Ethan.

"She found him?" He held her tight, his smile matching hers.

"No, not yet. Wendy dropped the charges. You're in the clear."

He frowned. "I thought you guys were looking for Hawk."

"I am. Ethan. Aren't you excited? No more charges against you. They'll cancel the warrant."

"Well, yeah, of course I am. How?"

"Mandy had a talk with Wendy. She pointed out how

easily a trial could get out of control with other men stepping up to swear Wendy had sex with them and turning
everything into a media circus." Sophie didn't mention that
she'd thought up the tactic during their drive. She'd told
Mandy, who thought it was a brilliant maneuver and volunteered to do the deed. "Of course Wendy didn't know
that you've been trying to keep it out of the media. I told
you. Mandy totally rocks."

Ethan smiled. The relief on his face lifted her spirits.
"Well, now that I've given Brian heart failure," he said,
"I'll call back and tell him to relax. What about Hawk?"

"The prick's real name is Floyd," she said, focusing on
the information on the screen. Sophie had finally realized
what she'd overlooked in his file. Annoyed with herself,
she shook her head. "We got you, you dumb ass."

She grabbed her phone again and while waiting for the
connection, glanced at Ethan.

He was watching her and frowning. "What?" she said.
But then Mandy answered. "He's twenty miles outside
Reno," Sophie told her. "The idiot was too lazy to walk
inside and pay for his gas with *our* money. He used his
credit card."

"Reno's a big place," Mandy said. "Any thoughts on
whether he's passing through or sticking around?"

"I think he'll be hanging around," she said. He'd had
some petty scrapes over gambling with a fake ID when
he was a kid. She should've figured he'd want to go play
big shot in a high-stakes poker game at a casino where
they'd kiss his ass.

"Have you told Lola yet?"

"No, but I bet he's bragged about something or other
that could point us in the right direction. Lola can help
us there."

"Or he's cried over being mistreated," Mandy said. "Either way, I say we meet in Reno."

"I agree." She looked over at Ethan, who of course was still watching her. Why hadn't he gone to call his agent? "Let me know after you book your flight. I'm kind of in the middle of nowhere. Driving might be quicker for me. I'll call Lola."

As soon as she hung up Ethan said, "We can check flights out of Billings and see if it's worth backtracking, but I think you're right. We'd be better off driving."

Hell no, she would not let him tag along. She felt guilty enough for the messes she'd created. Yes, they'd avoided one disaster, but they still needed to nail Floyd before he blew all their money. That was where her focus needed to be. Not on Ethan, who had to get himself mentally psyched for the finals.

Couldn't he see they were reaching the end of the road anyway? The thought hurt. She could barely think about it, so why prolong the agony?

"No. *I'll* be better off driving." She gathered her things. On the way out she'd call Lola. "I'd appreciate a ride to pick up a rental car, though. I'll be fine, Ethan." She wanted to kiss him, but better she stay detached. It was for his own good. And for hers. "You, on the other hand, are driving to Las Vegas."

ETHAN GLANCED AT Sophie's boots scuffing up his once-clean dashboard. "Are you going to sulk all the way to Reno?"

"Probably," she huffed. "Yes, I am. You deserve it. What part of *please drop me at the car rental office* did you not understand?"

Sighing, he nodded to himself. Yep, he knew she was a handful. Stubborn. Irritating. A real pain in the ass when she wanted to be. Sophie was also fiercely loyal. Smart as hell. And she was softhearted, which he could never say to her and expect to live.

She looked so damn tired it made his gut knot. He'd bet anything she was beating herself up over failing Lola. Which really wasn't the case. Not that Sophie would listen.

"It wouldn't hurt for you to get some shut-eye," he said. "Nothing's going to change because you're asleep."

"Why don't I drive for a while?"

"No, thanks."

"You are so damn stubborn."

He snorted. "You would know," he said, turning on the radio. He kept it low and found an easy-listening station.

She surprised him by not complaining. Ten minutes later, just as he'd hoped, she was asleep.

He drove for another hour and then stopped at a motel. Even if they slept for six hours, they had time to get to Reno and meet Mandy. The best flight she could get had two stopovers.

After checking them in and paying for the night, he drove them closer to the room. She slept through it all, even when he carried her inside and laid her on the bed. He thought about undressing her but decided that would be a bad idea. Yeah, they'd both better keep their clothes on or they wouldn't get any rest.

He lightly kissed her parted lips, hid the truck keys, just in case, then set the alarms and crawled in beside her.

THE PALACE CASINO AND HOTEL wasn't the snazziest of the large casinos in downtown Reno, but it looked to be the busiest.

A steady stream of mainly older folks led the way into the hotel, where dings and trills of electronic music mostly covered up the piped-in oldies. The purple carpeting and gold chandeliers had probably been daring in their day.

As they headed toward the front desk, Ethan took her hand, and a shiver ran up her spine. Such a simple touch brought so much pleasure. She'd add this moment to her mental scrapbook.

They had to wait in a short line to reach the front desk. But that was okay, because Mandy was still ten minutes away and Sophie wouldn't proceed without her. So she waited with Ethan, who stood right behind her, draping his arms over her shoulders. Her hands were on top of his where they met on her chest.

She'd meant it when she told him to head to Vegas, but she was still glad he was here. The feel of his body warm and comforting. She was a horrible, selfish person. By to-morrow he would have no more grace period. He'd have to leave first thing to check in for the finals.

"I could eat a whole buffet," he said. "Not including the desserts."

"That's the best part." Dammit, now she wanted chocolate.

It was their turn at the desk, and by the time Sophie explained the importance of speaking to the casino manager himself, Mandy had joined them.

When Sophie made the introductions Ethan thanked Mandy for her help in getting the charges dropped. She looked pleased with the recognition, and not surprised by their clasped hands.

It took a few minutes for the manager to arrive, and he was surprisingly young considering his title. Maybe late thirties? However, the way he sized them up before inviting them into his office said he was going to be a challenge.

His office was small, nothing ornate. Behind him, though, was a door opened just enough for them to see a wall of monitors showing every cash transaction, second by second.

"How can I help you?" Dan Pfizer asked, waving them to the seats in front of his desk.

Mandy took the lead. She showed him her ID, a picture of Floyd, and offered a video of the idiot emptying the company safe.

He stopped her when she brought out the flash drive. "It won't do you any good. Even if I watched him steal from you personally, without a valid warrant there's nothing I can do."

"We're going to call the police," Sophie said. "We already know you have private poker rooms, and that he's in one of them. Probably throwing all our money on the table."

"We saw his Harley close to the valet booth," Mandy added. "So we know he's here."

Pfizer shrugged. "Show me a warrant, and I'll be happy to call the police myself. You have no idea how many times I get asked to do this. Wives wanting their husbands to come home. Vice versa. My hands are tied."

"Actually you might want to reconsider, assuming you want to keep all this quiet. Do you know who this is?" Sophie asked, nodding at Ethan, who didn't even blink at her tactic.

"I'm afraid I don't," Pfizer said. "But I really do have to be—"

"He's the number-two-rated professional bull rider in the world. In fact, I saw a poster out there inviting people to watch the National Finals Rodeo on your HD TVs starting this weekend."

That got his attention. But it wasn't enough.

"Hey, if you can't help us, I understand," Ethan said, shrugging. "Just like you understand why we have to call the police. And since we don't have access to your poker room, I'm pretty sure they'll have no problem meeting us in front of the sports book. That is where people place bets, right?"

Picking up a pen and toying with it, Pfizer frowned.

Sophie could almost hear the wheels turning in his head. "We'll try not to make too big a fuss," she said with a smile.

"By the way," Ethan added, "I saw the odds you have posted out there. I'm the five-to-two favorite. Just out of curiosity, what happens if I get hung up and miss the finals?" His jaw tightened for a split second, and Sophie's heart slid right down to her toes. After that he didn't so much as blink. "Do you guys have to return the money people have already bet?"

And there it was. The look of a man defeated.

"If we could all step outside my office, I'll be with you in a few moments."

They did, and Mr. Pfizer in his neat suit and tie walked hastily toward the poker rooms in the back.

Mandy pulled out her phone and moved a few feet away to give them privacy while she called Lola.

Sophie turned to him. "Why did you say that?"

"Hey, it worked." He looked tired, but he smiled. "Don't tell me you're superstitious."

She didn't buy his act of indifference. He'd been worried about the finals all along. His concern hadn't suddenly disappeared. "No, just a bad-luck charm."

"Come on." He put an arm around her. "Knock it off. What were the chances you'd find Floyd as quickly as you did? That he was still here by the time we showed up? This was a best-case scenario."

No, it wasn't. She and Mandy here taking care of business while Ethan was already in Vegas was a best-case scenario. But she wouldn't argue. He looked so exhausted. Tonight he had to sleep. Tomorrow, if he was still tired, she'd talk him into catching a flight while she took care of his truck.

She dug up a smile from somewhere. "Thank you. Without you here, I don't know— You've been—" She inhaled deeply, hoping it would help keep her eyes dry.

"I would never have deserted you," he said, and squeezed her hand. "I told you I'd help any way I could."

Even if it had cost him the finals? Oh God. She would've just died. But in truth, he wasn't there yet. If she wanted to be a good person, a friend, she'd let him check in to the hotel alone. Sleep as much as he could without her distracting him.

She nodded. "I think it's okay for you to go right after they bring that moron out. If you don't want to stay here, I'm sure you'll find a room in another hotel."

Ethan frowned. "Don't you mean it's okay for *us* to go?"

Mandy, who'd approached and was now on the phone with the Reno cops, turned around again.

"You need sleep," Sophie said. "What you don't need is any more distractions."

"I'm a grown man. I'm pretty sure I know what I do and don't need."

"I didn't mean it like that. It's just— You know I can't go with you now. I have to go back to Wyoming. Once Floyd's arrested, we won't automatically get back what he's stolen. I can't leave everything to Lola." Most of that was true, but she had trouble meeting his eyes.

"Yo," Mandy said.

Walking toward them, right behind the casino manager, Floyd was staring daggers at her. But the two beefy security guards weren't about to let him make a move.

Pfizer stopped in front of Ethan. Behind him, on the

monitor on the wall, Sophie saw a man in a cowboy hat being interviewed. The closed caption said the broadcast was coming from Las Vegas. Her stomach turned over. She literally felt sick. Ethan had claimed he didn't need to be there yet.

"If you'll join us at the security office when you're ready," Pfizer said.

Mandy waited until the guards and Floyd had passed. "The cops will be here in about five minutes. I'll give them what we've got, and then we can head back."

Sophie nodded. "I'll be right there. Ethan has to get his butt to Vegas."

Mandy held out her hand, and Ethan took it. "Good luck. I bet a hundred bucks on you. So get some damn sleep, would you?"

"I'll try," he said, unsmiling.

Mandy shrugged, met Sophie's eyes, then started walking.

"You promised you'd come with me," he said.

"I did, but that was before all this crap happened." She swallowed hard. "I didn't know Floyd was going to rip us off, or that we'd actually find him. But Jesus, Ethan. You told me you didn't have to be in Vegas yet." She motioned to the monitor. "You should be up there being interviewed. Not here mixed up in my mess." She forced a smile. "Look, we had fun, right? But we knew it would end. Like you said, you know what you need to do, and I need to go home. It's as simple as that."

He stared at her as if she'd just ripped his heart out of his chest. "If it's that simple to you, then yeah, I sure did misunderstand."

Despite the pain that squeezed the life out of her, she nodded. He wasn't thinking clearly. She had to be strong for both of them. "I hope you win the title." She stepped back.

"That's it?" He looked stricken.

"I'll call," she said, wondering if she dared. Wanting so much to tell him all the things she couldn't say on the purple carpet of this damn casino. Like how he'd rocked her world. How she used to think she had it bad for him, but now? She'd never recover.

But he didn't need her as baggage or a distraction. He'd never forgive her if he missed the finals, and she'd never forgive herself, either.

Ethan stared, looking confused and angry. But then he turned and walked past the security office, past the police who were headed in to arrest Floyd.

And he just kept walking.

18

SOPHIE SAT IN front of her small TV and shoved another piece of chocolate into her mouth. She wasn't crazy about television. She didn't even have cable or satellite, but she'd watched most of the National Finals Rodeo. Well, she'd kept track of the bull riders, anyway. And now she was watching reruns of Ethan.

Sometimes it had been nearly impossible to watch. Two riders had suffered serious injuries. If Ethan had gotten hurt, she had no idea what she would've done. Except blame herself for having distracted him at the most important time of his entire career.

But she didn't have to worry about that. Ethan had won his second championship title. Last night had been the buckle ceremony.

She'd thought seriously about calling, just to congratulate him. But she couldn't bring herself to pick up her cell. She'd handled the goodbye at the casino so badly. It still stung.

She should've at least offered to drive his truck back to Wyoming. Drop him at the airport first. Sophie had replayed her words and the expression on his face a thousand times in the past two weeks. She'd sounded so cold. How he must hate her.

Seeing the cowboy being interviewed on the monitor had done something to her. Panic had taken over. And she knew if she'd given herself an inch, she would've done the thing she wanted to do instead of doing what was honorable. Intellectually she realized it wasn't completely her fault that he'd driven her to Reno when he should've gone to Las Vegas. She'd begged him to take her to a car rental office. But he'd insisted. And she hadn't fought him hard enough because she'd been thrilled he'd stayed with her.

Someone knocked at the apartment door. She grabbed something to throw at it. Then stared at the bag in her hand. What the hell was she thinking? Not the chocolate. That would make everything worse.

Another knock. It was either Lola or Mandy, most likely Lola. Mandy knew how to buy a clue.

"Go away," Sophie yelled loud enough to be heard by half the residents in the apartment complex.

"Not gonna happen."

"Goddammit, Lola," Sophie muttered, and got off the couch.

She opened the door and growled at her cousin.

Lola walked right in, uninvited, as usual. She surveyed Sophie's mess after three days of hibernation. Every glass she owned was sitting out somewhere.

Finally Lola eyed Sophie's baggy gray sweats and the sock with a hole over the big toe. "You look like shit."

"Should've saved yourself the trip. I could've told you that on the phone." Sophie plopped back down on the couch. Wincing, she lifted her butt and moved the bag of chocolate out of the way. "What do you want?"

"Get up and take a shower, then put on something nice. We're going out."

Sophie snorted a laugh. "Are you high?"

"Come on, Soph." Lola's gaze shifted briefly to the TV. "You can't keep moping."

"Yes, I can. Except I'm not moping."

Lola sighed. "Please get up and get ready. Mandy is meeting us at the—"

"Nice try. Mandy knows better. Yet she's only known me for a fraction of the time you have. Explain that." Sophie stretched her neck back. She'd stayed away from the gym too long. Tomorrow she'd get herself moving.

"The Reno police called. They found the brooch at a pawnshop."

Sophie shook her head. Anyone could tell the piece was an antique and too valuable to sell to a pawnbroker. Anyone but Floyd. "How much did he get for it? Did they tell you?"

"No. I didn't ask. I want this whole thing over with and I never want to hear his name again."

Sophie gave her a sympathetic nod. "I'm glad they recovered the brooch."

"You know what pisses me off, Sophie?"

"I'm coming in to work tomorrow. I'll be my old cheery self. Promise."

"That's not what I'm upset about." She sat at the edge of the couch. "Ethan is a really good man, and you're tossing him away. Do you have any idea what I'd do to find someone like him? What most single women would do? You've never been a quitter. I've always admired that about you."

Sophie had to look away. She wasn't good at hiding her emotions lately. "Not now. Okay, Lola?"

Her cousin sighed. "Please get dressed and come out. Would you do that for me?"

"I can't. I'm sorry."

Shrugging, Lola stood. "You can't say I didn't try."

Sophie watched sideways until Lola opened the door.

She would've felt worse if she thought her cousin really wanted a drinking buddy tonight. Lola was only trying to cheer her up.

Sophie turned her head. Lola had left. Why hadn't she closed the damn door?

Muttering a curse, she pushed to her feet.

Ethan appeared in the doorway. He looked at Sophie, glanced around the apartment and then looked at her again and laughed.

Her mouth wouldn't work. When it finally did, she said, "I'm going to kill her."

"Ah, right. She asked me to remind you that she tried."

"I'm still going to kill her. Stay right there." She skirted the coffee table, thought about taking some glasses and empty bags with her, but what was the point? "Right there," she repeated before disappearing into her bathroom.

She washed her face, brushed her hair and teeth in record time, then splurged with some mascara and scented body cream. She exchanged the sweatpants for jeans. Thank God she'd taken a shower earlier.

When she returned to the living room, plastic trash bag in hand, the door was closed and Ethan was sitting on the couch, staring at the TV. He hadn't pushed her crap to the side. He'd just made himself comfortable.

He looked up at her and smiled.

She pointed at the door. "I told you to stay there."

"You really have to quit being so damn bossy."

"I doubt that's going to stop," she said, sighing, and picked up empty cookie packages, dropping them into the trash bag. She hated feeling this awkward with him.

"I know," he said, his quiet tone making her look up. He nodded at the TV. "You've been watching the finals."

"Oh." She cleared her throat. "Congratulations, by the way." Should she give him a quick kiss or maybe a hug? A kiss wouldn't be out of line. She leaned over and he pulled her onto his lap.

Sophie let out a startled gasp.

"Is this okay?" he asked, uncertainty in his blue eyes.

"Uh-huh."

"I want to explain why I didn't call."

"You don't have to. I never expected you to—"

"Can you please just be quiet for a few minutes?"

She pressed her lips together and jerked a nod.

Ethan gave a short laugh. "At first I was really mad. And then I started thinking about the moment everything had gone sideways with us at the casino. I figured out you weren't trying to get rid of me but get me to Vegas. That was just before the first round.

"I was going to call then. Hash things out. But I knew the moment I heard your voice I'd lose my focus. And I couldn't afford to do that. I owed it to both of us to be on my game."

Sophie blinked. *Us?* A quiver started in her tummy. Like the feeling she'd gotten when she saw him wearing a helmet that first round. He'd worn it until the very end. She'd told herself he was doing it for her and then realized that was the fifteen-year-old inside her who still believed in fairy tales.

"Sophie…" He was watching her, waiting for her to look into his eyes. "Honey, I know you were trying to help get me to finals because you knew how important it was to me. But something had happened that shifted my priorities."

"Okay," she said. "What?"

"You."

"Me? How?"

"By believing in me. When you said my fans would believe me over Wendy, you were probably right. They'd rally around me. But they don't really know me. They just wouldn't want to believe their rodeo idol could be a thief. But you believed in *me*."

"Well, of course…"

"Look, you're a beautiful, capable woman who's built a business and a nice life. And I suspect you got here mainly by yourself. But you don't have to go a hundred miles an hour all the time. You don't have anything to prove. Now, how about believing in yourself, Sophie?"

Her mouth was so dry. Eleven years ago she'd been cowed and humiliated, and she'd been running so fast, so hard ever since to never be in a situation like that again. To be in control at all times. But she hadn't always succeeded. "May I speak now?"

"Go ahead."

"First of all, I'm obviously not all that capable, because I wasn't the one who helped you. It was Mandy. I couldn't even—"

"All right. Stop." He shook his head.

"What? Shouldn't I be able to have my say?"

"You can't expect me to sit here and listen to this crap. Remember, you're talking about someone I love."

The air left her lungs. "You can't love me."

Ethan's eyes blazed. He clearly did not like that response.

"I'm not saying I'm not lovable. I just meant, you don't really know me. You can't. Not after only four days."

He said nothing, just looked at her with a hint of sadness. "Sophie, I know all the things that matter about you. I promise you that. Even if it takes a year, two years, whatever it takes to prove it to you, I'm going to do that. I can be stubborn myself."

She held back a sob and dashed a tear away with impatience. "You're right."

"I am?" He smiled, looking so boyishly delighted, she laughed.

"I think you do know me. Maybe better than I do." She wasn't ready to explain that she had been trying to prove something she hadn't realized until now. She'd needed to feel she deserved the small kindness he'd shown her. Her teenage years had been so damn lonely.

He put his arms around her and pulled her back against him.

That alone made her want to cry as she curled up in his lap. She'd missed his arms so much.

"I owe you a congratulatory kiss." She turned her face, and their lips touched. He kissed her softly, eyes open. She kissed him back and heard the bag of candy scrunch. Now, how could she not love a man who'd seen her mess of an apartment, the mess of her life, and hadn't run in the other direction?

"Dammit, Ethan," she murmured against his lips.

"What?"

"I love you, too."

His smile could've lit the room. "With the finals money, I'm going ahead with the construction of the rodeo camp. And there's plenty of space for you to set up your martial arts studio. If you want to."

She kissed him again, so hard they both nearly fell off the couch. And when she finally caught her breath, she said, "I know the important parts about you, too, Ethan Styles. But it'll be fun to explore the rest."

"I'd like to do a little exploring myself." He stood with her still in his arms. "I'm guessing you have a bedroom somewhere in here."

Sophie grinned. She might not be the best bounty hunter in the world, but she'd set out to get her man and ended up with the man of her dreams. "You can have me anywhere, cowboy."

* * * * *

*Gage Ringer: Powerful, fierce, unforgettable...
and temporarily sidelined from his MMA career
with an injury. Back home, he has one month
to win over the woman he could never forget...*

Read on for New York Times *bestselling author
Lori Foster's*

HARD KNOCKS

*The stunning prequel novella for
her* ULTIMATE *series!*

HARD KNOCKS

Lori Foster

CHAPTER ONE

GAGE RINGER, better known as Savage in the fight world, prowled the interior of the rec center. His stride was long, his thoughts dark, but he kept his expression enigmatic to hide his turmoil from onlookers. He didn't want to be here tonight. He'd rather be home, suffering his bad mood alone instead of covering up his regret, forced to pretend it didn't matter. His disappointment was private, damn it, and he didn't want to advertise it to the world. Shit happened.

It had happened to him. So what?

Life went on. There would be other fights, other opportunities. Only a real wimp would sit around bellyaching about what could have been, but wasn't. Not him. Not publicly anyway.

Tonight the rec center would overflow with bodies of all shapes, sizes and ages—all there for different reasons.

Cannon Coulter owned the rec center. It was a part of Cannon's life, a philanthropic endeavor that, no matter how big Cannon got, how well-known he became in the Supreme Battle Championship fight world, would always be important to him.

Armie Jacobson, another fighter who helped run the rec center whenever Cannon had to travel for his career, had planned a long night of fun. Yay.

Not.

At least, not for Gage.

Earlier they'd had a party for the kids too young to stick

around and watch the pay-per-view event that night on the big screen. One of Cannon's sponsors had contributed the massive wall-mounted TV to the center.

So that they wouldn't feel left out, Armie had organized fun activities for the younger kids that had included food, games and some one-on-one play with the fighters who frequented the rec center, using it as a gym.

With the kiddie party now wrapping up, the more mature crowd would soon arrive, mixing and mingling while watching the fights.

The rec center had originally opened with very little. Cannon and some of his friends had volunteered to work with at-risk youths from the neighborhood to give them an outlet. They started with a speed bag, a heavy bag, some mats and a whole lot of donated time and energy.

But as Cannon's success had grown, so too had the rec center. Not only had Cannon added improvements, but his sponsors loved to donate anything and everything that carried their brand so that now the size of the place had doubled, and they had all the equipment they needed to accommodate not only a training camp for skilled fighters, but also dozens of boys, and a smattering of girls, of all ages.

Gage heard a distinctly female laugh and his gaze automatically went to Harper Gates.

So she had arrived.

Without meaning to, he inhaled more deeply, drawing in a calming breath. Yeah, Harper did that to him.

He watched as Harper assisted Armie in opening up folding chairs around the mats. Together they filled up every available speck of floor space. She stepped around a few of the youths who were still underfoot, racing around, wrestling—basically letting off steam with adult supervision, which beat the hell out of them hanging on street corners, susceptible to the thugs who crawled out of the shadows as the sun went down.

Gage caught one boy as he recklessly raced past. He twirled him into the air, then held him upside down. The kid squealed with laughter, making Gage smile, too.

"You're moving awfully fast," Gage told him.

Bragging, the boy said, "I'm the fastest one here!"

"And humble, too," he teased.

The boy blinked big owl eyes at him while grinning, showing two missing teeth. He was six years old, rambunctious and considered the rec center a second home.

"I need you to take it easy, okay? If you're going to roughhouse, keep it on the mats."

"'Kay, Savage."

Gage glanced at a clock on the wall. The younger crowd would be heading out in a few more minutes. Still holding the boy suspended, he asked, "Who's taking you home?"

"My gram is comin' in her van and takin' all of us."

"Good." Luckily the grandmother was reliable, because the parents sure as hell weren't. And no way did Gage want the boys walking home. The rec center was in a decent enough area, but where the boys lived...

The kid laughed as Gage flipped him around and put him back on his feet.

Like a shot, he took off toward Miles, who was already surrounded by boys as he rounded them up.

Grandma would arrive soon. She'd probably appreciate how the kids had been exercised in the guise of play, schooled on control and manners, and fed. The boys always ate like they were starving. But then, Gage remembered being that age and how he could pack it away.

Briefly, his gaze met Harper's, and damn it, he felt it, that charged connection that had always existed between them. She wore a silly smile that, despite his dark mood, made him want to smile, too.

But as they looked at each other, she deliberately wiped the smile away. Pretending she hadn't seen him at all, she got back to work.

Gage grunted. He had no idea what had gotten into her, but in his current frame of mind, better that he just let it go for now.

Very shortly, the most dedicated fight fans would arrive to catch the prelims. By the time the main card started, drawing a few high school seniors, some interested neighbors and the other fighters, there'd be bodies in all the chairs, sprawled on the mats and leaning up against the concrete walls. Equipment had been either moved out of the way or stored for the night.

This was a big deal. One of their own was competing tonight.

The high school guys were looking forward to a special night where they'd get to mingle more with their favorite fighters.

A dozen or more women were anxious to do some mingling of their own.

Armie, the twisted hedonist, had been judicious in handing out the invites: some very hot babes would be in attendance, women who'd already proven their "devotion" to fighters.

Gage couldn't have cared less. If he hadn't been fucked by karma, he'd be there in Japan, too. He didn't feel like celebrating, damn it. He didn't want to expose anyone to his nasty disposition.

The very last thing he wanted was a female groupie invading his space.

Actually, he'd been so caught up in training, he'd been away from female company for some time now. You'd think he'd be anxious to let off steam in the best way known to man.

But whenever he thought of sex...

Harper laughed again, and Gage set his back teeth even while sneaking a peek to see what she found so funny. Armie said something to her, and she swatted at him while smiling widely.

Gage did a little more teeth grinding.

Like most of the fighters, Armie understood Gage's pre-occupation and ignored him. Now if he would just ignore Harper, too, Gage could get back to brooding.

Instead, he was busy thinking of female company—but there was only one woman who crowded his brain.

And for some reason, she seemed irritated with him.

His dark scowl made the stitches above his eye pull and pinch, drawing his thoughts from one problem and back to another.

One stupid mistake, one botched move during prac-tice, and he had an injury that got him kicked out of the competition.

Damn it all, he didn't want to be here tonight, but if he hadn't shown up, he'd have looked sad and pathetic.

"Stop pacing," Harper said from right behind him. "It makes you look sad and pathetic."

Hearing his concern thrown right back at him, Gage's left eye twitched. Leave it to Harper to know his exact thoughts and to use them as provocation. But then, he had to admit, she provoked him so well....

He'd missed the fights. And he'd missed Harper.

The only upside to heading home had been getting to see her. But since his return three days ago, she'd given him his space—space he wanted, damn it, just maybe not from her. At the very least, she could have *wanted* to see him, instead of treating him like one of the guys.

Relishing a new focus, Gage paused, planning what he'd say to her.

She didn't give him a chance to say anything.

With a hard whop to his ass, she walked on by and sashayed down the hall to the back.

Gage stood there, the sting of her swat ramping up his temper...and something else. Staring after her, he suffered the sizzling clench of emotions that always surfaced whenever Harper got close—which, since he'd returned home with his injury, had been rare.

He'd known her for years—grown up with her, in fact—and had always enjoyed her. Her wit. Her conversation. Her knowledge of mixed martial arts competition.

Her cute bod.

They'd recently taken their friendship to the next level, dating, spending more private time together. He'd enjoyed the closeness...

But he'd yet to enjoy her naked.

Time and circumstances had conspired against him on that one. Just when things had been heating up with Harper, just when it seemed she was ready to say "yes" instead of "not yet," he'd been offered the fight on the main card in Japan. He'd fought with the SBC before. He wasn't a newbie.

But always in the prelims, never on the highly publicized, more important main card. Never with such an anticipated event.

In a whirlwind, he'd gone off to a different camp to train with Cannon, getting swept up in the publicity and interviews that went with a main card bout...

Until, just a few lousy days ago—*so fucking close*—he'd miscalculated in practice and sustained a deep cut from his sparring partner's elbow.

A cut very near his eye that required fifteen stitches.

It made him sick to think of how quickly he'd been pro-
nounced medically ineligible. Before he'd even caught his
breath the SBC had picked his replacement.

That lucky bastard was now in Japan, ready to compete.

And Gage was left in Ohio. Instead of fighting for
recognition, he fought his demons—*and got tweaked by
Harper.*

He went after her, calling down the empty hallway, "I
am not pathetic."

From inside a storage room, he heard her loud "Ha!"
of disagreement.

Needing a target for his turbulent emotions and deciding Harper was perfect—in every way—he strode into
the room.

And promptly froze.

Bent at the waist, Harper had her sexy ass in the air
while she pulled disposable cups off the bottom shelf.

His heart skipped a beat. Damn, she was so hot. Except
for bad timing, he'd be more familiar with that particular,
very perfect part of her anatomy.

Not sleeping with her was yet another missed opportunity, one that plagued him more now that he didn't have
the draining distraction of an upcoming fight. His heart
started punching a little too hard. Anger at his circumstances began to morph into red-hot lust as he considered
the possibilities.

But then, whenever he thought of Harper, lust was the
least confusing of his emotions.

Now that he was home, he'd hoped to pick up where
they'd left off. Only Harper had antagonism mixed with
her other more welcoming signals, so he had to proceed
with caution.

"What are you doing?" he asked, because that sounded
better than saying, *"Damn, girl, I love your ass."*

Still in that tantalizing position, she peeked back at him, her brown hair swinging around her face, her enormous blue eyes direct. With her head down that way, blood rushed to her face and made her freckles more noticeable.

There were nights he couldn't sleep for wondering about all the places she might have freckles. Many times he'd imagined stripping those clothes off her, piece by piece, so he could investigate all her more secret places.

Like him, she was a conservative dresser. Despite working at a secondhand boutique clothing store she always looked casual and comfortable. Her jeans and T-shirts gave an overview of sweet curves, but he'd love to get lost in the details if he could ever get her naked.

She straightened with two big boxes in her hands. "Armie had small juice containers out for the kids, but of course adults are going to want something different to drink. Same with the snacks. So I'm changing up the food spread."

Due to her schedule at the boutique, Harper had been unable to attend the party with the youngsters, but she'd sent in snacks ahead of time. She had a knack for creating healthy treats that looked fun and got gobbled up. Some of the options had looked really tasty, but if she wanted to switch them out, he could at least help her.

She glanced at the slim watch on her wrist. "Lots to do before everyone shows up for the prelims."

Since pride kept him at the rec center anyway...

"What can I do to help?"

Her smile came slow and teasing. "All kinds of things, actually. Or—wait—do you mean with the setup?"

"I... What?" Was that a come-on? He couldn't tell for sure—nothing new with Harper. Clearly she'd been pissed at him about something, but now, at her provocative words, his dick perked up with hopes of reconciliation.

Snickering, she walked up to him, gave him a hip bump, then headed out of the room. "Come on, big boy. You can give me a hand with the folding tables."

As confusion warred with disgruntlement, he trailed after her. "All right, fine." Then he thought to remind her, "But I'm not pathetic."

Turning to face him, she walked backward. "Hit home with that one, did I?"

"No." *Yes.*

"I can help you to fake it if you want."

Despite the offhand way she tossed that out, it still sounded suggestive as hell. "Watch where you're going." Gage reached out, caught her arm and kept her from tripping over the edge of a mat.

Now that he had ahold of her, he decided to hang on. Where his fingers wrapped around her arm just above her elbow, she was soft and sleek and he couldn't stop his thumb from playing over the warm silk of her skin.

"Thanks," she said a little breathlessly, facing forward again and treading on.

"So." Though he walked right beside her, Gage couldn't resist leaning back a bit to watch the sway of her behind. "How would we fake it? Not that I need to fake shit, but you've got me curious."

Laughing, she leaned into him, smiled up at him, and damn it, he wanted her. *Bad.*

Always had, probably always would.

He'd had his chance before he left for the new camp. Even with the demands of training, he'd wanted her while he was away. Now he was back and the wanting boiled over.

Her head perfectly reached his shoulder. He stood six-three, nine inches taller than her, and he outweighed her by more than a hundred pounds.

But for a slim woman, she packed one hell of a punch. "Harper," he chided. She was the only person he knew who seemed to take maniacal delight in tormenting him.

Rolling her eyes, she said, "You are such a grouch when you're being pathetic." She stepped away to arrange the cups on a long table placed up against the wall. "Everyone feels terrible for you. And why not? We all know you'd have won. Maybe even with a first-round knockout."

Did she really believe that? Or was she just placating him? "Darvey isn't a slouch." Gage wouldn't want an easy fight. What the hell would that prove?

"No," she agreed, "but you'd have creamed him."

"That was the plan." So many times he'd played it out in his head, the strategy he'd use, how he'd push the fight, how his cardio would carry him through if it went all three rounds. Darvey wasn't known for his gas tank. He liked to use submissions, manipulating an arm or leg joint to get his opponent to tap before something broke. His plan was always to end things fast. But Gage knew how to defend against submissions, how to make it *his* fight, not anyone else's.

"Sucks that you have to sit this one out," Harper continued. "But since you do, I know you'd rather be brimming with confidence, instead of moping around like a sad sack."

Folding his arms over his chest, he glared down at her. "I don't mope."

She eyed his biceps, inhaled slowly, blew the breath out even slower.

"Harper."

Brows raised, she brought those big blue eyes up to focus on his face. "What?"

He dropped his arms and stepped closer, crowding her,

getting near enough to breathe in her unique scent. "How do you figure we'd fake things?"

"Oh, yeah." She glanced to one side, then the other. "People are looking at us."

"Yeah?" Currently the only people in the gym were the guys helping to set it up for the party. Armie, Stack, Denver, a few others. "So?"

"So…" She licked her lips, hesitated only a second, then came up against him. In a slow tease, her hands crawled up and over his chest. Fitted against him, she went on tiptoe, giving him a full-body rub.

Without even thinking about it, Gage caught her waist, keeping her right there. Confusion at this abrupt turnaround of hers stopped him from doing what came naturally.

Didn't bother her, though.

With her gaze locked on his, she curled her hands around his neck, drew him down to meet her halfway and put that soft, lush, taunting mouth against his.

Hell, yeah.

Her lips played over his, teasing, again provoking. They shared breath. Her thighs shifted against his. Her cool fingers moved over his nape and then into his hair. The kiss stayed light, slow and excruciating.

Until he took over.

Tilting his head, he fit his mouth more firmly against her, nudged her lips apart, licked in, deeper, hotter…

"Get a room already."

Gasping at the interruption, Harper pulled away. Embarrassed, she pressed her face against his chest before rearing back and glaring at Armie.

Gage just watched her. He didn't care what his dipshit friends said.

But he'd love to know what Harper was up to.

"Don't give me that look," Armie told her. "We have high school boys coming over tonight."

"The biggest kids are already here!"

"Now, I know you don't mean me," Armie continued, always up for ribbing her. "You're the one having a tantrum."

Gage stood there while they fussed at each other. Harper was like that with all the guys. She helped out, gave as good as she got, and treated them all like pesky brothers that she both adored and endured.

Except for Gage.

From the get-go she'd been different with him. Not shy, because seriously, Harper didn't have a shy bone in her hot little body. But maybe more demonstrative. Or rather, demonstrative in a different way.

He didn't think she'd smack any of the other fighters on the ass.

But he wasn't stupid. Encouraged or not, he knew guys were guys, period. They'd tease her, respect her boundaries, but every damn one of them had probably thought about sleeping with her.

For damn sure, they'd all pictured her naked.

Those vivid visuals were part of a man's basic DNA. Attractive babe equaled fantasies. While Harper hustled around the rec center helping out in a dozen different ways, she'd probably been mentally stripped a million times.

Hell, even while she sniped back and forth with Armie, Gage pictured her buck-ass, wondering how it'd feel to kiss her like that again, but without the barrier of clothes in the way.

"You need a swift kick to your butt," Harper declared.

"From you?" Armie laughed.

Fighting a smile, she said, "Don't think I won't."

"You wanna go?" Armie egged her on, using his finger-tips to call her forward. "C'mon then, little girl. Let's see what you've got."

For a second there, Harper looked ready to accept, so Gage interceded. "Children, play nice."

"Armie doesn't like *nice*." She curled her lip in a taunt. "He likes *kinky*."

In reply, Armie took a bow.

True enough, if ever a man liked a little freak thrown into the mix, it was Armie. He'd once been dropped off by a motorcycle-driving chick dressed in leather pants and a low-cut vest, her arms circled with snake tattoos. She'd sported more piercings than Gage could count—a dozen or so in her ears, a few in her eyebrows, lip, nose. The whole day, Armie had limped around as if the woman had rid-den him raw. He'd also smiled a lot, proof that whatever had happened, he'd enjoyed himself.

Unlike Gage, Armie saw no reason to skip sex, ever. Not even prior to a fight. The only women he turned down were the ones, as Harper had said, that were too nice.

"Come on." She took Gage's hand and started dragging him toward the back.

"Hey, don't leave my storage closet smelling like sex," Armie called after them. "If you're going to knock boots, take it elsewhere!"

Harper flipped him the bird, but she was grinning. "He is so outrageous."

"That's the pot calling the kettle black." Just where was she leading him?

"Eh, maybe." She winked up at him. "But I just act out-rageous. I have a feeling it's a mind-set for Armie."

Ignoring what Armie had said, she dragged him back into the storage closet—and shut the door.

Gage stood there watching her, thinking things he shouldn't and getting hard because of it. Heart beating slow and steady, he asked, "Now what?"

CHAPTER TWO

COULD A MAN look sexier? No. Dumb question. Harper sighed. At twenty-five, she knew what she wanted. Whether or not she could have it, that was the big question.

Or rather, could she have it for the long haul.

"Is that for me?" She nodded at the rise in his jeans.

Without changing expressions, Gage nodded. "Yeah." And then, "After that kiss, you have to ask?"

Sweet. "So you like my plan?"

Looking far too serious, his mellow brown gaze held hers. "If your plan is to turn me on, yeah, I like it."

As part of her plan, she forced a laugh. She had to keep Gage from knowing how badly he'd broken her heart.

Talk about pathetic.

Gage was two years older, which, while they'd been in school, had made him the older, awesome star athlete and popular guy that *every* girl had wanted. Her included.

Back then, she hadn't stood a chance. He'd dated prom queen, cheerleader, class president material, not collect-for-the-homeless Goody Two-shoes material.

So she'd wrapped herself in her pride and whenever they'd crossed paths, she'd treated him like any other jock—meaning she'd been nice but uninterested.

And damn him, he'd been A-OK with that, the big jerk.

They lived in the same small neighborhood. Not like Warfield, Ohio, left a lot of room for anonymity. Everyone knew everyone, especially those who went through school together.

It wasn't until they both started hanging out in the rec center, her to help out, him to train, that he seemed to really tune in to her. Course, she hadn't been real subtle with him, so not noticing her would have required a deliberate snub.

She was comfortable with guys. Actually, she was comfortable with everyone. Her best friend claimed she was one of those nauseatingly happy people who enjoyed life a little too much. But whatever. She believed in making the most of every day.

That is, when big, badass alpha fighters cooperated.

Unfortunately, Gage didn't. Not always.

Not that long ago they'd been dating, getting closer. Getting steamier.

She'd fallen a little more in love with him every day.

She adored his quiet confidence. His motivation and dedication. The gentle way he treated the little kids who hung out at the center, how he coached the older boys who revered him, and the respect he got—and gave—to other fighters.

She especially loved his big, rock-solid body. Just thinking about it made her all twitchy in private places.

Things had seemed to be progressing nicely.

Until the SBC called and put him on the main card for freaking other-side-of-the-world Japan, and boom, just like that, it seemed she'd lost all the ground she'd gained. Three months before the fight, Gage had packed up and moved to Harmony, Kentucky, to join Cannon in a different camp where he could hone his considerable skills with a fresh set of experienced fighters.

He'd kissed her goodbye first, but making any promises about what to expect on his return hadn't been on his mind. Nope. He'd been one big obsessed puppy, his thoughts only on fighting and winning.

Maybe he'd figured that once he won, his life would get too busy for her to fit into it.

And maybe, she reminded herself, she was jumping ahead at Mach speed. They hadn't even slept together yet.

But that was something she could remedy.

Never, not in a million years, would she have wished the injury on him. He'd fought, and won, for the SBC before. But never on the main card. Knowing what that big chance had meant to him, she'd been devastated on his behalf.

Yet she'd also still been hurt that the entire time he was gone, he hadn't called. For all she knew, he hadn't even thought about her. Ignoring him had seemed her best bet—until she realized she couldn't. Loving him made that impossible.

And so she decided not to waste an opportunity.

Gage leaned against the wall. "I give up. How long are you going to stand there staring at me?"

"I like looking at you, that's all." She turned her back on him before she blew the game too soon. "You're terrific eye candy."

He went so silent, she could hear the ticking of the wall clock. "What are you up to, Harper?"

"No good." She grinned back at him. "Definitely, one hundred percent no good." Locating napkins and paper plates on the shelf, she put them into an empty box. Searching more shelves, she asked, "Do you see the coffeemaker anywhere?"

His big hands settled on her waist. "Forget the coffeemaker," he murmured from right behind her. Leaning down, he kissed the side of her neck. "Let's talk about these no-good plans of yours."

Wow, oh, wow. She could feel his erection against her

tush and it was so tantalizing she had to fight not to wiggle. "Okay."

He nuzzled against her, his soft breath in her ear, his hands sliding around to her belly. Such incredibly large hands that covered so much ground. The thumb of his right hand nudged the bottom of her breast. The pinkie on his left hovered just over the fly of her jeans.

Temptation was a terrible thing, eating away at her common sense and obscuring the larger purpose.

He opened his mouth on her throat and she felt his tongue on her skin. When he took a soft, wet love bite, she forgot she had knees. Her legs just sort of went rubbery.

To keep her upright, he hugged her tighter and rested his chin on top of her head. "Tell me what we're doing, honey."

Took her a second to catch her breath. "You don't know?" She twisted to face him, one hand knotted in his shirt to hang on, just in case. "Because, seriously, Gage, you seemed to know exactly what you were doing."

His smile went lazy—and more relaxed than it had been since he'd found out he wouldn't fight. He slipped a hand into her hair, cupping the back of her head, rubbing a little. "I know I was making myself horny. I know you were liking it. I'm just not sure why we're doing this here and now."

"Oh." She dropped against him so she could suck in some air. "Yeah." Unfortunately, every breath filled her head with the hot scent of his powerful body. "Mmm, you are so delicious."

A strained laugh rumbled in his chest. "Harper."

"Right." To give herself some room to think, she stepped back from him. So that he'd know this wasn't just about sex, she admitted, "I care about you. You know that."

Those gorgeous brown eyes narrowed on her face. "Ditto."

That kicked her heart into such a fast rhythm, she almost gasped. *He cared about her.* "And I know you, Gage. Probably better than you think."

His smile softened, and he said all dark and sensuous-like, "Ditto again, honey."

Damn the man, even his murmurs made her hot and bothered. "Yeah, so…" Collecting her thoughts wasn't easy, not with a big hunk of sexiness right there in front of her, within reach, ready and waiting. "I know you're hammered over the lost opportunity."

"The opportunity to have sex with you?"

Her jaw loosened at his misunderstanding. "No, I meant…" Hoping sex was still an option, she cleared her throat. "I meant the fight."

"Yeah." He stared at her mouth. "That, too."

Had he somehow moved closer without her knowing it? Her back now rested against the shelving and Gage stood only an inch from touching her. "So…" she said again. "It's understandable that you'd be stomping around in a bad mood."

He chided her with a shake of his head. "I was not stomping."

"Close enough." Damn it, now she couldn't stop staring at his mouth. "But I know you want to blow it off like you're not that upset."

"I'm not *upset.*" He scoffed over her word choice. "I'm disappointed. A little pissed off." His feet touched hers. "I take it you have something in mind?"

She shifted without thinking about it, and suddenly he moved one foot between hers. His hard muscled thigh pressed at the apex of her legs and every thought she had, every bit of her concentration, went to where they touched.

Casual as you please, he braced a hand on the shelf beside her head.

Gage was so good at this, at stalking an opponent, at gaining the advantage before anyone realized his intent.

But she wasn't his opponent. Keeping that in mind, she gathered her thoughts, shored up her backbone and made a proposal. "I think we should fool around." Before he could reply to that one way or the other, she added, "Out there. Where they can all see." *And hopefully you'll like that enough to want to continue in private.*

He lifted one brow, the corner of his mouth quirking. "And you called Armie kinky."

Heat rushed into her face. "No, I don't mean anything really explicit." But that was a lie, so she amended, "Well, I mean, I do. But not with an audience."

Again his eyes narrowed—and his other hand lifted to the shelving. He effectively confined her, not that she wanted freedom. With him so close, she had to tip her head back to look up at him. Her heart tried to punch out of her chest, and the sweetest little ache coiled inside her.

"I'm with you so far," he whispered, and leaned down to kiss the corner of her mouth.

"I figured, you know…" How did he expect her to think while he did that? "We could act all cozy, like you had other things on your mind. Then no one would know how distressed you are over missing the fight."

"First off, I'm not acting." His forehead touched hers. "Second, I am *not* distressed. Stop making me sound so damned weak."

Not acting? What did that mean? She licked her lips—and he noticed. "I know you're not weak." Wasn't that her point? "So…you don't like my plan?"

"I like it fine." His mouth brushed her temple, his tongue touched the inside of her ear—*Wow, that curled her toes!*—then he nibbled his way along her jaw, under her chin. "Playing with you will make for a long night."

"Yes." A long night where she'd have a chance to show him how perfect they were for each other. And if he didn't see things the same as she did, they could still end up sharing a very special evening together. If she didn't have him forever, she'd at least have that memory to carry her through.

But before she settled for only a memory, she hoped to—

A sharp rap on the door made her jump.

Gage just groaned.

Through the closed door, Armie asked, "You two naked?"

Puffing up with resentment at the intrusion, Harper started around Gage.

Before she got far, he caught her. Softly, he said, "Don't encourage him," before walking to the door and opening it. "What do you want, Armie?"

"Refreshments for everyone." Armie peeked around him, ran his gaze over Harper, and frowned. "Damn, fully clothed. And here I was all geared up for a peep show."

Harper threw a roll of paper towels at him.

When Armie ducked, they went right past him and out into the hall.

Stack said, "Hey!"

And they all grinned.

Getting back to business, she finished filling the box with prepackaged cookies, chips and pretzels, then shoved it all into Armie's arms, making him stumble back a foot.

He just laughed at her, the jerk.

"Where did you hide the coffeemaker?" Harper asked, trying to sound normal instead of primed.

"I'll get it." Armie looked at each of them. "Plan to join us anytime soon?"

Unruffled by the interruption, Gage said, "Be right there."

"Not to be a spoilsport, but a group of the high school boys have arrived, so, seriously, you might want to put a lid on the hanky-panky for a bit."

"People are here already?" She'd thought she had an hour yet. "They're early."

Armie shrugged. "Everyone is excited to watch Cannon fight again." He clapped Gage on the shoulder. "Sucks you're not out there, man."

"Next time," Gage said easily with no inflection at all.

Harper couldn't help but glance at him with sympathy.

"If you insist on molesting him," Armie said, "better get on with it real quick."

She reached for him, but he ducked out laughing.

She watched Armie go down the hall.

Gage studied her. "You going to molest me, honey?"

Did he want her to? Because, seriously, she'd be willing. "Let's see how it goes."

His eyes widened a little over that.

She dragged out a case of cola. Gage shook off his surprise and took it from her, and together they headed back out.

A half hour later they had everything set up. The colas were in the cooler under ice, sandwiches had been cut and laid out. A variety of chips filled one entire table. More people arrived. The boys, ranging in ages from fifteen to eighteen, were hyped up, talking loudly and gobbling down the food in record time. The women spent their time sidling up to the guys.

The guys spent their time enjoying it.

"Is there more food in the back room?"

Harper smiled at Stack Hannigan, one of the few fighters who hadn't yet staked out a woman. "Yeah, but I can get it as soon as I finish tidying up here." Every ten minutes she needed to reorganize the food. Once the fights started, things would settle down, but until then it was pure chaos.

Stack tugged on a lock of her hair. "No worries, doll. Be right back." And off he went.

Harper watched him walk away, as always enjoying the show. Long-legged with a rangy stride, Stack looked impressive whether he was coming or going—as all of them did.

In some ways, the guys were all different.

Stack's blond hair was darker and straighter than Armie's. Denver's brown hair was so long he often contained it in a ponytail. Cannon's was pitch-black with a little curl on the ends.

She preferred Gage's trimmed brown hair, and she absolutely loved his golden-brown eyes.

All of the fighters were good-looking. Solid, muscular, capable. But where Stack, Armie and Cannon were light heavyweights, her Gage was a big boy, a shredded heavyweight with fists the size of hams. They were all friends, but with different fighting styles and different levels of expertise.

When Stack returned with another platter of food, he had two high school wrestlers beside him, talking a mile a minute. She loved seeing how the older boys emulated the fighters, learning discipline, self-control and confidence.

With the younger kids, it sometimes broke her heart to see how desperate they were for attention. And then when one or more of the guys made a kid feel special, her heart expanded so much it choked her.

"You're not on your period, are you?" Armie asked from beside her.

Using the back of her hand to quickly dash away a tear, Harper asked him, "What are you talking about?"

"You're all fired up one minute, hot and bothered the next, now standing here glassy-eyed." Leaning down to better see her, he searched her face and scowled. "What the hell, woman? Are you *crying?*"

She slugged him in the shoulder—which meant she hurt her hand more than she hurt him. Softly, because it wasn't a teasing subject, she said, "I was thinking how nice this is for the younger boys."

"Yeah." He tugged at his ear and his smile went crooked. "Makes me weepy sometimes, too."

Harper laughed at that. "You are so full of it."

He grinned with her, then leveled her by saying, "How come you're letting those other gals climb all over Gage?"

She jerked around so fast she threw herself off balance. Trapped by the reception desk, Gage stood there while two women fawned over him. Harper felt mean. More than mean. "What is he doing now?"

"Greeting people, that's all. Not that the ladies aren't giving it the old college try." He leaned closer, his voice low. "I approve of your methods, by the way."

"Meaning what?"

"Guys have to man up and all that. Be tough. But I know he'd rather be in the arena than here with us."

Than here—with her. She sighed.

Armie tweaked her chin. "Don't be like that."

"Like what?"

"All 'poor little me, I'm not a priority.' You're smarter than that, Harper. You know he's worked years for this."

She did know it, and that's why it hurt so much. If it wasn't so important to him, she might stand a chance.

"Oh, gawd," Armie drawled, managing to look both disgusted and mocking. "You're deeper down in the dumps than he is." He tipped up her chin. "You know, it took a hell of a lot of discipline for him to walk away from every-one, including you, so he could train with another camp."

She gave him a droll look rife with skepticism.

Armie wasn't finished. "It's not like he said goodbye to you and then indulged any other women. Nope. It was celibacy all the way."

"That's a myth." She knew because she'd looked it up. "Guys do not have to do without in order to compete."

"Without sex, no. Without distractions, yeah. And you, Harper Gates, are one hell of a distraction."

Was she? She just couldn't tell.

Armie leaned in closer, keeping his voice low. "The thing is, if you were serving it up regular-like, it'd prob-ably be okay."

She shoved him. "Armie!" Her face went hot. Did everyone know her damn business? Had Gage talked? Complained?

Holding up his hands in surrender, Armie said, "It's true. Sex, especially good sex with someone important, works wonders for clearing the mind of turmoil. But when the lady is holding out—"

She locked her jaw. "Just where did you get this info?"

That made him laugh. "No one told me, if that's what you're thinking. Anyone with eyes can see that you two haven't sealed the deal yet."

Curious, eyes narrowed in skepticism, she asked, "How?"

"For one thing, the way Gage looks at you, like he's waiting to unwrap a special present."

More heat surfaced, coloring not only her face, but her throat and chest, too.

"Anyway," Armie said, after taking in her blush with a brow raised in interest, "you want to wait, he cares enough not to push, so he did without. It's admirable, not a reason to drag around like your puppy died or something. Not every guy has that much heart." He held out his arms. "Why do you think I only do local fighting?"

"You have the heart," Harper defended. But she added, "I have no idea what motivates you, I just know it must be something big."

Pleased by her reasoning, he admitted, "You could be right." Before she could jump on that, he continued. "My point is that Gage is a fighter all the way. He'll be a champion one day. That means he has to make certain sacrifices, some at really inconvenient times."

Oddly enough, she felt better about things, and decided to tease him back a little. "So I was a sacrifice?"

"Giving up sex is always a sacrifice." He slung an arm around her shoulders and hauled her into his side. "Especially the sex you haven't had yet."

"Armie!" She enjoyed his insights, but he was so cavalier about it, so bold, she couldn't help but continue blushing.

"Now, Harper, you know…" Suddenly Armie went quiet. "Damn, for such a calm bastard, he has the deadliest stare."

Harper looked up to find Gage scrutinizing them. And he did look rather hot under the collar. Even as the two attractive women did their best to regain his attention, Gage stayed focused on her.

She tried smiling at him. He just transferred his piercing gaze to Armie.

"You could go save him from them," Harper suggested.

"Sorry, honey, not my type."

"What?" she asked as if she didn't already know. "The lack of a Mohawk bothers you?"

He laughed, surprised her with a loud kiss right on her mouth and a firm swat on her butt, then he sauntered away.

CHAPTER THREE

GAGE LOOKED READY to self-combust, so Harper headed over to him. He tracked her progress, and even when she reached him, he still looked far too intent and serious.

"Hey," she said.

"Hey, yourself."

She eyed the other ladies. "See those guys over there?" She pointed to where Denver and Stack loitered by the food, stuffing their faces. "They're shy, but they're really hoping you'll come by to say hi."

It didn't take much more than that for the women to depart.

Gage reached out and tucked her hair behind her ear. "Now why didn't I think of that?"

"Maybe you were enjoying the admiration a little too much."

"No." He touched her cheek, trailed his fingertips down to her chin. "You and Armie had your heads together long enough. Care to share what you two talked about?"

She shrugged. "You."

"Huh." His hand curved around her nape, pulling her in. "That's why he kissed you and played patty-cake with your ass?"

She couldn't be this close to him without touching. Her hands opened on his chest, smoothing over the prominent muscles. What his chest did for a T-shirt should be illegal. "Now, Gage, I know you're not jealous."

His other hand covered hers, flattening her palm over his heart. "Do I have reason to be?"

"Over *Armie?*" She gave a very unladylike snort. "Get real."

He continued to study her.

Sighing, she said, "If you want to know—"

"I do."

Why not tell him? she thought. It'd be interesting to see his reaction. "Actually, it's kind of funny. See, Armie was encouraging me to have sex with you."

Gage's expression went still, first with a hint of surprise, then with the heat of annoyance. "What the hell does it have to do with him?"

No way could she admit that Armie thought they were both sad sacks. "Nothing. You know Armie."

"Yeah." He scowled darker. "I know him."

Laughing, she rolled her eyes. "He's lacking discretion, says whatever he thinks and enjoys butting in." She snuggled in closer to him, leaning on him. Loving him. "He wants you happy."

"I'm happy, damn it."

She didn't bother telling him how *un*happy he sounded just then. "And he wants me happy."

Smoothing a hand down her back, pressing her closer still, he asked, "Sex will make you happy?"

Instead of saying, *I love you so much, sex with you would make me ecstatic,* she quipped, "It'd sure be better than a stinging butt, which is all Armie offered."

"Want me to kiss it and make it better?"

She opened her mouth, but nothing came out.

With a small smile of satisfaction, Gage palmed her cheek, gently caressing. "I'll take that as a yes."

She gave a short nod.

He used his hand on her butt to snug her in closer. "Armie kissed you, too."

Making a face, she told him, "Believe me, the swat was far more memorable."

"Good thing for Armie."

So he *was* jealous?

"Hey," Stack called over to them. "We're ready to get things started. Kill the overhead lights, will you?"

Still looking down at her, Gage slowly nodded. "Sure thing." Taking Harper with him, he went to the front desk and retrieved the barrel key for the locking switches.

The big TV, along with a security lamp in the hallway, would provide all the light they needed. When Gage inserted the key and turned it, the overhead florescent lights clicked off. Given that they stood well away from the others, heavy shadows enveloped them.

Rather than head over to the crowd, Gage aligned her body with his in a tantalizing way. His hand returned to her bottom, ensuring she stayed pressed to him. "Maybe," he whispered, "I can be more memorable."

As he moved his hand lower on her behind—his long fingers seeking inward—she went on tiptoe and squeaked, "*Definitely.*"

Smiling, he took her mouth in a consuming kiss. Combined with the way those talented fingers did such incredible things to her, rational thought proved impossible.

Finally, easing up with smaller kisses and teasing nibbles, he whispered, "We can't do this here."

Her fingers curled in against him, barely making a dent in his rock-solid muscles. "I know," she groaned.

He stroked restless hands up and down her back. "Want to grab a seat with me?"

He asked the question almost as if a big *or* hung at the

end. Like... *Or should we just leave? Or should we find an empty room?*

Or would you prefer to go anywhere private so we can both get naked and finish what we started?

She waited, hopeful, but when he said nothing more, she blew out a disappointed breath. "Sure."

And of course she felt like a jerk.

He and Cannon were close friends. Everyone knew he wanted to watch the fights. Despite his own disappointment over medical ineligibility, he was excited for Cannon's competition.

Her eyes were adjusting and she could see Gage better now, the way he searched her face, how he...waited.

For her to understand? Was Armie right? Maybe more than anything she needed to show him that she not only loved him, but she loved his sport, that she supported him and was as excited by his success as he was.

"Yes, let's sit." She took his hand. "Toward the back, though, so we can sneak away later if we decide to." Eyes flaring at that naughty promise, he didn't budge.

"Sneak away to where?"

"The way I feel right now, any empty room might do." Hiding her smile, Harper stretched up to give him a very simple kiss. "That is, between fights. We don't want to miss anything."

His hand tightened on hers, and she couldn't help thinking that maybe Armie's suggestion had merit after all.

GAGE GOT SO caught up in the prefights that he almost— *almost*—forgot about Harper's endless foreplay. Damn, she had him primed. Her closeness, the warmth of her body, the sweet scent of her hair and the warmer scent of her skin, were enough to make him edgy with need. But every so often her hand drifted to his thigh, lingered, stroked. Each time he held his breath, unsure how far she'd go.

How far he wanted her to go.

So far, all he knew was that it wasn't far enough.

Once, she'd run her hand up his back, just sort of feeling him, her fingers spread as she traced muscles, his shoulder blades, down his spine...

If he gave his dick permission, it would stand at attention right now. But he concentrated on keeping control of things—himself and, when possible, Harper, too.

It wasn't easy. Though she appeared to be as into the fights as everyone else, she still had very busy hands.

It wasn't just the sexual teasing that got to him. It was emotional, too. He hated that he wasn't in Japan with Cannon, walking to the cage for his own big battle. He'd had prelim fights; he'd built his name and recognition.

He'd finally gotten that main event—and it pissed him off more than he wanted to admit that he was left sitting behind.

But sitting behind with Harper sure made it easier. Especially when he seemed so attuned to her.

If her mood shifted, he freaking felt it, deep down inside himself. At one point she hugged his arm, her head on his shoulder, and something about the embrace had felt so damn melancholy that he'd wanted to lift her into his lap and hold her close and make some heavy-duty spur-of-the-moment promises.

Holding her wouldn't have been a big deal; Miles had a chick in his lap. Denver, too.

With Harper, though, it'd be different. Everyone knew a hookup when they saw one, and no way did Gage want others to see her that way. Harper was like family at the rec center. She was part of the inner circle. He would never do anything to belittle her importance.

Beyond that, he wanted more than a hookup. He cared about her well beyond getting laid a single time, well beyond any mere friendship.

Still, as soon as possible, he planned to get her alone and, God willing, get her under him.

Or over him.

However she liked it, as long as he got her. Not just for tonight, but for a whole lot more.

Everyone grimaced when the last prelim fight ended with a grappling match—that turned into an arm bar. The dominant fighter trapped the arm, extended it to the breaking point while the other guy tried everything he could to free himself.

Squeezed up close to his side, peeking through her fingers, Harper pleaded, "Tap, tap, tap," all but begging his opponent to admit defeat before he suffered more damage. And when he did, she cheered with everyone else. "Good fight. Wow. That was intense."

It was so cute how involved she got while watching, that Gage had to tip up her chin so he could kiss her.

Her enthusiasm for the fight waned as she melted against him, saying, "Mmm…"

He smiled against her mouth. "You're making me a little nuts."

"Look who's talking." She glanced around with exaggerated drama. "If only we were alone."

Hoping she meant it, he used his thumb to brush her bottom lip. "We can be." His place. Her place. Either worked for him. "It'll be late when the fights end, but—"

"I really have to wait that long?"

Yep, she meant it. Her blue eyes were heavy, her face flushed. She breathed deeper. He glanced down at her breasts and saw her nipples were tight against the material of her T-shirt.

Okay, much more of that and he wouldn't be able to keep it under wraps.

A roar sounded around them and they both looked up to see Cannon on the screen. Gage couldn't help but grin. Yeah, he wanted to be there, too, but at the same time, he was so damn proud of Cannon.

In such a short time, Cannon had become one of the most beloved fighters in the sport. The fans adored him. His peers respected him. And the Powers That Be saw him as a big draw moneymaker. After he won tonight, Gage predicted that Cannon would be fighting for the belt.

He'd win it, too.

They showed footage of Cannon before the fight, his knit hat pulled low on his head, bundled under a big sweatshirt. Keeping his muscles warm.

He looked as calm and determined as ever while answering questions.

Harper squeezed his hand and when she spoke, Gage realized it was with nervousness.

"He'll do okay."

Touched by her concern, he smiled. "I'd put money on it."

She nodded, but didn't look away from the screen. "He's been something of a phenomenon, hasn't he?"

"With Cannon, making an impact comes naturally."

"After he wins this one," she mused, "they'll start hyping him for a title shot."

Since her thoughts mirrored his own, he hugged her. Her uncanny insight never ceased to amaze him. Then again, she was a regular at the rec center, interacted often with fighters and enjoyed the sport. It made sense that she'd have the same understanding as him.

"Cannon's earned it." Few guys took as many fights as he did, sometimes on really short notice. If a fighter got sick—or suffered an injury, as Gage had—Cannon was there, always ready, always in shape, always kicking ass. They called him the Saint, and no wonder.

Gage glanced around at the young men who, just a few years ago, would have been hanging on the street corner looking for trouble. Now they had some direction in their lives, the attention they craved, decent role models and a good way to expend energy. But the rec center was just a small part of Cannon's goodwill.

Whenever he got back to town, he continued his efforts to protect the neighborhood. Gage had enjoyed joining their group, going on night strolls to police the corruption, to let thugs know that others were looking out for the hardworking owners of local family businesses. Actual physical conflicts were rare; overall, it was enough to show that someone was paying attention.

It didn't hurt that Cannon was friends with a tough-as-nails police lieutenant and two detectives. And then there was his buddy at the local bar, a place where Cannon used to work before he got his big break in the SBC fight organization. The owner of the bar had more contacts than the entire police department. He influenced a lot of the other businesses with his stance for integrity.

Yeah, Cannon had some colorful, capable acquaintances—which included a diverse group of MMA fighters.

Saint suited him—not that Cannon liked the moniker. It wasn't nearly as harsh as Gage's own fight name.

Thinking about that brought his attention back to Harper. She watched the TV so he saw her in profile, her long lashes, her turned up nose, her firm chin.

That soft, sexy mouth.

He liked the freckles on her cheekbones. He liked everything about her—how she looked, who she was, the way she treated others.

He smoothed Harper's hair and said, "Most women like to call me Savage."

She snorted. "It's a stupid nickname."

Pretending great insult, he leaned away. "It's a fight name, not a nickname. And it's badass."

She disagreed. "There's nothing savage about you. You should have been named Methodical or Accurate or something."

Grinning, he shook his head. "Thanks, but no thanks."

"Well," she muttered, "you're not savage. That's all I'm saying."

He'd gotten the name early on when, despite absorbing several severe blows from a more experienced fighter, he'd kept going. In the end, he'd beaten the guy with some heavy ground and pound, mostly because he'd still been fresh when the other man gassed out.

The commentator had shouted, *He's a damn savage*, and the description stuck.

To keep himself from thinking about just how savage Harper made him—with lust—he asked, "Want something to eat?"

She wrinkled her nose. "After those past few fights? Bleh."

Two of the prelim fights were bloody messes, one because of a busted nose, but the other due to a cut similar to what Gage had. Head wounds bled like a mother. During a fight, as long as the fighter wasn't hurt that badly, they wouldn't stop things over a little spilled blood. Luckily for the contender, the cut was off to the side and so the blood didn't run into his eyes.

For Gage, it hadn't mattered. If only the cut hadn't been so deep. If it hadn't needed stitches. If it would have been somewhere other than right over his eye. If—

Harper's hand trailed over his thigh again. "So, *Savage*,"

she teased, and damned if she didn't get close to his fly. "Want to help me bring out more drinks before the main event starts?"

Anything to keep him from ruminating on lost opportunities, which he was pretty sure had been Harper's intent.

"Why not?" He stood and hauled her up with him.

They had to go past Armie who stood with two very edgy women and several teenagers, munching on popcorn and comparing biceps.

Armie winked at Harper.

She smiled at him. "We'll only be a minute."

The idiot clutched his chest. "You've just destroyed all my illusions and damaged Savage's reputation beyond repair."

Gage rolled his eyes, more than willing to ignore Armie's nonsense, but he didn't get far before one of the boys asked him about his cut. Next thing he knew, he was surrounded by wide eyes and ripe curiosity. Because it was a good opportunity to show the boys how to handle disappointment, he lingered, letting them ask one question after another.

Harper didn't complain. If anything, she watched him with something that looked a lot like pride. Not exactly what he wanted from her at this particular moment, but it felt good all the same.

He didn't realize she'd gone about getting the drinks without him until Armie relieved her of two large cartons of soft drinks. Together they began putting the cans in the cooler over ice. They laughed together, and even though it looked innocent enough, it made Gage tense with—

"You two hooking up finally?"

Thoughts disrupted, Gage turned to Denver. Hard to believe he hadn't noticed the approach of a two-hundred-and-twenty-pound man. "What?"

"You and Harper," Denver said, while perusing the food that remained. "Finally going to make it official?"

"Make what official?"

"That you're an item." Denver chose half a cold cut sandwich and devoured the majority of it in one bite.

Gage's gaze sought Harper out again. Whatever Armie said to her got him a shove in return. Armie pulled an exaggerated fighter's stance, fists up, as if he thought he'd have to defend himself.

Harper pretended a low shot, Armie dropped his hands to cover the family jewels, and she smacked him on top of the head.

The way the two of them carried on, almost like siblings, made Gage feel left out.

Were he and Harper an item? He knew how he felt, but Harper could be such a mystery.

Denver shouldered him to the side so he could grab some cake. "Gotta say, man, I hope so. She was so glum while you were away, it depressed the hell out of everyone."

Hard to imagine a woman as vibrant as Harper ever down in the dumps. When he'd left for the camp in Kentucky, she'd understood, wishing him luck, telling him how thrilled she was for him.

But since his return a few days ago, things had been off. He hadn't immediately sought her out, determined to get his head together first. He didn't want pity from anyone, but the way he'd felt had been pretty damned pitiful. He'd waffled between rage at the circumstances and mind-numbing regret. No way did he want others to suffer him like that, most especially Harper.

He knew he'd see her at the rec center and had half expected her to gush over him, to fret over his injury, to sympathize.

She hadn't done any of that. Mostly she'd treated him

the same as she did the rest of the guys, leaving him confused and wallowing in his own misery.

Until tonight.

Tonight she was all about making him insane with the need to get her alone and naked.

"You listening to me, Gage?"

Rarely did another fighter call him by his given name. That Denver did so now almost felt like a reprimand from his mom. "Yeah, *Denver,* I'm listening."

"Good." Denver folded massive arms over his massive chest, puffing up like a turkey. "So what's it to be?"

If Denver expected a challenge, too bad. Gage again sought out Harper with his gaze. "She was really miserable?"

Denver deflated enough to slap him on the back. "Yeah. It was awful. Made me sad as shit, I don't mind telling you."

"What was she miserable about?"

"Dude, are you that fucking obtuse?"

Stack stepped into the conversation. "Hell, yeah, he is." Then changing the subject, Stack asked, "Did Rissy go to Japan with Cannon?"

Denver answered, saying, "Yeah, he took her and her roommate along."

Merissa, better known as Rissy, was Cannon's little sis. A roommate was news to Gage, though. "If you have ideas about his sister, you're an idiot."

Stack drew back. "No. Hell, no. Damn man, don't start rumors."

Everyone knew Cannon as a nice guy. More than nice. But he was crazy-particular when it came to Merissa. For that reason, the guys all looked past her, through her or when forced to it, with nothing more than respect. "Who's the roommate?"

"Sweet Cherry Pie," Denver rumbled low and with feeling.

Stack grinned at him.

Gage totally missed the joke. "What?"

"Cherry Payton," Denver said, and damn if he didn't almost sigh. "Long blond hair, big chocolate-brown eyes, extra fine body…"

"Another one bites the dust," Stack said with a laugh.

"Another one?"

"Obtuse," Denver lamented.

Stack nodded toward Harper. "You being the first, dumb ass."

"We all expect you to make her feel better about things."

Confusion kicked his temper up a notch. "What *things?*"

Slapping a hand over his heart, Stack said, "How you feel."

Striking a similar pose, Denver leaned into Stack. "What you want."

Heads together, they intoned, *"Love."*

"You're both morons." But damn it, he realized that he did love her. Probably had for a long time. How could he not? Priorities could be a bitch and he hated the idea that he'd maybe made Harper unhappy by not understanding his feelings sooner.

He chewed his upper lip while wondering how to correct things.

"Honesty," Stack advised him. "Tell her how the schedule goes, what to expect and leave the rest up to her."

"Harper's smart," Denver agreed. "She'll understand."

It irked Gage big-time to have everyone butting into his personal business. "Don't you guys have something better to do than harass me?"

"I have some*one* better to do," Stack told him, nodding toward one of the women who'd hit on Gage earlier.

"Butting in to your business was just my goodwill gesture of the day." And with that he sauntered off.

Denver leaned back on the table of food. "We all like Harper, you know."

Gage was starting to think they liked her a little too much. "Yeah, I get that."

"So quit dicking around, will you?" He grabbed up another sandwich and he, too, joined a woman.

Gage stewed for half a minute, turned—and almost ran into Harper.

CHAPTER FOUR

GAGE CAUGHT HER ARMS, steadying them both. "Why does everyone keep sneaking up on me?"

She brushed off his hands. "If you hadn't been ogling the single ladies, maybe you'd be more aware."

She absolutely had to know better than to think that, but just in case... "How could I notice any other woman with you around?"

She eyed him. "Do you notice other women when I'm not around?"

Damn, he thought, did she really *not* know how much he cared? Worse, had she been sad while he was away?

The possibility chewed on his conscience. "No, I don't." He drew her up to kiss her sweetly, and then, because this was Harper, not so sweetly.

To give her back a little, he shared his own complaint. "You spend way too much time horsing around with Armie."

Shrugging, she reached for a few chips. "I was trying not to crowd you."

"What does that mean?"

While munching, she gestured around the interior of the rec center. "This is a fight night. You're hanging with your buds. When I see you guys talking, I don't want to horn in."

Whoa. Those were some serious misconceptions. To help clear things up, he cupped her face. "You can't."

"Can't what?"

"Horn in. Ever."

Brows pinching in disgruntlement, she shoved away from him. "I just told you I wouldn't."

He hauled her right back. "I'm not saying you shouldn't, honey, I'm saying you can't because there's never a bad time for you to talk to me. Remember that, okay?"

Astonished, she blinked up at him, and he wanted to declare himself right then. Luckily the first fight on the main card started and everyone went back to their seats, saving him from rushing her.

This time, Gage had a hard time concentrating. He saw the fight, he cheered, but more of his attention veered to Harper, to how quiet she was now.

Thinking about him?

The fight ended in the first round with a knockout.

Instead of reacting with everyone else, Harper turned her face up to his. As if no time had passed at all, she said, "That's not entirely true."

Damn, but it was getting more difficult by the second to keep his hands off her. He contented himself by opening his hand on her waist, stroking up to her ribs then down to her hip. "What's that?"

"There are plenty of times when I can't intrude."

She was still stewing about that? "No."

Like a thundercloud, she darkened. Turning to more fully face him, she said low, *"Yes."* Before he could correct her, she insisted, "But I want you to know that I understand."

Apparently she didn't. "How so?"

Leaning around him, she glanced at one and all to ensure there were no eavesdroppers. As if uncertain, she puckered her brows while trying to find the right words. "I know when you're in training—"

"I'm pretty much always in training."

She looked like she wanted to smack him. "There's training and then there's *training*."

True enough. "You mean when I go away to another camp."

"That, and when you're close to a fight."

Should he tell her how much he'd enjoy coming home to her—every night, not just between fights? Would she ever be willing to travel with him? Or to wait for him when she couldn't?

He had a feeling Harper would fit seamlessly into his life no matter what he had going on.

Being as honest as he could, Gage nodded. "There will be times when my thoughts are distracted, when I have to focus on other stuff. But that doesn't mean I don't care. It sure as hell doesn't mean you have to keep your distance."

The next fight started and though a few muted conversations continued, most in attendance kept their comments limited to the competition. Beside him, Harper fell silent. Gage could almost feel her struggling to sort out everything he'd said.

Again, he found himself studying her profile; not just her face, but her body, too. Her breasts weren't large, but they fit her frame, especially with her small waist and the sexy flare of her hips. She kept her long legs crossed, one foot nervously rocking. She drew in several deep breaths. A pulse tripped in her throat.

By the second the sexual tension between them grew.

The end of the night started to feel like too many hours away. They had at least three more fights on the main card. Cannon's fight would be last. It wasn't a title fight, but it'd still go five rounds.

The current match went all three rounds and came down to a split decision. Gage no longer cared; hell, he'd missed more of the fight than he'd seen.

Around him, voices rose in good-natured debate about how the judges had gotten it right or wrong.

"What do you think?" Gage asked Harper.

She shrugged. "Depends on how the judges scored things. The guy from Brazil really pushed the fight, but the other one landed more blows. Still, he didn't cause that much damage, and the Brazilian got those two takedowns—"

Gage put a finger to her mouth. "I meant about us."

Her wide-eyed gaze swung to his. "Oh." She gulped, considered him, then whispered, "I like it."

"It?"

"There being an 'us.'"

Yeah, he liked it, too, maybe more than he'd realized before now. "I missed you while I was away."

She scoffed. "You were way too busy for that."

"I worked hard, no denying it. But it wasn't 24/7. I found myself alone with my thoughts far too often."

She forced a smile. "I'm sure at those times you were obsessed about the SBC, about the competition, about winning."

"All that—plus you." When it came to priorities, she was at the top. He'd just made too many assumptions for her to realize it.

She looked tortured for a moment before her hand knotted in his shirt and she pulled him closer. With pained accusation, she said, "You didn't call."

Hot with regret, Gage covered her hand with his own. "I was trying to focus." Saying it out loud, he felt like an ass.

But Harper nodded. "That's what I'm saying. There will be times when I need to stay out of your way so I don't mess with that focus."

He hated the idea of her avoiding him.

Almost as much as he hated the thought of ever leaving her again. Yet that was a reality. He was a fighter; he would go to other camps to train, travel around the country, around the world.

He'd go where the SBC sent him.

"You have to know, Gage. I'd never get in your way, not on purpose."

He almost groaned.

"I'm serious! I know how important your career is and I know what a nuisance it can be to—"

Suddenly starved for the taste of her, for the feel of her, Gage took her mouth in a firm kiss.

But that wasn't enough, so he turned his head and nibbled her bottom lip until she opened. When he licked inside her warm, damp mouth, her breath hitched. Mindful of where they were, he nonetheless had a hell of time tempering his lust.

Damn it.

The next fight started. Cannon would be after that.

In a sudden desperate rush, Gage left his chair, pulling her up and along with him as he headed toward the dimly lit hallway. He couldn't wait a second more. But for what he had to say, had to explain, he needed the relative privacy of a back room.

Luckily she'd seated them at the end of the back row. In only a few steps, and without a lot of attention, he had them on their way.

Tripping along with him, Harper whispered, *"Gage."*

"There are high school boys out there," he told her. He glanced in the storage room, but no, that was too close to the main room and the activity of the group.

"I know. So?"

He brought her up and alongside him so he could slip an arm around her. "So they don't need to see me losing my head over you."

She stopped suddenly, which forced him to stop.

Looking far too shy for the ballsy woman he knew her to be, she whispered, "Are you?"

This time he understood her question. "Losing my head over you?" Gently, he said, "No."

Her shoulders bunched as if she might slug him.

Damn, but he adored her. "I lost it a long time ago. I just forgot to tell you."

Suspicious, she narrowed her eyes. "What does that mean exactly?"

Not about to declare himself in a freaking hallway, he took her hands and started backing up toward the office. "Come along with me and I'll explain everything." This particular talk was long overdue.

She didn't resist, but she did say, "The fight you should have been in is next. And Cannon will be fighting soon after that."

"I know." At the moment, seeing the fight he'd missed was the furthest thing from his mind. As to Cannon, well, he'd be in a lot of fights. This wasn't his first, wouldn't be his last. If all went well, Gage would get her commitment to spend the night, and more, before Cannon entered the cage. "The thing is, I need you."

She searched his face. "Need me...how?"

In every way imaginable. "Let me show you."

Her gaze went over his body. "Sounds to me like you're talking about sex."

Did lust taint his brain, or did she sound hopeful? They reached the office door and he tried the handle. Locked, of course. Trying not to think about how the night would end, he said, "Seriously, Harper, much as I love that idea, we're at the rec center."

"So?"

Damn, she knew how to throw him. He sucked in air and forged on. "I thought we'd talk." Digging in his pocket, he found the keys he'd picked up earlier when he shut off the lights.

Sarcasm added a wicked light to her beautiful blue eyes. "Talk? That's what you want to do? Seriously?"

"Yeah. See, I need to explain a few things to you and it's better done in private." The door opened and he drew her in.

Typical of Harper, she took the initiative, shutting and locking the door, then grabbing him. "We're alone." Her mouth brushed his chin, his jaw, his throat. "Say what you need to say."

"I love you."

She went so still, it felt like he held a statue. Ignoring her lack of a response, Gage cupped her face. "I love you, Harper Gates. Have for a while now. I'm sorry I didn't realize it sooner. I'm especially sorry I didn't figure it out before I took off for Kentucky."

Confused, but also defending him, she whispered, "You were excited about the opportunity."

She made him sound like a kid, when at the moment he felt very much like a man. "True." Slowly, he leaned into her, pinning her up against the door, arranging her so that they fit together perfectly. She was so slight, so soft and feminine—when she wasn't giving him or one of the other fighters hell. "I thought it'd be best for me to concentrate only on the upcoming fight, but that was asinine."

"No," she said, again defending him. "It made sense."

"Loving you makes sense." He took her mouth, and never wanted to stop kissing her. Hot and deep. Soft and sweet. With Harper it didn't matter. However she kissed him, it blew his mind and pushed all his buttons.

He brushed damp kisses over to the side of her neck, up to her ear.

On a soft wail, Harper said, "How can you love me? We haven't even had sex yet."

"Believe me, I know." He covered her breast with his hand, gently kneading her, loving the weight of her, how her nipple tightened. He wanted to see her, wanted to take her in his mouth. "We can change that later tonight."

"I'll never last that long." She stretched up along his body, both hands tangled in his hair, anchoring him so she could feast off his mouth.

No way would he argue with her.

Everything went hot and urgent between them.

He coasted a hand down her side, caught her thigh and lifted her leg up alongside his. Nudging in against her, knowing he could take her this way, right here, against the door, pushed him over the edge.

Not what he would have planned for their first time, but with Harper so insistent, he couldn't find the brain cells to offer up an alternative.

"Are you sure?" he asked, while praying that she was.

"Yes. Now, Gage." She moved against him. "Right now."

HARPER GRABBED FOR his T-shirt and shoved it up so she could get her hands on his hot flesh, so she could explore all those amazing muscles. Unlike some of the guys, he didn't shave his chest and she loved—*loved, loved, loved*—his body hair.

God, how could any man be so perfect?

She got the shirt above his pecs and leaned in to brush her nose over his chest hair, to deeply inhale his incredible scent. It filled her head, making her dazed with need.

When she took a soft love bite, he shuddered. "Take it easy."

No, she wouldn't.

"We have to slow down or I'm a goner."

But she couldn't. Never in her life had she known she'd miss someone as much as she'd missed him when he'd left. Now he was back, and whether he really loved her or was just caught up in the moment, she'd worry about it later.

She needed him. All of him.

She cupped him through his jeans and heard him groan. He was thick and hard and throbbing.

He sucked in a breath. "Harper, baby, seriously, we have to slow down." Taking her wrist, he lifted her hand away. "You need to catch up a little."

"I'm there already." She'd been there since first deciding on her course of action for the night.

"Not quite." Gage carried both her hands to his shoulders before kissing her senseless, giving her his tongue, drawing hers into his mouth.

She couldn't get enough air into her starving lungs but didn't care. Against her belly she felt his heavy erection, and she wanted to touch him again, to explore him in more detail.

He caught the hem of her T-shirt, drawing it up and over her head. Barely a heartbeat passed before he flipped open the front closure on her bra and the cups parted.

Taking her mouth again, he groaned as his big hands gently molded over her, his thumbs teasing her nipples until she couldn't stop squirming. She wasn't one of the overly stacked groupies who dogged his heels, but she didn't dislike her body, either.

She'd always considered herself not big, but big enough.

Now, with his enormous hands on her, she felt delicate—even more so when he scooped an arm under her behind and easily lifted her up so he could draw one nipple into his hot mouth.

Harper wrapped her legs around his waist, her arms

around his neck. He took his time, drawing on her for what felt like forever, until she couldn't keep still, couldn't contain the soft cries of desperate need.

From one breast to the other, he tasted, teased, sucked, nibbled.

"Gage…" Even saying his name took an effort. "Please."

"Please what?" he asked, all full of masculine satisfaction and a fighter's control. He licked her, circling, teasing. "Please more?"

"Yes."

Back on her feet, she dropped against the door. He opened her jeans and a second later shoved them, and her panties, down to her knees.

Anticipation kept her still, kept her breath rushing and her heart pounding. But he just stood there, sucking air and waiting for God knew what.

"Gage?" she whispered with uncertainty.

One hand flattened on the wall beside her head, but he kept his arm locked out, his body from touching hers. "I should take you to my place," he rasped, sounding tortured. "I should take you someplace with more time, more privacy, more—"

Panic tried to set in. "Don't you even *think* about stopping now." No way could he leave her like this.

His mouth touched her cheek, the corner of her lips, her jaw, her temple. "No, I won't. I can't."

A loud roar sounded from the main part of the room. Knowing what that meant, that Cannon's fight was about to start, guilt nearly leveled Harper. "I forgot," she admitted miserably.

"Doesn't matter," he assured her.

But of course it did. He was here to watch Cannon compete, to join in with his fight community to celebrate a close friend.

She was here to show him she wouldn't interfere and yet, that's exactly what she'd done. "We could—"

"No, baby." Need made his short laugh gravelly. "Believe me when I say that I *can't*."

"Oh." Her heart started punching again—with excitement. "We'll miss the fight."

"We'll catch the highlights later. Together." He stroked her hair with his free hand, over her shoulder, down the side of her body.

"You're sure?"

Against her mouth, he whispered, "Give or take a bed for convenience, I'm right where I want to be." His kiss scorched her, and he added, "With you."

Aww. Hearing him say it was nice, but knowing he meant it multiplied everything she felt, and suddenly she couldn't wait. She took his hand and guided it across her body.

And between her legs.

They both groaned.

At first he just cupped her, his palm hot, his hand covering so much of her. They breathed together, taut with expectation.

"It seems like I've wanted you forever," he murmured at the same time as his fingers searched over her, touching carefully. His forehead to hers, he added, "Mmm. You're wet."

Speaking wasn't easy, but he deserved the truth. "Because I *have* wanted you forever."

"I'm glad, Harper." His fingers parted her swollen lips, stroked gently over her, delved. "Widen your legs a little more."

That husky, take-charge, turned-on tone nearly put her over the edge. Holding on to his shoulders, her face tucked into his throat, she widened her stance. Using two fingers, he glided over her, once, twice, testing her readiness—and he pressed both fingers deep.

Legs stiffening, Harper braced against the door.

"Stay with me," Gage said before kissing her throat.

She felt his teeth on her skin, his hot breath, those oh-so-talented fingers.

"Damn, you feel good. Tight and wet and perfect." He worked her, using his hand to get her close to climax. "Relax just a little."

"Can't." Her fingernails bit into his shoulders. "Oh, God."

"If we were on a bed," he growled against her throat, "I could get to your nipples. But you're so short—"

"I'm not," she gasped, unsure whether she'd be able to take that much excitement. "You're just so damn big."

"Soon as you come for me," he promised, "I'll show you how big I am."

Such a braggart. Of course, she'd already had a good idea, given she often saw him in nothing more than athletic shorts. And she'd already had her hands on him. Not long enough to do all the exploring she wanted to do, but enough to—

He brought his thumb up to her clitoris, and she clenched all over.

"Nice," he told her. "I can feel you getting closer."

Shut up, Gage. She thought it but didn't say it, because words right now, at this particular moment, would be far too difficult.

He cupped her breast and, in keeping with the accelerated tempo of the fingers between her legs, he tugged at her nipple.

The first shimmer of approaching release took her to her tiptoes. *"Gage."*

"I've got you."

The next wave, stronger, hotter, made her groan in harsh pleasure.

"I love you, Harper."

Luckily, at that propitious moment, something happened in the fight because everyone shouted and cheered—and that helped to drown out the harsh groans of Harper's release.

CHAPTER FIVE

GAGE BADLY WANTED to turn on lights, to strip Harper naked and then shuck out of his own clothes. He wanted to touch her all over, taste her everywhere, count her every freckle while feeling her against him, skin on skin, with no barriers.

Even with her T-shirt shoved up above her breasts and her jeans down around her knees, holding Harper in his arms was nice. Her scent had intensified, her body now a warm, very soft weight limp against him. He kept one hand tangled in her hair, the other cupping her sexy ass.

He let her rest while she caught her breath.

If he'd found a better time and place for this, he could stretch her out on a bed, or the floor or a table—didn't matter as long as he could look at every inch of her, kiss her all over.

Devour her slowly, at his leisure.

But they were in an office, at the rec center, with a small crowd of fighters and fans only a hallway away.

He kissed her temple, hugged her protectively.

His cock throbbed against her belly. He badly wanted to be inside her, driving them both toward joint release.

But this, having Harper sated and cuddling so sweetly... yeah, that was pretty damn special.

"Mmm," she murmured. "I lost my bones somewhere."

"I have one you can borrow."

He felt her grin against his throat, then her full-body

rub as she wiggled against him. "Yes," she teased. "Yes, you do."

"I like hearing you come, Harper." With small pecks, he nudged up her face so he could get to her mouth. "Whatever you do, you do it well."

That made her laugh, so the kiss was a little silly, tickling.

She drew in a deep breath, shored up her muscles, and somewhat stood on her own. "The fight is still going on?"

"Sounds like."

"So all that excitement before—"

"You coming?"

She bit his chest, inciting his lust even more. "No, I meant with everyone screaming."

"Probably a near submission. Cannon is good on the ground, good with submissions." Good with every facet of fighting. "But let's not talk about Cannon right now."

"You really don't mind missing his fight?"

"Jesus, woman, I'm about to bust my jeans. Cannon is the furthest thing from my mind."

Happy with his answer, she said, "Okay, then, let's talk about you." She nibbled her way up to his throat. "There is just so much of you to enjoy."

"You could start here," he said, taking one of her small, soft hands down to press against his fly.

"I think I will." With her forehead to his sternum, she watched her hands as she opened the snap to his jeans, slowly eased down the zipper. "I wish we had more light in here."

Because that mirrored his earlier thought, he nodded. "You can just sort of feel your way around."

"Is that what you did?" Using both hands, she held him, so no way could he reply. She stroked his length, squeezed him. "You are so hard."

"Yup." He couldn't manage anything more detailed than that.

"You have a condom?"

"Wallet."

Still touching him, she clarified, "You have a condom in your wallet?"

"Yup."

She tipped her face up to see him, and he could hear the humor in her voice. "A little turned on?"

"A *lot* turned on." He covered her hand with his own and got her started on a stroking rhythm he loved. *"Damn."*

Harper whispered, "Kiss me."

And he did, taking her mouth hard, twining his tongue with hers, making himself crazy by again exploring her, the silky skin of her bottom, the dampness between her thighs, her firm breasts and stiffened nipples.

Harper released him just long enough to say, "Shirt off, big boy." She tried shoving it up, but Gage took over, reaching over his back for a fistful of cotton and jerking the material away. Anticipating her hands, her mouth, on his hot skin, he dropped the shirt.

She didn't disappoint. Hooking her fingers in the waistband of his jeans, she shoved down the denim and his boxers, too, then started feeling him all over. His shoulders to his hips. His pecs to his abs. She grazed her palms over his nipples, then went back to his now throbbing cock.

"You are so impressive in so many ways."

He tried to think up a witty reply, but with her small, soft hands on him, he could barely breathe, much less banter.

"I've thought about something so many times…" And with no more warning than that, she sank to her knees.

Oh, God. Gage locked his muscles, one hand settling on top of her head.

Holding him tight, Harper skimmed her lips over the sensitive head, licked down the length of his shaft.

Never one for half measures, she drew her tongue back up and slid her mouth over him.

A harsh groan reverberated out of his chest. "Harper."

Her clever tongue swirled over and around him—and she took him deep again.

Too much. Way too much. He clasped her shoulder. "Sorry, honey, but I can't take it."

She continued anyway.

"Harper," he warned.

She reached around him, clasping his ass as if she thought she could control him.

But control of any kind quickly spiraled away. Later, he thought to himself, he'd enjoy doing this again, letting her have her way, giving her all the time she wanted.

Just not now, not when he so desperately wanted to be inside her.

"Sorry, honey." He caught her under the arms and lifted her to her feet, then set her away from him while he gasped for breath. As soon as he could, he dug out his wallet and fumbled for the condom.

Sounding breathless and hot, she whispered, "You taste so good."

He'd never last. "Shh." He rolled on the condom with trembling hands. Stepping up to her in a rush, he stripped away her shirt and bra, shoved her jeans lower. "Hold on to me."

Hooking her right knee with his elbow, he lifted her leg, opening her as much as he could with her jeans still on, his still on. He moved closer still, kissing her until they were both on the ragged edge.

"Now," Harper demanded.

He nudged against her, found his way, and sank deep in one strong thrust.

More cheers sounded in the outer room, but neither of them paid much attention. Already rocking against her, Gage admitted, "I'm not going to last."

She matched the rhythm he set. "I don't need you to… *Gage!*"

Kissing her, he muffled her loud cries as she came, holding him tight, squeezing him tighter, her entire body shimmering in hot release. Seconds later he pinned her to the door, pressed his face into her throat, and let himself go.

For several minutes he was deaf and blind to everything except the feel of Harper in his arms where she belonged.

Little aftershocks continued to tease her intimate muscles, and since he remained joined with her, he felt each one. Their heartbeats danced together.

Gradually he became aware of people talking in the outer room. They sounded happy and satisfied, telling him the fight had ended.

Harper came to the same realization. "Oh, no. We missed everything?"

"Not everything." After a nudge against her to remind what they hadn't missed, he disengaged their bodies. Slowly he eased her leg down, staying close to support her—which was sort of a joke, given how shaky he felt, too.

"Do you think Cannon won?"

"I know he did."

Her fingers moved over his face, up to the corner of his eye near his stitches. "You're sure?"

"Absolutely." He brought her hand to his mouth and kissed her palm. "I was sure even before the fight started."

Letting out a long breath, she dropped her head. "I'm sorry we missed it."

"I don't have any regrets."

She thought about that for a second, then worried aloud, "They'll all know what we were doing."

"Yeah." There was barely enough light to see, but he located paper in the printer, stole a sheet, and used it to wrap up the spent condom. He pitched it into the metal waste can.

"I hope they didn't hear us."

Gage tucked himself away and zipped his jeans. "Even if they did—"

She groaned over the possibility. "No, no, no."

Pulling her back into his arms, he teased, "They won't ask for too many details."

Her fisted hands pressed against his chest. "I swear, if Armie says a single word, I'll—"

Gage kissed her. Then touched her breasts. And her belly.

And lower.

"Gage," she whispered, all broken up. "We can't. Not now."

"Not here," he agreed, while paying homage to her perfect behind. "Come home with me."

"Okay."

He'd told her that he loved her. She hadn't yet said how she felt. But while she was being agreeable… "I'll fight again in two months."

Gasping with accusation, she glared at him. "You knew you'd fight again—"

"Of course I will." He snorted. "I got injured. I didn't quit."

"Yeah, I know. But…" Her confusion washed over him. "I didn't realize things were already set. Why didn't you tell me?"

"Didn't come up." He kissed the end of her nose. "And

honestly, I was too busy raging about the fight I'd miss to talk about the next one."

He felt her stillness. "You're not raging anymore?"

"Mellow as a newborn kitten," he promised. "Thank you for that."

Thinking things through, she ran her hands up his chest to his collarbone. "Where?"

"Canada."

Gage felt her putting her shoulders back, straightening her spine, shoring herself up. "So when you leave again—"

Before she could finish that thought, he took her mouth, stepping her back into the door again, unable to keep his hands off her ass. When he came up for air, he said, "If you can, I'd love it if you came with me."

She was still all soft and sweet from his kiss. "To Canada?"

"To wherever I go, whenever I go. For training. For fighting." He tucked her hair behind her ear, gave her a soft and quick kiss. "For today and tomorrow and the year after that."

Her eyes widened and her lips parted. "Gage?"

"I told you I love you. Did you think I made it up?"

In a heartbeat, excitement stripped away the uncertainty and she threw herself against him, squeezing tight. With her shirt still gone, her jeans still down, it was an awesome embrace.

A knock sounded on the door, and Armie called, "Just about everyone is gone if you two want to wrap it up."

"He loves me," Harper told him.

Armie laughed. "Well, duh, doofus. Everyone could see that plain as day."

Gage cupped her head in his hands, but spoke to Armie. "Any predictions on how she feels about me?"

"Wow." The door jumped, meaning Armie had probably just propped his shoulder against it. "Hasn't told you yet, huh?"

"No."

"Cruel, Harper," he chastised her. "Really cruel. And here I thought you were one of those *nice* girls."

Lips quivering, eyes big and liquid, she stared up at him. "I love you," she whispered.

"Me or Gage?" Armie asked with facetious good humor.

Harper kicked the door hard with her heel, and Armie said, "Ow, damn it. Fine. I'm leaving. But Gage, you have the keys so I can't lock up until—"

"Five minutes."

"And there go my illusions again."

The quiet settled around them. They watched each other. Gage did some touching, too. But what the hell, Harper was mostly naked, looking at him with a wealth of emotion.

"I should get dressed."

"You should tell me again that you love me."

"I do. *So much,*" Harper added with feeling. "I have for such a long time."

Nice. "The things you do to me…" He fumbled around along the wall beside the door and finally located the light switch.

She flinched away at first, but Harper wasn't shy. God knew she had no reason to be.

Putting her shoulders back, her chin up, she let him look. And what a sight she made with her jeans down below her knees and her shirt gone. He cupped her right breast and saw a light sprinkling of freckles decorating her fair skin.

"Let's go," he whispered. "I want to take you home and look for more freckles."

That made her snicker. As she pulled up her jeans, she said, "I don't really have that many."

"Don't ruin it for me. I'll find out for myself."

By the time they left the room, only Armie, Stack and Denver were still hanging around.

With his arm around Harper, Gage asked, "You guys didn't hook up?"

"Meeting her in an hour," Stack said.

"She's pulling her car around," Denver told him.

Armie shrugged toward the front door. "Those two are waiting for me."

Two? Everyone glanced at the front door where a couple of women hugged up to each other. One blonde, one raven-haired.

"Why does she have a whip in her belt?" Harper asked.

"I'm not sure," Armie murmured as he, too, watched the women. "But I'm intrigued."

"Are they fondling each other?" Gage asked.

"Could be." Armie drew his gaze back to Harper and Gage, then grinned shamelessly. "But I don't mind being the voyeuristic third wheel."

The guys all grinned with amusement. They were well used to Armie's excesses.

A little shocked, Harper shook her head. "One of these days a nice girl will make an honest man of you. That is, if some crazy woman doesn't do you in first."

"At least I'd die happy." Leaning against the table, arms folded over his chest, Armie studied them both. "So. You curious about how your match went?"

"Wasn't my match," Gage said.

"Should have been. And just so you know, Darvey annihilated your replacement."

"How many rounds?"

"Two. Referee stoppage."

Gage nodded as if it didn't matter all that much. Darvey had gotten off easy because Gage knew he'd have won the match.

Then Armie dropped a bombshell. "Cannon damn near lost."

Because he'd been expecting something very different, Gage blinked. "No way."

Armie blew out a breath. "He was all but gone from a vicious kick to the ribs."

"Ouch." Gage winced just thinking of it. If the kick nearly took Cannon out, it must have been a liver kick, and those hurt like a mother, stole your wind and made breathing—or fighting—impossible.

Stack picked up the story. "But you know Cannon. On his way down he threw one last punch—"

"And knocked Moeller out cold," Denver finished with enthusiasm. "It was truly something to see. Everyone was on their feet, not only here but at the event. The commentators went nuts. It was crazy."

"Everyone waited to see who would get back on his feet first," Stack finished.

And obviously that was Cannon. Gage half smiled. Every fighter knew flukes happened. Given a fluke injury had taken him out of the competition, he knew it better than most. "I'm glad he pulled it off."

"That he did," Armie said. "And if you don't mind locking up, I think I'll go pull off a few submissions of my own."

Harper scowled in disapproval, then flapped her hand, sending him on his way.

A minute later, Denver and Stack took off, too.

Left alone finally, Gage put his arm around Harper. "Ready to go home?"

"My place or yours?"

"Where doesn't matter—as long as you're with me."

She gave him a look that said *"Awww!"* and hugged him tight. Still squeezed up close, she whispered with worry, "I can't believe Cannon almost lost."

Gage smoothed his hand down her back. "Don't worry about it. We fighters know how to turn bad situations to our advantage."

"We?" She leaned back in his arms to see him. "How's that?"

"For Cannon, the near miss will only hype up the crowd for his next fight." He bent to kiss the end of her freckled nose. "As for me, I might have missed a competition, but I got the girl. There'll be other fights, but honest to God, Harper, there's only one *you*. All in all, I'd say I'm the big winner tonight."

"I'd say you're *mine*." With a trembling, emotional smile, Harper touched his face, then his shoulders, and his chest. As her hand dipped lower, she whispered, "And that means we're both winners. Tonight, tomorrow and always."

* * * * *

Want more sizzling romance from
New York Times *bestselling author Lori Foster?*
Pick up every title in her Ultimate series:

HARD KNOCKS
NO LIMITS
HOLDING STRONG
TOUGH LOVE

Available now from HQN Books!

COMING NEXT MONTH FROM

HARLEQUIN *Blaze*

Available September 15, 2015

#863 TEASING HER SEAL
Uniformly Hot!
by Anne Marsh
SEAL team leader Gray Jackson needs to convince Laney Parker to leave an island resort before she gets hurt—and before his cover is blown. But as his mission heats up, so do their nights...

#864 IF SHE DARES
by Tanya Michaels
Still timid months after being robbed at gunpoint, Riley Kendrick wants to rediscover her fun, daring side, and Jack Reed, her sexy new neighbor, has some wicked ideas about how to help.

#865 NAKED THRILL
The Wrong Bed
by Jill Monroe
They wake up in bed together. Naked. And with no memory. So Tony and Hayden follow a trail of clues to piece together what—or *who*—they did on the craziest night of their lives.

#866 KISS AND MAKEUP
by Taryn Leigh Taylor
Falling into bed with a sexy guy she met on a plane is impulsive even for Chloe. But when Ben's client catches them together, she does something even more impulsive: she pretends to be his wife!

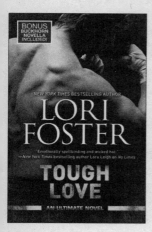

Limited time offer!

$1.⁰⁰ OFF

TOUGH LOVE

New York Times Bestselling Author

LORI FOSTER

She's playing hard to get...to win the MMA fighter of her ultimate fantasies.

*Available August 25, 2015,
wherever books are sold.*

HQN™

- ✂

$1.⁰⁰ OFF
**the purchase price of
TOUGH LOVE by Lori Foster.**

Offer valid from August 25, 2015, to September 30, 2015.
Redeemable at participating retail outlets. Not redeemable at Barnes & Noble.
Limit one coupon per purchase. Valid in the U.S.A. and Canada only.

52612796

5 65373 00076 2   (8100)0 12073

PHLF0915COUP

SPECIAL EXCERPT FROM

HARLEQUIN

Blaze

*US Navy SEAL Gray Jackson is undercover...posing as
a massage therapist at a sultry Caribbean resort. But
when he gets his hands on Dr. Laney Parker, can he
keep his mind on his mission?*

*Read on for a sneak preview of
TEASING HER SEAL,*
Anne Marsh's *latest story
about supremely sexy SEALs in the
UNIFORMLY HOT! miniseries*

Gray had magic hands. Laney should have gone for sixty
or even the full ninety minutes instead of the paltry thirty
minutes she'd ponied up for. He was that good.

"You're tight here." He pressed a particularly tense spot
on her back, and she stopped caring that she was stretched
out, bare-ass naked and vulnerable. God, he was good.

"Trigger point." Not, apparently, that she needed to tell
him. The man knew what he was doing.

"Are you a doctor?"

"Trauma surgeon." Was that sultry whisper her voice?
Because, if so, Gray was definitely a miracle worker. She
felt herself melting under his touch and, wow, how long
had it been since she'd done that?

He found and pressed against another knot. "So I
should call you Dr. Parker."

He moved around to the front of the massage bed. The
ad one of those circle doughnut things that she'd

always thought were awkward. She opened her eyes as Gray's feet moved into view. She'd never had a foot fetish before, but he was barefoot, and his feet were sun-bronzed and strong-looking. Those few inches of bare skin made her want to see more. She'd bet the rest of him was every bit as spectacular.

It was probably bad she found his feet sexy. He was just doing a job.

Really, really well.

He gently pulled her ponytail free before running his hands through her hair, pressing his fingertips against her scalp. Maybe she'd been a cat in a former life, because she'd always loved having her hair played with. For long minutes, Gray rubbed small sensual circles against her scalp. She bit back a moan. *Just lie here. Keep still.* She probably wasn't supposed to arch off the table, screaming *more, more, more.* Although she could. She definitely could.

He moved closer, his thighs brushing against the bed. If she lifted her head, the situation could get awkward fast. Thinking about that made her stiffen up again, but then he cupped the back of her neck, pressing and rotating. And oh, she could feel the tension melting away. The small tugs on her hair sent a prickle of excitement through her entire body.

"Should I call you *Doctor*?" he prompted.

Don't miss
TEASING HER SEAL by Anne Marsh.
Available October 2015 wherever
Harlequin® Blaze® books and ebooks are sold.

www.Harlequin.com

A hot shade of lipstick calls for a hot, sexy guy...

Falling into bed with a sexy guy she met on a plane is impulsive even for Chloe. But when Ben's client catches them together, she does something even more impulsive: she pretends to be his wife!

SAVE $1.00

on the purchase of KISS AND MAKEUP by Taryn Leigh Taylor {available Sept. 15, 2015} or any other Harlequin® Blaze® book.

Redeemable at participating outlets in the U.S. and Canada only. Not redeemable at Barnes & Noble stores. Limit one coupon per customer.

52612884

Canadian Retailers: Harlequin Enterprises Limited will pay the face value of this coupon plus 10.25¢ if submitted by customer for this product only. Any other use constitutes fraud. Coupon is nonassignable. Void if taxed, prohibited or restricted by law. Consumer must pay any government taxes. Void if copied. Inmar Promotional Services ("IPS") customers submit coupons and proof of sales to Harlequin Enterprises Limited, P.O. Box 3000, Saint John, NB E2L 4L3, Canada. Non-IPS retailer—for reimbursement submit coupons and proof of sales directly to Harlequin Enterprises Limited, Retail Marketing Department, 225 Duncan Mill Rd., Don Mills, Ontario M3B 3K9, Canada.

U.S. Retailers: Harlequin Enterprises Limited will pay the face value of this coupon plus 8¢ if submitted by customer for this product only. Any other use constitutes fraud. Coupon is nonassignable. Void if taxed, prohibited or restricted by law. Consumer must pay any government taxes. Void if copied. For reimbursement submit coupons and proof of sales directly to Harlequin Enterprises Limited, P.O. Box 880478, El Paso, TX 88588-0478, U.S.A. Cash value 1/100 cents.

5 65373 00076 2   (8100)0 12081

COUPON EXPIRES DEC. 15, 2015

Available wherever books are sold, including most bookstores, supermarkets, drugstores and discount stores.

www.Harlequin.com

STAR TREK®

THE BRAVE AND THE BOLD

BOOK ONE

KEITH R.A. DeCANDIDO

Based upon *Star Trek*®
created by Gene Roddenberry,
Star Trek: Deep Space Nine®
created by Rick Berman & Michael Piller,
and *Enterprise*™
created by Rick Berman & Brannon Braga

POCKET BOOKS
New York   London   Toronto   Sydney   Singapore

An *Original* Publication of POCKET BOOKS

POCKET BOOKS, a division of Simon & Schuster, Inc.
1230 Avenue of the Americas, New York, NY 10020

STAR TREK is a Registered Trademark of Paramount Pictures.

This book is published by Pocket Books, a division of Simon & Schuster, Inc., under exclusive license from Paramount Pictures.

ISBN: 0-7434-1922-7

First Pocket Books printing December 2002

10 9 8 7 6 5 4 3 2 1

POCKET and colophon are registered trademarks of Simon & Schuster, Inc.

For information regarding special discounts for bulk purchases, please contact Simon & Schuster Special Sales at 1-800-456-6798 or business@simonandschuster.com

Printed in the U.S.A.

On 11 September 2001, I was in the midst of writing Part 1 of this book when the World Trade Center and the Pentagon were brutally attacked. The WTC was destroyed, killing thousands, and scarring the skyline of my hometown forever.

This book is sadly but emphatically dedicated to those whose lives were lost on that awful day.

ENTERPRISE™

Prelude: Discovery

2151

This portion of the story takes place shortly before the
Enterprise first-season episode "Breaking the Ice."

Chapter One

"CAPTAIN, I believe you should come down to see this."

The captain of the *Enterprise* smiled at what almost sounded like enthusiasm coming from his Vulcan science officer, filtered through the intercom speakers in his quarters.

"See what, T'Pol?" Captain Jonathan Archer asked. He was currently kneeling on the floor, scratching his beagle Porthos behind one floppy ear.

"I believe that we have found evidence that this planet is, in fact, the homeworld of the Zalkat Union."

The planet to which the Vulcan sub-commander referred was Beta Aurigae VII. *Enterprise,* the still largely experimental flagship of Earth's nascent Starfleet space service, had been given a mandate to explore new worlds, and the Beta Aurigae system was

3

full of them. The seventh planet even had an oxygen/nitrogen atmosphere (what the Vulcans referred to as a "Minshara-class" planet), so Archer had authorized T'Pol to lead a team to explore the surface—after a thorough scan, naturally. Archer had made the mistake of not making sufficient preparations for visiting an Earth-type world once, and several members of his crew almost paid for that with their lives. Jonathan Archer liked to think that he learned from his mistakes.

They had not detected any sentient animal life—indeed, the largest animal they'd been able to detect was an insect—nor anything especially dangerous to humanoids. There was plenty of plant life, and the probe and sensor readings indicated a scattering of refined metals and the remnants of a system of roads.

"Let me guess," Archer said, standing upright, thus prompting a hurt look from Porthos, "the Alley Cat Union's another one of those races we're not meant to know about yet?" He reached for the cup of coffee on the nightstand as Porthos started sniffing his boots.

"Zalkat, not 'alley cat,' Captain, and hardly," T'Pol said in the tone that Archer had come to recognize as the one she used when he was being annoyingly human. As far as he could tell, those times were roughly whenever Archer was awake. Sometimes, however, the teasing was impossible for him to resist, hence his deliberate malapropism.

She continued: *"Archaeological evidence of the Union has been found on several worlds throughout*

the sector—and all of it indicates that the Union's heyday was over ninety thousand years ago."

Archer almost sputtered his coffee. "Ninety thousand?"

"Yes, sir."

"Wow." It took Archer a moment to wrap his mind around the number. Ninety thousand years ago, *Homo sapiens* didn't even exist. "What have you found?"

"The remains of a building that, as best I can tell, was recently unearthed. I've been extrapolating the weather patterns, and it would seem that erosion has been caused—"

"T'Pol," he said with a smile, "please tell me you didn't call to talk about the weather."

"Excuse me?" she said archly.

Archer sighed. "Just give me the basics of what you found. Save the details for your written report."

A noise that Archer chose to interpret as static rather than a *tcha* of disapproval preceded T'Pol's next statement. *"We have found several items containing markings consistent with other Zalkatian artifacts, as well as humanoid bone fossils that are consistent with those found at other Zalkatian sites. Ensign Sato has also discovered a box."*

"A box?" Archer prompted when no further details were forthcoming.

"Yes, sir. Mr. Reed has been attempting to gain ingress to the box, thus far with minimal success."

"What, blasting it open with a phase pistol didn't work?" Archer said with a laugh.

"No."

Archer blinked. "T'Pol, I was kidding."

So was Mr. Reed when he first made the suggestion. However, after all other avenues were exhausted, he did attempt to, as you so eloquently put it, blast it open. That proved as fruitless. The box is made of a material impervious to coherent phased light.

After gulping down the remainder of his coffee, Archer asked, "What's the big deal about this box anyhow?" At Porthos's pleading look, Archer disposed of the coffee cup and then knelt down to scratch the canine behind the ears some more. "You're not getting any cheese, so stop giving me that look," he said to the puppy.

"Sir?"

"Nothing," he said quickly. "What about the box?"

"Ensign Sato has concluded, based on a very limited linguistic database that I provided, that the box contains critical documents relating to Malkus the Mighty."

"Dare I ask what Malkus the Mighty is?"

"Was, Captain. Several of the documents that have been recovered from Zalkatian sites have made reference to Malkus—apparently a tyrant who ruled for many years. Accounts have chronicled his reign at anywhere from ten years to a thousand years—the former is more likely, though the latter more prevalent in the accounts. The box is probably of the same tenor as most other documents relating to Malkus: tributes to his glory, accounts of his greatness, and other such emotional outpourings."

Grinning, Archer asked, "Is that distaste I hear in your tone, Sub-commander?"

"Certainly not," T'Pol said indignantly.

"In any case, you've sold me."

"Sir?"

"Sounds like this is a major archaeological find." He cradled Porthos in his arms and then stood upright. The dog made a happy bleating noise in response and licked Archer's hand. "I'd like to get a good look at it. Mr. Tucker, Porthos, and I will be on the next pod down."

"Sir, I don't think it's necessary for you to bring—"

Archer sighed as he interrupted. "Are we going to start this again? Porthos is a beagle. He's spent most of his time sitting patiently in my cabin when every instinct in his little canine body pushes him to run yapping all over the ship. I'd say he's earned another chance to run free in the great outdoors for a while."

After a brief pause, T'Pol said slowly, *"If you'd let me finish, sir, you'd have known that I have no objection to bringing your animal down—assuming he is kept out of the main archaeological site we have established. My objection was to the presence of Mr. Tucker."*

"I can't see why—you two haven't gotten into an argument for hours," Archer said dryly. "You must be suffering withdrawal."

"I simply do not see what Mr. Tucker can contribute to the landing party—plus it would place Enterprise's *four seniormost crew members off-ship."*

"Travis can handle the conn while we're gone. And Trip's an engineer. They're good at opening things that don't want to be opened—in fact, that's a particular talent of Trip's."

"Really?" The dubiousness practically dripped from T'Pol's voice.

"Really. We'll be down within the hour. Archer out." After cutting off that connection, he opened another. "Archer to Tucker."

"Tucker here."

"How'd you like to take a little trip, Trip?"

There was a pause, then a snort of what might have almost been laughter. *"Cap'n, however long you been waitin' to use that line—you shoulda waited longer."*

It took Charles "Trip" Tucker all of forty-five seconds to open the box.

Malcolm Reed stared daggers at him. "How in the hell did you do that, Commander?"

"Sorry, trade secret," Tucker said with his toothy smile.

"Look, I went at that thing for the better part of an hour," Reed said, his normally dry face looking positively sour. "I think—"

"Forget it, Malcolm," Archer said with a grin. "Trip's not one to reveal a trade secret."

As his security chief continued to regard his chief engineer with disdain, Archer looked around the dig site. One of Reed's people had been detailed with keeping an eye on Porthos as he ran around a bushy area. Archer, meanwhile, looked admiringly at a pile of stones that vaguely resembled pictures of Greek ruins he'd seen. The architectural style was completely different, of course, but it evoked the same feeling of treading on ancient ground. *Ninety thousand years,* he thought, still in awe of the number. Once, this barren, brown kilometer-wide patch of dirt was probably a

thriving metropolis. Now there was nothing but an assortment of rocks and broken trinkets. *Look upon my works, ye mighty, and despair,* he thought, recalling the Percy Bysshe Shelley poem.

T'Pol had collected several items—some seemingly ordinary pieces of rock, others that appeared to have a particular shape—into a sample case, each tagged with a notation written in the severe Vulcan script. Archer instinctively wanted to rebuke her for that—*Enterprise* was an Earth ship, so to Archer's mind the documentation should have been in an Earth language—but he realized immediately how foolish that was. The two people who were going to be spending the most time with the artifacts from this dig were T'Pol and the ship's linguist, Ensign Hoshi Sato. It mattered only that those two could read the notes. Their reports would be in English in any case.

Speaking of the young ensign, she was now kneeling down in front of the box, pawing through its contents, her hands clad in sterile gloves. "I was right! These have the same markings as the box." She held something up to T'Pol, who stood next to her. Archer leaned in close to see a very small cube—barely two centimeters on a side—with surprisingly elaborate markings, given its size. Sato easily held the cube between her forefinger and thumb. "See? That glyph is definitely the symbol for 'mighty,' " she added, pointing to a marking on one side, then pointed to the opposite side, "and that's the one for 'story.' It's got to be more of those Malkus Chronicles."

T'Pol, her hands also gloved, took the cube. "The evidence does seem to point to that conclusion."

"The word 'mighty' shouldn't be a clue all by itself," Archer said. "I mean, this Malkus guy can't have been the only person to whom that word would apply."

"Actually it is," Sato said sheepishly. "See, that," she said, pointing to one corner of the glyph, "indicates that it's a proper name, and belongs to a great personage."

T'Pol added, "The word 'mighty' written in that particular style has thus far been exclusively found in relation to Malkus. It would seem that Ensign Sato's hypothesis was correct."

Smiling, Sato stood up. "Told you."

"This is an even greater find than you might think," T'Pol said. "These are a type of data storage. Other such items have been found—many of them fragments of the so-called Malkus Chronicles. Until now, however, we have not found any units in such pristine condition."

"They were certainly well preserved in that damn box," Reed muttered. Then, louder, he added, "Actually, that's probably why that box was so bloody hard to get into. If it was related to such an important figure . . ."

T'Pol nodded. "That is a logical deduction."

"Pristine or not," Archer said, "it doesn't do us any good if we can't read it. I don't think we have anything on board that'll interface with that thing."

Tucker walked over to the box. "Lemme take a look at that."

Sato grabbed the box and moved it away from Tucker. "Not until you get some gloves on."

"Whoa there, Ensign Squeaky Clean, I took a shower 'fore I came down."

"I don't care if you dipped yourself in a vat of decon gel, you're not touching my artifacts without gloves on."

"*Your* artifacts?" Tucker said with a laugh. "You said they had this Malkus fella's name on 'em, not yours."

"Malcolm, give the commander a pair of gloves," Archer said before the argument went on.

"Fine, fine, gimme the damn gloves," Tucker said with a look at Sato. For her part, Sato continued to look defiant. She had obviously taken a personal interest in this find.

Reed smiled as he went to the supply box, and said in a perfect imitation of Tucker's drawl, "Keep your shirt on."

Archer managed to maintain a straight face, as, naturally, did T'Pol. Sato had somewhat less discipline, and burst into a giggle.

Tucker turned to Archer. "Y'know, if I wanted abuse, I coulda stayed home. Next time, open y'own damn boxes." However, he took the gloves Reed proffered a moment later, put them on, then looked at Sato. "May I?"

Presenting him with the box, Sato said with a smile, "Knock yourself out, Commander."

Tucker studied one of the cubes for several seconds, then said, "I think I might be able to modify one of the readers. It'll take a couple hours, though—and I'll need to take one of these with me."

"All right, take them back up to *Enterprise*," Archer said. "T'Pol, go with him and give him a hand."

"Captain," Sato said, "request permission to go back—"

"Denied—for now," he added at the ensign's forlorn look. "Once they've rigged the reader up, then I'll want you in orbit translating what's on these cubes, but until then, with T'Pol going back to the ship, I want you down here cataloging what we find."

"Yes, sir."

"You will be remaining as well?" T'Pol asked Archer.

The captain nodded. "Not quite a first contact, but close enough for me. I'd like to learn more about this Zalkat Union. Besides," he added with a smile, "Porthos could use a little more running-around time."

Five hours later, Archer took a pod back up to *Enterprise,* along with Reed, the rest of the archaeological crew, a crate full of samples, and a very content beagle (who spent the entire trip from the surface asleep in Archer's lap). An hour prior to that, T'Pol had sent a pod down to fetch Sato, and by the time Archer had settled back onto *Enterprise,* the two of them had a preliminary report for him.

The captain sat behind his desk. T'Pol stood calmly on the other side of the desk, while Sato was pacing around the cramped space, seemingly ready to burst. Archer found it an amusing contrast.

T'Pol said, "This chronicle is somewhat different from the others that have been unearthed."

"It was written *after* Malkus was overthrown," Sato added excitedly.

"I have to say, Ensign," Archer said with a smile,

"you're remarkably enthusiastic for someone who'd never heard of the Zalkat Union two days ago."

"It's a fascinating culture, Captain," Sato said, now sounding a bit more sheepish. "I could spend days just listening to their language—it has so many layers and nuances. They took their words very seriously. And their sculpture—what we were able to unearth and what the sub-commander's shown me in some other records—it's just *amazing.*"

Smiling indulgently, Archer said, "Continue your report, Sub-commander."

After a brief nod, T'Pol said, "Ensign Sato is correct in that this chronicle was written after Malkus was overthrown. In addition, it also provided the first evidence of how Malkus was able to rule for so long."

"How long?"

"Apparently," and here, it seemed to Archer, T'Pol spoke with the greatest reluctance, "he truly did reign for the rough equivalent of one thousand years. Malkus had four items constructed which served as the instruments of his rule. They were devices of impressive power—far in excess of the Union's baseline technology level."

"Did he steal the technology from another spacefaring power?"

"Unknown—and unlikely. Based on the descriptions that Ensign Sato and I have translated, it is in keeping with the Union's technology curve, simply farther along on that curve than the rest of the Union of that era. To give an Earth analogy, the creator of these devices was the Zalkatian equivalent of Leonardo da Vinci. Unlike da Vinci, however, who could not con-

struct the ornithopter he designed, Malkus was able to provide the material for these devices to be created."

"So what do they do?" Archer asked, shifting uncomfortably in his chair.

"One was capable of controlling the weather, one imparted a fatal virus, one served as an immensely powerful energy weapon, and the final device could be used to channel telepathy."

Archer sat up. "Mind control?"

"Yes, sir."

"Basically," Sato said as she paced back and forth past the images of other, older ships named *Enterprise* on the office wall, "he could force people to do what he wanted, and if they still didn't obey, they had their choice of dying by disease, tornado, or being blasted into oblivion."

"That's quite a combination." Archer knew his words didn't do their meaning justice. He thought back to the tyrants of human history, and imagined what Julius Caesar, Genghis Khan, Napoleon Bonaparte, Adolf Hitler, or Colonel Green would have done with even one of those devices, much less all four. *Hell,* he thought, *any sufficiently crazed Japanese shōgun or Russian czar would have a field day.* "So what happened to the devices after Malkus was overthrown?" He snorted. "For that matter, *how* was he overthrown?"

"We haven't found that part, yet," Sato said. She had moved to stand next to T'Pol. "Captain, each of the cubes we found had different things on it, but the information we're giving you about Malkus's devices is on *all* of them. I think that's why the box was so well

preserved—the Zalkatians wanted someone to find these chronicles in the future."

"Why?"

T'Pol said, "As a warning. The devices proved impossible to destroy. According to the chronicle, they tried every method they could imagine, including dropping the devices into a sun."

"That didn't work either?" Archer asked, surprised.

"No. The devices were able to resist the gravitational forces of the sun and drift back out, unscathed. However, the Zalkatians could not risk another possessing even one of them, much less all four."

"Smart move. So what'd they do?"

"Spread them to the nine winds," Sato said with a grim smile. She started pacing again. "The Zalkat Union was *huge*, Captain. It included parts of the galaxy we're probably never gonna see in our lifetime. And the rebels buried them in four different places on the outskirts of their territory."

"Where?"

"That information was deliberately withheld," T'Pol said, "in order to keep anyone from finding them. The only definitive information is that they are in four separate locations and that they are simple black boxes."

A wry smile played across Archer's face. "The Zalkatians have a thing for ordinary-looking boxes, don't they?"

Sato also smiled.

T'Pol, of course, did not, but simply went on as if Archer hadn't commented. "This rather generic form makes recognizing the devices visually difficult. How-

ever, the devices do give off a distinctive energy signature when they're active. That signature is encoded into all of the cubes we found, and can easily be programmed into *Enterprise*'s sensors."

Archer stood up. "We need to do more than that."

Sato frowned. "Sir?"

"Think about it, Ensign—we're not the only ship out here. More to the point, we're not the last Earth ship to explore; we're the first. If someone comes across one of these devices when it's active, they need to know what it is—especially if they're so unassuming looking."

The look of trepidation on Sato's face showed that she was thinking about it now, and understood the potential danger.

"Ensign, prepare a message to Admiral Forrest. I want him to know everything you just told me—along with my strong recommendation that the information about these devices be programmed into *every* Starfleet ship and also be made available to any civilian ship."

T'Pol nodded what Archer guessed was an approving nod, and said, "I would like you to prepare a similar message to the Vulcan High Command, Ensign."

Archer's eyes widened as an idea hit him. "Actually, I think the recommendations to both Earth and Vulcan should come from both of us, Sub-commander. And we might want to provide this information to the Axanar, too—as a goodwill gesture to our new friends."

Another approving nod. "An excellent idea, Captain." *Enterprise* had made first contact with the Axanar only a couple of weeks earlier. At last report, diplomatic relations with them were going well.

Sato headed toward the door. "I'll start preparing the message right away, sir."

"One other thing, Ensign," Archer said. Sato stopped, her arm hovering over the door control. "I also want to recommend to the admiral that a general order is created that requires any Starfleet vessel that does encounter this energy signature be ordered to confiscate the device immediately."

"Yes, sir." Sato touched the control to open the door and departed.

"Another excellent idea, Captain," T'Pol said.

"Twice in one lifetime, Sub-commander," Archer said with a wide grin. "When you're hot, you're hot."

Archer waited expectantly for some kind of comeback. When none was forthcoming, he realized that T'Pol knew that Archer was expecting some kind of rebuke, and she had decided not to give him the satisfaction of rising to the bait.

Well, I did *bring her along to keep me on my toes.* "What say we head belowdecks so you can take a look at the other goodies we dug up down there?" Archer asked, heading for the door.

T'Pol nodded in acknowledgment. "After you, Captain."

STAR TREK®

Part 1: The First Artifact

2266

This portion of the story takes place shortly before the
Star Trek first-season episode "Balance of Terror."

Chapter Two

SHE WAS PRETTY SURE the vacation sounded good when Alvaro suggested it. As the wind sliced through her thermal suit and snow obscured her goggles, however, it didn't sound nearly as appealing at the moment.

Pirenne's Peak had gotten warm enough to be habitable to humans only in the last few years. It was almost virgin territory. She had always liked hiking and climbing, and finding a new mountainous area of Alpha Proxima II to explore was certainly tempting.

And it wasn't like she had anything better to do now.

Of course, "habitable to humans" was a relative term. Proxima was a colony world, after all, and, though it was Class-M, no sentient life had ever evolved on it. That was, many felt, because it was so hot on most of the surface. There were exceptions, of

course: the parts of the northern continent where the colony had been founded and now, almost a century later, thrived; and the mountaintops, above the cloud layer, where temperatures plunged to well below the freezing point.

After spending so long in the oppressive heat of Sierra City, she had thought she would welcome the cold. It matched her mood.

Damn them all to hell.

It's normal, they said. This sort of thing always happens when someone new takes over, they said.

But someone new *shouldn't* have taken over, didn't they understand that? That job was *hers,* by every right. *Hers,* dammit, and they had *no right* to take it away from her.

Take a vacation, they said. You'll feel better, they said.

Right now, she didn't feel better. She felt cold and miserable and like she was being attacked by wind and snow and she wanted it to stop.

The path she was on would lead to the top of the peak. It had been cleared by the tourist bureau as a way of encouraging hikers like herself to come to the peak. Unfortunately, the path made things *too* easy. If she had had to work a bit harder to get up to the top by navigating the natural crevices and outcroppings, she might have been able to actually accomplish what Alvaro had suggested: keep her mind off her recent misfortunes.

Misfortunes? Hell, it was thievery. That job was mine, dammit, mine! They had no right!

She touched a control on the lining of the glove of her thermal suit. A display appeared on the inside of

her goggles, showing the route that would take her to the top. She then had the image pull back and expand to show the entire region.

As she had hoped, there was another way to the top. It would take twice as long, and involve clambering over ground much more treacherous than this path—including at least one section that, according to the map, was covered in ice. But she was hardly in a rush—it wasn't as if she had a job to go home to—and she'd been in far more dangerous climbs when she was a child. This would be easy.

Half an hour later, sweat poured down her forehead, staining her goggles (which obediently cleaned themselves), her arm and leg muscles ached from the exertion of climbing in the bulky suit, and she hadn't thought about the misery her life had turned into for the entire time.

She paused, having found a small rock to sit on. Using one control to call up the map, she used another to activate the water dispenser. As refreshing water poured through a straw into her dry mouth, she looked over the display. *Only about another twenty minutes or so,* she thought. Had she taken the beaten path, as it were, she would have been there ten minutes ago. She preferred this.

I'll just wait here for a few minutes, get my breath back, then go on.

The cold and the snow and the wind somehow didn't matter as much now. Finally, she had found something to distract her. To make her forget her misery and what they took from her.

23

You can do better.

She sat up. "Who said that?" she asked aloud, not sure that anyone would even be able to hear her in the fierce wind.

You can get revenge.

Now she stood up. "Who is this?"

I can help you.

Almost against her will, she found herself looking between the rock she sat on and the one next to it. She squinted, and saw a faint green glow.

You can have your revenge. Just take me with you and everything you want will be yours.

Her arm just barely fit between the two rocks. She reached in, felt around near where the green glow was. She felt the metal shape, which was warm even through the protection of her gloves.

Unfortunately, she couldn't fit it through the small space between the rocks. Indeed, she could barely fit her hand through.

Consumed suddenly by an all-encompassing *need* to get the whatever-it-was out from between the rocks, she clambered off the rock, got on her knees, and examined the space. The rocks were close together, but the gap between them widened closer to the ground. They were also buried in snow. *Maybe if I dig down a bit, they're farther apart!*

No. Not maybe. They *were* farther apart. She just had to dig into the snow. Somehow, she *knew* this.

On her knees, the peak, the vacation, the climb, everything forgotten, she started to dig with her hands, clearing away the snow at a great rate.

She had no idea how much time passed before she cleared out enough room to reach in between the rocks and grab the item. But as soon as she had, she did so.

It was a black box. It felt amazingly warm in her hands.

Now you can have your revenge.

She smiled.

"Y'know, I really hate the night shift, Dad."

Sitting in his quarters on the *U.S.S. Constellation*, Commodore Matthew Decker laughed at the image of his son set in the desk monitor. Commander Willard Decker—whom his father would have sworn was only a child a week ago—sat in the operations center of Starbase 6, where he served as Admiral Borck's adjutant.

"It's space, son, it's—"

"—always night," he finished, *"I know, I know."*

Both father and son laughed. It was an old joke dating back to when Will was four. His parents had told him it was time for bed because it was night. Even then, Will had been thinking about following his father's footsteps into Starfleet, and he had said, "Mommy, Daddy, when I go to space I'm'na have to sleep all the time. 'Cause, in space it's *always* night!"

"C'mon, son, it's only for another day."

"I know, I know. I just prefer to be in the thick of things." Will leaned back in his chair and sighed. He looked, his father had to admit, good in his gold shirt. *Won't be long before he has a command of his own.*

Something on the console behind Will beeped. He brushed a lock of blond hair off his forehead and

checked the console. *"Damn—I've got to take care of that. I'll talk to you later, okay, Dad?"*

"That's Commodore Dad to you, mister!" Decker said with mock authority.

Will saluted sloppily. *"Yes, sir, Commodore Dad, sir!"* Then he nodded. *"Starbase 6 out."*

The monitor on Matt Decker's desk faded to black. The commodore leaned back in his chair. He was proud of his son. The boy's record was spotless. Truth be told, it was cleaner than his old man's, which had enough reprimands to choke a *sehlat*. Matt Decker had clawed his way through the ranks. His Academy professors had deemed him not fit to be command material. He came up through security, and wasn't expected to advance all that far. Most of his commanding officers considered him to be insubordinate—though never to the point of court-martial—and overly opinionated.

No one was more surprised than he when Admiral Fitzgerald gave him his captain's braid and command of the *Constellation* all those years ago.

Will, though, was a Starfleet poster boy. Although Decker hadn't told his son this, the next high-level starship first officer position to become available was probably going to go to Willard Decker.

The commodore got up and pulled his golden uniform shirt over his head. As he did so, he felt like all the energy drained out of his body—almost as if the shirt had been keeping him awake. It had been another long day on their two-week scientific mission examining the emissions from the neutron star in the Beta Proxima system. His second officer, Lieutenant

Guillermo Masada, had been pushing his people pretty hard to get all the readings that they could before their next assignment three days hence—the oh-so-exciting hosting of a diplomatic conference in the Crellis Cluster. Even as Masada had been gathering enough sensor readings to challenge the storage capacity of the *Constellation* computer, Decker's first officer, Commander Hiromi Takeshewada, had been working with security to get all the details ready for the conference.

Bleary-eyed, Decker looked at himself in the mirror, scratching his rough, stubble-covered cheek.

"Bridge to captain."

It was Masada. Decker was about to ask what he was still doing up, then realized it was a silly question. *Guillermo has hardly slept since we warped into Beta Proxima.*

Thumbing the intercom on his desk, he said, "Decker here." Then he winced, realizing how slurred his words were. He wondered if he had sounded that bad when talking to Will.

"Sir, we're picking up a distress call from Alpha Proxima II."

In an instant, he was wide awake. Alpha Proxima was almost literally the star system next door to the *Constellation*'s present location, so they were ideally situated to respond to the call. "Specifics?"

"Medical emergency—some kind of plague has broken out. That's all we've got."

"That's enough. Set a course, maximum warp, and have Commander Takeshewada and Dr. Rosenhaus report to the bridge. I'll be right up. Decker out."

"Sir, I—"

Decker thumbed the intercom off before Masada could finish the sentence. He knew that tone in his science officer's voice. He was going to try to talk Decker out of changing course until they had more information so he could squeeze more sensor readings out of the neutron star. But the star wasn't going anywhere, and he had a duty to respond to the medical emergency immediately.

Throwing his shirt back on, he went out into the corridor, rubbing the sleep that had already started collecting in his eyes. *I haven't even gone to bed yet, and I feel like I just woke up.*

He approached the turbolift just as Hiromi Takeshewada did likewise from an adjacent corridor. Decker nodded down at her by way of greeting. Decker was a tall man, relatively broad shouldered, and starting to get the inevitable paunch that all the men in his family got after they hit fifty-five. In complete contrast, the slim Takeshewada only came up to Decker's shoulder. Where Decker's lined (and, at the moment, stubbly) face had all his years etched on it, Takeshewada's porcelain-like features probably allowed her to still pass for a cadet. Some had even been foolish enough to not take her completely seriously because of that—though never twice.

Right now, she looked as tired as Decker felt. "I take it you were roused out of bed, Number One?" Decker said with a smirk.

"Not quite," she said. "I was *heading* for bed. I could *see* my bed from where I was standing when Guillermo called me. But no, I didn't actually make it *to* the bed." As the turbolift doors opened and they en-

tered, she looked up at Decker's face. "So you gonna grow that beard, or what?"

Decker chuckled as he grabbed the turbolift's handle and said, "Bridge." Takeshewada had been on him to simply grow a beard. Decker hadn't been entirely comfortable with the idea, but he also hated shaving. "Still thinking about it."

As soon as the doors opened to the bridge, Decker noticed that any signs of fatigue were erased from Takeshewada's smooth features. Nodding his approval, they both entered the *Constellation*'s nerve center. "Report," Takeshewada said to Masada, who had been sitting in the command chair, and vacated it for Decker.

Masada, whose normally well-trimmed beard was now thick enough to obscure his lips, ran his hand over his receding salt-and-pepper hair as he moved to the science console. "Alpha Proxima II reports that a plague of some kind has broken out and they need medical attention. Like I told the commodore, that's all the detail we've gotten so far."

As Decker sat in his command chair, Yeoman Guthrie appeared at his side with a cup of coffee—milk, no sugar. Decker accepted the cup with a grateful smile.

Takeshewada walked to the console directly behind Decker, where the night-shift communications officer—whose name Decker could not for the life of him remember—sat pushing several buttons. Before the first officer could say anything, the young ensign said, "I've been trying to raise Proxima since we received the distress signal, Commander. They have yet to respond."

"Have any other ships answered the distress call?"

He nodded. "The *Enterprise*."

Decker turned around. "Isn't that Chris Pike's ship?"

"No, Jim Kirk has her now," Takeshewada said. "Has since Pike was promoted to fleet captain."

Grunting, Decker turned to the navigation console. "ETA to Proxima?"

The helm officer, another fresh-faced young officer Decker didn't recognize, said, "Twenty minutes, sir."

"Something wrong, Ensign?" Takeshewada said.

Decker turned to see that the comm officer looked vexed, which had prompted the first officer's question.

The communications officer touched the receiver in his ear. "I'm not sure. The comm traffic on Proxima is tremendous, but none of it is on the official frequencies. In fact, the official government channel is dead."

As he spoke, the turbolift doors opened to reveal the smooth, unlined face of Dr. Lewis Rosenhaus. Only a few years removed from his graduation with honors from Starfleet Medical, Rosenhaus had been something of a prodigy. After Decker's previous chief medical officer retired a month ago, Admiral Fitzgerald had all but forced Rosenhaus upon the *Constellation,* claiming he was one of the best. Decker's sole impression of the young man so far was that he was a bit too eager. He also hadn't had to do much beyond routine physicals to acquaint himself with his four hundred new patients. *I suspect,* Decker thought with some trepidation, *that this will be a test for him. Let's hope to hell he passes it.* Idly, he wondered who the *Enter-*

prise CMO was, and hoped it was a more experienced hand.

His presence led to some chuckling around the bridge, as the doctor hadn't bothered to change into uniform, and his wavy red hair was sticking up in all directions. He was still wearing his pajamas—silk, Decker noticed, or something similar.

"What's happening?" the young man asked. "Lieutenant Masada said it was some kind of medical crisis."

"We don't have any details yet, Doctor," Takeshewada said. "So far, all we know is that Alpha Proxima II has been hit with a medical emergency of some kind."

"That could be anything," Rosenhaus said prissily.

"The word 'plague' was used, Doctor," Decker said. "Does that help?"

"Not especially, no. Hard to prepare sickbay when I don't know what to prepare it *for.*"

Takeshewada turned to Masada. "Talk to me about Proxima, Guillermo."

Masada reached behind his head and yanked on his ponytail, which he always did right before giving a report. "Your basic Class-M planet—part of the big colonization push after warp drive was discovered, made part of the Federation, gobby gobby gobby. Nothing particularly notable."

Decker could hear the undercurrent in Masada's voice, and knew he was dying to add, *Unlike, say, a neutron star.* "Guillermo, knock it off."

Sounding nonplussed, Masada said, "Sir?"

"We know you're angry about cutting the neutron star survey short. Get over it and give a proper report."

Straightening in his chair, Masada pulled on his ponytail again. "Yes, *sir,*" he said quickly, and peered into his sensor hood. Blue light shone on his features as he read off the data contained therein. "Alpha Proxima II was colonized in 2189 by the *S.S. Esperanza.* They set up two cities, both on the northern continent. In fact, the northern polar region's the only place that's really comfortable for humans—rest of the planet's either too hot or covered in water. Current population is about one million four hundred thousand. The government consists of a planetary council run by a chief speaker, and they also have representation on the Federation Council." He looked up. "You want their chief exports?"

Chuckling, Decker said, "I'll pass, thanks."

Then Masada's console beeped. "What the—?"

"Report," Takeshewada said.

Masada peered back into the sensor hood. "That's weird." He looked up at Takeshewada, who was now standing behind him. "We're picking up an energy signature from Proxima, one that triggered a flag in the computer relating to Starfleet General Order 16."

Decker frowned. "I don't remember that one."

"Neither do I," Takeshewada said, sounding ashamed at the lapse.

Masada snorted. "Honestly, if the computer hadn't just shoved it in my face, I wouldn't have remembered it, either. But if this sensor reading is accurate, we may have stumbled across a deadly weapon."

"What kind?" Takeshewada asked.

"Not sure," Masada said, shaking his head and start-

ing to work his console, "but I'll have something by the time we get there."

Decker turned away from Masada and smiled. Now that he had a problem to solve, Masada was sounding less petulant. *Good,* he thought. *Last thing I need is Guillermo feeling sorry for himself when we've got a medical crisis* and *some unknown weapon. . . .*

The *Constellation*'s Sensor Control Center—or "sensor room," as it was more commonly known—was not normally a hotbed of activity. Someone was always on duty to make sure everything was working. However, that person was often alone. Located on deck twelve, all the sensor information from the ship came through this room. Unlike the bridge sciences station—where the duty officer could pick and choose what to focus on—the consoles in this room took in and recorded everything. Its functions were generally automatic.

Since the *Constellation* had arrived at Beta Proxima eleven days ago, though, there had never been fewer than four people in the sensor room at any given time, and sometimes up to ten. Lieutenant (j.g.) Chaoyang Soo had joked that the science staff had spent more time in the room in those eleven days than they had during their entire collective tours on the *Constellation.*

Right now, Soo was frowning at a new reading that had come in. With the sudden departure to respond to a medical emergency, Soo had taken it upon himself to dismiss the staff—mostly noncommissioned scientists who had spent the last eleven days being harangued by

Lieutenant Masada—leaving only himself and Ensign Sontor. Were Sontor not a Vulcan, Soo would have dismissed him, too. However, he had apparently altered his metabolism so he would not need to sleep at all for the two-week period of the mission. It was a move that some viewed as showing off, but it also made dismissing him so he could get some sleep more or less pointless.

"Curious."

Soo, who had been gazing at the lateral sensor array, walked over to stand behind Sontor, who was staring at the same anomalous reading. "What do you make of it?"

"We have detected the energy signature of one of the Malkus Artifacts."

"You say that like I have the first clue what that is." Soo realized after he said it that he sounded more irritated than he should have. *Ah, hell, it's not like Sontor'll care.*

"My apologies. I had, of course, assumed that you would be familiar with the major archeological find on Beta Aurigae VII one hundred and fifteen years ago, since it relates to the sixteenth of Starfleet's General Orders." Sontor's right eyebrow shot up. "Obviously, my assumption was in error."

Soo closed his eyes and counted to ten in English, French, and Mandarin. Then he opened them again. "Ensign Sontor, would you be *so* kind as to enlighten me as to what a 'Malkus Artifact' is?"

"Masada to sensor room."

"Our master speaks," Soo muttered, then thumbed the intercom. "Sensor room, this is Soo."

"I need everything on Starfleet General Order 16 and what it has to do with emissions we're getting from Alpha Proxima II, and I need it yesterday."

With a look at Sontor, Soo said, "I don't think that'll be a problem, sir."

"So you're saying that this plague may be caused by this—this artifact?"

Decker felt dubious about the story that Ensign Sontor was relaying to him on the bridge now. On the other hand, Starfleet didn't issue general orders without a reason. Obviously whoever issued the order—and, according to Sontor, it dated back to when Starfleet was Earth's space exploration arm before the forming of the Federation—thought the threat of these four artifacts was real enough. Even if the distress call turned out to be a false alarm, just detecting those emissions meant that the *Constellation* and the *Enterprise* were now obligated to find and confiscate the artifact or artifacts. "Do we know what type of disease the artifact can cause?" he asked.

"No, sir. Only that the disease in question is fatal." Sontor hesitated. "If I may say so, sir, this is a fascinating discovery, of great scientific importance."

"You may say that, Mr. Sontor, but I'm a bit more concerned about the loss of life on Proxima."

"Of course, sir," Sontor said quickly, though he didn't sound nearly contrite enough to suit Decker.

Oh lay off the kid, he admonished himself. *He's just being Vulcan. He wouldn't know contrite if it bit him on the rear.*

The ensign at helm said, "Entering Alpha Proxima system, sir."

"Come out of warp and bring us into standard orbit of the second planet." He turned to Masada. "Guillermo?"

Peering into the sensor hood, Masada said, "Several artificial satellites and small vessels in orbit, all matching what should be there. Also reading a *Constitution*-class starship in a standard orbit, registry NCC-1701—that'd be the *Enterprise*. I can also now verify the presence of the energy signature from General Order 16 on-planet—but I can't localize it. At least, not yet."

Decker turned to communications. "Any luck raising anyone in authority, Ensign?"

The ensign shook his head. "No, sir, but I'm getting a signal from the *Enterprise*."

"Good." He turned to Takeshewada. "What's the captain's name again?"

She rolled her eyes in the long-suffering manner that Decker had long since learned to ignore. "Kirk."

"Right. Ensign, open a channel."

When they came out of warp, the viewscreen had provided an image of Alpha Proxima II—a gold-and-yellow-tinged planet—and a ship of the same class as the *Constellation* in orbit around it. Within moments, that image was replaced by a bridge that was also of the same design as the *Constellation*.

In the center seat sat a man who was barely in his thirties. *My God, they're letting* children *captain starships.* "I'm Commodore Matt Decker of the *Constellation*."

"*James T. Kirk, captain of the* Enterprise. *It's a*

pleasure, Commodore—I'm just sorry we can't meet under better circumstances."

"Likewise," Decker said quickly. "Have you been able to get anything from the planet?"

Kirk nodded. *"Not from the government, but my chief medical officer has been in touch with the chief of staff of one of the hospitals. I'm afraid the news isn't good, Commodore. Right now, over thirty percent of the population is either incapacitated or dead from this virus."*

"My God." That was Rosenhaus, who still stood by the turbolift, still in his nightclothes.

"Unfortunately, most of the planet's public officials are among that thirty percent."

Decker blinked. "How is that possible?"

"My first officer is working on that right now, though he has a theory based on some emissions we've received."

Nodding, Decker said, "The Malkus Artifacts? General Order 16?"

Again, Kirk nodded.

"All right, I want you, your first officer, and your CMO to beam over here in fifteen minutes. Bring everything you know about the situation, both on Proxima and regarding these artifacts. We'll do likewise."

"Of course, Commodore." Kirk sounded as nonplussed as Masada had when Decker dressed him down earlier. *"We'll see you in fifteen minutes.* Enterprise *out."*

Without turning to look at Rosenhaus, Decker said,

"Doctor, that gives you fifteen minutes to put a uniform on and get to the briefing room."

"Hm? Oh, right. Sorry," he said sheepishly, and went into the turbolift.

Takeshewada stepped down to the lower portion of the bridge and stood next to Decker. "A little rough on the kid, weren't you?"

"He showed up on the bridge in his jammies, Number One, that—"

She smiled. "I don't mean Rosenhaus, I mean Kirk."

Decker snorted. "I'm the ranking officer here. Besides, Kirk doesn't look old enough to shave."

"You *do* know that he's got a list of commendations about a kilometer long, not to mention the Medal of Honor, the Silver Palm, a Kragite, and probably some others I'm forgetting, don't you?"

Decker grinned. "Yeah, but I bet I've got more reprimands." He hauled himself up from his chair and drained his coffee cup. Handing it to Guthrie, he said, "Yeoman, make sure there's a full pot in the briefing room. We're gonna need it."

"Yes, sir," the yeoman said, taking the now-empty cup.

"Masada, Sontor, let's go." He turned—and realized that he didn't have a clue what the names of any of the officers left on the bridge were. He had enough trouble keeping track of alpha shift, much less the near-strangers from gamma shift presently staffing the duty stations.

Takeshewada, bless her, whispered the word "Alamanzar" in his ear.

"Alamanzar," he said without missing a beat, and wondering which face that name belonged to, "you have the conn."

Decker spent the time waiting for the *Enterprise* contingent and Rosenhaus to show up taking a quick glance at Kirk's service record. Although the commodore was appalled to see that Kirk was only a few years older than Decker's son, he was also impressed with the young man's service record. Kirk had several citations besides the ones Takeshewada mentioned.

Still think he's too damn young to be a ship captain . . .

The man himself came in a moment later, followed by two men in blue uniforms, one Vulcan, one human; they were led in by a security guard, whom Decker dismissed with a nod.

Decker stood up and offered his hand. "Captain Kirk."

"Commodore. May I present my first officer, Mr. Spock, and my chief surgeon, Dr. Leonard McCoy."

The first officer's wearing blue? What the hell kind of ship is this kid running? The ship's second-in-command should have been in command gold, not the blue of the sciences. Aloud, he said, "This is Commander Hiromi Takeshewada, my XO; Lieutenant Guillermo Masada, my second officer; and Ensign Sontor, one of my science officers. We're still waiting on—"

The door opened and Rosenhaus ran in, tugging on a blue uniform shirt that looked like it had been hastily

thrown on. He was also trying to smooth his red hair down, and only partially succeeding.

"—my CMO," Decker finished with a smile. "Dr. Lewis Rosenhaus."

"A pleasure, sirs," Rosenhaus said breathlessly.

Within moments, they were all seated around the table. "Dr.—McCoy?" Decker said. When the doctor nodded affirmation, he continued. "Since you've been in touch with the surface . . ."

McCoy nodded. "According to Dr. Baptiste, the head of the Sierra City Medical Center—and, for all intents and purposes, the surgeon general down there, since the S.G.'s one of the ones who's down for the count—what we're dealing with here appears to be a virus that stimulates the adrenal gland. The body can only handle so much of that, naturally, and eventually the organs become overworked. The most common actual cause of death is heart failure—the heart almost literally explodes from the intensity of the blood being pumped through it." The doctor made a snorting noise. "In fact, most of the people who have died from this did so before anyone realized something was wrong. Damn difficult to diagnose a disease whose symptoms include feeling energetic, unusual vigor, and general excitement."

Rosenhaus asked, "What finally led them to realize it then?"

"Over a dozen seemingly unrelated deaths with the same cause within a close time frame. Law-enforcement types tend to notice that kinda thing," McCoy said dryly. "The autopsies revealed the presence of the

virus, and they started treating it and asking anyone with the symptoms to report to the nearest hospital immediately."

Decker leaned back in his chair. "Which meant the hospitals were flooded with healthy people who felt good and thought their hearts would blow up."

McCoy half-smiled. "Exactly. But the virus is fairly easy to identify."

"So what's the problem?" Rosenhaus asked.

"No one's been able to find a cure is the damn problem," McCoy snapped at the younger doctor. Decker had to hide a smile. McCoy went on: "Dr. Baptiste is sending us all his lab work. They're treating with sedation and anti-adrenal medications, but that's only temporary. The virus works past that eventually. It also inhibits any attempt to put the body into stasis. Even under sedation, it won't allow body functions to slow down enough for that."

"Impressive disease," Rosenhaus said. "It knocks out the best method of staving it off, and badly cripples the second-best. Have they tried using brolamine?"

McCoy frowned. "You can't use brolamine in these cases."

"Of course you can—according to—"

Both Kirk and Decker said, "Gentlemen," simultaneously. Decker smirked and added, "You two'll have plenty of time to kibbitz later. Doctor, if you could please have that lab work sent over to us as well, so Dr. Rosenhaus can argue with authority."

"Of course," McCoy said. "The other problem," he said before Decker could then turn to Kirk and ask him

for a report—Decker had thought McCoy to be finished, "is that there's no pattern to the distribution of the virus."

"It's not airborne?" Rosenhaus asked.

"No, and it's not being transmitted by contact, either. In fact, as far as Baptiste has been able to tell, it's not in the least bit contagious. But suddenly, without any kind of warning, a group of people in a certain geographic area all contract it."

"Dr. McCoy is correct," the Vulcan first officer—*what the hell is his name?* Decker thought in a mild panic—said. "The size of the area targeted varies from incident to incident. One of those targets was Sierra City, the colony's capital, during a full council session. Most of the representatives of the government are now ill—and several of them are dead, including the Chief Representative, who was the head of the government."

Turning to Kirk, Decker said, "So what's the situation planetside?"

"In a word, Commodore, chaos. The government's ground to a halt. We may need to take drastic actions."

Sontor spoke up then. "It is likely that the Malkus Artifact is indeed responsible for the virus."

The Vulcan from the *Enterprise* said, "Agreed. The logical deduction would be that someone has unearthed the artifact and is using it to foment chaos."

"Or at least strife," Kirk said. "Chaos is random, and there was nothing random about the attack on the government."

Masada tugged on his ponytail. "I've picked up the artifact's energy pattern, but I haven't been able to localize it."

"Nor have I," Kirk's first officer said.

"In that case, Mr. Spock," Kirk said with a small smile, "the logical course would be for you and Mr. Masada to pool your resources. And see if there's any more information about the Zalkat Union."

"That goes for our doctors, too," Decker said. "Time to prove if two heads really are better than one. One question, Doctor—if it's not contagious, do we need to quarantine the planet?"

McCoy fidgeted with a stylus. "I'd still recommend it, Commodore. All right, so it's being transmitted to a person with some kind of artifact instead of traveling on microbes through the air—that's *still* transmission of a disease, and it still calls for a full quarantine. No ships leave orbit, no ships come into orbit. That includes us."

"Very well—put that into motion as soon as we're done here." He turned to Kirk. "In the meantime, Captain—"

Decker's words were cut off by the comm officer. *"Bridge to Decker."*

He thumbed the intercom, and the young ensign's face appeared on the three-screen monitor in the center of the briefing room table. "Decker here."

"We're getting an emergency distress call from a Chief Bronstein on the planet. She's apparently the head of the Proximan Police Department. Riots have broken out in Sierra City, and they're requesting immediate assistance."

"Tell her we'll be sending a party down. Decker out." He stood up. "Captain, I suggest you and I both

beam down and assess the situation in person and put both our security staffs on standby."

"Commodore, if there are riots breaking out—" Takeshewada started.

"I'm a big boy, Number One, I can handle myself. You have the conn while I'm gone." Decker noticed that this Spock person didn't put up the same argument. He wondered if that was because he was spineless, or just knew better than to argue with his captain—and if the latter, did that mean Kirk was stubborn or that Spock just knew him too well?

Of course, Hiromi knows me too well, and I'm pretty damn stubborn, but so's she. She'll keep beating her head against the same wall, figuring it'll fall sometime . . .

However, that was speculation that could wait. "Let's go, people."

Chapter Three

"Chief, we've got more problems."

"Oh, good," Anna Bronstein said through gritted teeth. Her chief deputy had just entered her too-cramped office with this unwelcome news. The chief of police for the Alpha Proxima II colony had been up for thirty-six straight hours dealing with crisis after crisis. Keeping order at the hospitals alone was proving to be a nightmarish duty, and that was only the tip of the iceberg—and now people were rioting in the streets. Her shoulder-length brown hair, normally tied up and neat, was loose and tangled, her head felt as if someone had taken a welding laser to it, and her uniform was starting to take on a rather unfortunate odor of sweat and grime.

I should've joined Starfleet like Aunt Raisa, she thought crankily. She had only been on the job for a

month, was still learning half the regular procedures, and now she was scrambling to implement the emergency ones.

"I was just thinking I needed more problems. What is it *this* time?"

Deputy Armando Ramirez ran a hand through his thinning black hair. "Well, first of all, the people we have guarding the water reclamation plant are about to go off-shift, and we don't have anyone to relieve them."

"Can't they work another shift?"

"All of them are on their second shift—some of them on their third. They're gonna collapse soon."

"Is there anywhere we can divert?"

Ramirez snorted. "That was a joke, right?"

"I had my sense of humor surgically removed when I took this job, 'Mando."

"That explains a lot, Chief."

Bronstein glowered at Ramirez, then started gnawing on her fingernail again. "Have half of 'em work half the shift. Let the other half get some rest, then switch 'em off. What else?" The nail broke off, and she looked at the finger like it had betrayed her.

"Nobody's showing up to run the cargo transporter downtown."

"So?"

"Nobody *at all*. That's the one they use to get the food and stuff to Arafel County. If nobody shows up, they don't get their food."

Bronstein frowned. "Doesn't Arafel have an emergency supply?"

"Well, yeah, but that'll only last a couple days, and—"

"In a couple of days, we'll probably all be dead, 'Mando. That's not a priority." She started nibbling on her middle finger's nail. "How's Stephopolous coming with his investigation?"

"It's definitely murder. Stephopoulos figures that it was the roommate."

Bronstein got up from behind her desk, which was presently so covered with reports and other items that she couldn't tell what the desk was made of anymore, and started to pace. "Why is it that the first wrongful death this planet has had in six years has to happen when the planet's falling apart at the seams?"

Ramirez scratched his ear and started to answer when Bronstein said, " 'Mando, that was a *rhetorical* question. Anything else?"

Before Ramirez could answer, she heard a familiar sound—that of a transporter. She whirled around to see two patterns starting to coalesce in the doorway to her office. Without hesitating, she unholstered her phaser. Ramirez did likewise.

The patterns became two white males in gold Starfleet uniforms. *That means either two people from those ships that responded to our distress call or two imposters.*

"Identify yourselves *now*," she said without lowering the phaser.

The younger of the two men held his arms out in a conciliatory gesture. "I'm James T. Kirk, captain of the *Enterprise.* This is Commodore Matt Decker of the *Constellation.* We don't mean you any—"

"Don't move," Bronstein said when Kirk started moving forward.

He stopped moving. "I'm sorry. We're here in response to your distress call. We've both got security teams standing by, but we need you to tell us where to put them."

Decker put in, "We figured that beaming down in the middle of the street might cause more problems than it would solve."

Well, if they are Starfleet, at least they're not idiots. "Ramirez?" she asked, not taking her eye off of Decker and Kirk.

She could hear the whirring of Ramirez's tricorder. "The transporter beam did originate from orbit, and not from a position that matches any of the satellites or local ships."

Bronstein let out a breath she hadn't realized she was holding and lowered her phaser. "I'm sorry, Captain, Commodore, but the way things have been—"

"Say no more, Chief, we understand," Kirk said with a nice smile and in a gentle, reassuring tone—and, to Bronstein's surprise, she actually felt reassured, an emotion she would not have given herself credit for feeling.

The commodore, though, didn't smile when he asked, "So where *can* we put our people down?"

Indicating the west wall, she said, "Take a look." The wall contained a map of Sierra City, with sections marked in red and blue. The amount of red far exceeded the blue. "The red areas are where the worst of the rioting is—the blue areas are the ones we've got contained. Everything else is stable, for now. We've

been trying to keep people indoors, but we've got everybody working double and triple shifts. Not surprisingly, the worst is at Government Center, since people want their elected officials to actually, y'know, *do* something. Second-worst is the two hospitals." She shook her head. "Can't tell *what* they're thinking."

"They're not," Decker said. "They're a mob, Chief—mobs don't think, they just act."

Bronstein sighed in acknowledgment.

Taking out his communicator, Kirk said, "We'll try to provide you with some relief. Kirk to *Enterprise*."

Decker also took his communicator out, and they each spoke with their security chiefs. While they did so, Bronstein said, "Ramirez, get in touch with the OICs at all the sites and tell them to expect some help."

Nodding, Ramirez headed back to his desk in order to contact the officers in charge.

"We'll have people in place within the next minute," Decker said. "Their phasers are on stun and they'll be able to pacify the crowd."

"Great—then what?" Bronstein said. "We don't have holding facilities for this many people, and I can't just leave them lying in the street." She sighed. "Running this place is supposed to be a straightforward operation. I've only been here four weeks, and I specifically came here because it was supposed to be calm and relaxing. The worst thing I have to deal with is crowd control during holidays and major sporting events. Now, I have to—"

"Excuse me?" came a small voice from doorway. Bronstein turned to see a short, pale man wearing an

ugly one-piece brown suit. "I'm looking for Chief Bronstein?"

"That would be me. You are?"

The little man entered, gave Kirk and Decker a surprised look, then offered his hand to Bronstein. "My name is Johan Trachsel, and I'm one of the directors of the Sierra City Medical Center. I was told to come see you about authorizing an Emergency Powers Act for the hospital so SCMC can simply treat everyone who walks in without having to go through the usual entry process."

"You mean you haven't been?" Kirk asked, sounding as surprised as Bronstein felt.

"I'm afraid not—or, rather, some of the doctors have, but it's been haphazard. We'd rather it was official to save problems down the line."

Decker snorted. "Assuming there *is* a 'down the line.' "

"We prefer to remain optimistic, sir." He turned to Bronstein. "In any case, I'll need you to sign off on this."

Bronstein blinked. *"Me?* Why me?"

Trachsel went wide-eyed. "You don't know?"

"Don't know *what?"* Bronstein asked, exasperated.

"Uhm, well, you see—you're in charge now."

Again, Bronstein blinked. "In charge of what?"

"The planet. The entire council has been either hospitalized or is dead. According to the Proxima charter, in the event of something like this happening, power then goes into the hands of the chief of police."

Bronstein stupidly looked down at her hands, as if Trachsel had spoken literally. Casting her mind back,

she remembered something during her orientation about the fact that the chief of police was next in line if the entire government was incapacitated, but she hadn't taken it very seriously—after all, how likely was *that* to happen in real life?

Then she looked up. "Me? In charge?"

"I'm afraid so, ma'am."

She found herself looking helplessly at Kirk and Decker. Decker was inscrutable, but Kirk looked sympathetic. "I'm barely able to do *my* job, now I'm supposed to do the whole government's?"

Trachsel was holding out a copy of the executive order and a stylus. "Please, ma'am, if you can sign this, we can streamline the treatment of the sick."

"Right, fine," she said, grabbing the stylus and signing in the appropriate spot. "Someone may want to mention this to the lunatics throwing things at Government Center . . ."

Soon, they'll all be dead.

She stared out the window. It all looked so peaceful. So quiet.

But she knew better.

She had been watching the newsfeeds. They were rioting now. Maybe not here, near her house, but elsewhere in Sierra City, oh, yes.

Cowards. Weaklings.

They had had it *so* easy, and now they were falling apart at the seams.

And it was all her doing.

Sure, they went through the motions, pretending to

be civilized. But introduce a little bit of death into their perfect lives, and they become savages.

Their lives had been disrupted. Just as hers was. They stole her life from her, now she was stealing their lives from them.

She turned on the newsfeeds, curious as to whether things had gotten any more entertaining in the last fifteen minutes.

"According to the latest reports, Starfleet security personnel have been sighted near Government Center as well as at Kurkjian Memorial and SCMC. It is hoped that the presence of additional forces from Starfleet will help curb the tide of violence, though some are questioning the presence of Starfleet under these circumstances, and wondering what that means in terms of the search for a cure. Presently, two starships are in orbit, the U.S.S. Constellation *and the* U.S.S. Enterprise. *Both ships have impressive security staffs and heavy armaments. They also have medical facilities that rival our own, and have the benefit of not being inundated with rioting citizens. Further—"*

She turned it off in disgust. *Damn Starfleet, anyhow, who asked for* them *to stick their noses into this?*

Not that it mattered. She'd just have to use the gift again.

The gift that gave her power.

The wonderful black box with the green glow.

Take my power away from me? I'll show you power, my friends. I have the power to make you dead—and turn the rest of you into a band of raving lunatics.

She laughed. People used to say that she didn't have

a sense of humor, which wasn't true. She just didn't like to laugh very much. When she did laugh it was always awkward and painful-sounding.

Now, though, she laughed with the greatest of ease.

It had been difficult to not run all the way down Pirenne's Peak after she had found the gift. But that was dangerous, both to herself and to her ability to keep the gift secret. After all, it was *her* gift. She couldn't share it, not with anyone—not even Alvaro. No, it was *hers.* Her gift, her salvation, her instrument of revenge.

So she had calmly made her way back down the trail, moving as fast as she could without raising suspicion, and then had waited impatiently in the queue for the transporter that would take her home.

She held the gift in her hand and contemplated it. She wondered who to use it on next. *Maybe I'll use it on the rioters. That would be so wonderfully ironic, wouldn't it?*

Again, she laughed.

Soon, they'll all be dead.

Never thought I'd love the sound of a transporter so much, Matt Decker thought.

He stood with Jim Kirk on the roof of Police Headquarters, which afforded them a fine view of the Government Center. Not to mention the hundreds of people who were yelling, screaming, holding signs, throwing things, and pushing against the barely adequate cordon of exhausted-looking police officers. That cordon was all that kept the mob from pouring into the GC.

Then Decker heard the familiar whine of a transporter beam, only amplified to a much greater degree than what he was used to. As the sound increased, the noise from the mob quieted down proportionately. No one was sure what the noise was, at first, but they didn't seem to think it was good.

After a moment, the noise reached a crescendo, and some forty humanoid figures started to coalesce.

The transporter whine died down, but a concomitant noise increase from the crowd did not occur—mainly due to the fact that the transporter had heralded the arrival of two score people wearing red Starfleet uniforms and each holding a phaser rifle. These were Kirk's people, so Decker didn't recognize any of them—the *Constellation* security detail was assigned to the hospitals—but they looked sufficiently menacing.

Some people continued to shout, but the efforts were much more half-hearted.

Decker remembered a skirmish with a Klingon patrol several years earlier—the Klingon transporters, he had noted then, were almost totally silent. At the time, Decker had envied that discrepancy—especially since it had almost got him killed. Today he was grateful for it. The noise had had much more of an effect than even the presence of armed Starfleet personnel.

"Attention, citizens of Sierra City," came a voice from everywhere. Again, Decker didn't recognize the voice, but he assumed it to be that of Kirk's security chief, doing what he was supposed to do: using an amplifier on his voice as he tried to talk them down. True,

they could have just stunned everyone from orbit, but that had a certain ruthlessness that both Decker and Kirk wanted to avoid if possible. Besides, as Bronstein had pointed out, that would raise the question of what to do with the unconscious bodies. Better to at least attempt to pacify with words rather than phaser beams. *And we can still knock 'em out from orbit if we need to.*

The security chief continued: "Please disperse and return to your homes. The Proximan government is doing everything it can to alleviate the current crisis, but it cannot function under these conditions. If you do not comply, we *will* use force. Please do not put us in that position."

With that, the *Enterprise* security personnel started moving forward—but with their phasers lowered. Emboldened, the Sierra City police did likewise, with their weapons holstered, guiding people away from the GC.

Amazingly enough, it worked. Where the mob probably figured it could handle a few local cops, a cadre of Starfleet security was a completely different matter.

"Everything is being done to alleviate the crisis," the *Enterprise* security chief said. "Please return to your homes and await further word. With your help, we will get through this and cure the disease, but we can't accomplish anything with actions like this going on."

Ever so slowly, the crowd started to disperse. People lowered the signs, pocketed items they intended to throw, and started to move off. Some still shouted the occasional epithet, but without the white noise of the screaming crowd to back them up, they came across as petty and weak rather than threatening.

Decker turned to Kirk. "Nice job your man did there."

"Thanks," Kirk said absently. "Commodore, are you by any chance related to Will Decker?"

Feeling his face crack with a smile of paternal pride, Decker said, "Yes, he's my son."

"I met him when we had a layover at Starbase 6. He's a good man."

"Thank you," Decker said, but he could tell from Kirk's distracted tone that that was not what he'd intended to ask the commodore about. "Kirk, you've obviously got something on your mind. Nice as it is to know you think well of my son, I'd rather you just come out and tell me what you're thinking."

Kirk took a moment to answer, then indicated the crowd below with a gesture. "This is only a temporary solution. These sorts of things are going to keep happening, especially if whoever has that artifact decides to infect more people. Chief Bronstein can barely handle her own duties without our help, much less run the government." He finally turned to look at Decker. His face had a somber quality that Decker frankly wouldn't have credited so young an officer—even a starship captain—as being capable of. "Commodore, with respect, I strongly recommend that we put Proxima under martial law."

Decker almost flinched. As it was, he did take a step backward, as though Kirk's words were a physical attack. "Are you joking?"

"Not about something like this, believe me."

"Kirk, we can't—"

"I don't make this request lightly, Commodore,"

Kirk interrupted. "I've *lived* under martial law. You familiar with Tarsus IV?"

"Of course," Decker said. Kirk didn't need to be any more specific—Decker knew that Kirk was referring to what happened on that colony world twenty years earlier. Decker had been serving as security chief on Starbase 4 at the time. A fungus had wiped out the food supply, and the planetary governor, a lunatic named Kodos, had declared martial law and ordered half the population—some four thousand people—put to death. It had been his way of preserving the entire colony, murdering some so the others could survive. With those four thousand taken out of the equation, the remaining populace could survive on the remaining available food stores. From a eugenics standpoint, it made a certain amount of sense, if one had a sufficiently diseased mind, but from a human standpoint it was one of the most appalling acts committed since the Federation's founding a century earlier.

"You were there?" Decker asked. After Kirk nodded, Decker did the math. "You must've only been a teenager."

Again, Kirk nodded. "I've never forgotten Kodos. For a long time I associated the very concept of martial law with the death of thousands of people." Kirk got a faraway look in his eyes. Then he blinked, and looked at Decker. "But right here, right now, what we're looking at is anarchy. Under regulations, our only recourse is to declare martial law." He took a deep breath. "It's your call, Commodore—you're the ranking officer. But just because this has been done wrong by people like Kodos doesn't mean it can't be done right. It isn't

martial law that's evil, it's those who abuse it. I'd like to think that you and I are capable of rising above the temptations and using the power wisely."

Decker looked into the eyes of the younger man. He saw a determination that belied the captain's age. *Or maybe I'm just not being fair—being under forty doesn't automatically make you an idiot,* he admonished himself.

He pulled out his communicator. "Decker to *Constellation.*"

"Constellation. *Takeshewada here.*"

"Number One, please note in the ship's log that, due to the crisis on Alpha Proxima II, I, as ranking Starfleet officer, have been forced to take extraordinary action. As of this moment, Proxima is hereby under martial law, to be jointly administered by myself and Captain Kirk until such a time as we have deemed the crisis to have passed. Inform Starfleet Command of this immediately."

"Commodore—Matt, are you sure—"

"That's an order, Number One!" Decker barked. Then he took a breath. "Hiromi, believe me, this way is best. Kirk and I'll stay down here. You're in charge of the *Constellation.* Ride herd on Rosenhaus and McCoy to find a cure for this thing, and I want Masada and Spock working round-the-clock to find that damned artifact."

"Understood, Commodore," Takeshewada said in a tone that Decker recognized as her we're-going-to-talk-about-this-later tone. *Well, at least she's not giving me a hard time now.*

Indicating the doorway back into the building, Kirk

said, "We need to tell Chief Bronstein, then inform the general population."

"And won't *that* go over like a lead balloon," Decker muttered. "I doubt most folks even know that the government's been laid low by the virus."

With a small smile, Kirk said, "It's a challenge, Commodore."

Chapter Four

LEWIS ROSENHAUS could barely contain himself as he beamed over to the *Enterprise.* He had copies of several notes and papers with him, including case studies he'd done at the Academy that he thought might be relevant. This was the moment he'd been waiting for since Admiral Fitzgerald had first given him the assignment to the *Constellation* last month.

And not waiting very patiently, either. He had graduated at the top of his class at Starfleet Medical, only to find himself languishing in a research position on Earth. Rosenhaus distinguished himself as much as he could in so dreary a place, but what he longed for was to be out in space, exploring strange new worlds, seeking out new life and new diseases, and coming up with brilliant methods of curing them.

That was his whole reason for joining Starfleet in the first place.

Finally they put him on one of the twelve *Constitution*-class vessels—the elite of the fleet. These were the massive starships that were spearheading the Federation's expansion, making first contacts, making *history*. The *Constellation*'s CMO had retired, and Fitzgerald himself had contacted him and cut him his new orders to report to Commodore Decker.

So how've I spent my first month on the job? Doing physicals. Not a single new world, not a solitary biological phenomenon. Instead, they'd spent almost two weeks studying a neutron star. Of what possible benefit could *that* be to humanity?

Now, though, he had a virus he could sink his teeth into. Better still, he'd be working with Leonard McCoy, a Starfleet veteran, who had already pioneered several revolutionary surgical techniques. This was a colleague, not those sycophants on the medical staff of the *Constellation*—lab techs with no brains, nurses with no good sense, and a junior physician with all the skills of a twentieth-century suturer.

The instant the transporter fully materialized him onto the *Enterprise* platform, he was down the stairs and ready to run out the door. He was stopped by a blonde woman in a blue uniform. "You must be Dr. Rosenhaus," she said in a pleasant voice. "I'm Nurse Chapel. If you'll come with me, I'll take you to sickbay."

"Ah, thanks," Rosenhaus said, surprised. "But, uh, I already know my way there. Our ships have the same design, y'know."

"Perhaps, but Dr. McCoy thought it would be best for you to have an escort."

Rosenhaus shrugged. "Fine, if that's what he wants. It's good manners, I guess, if nothing else." As they exited the transporter room, he took another look at the nurse. "Waitasec—are you *Christine* Chapel? The one who cowrote that paper on practical applications of the records found in the Orion ruins—oh, hell, what was that called?" He started racking his brain.

"That was a long time ago," Chapel said quietly.

"Not *that* long. You wrote it with Roger Korby, right?"

"Uh, yes, but—"

"You both did some great work. What are you doing serving in Starfleet as a *nurse?* The work you and Korby did was years ahead of its time."

"Thank you, but—Dr. Korby has been missing for several years. I—I really don't want to talk about it, Doctor, if it's all the same to you."

Open mouth, insert foot. Nice work, Lew. "Oh my God, Nurse Chapel, I'm *so* sorry, I had *no* idea."

"That's quite all right," Chapel said as they turned a corner and entered sickbay. Her tone of voice belied her words, but Rosenhaus decided it was best not to say anything further.

They entered the laboratory area, where McCoy was already working, looking over a bio sample. "Dr. McCoy, I see you've started without me," he said with what he hoped was his best smile.

McCoy didn't even look up as he snapped, "Under the circumstances, I didn't think waiting would be

such a good idea considering people might *die* in the interim."

Rosenhaus blinked. "I'm sorry, Doctor, I was just trying—"

Looking up from his sample, McCoy waved his hand. "No, never mind, I'm the one who should be apologizing. Been a *long* day. Let me show you what we've gotten from the surface."

They started going over the data, which McCoy had called up on the lab desk monitor. Rosenhaus sat in front of the monitor—McCoy, for some reason, preferred to stand.

"What the virus does," McCoy explained as he paced back and forth on the other side of the lab desk, "is attach itself to the adrenal medulla and starts causing it to generate epinephrine and norepinephrine, independent of the usual stimuli. As far as I can tell, the damn thing actually consumes some of it, but only a minuscule portion of what's generated—maybe ten percent."

Rosenhaus nodded as he peered at the screen. He was grateful for the more clinical analysis. McCoy had translated the diagnosis into lay language for the briefing on the *Constellation*—a necessary survival skill when serving with nonmedicos, as Rosenhaus had learned early on in his Starfleet career—but that gave it an imprecision that irked the younger man. "So the rest of it gets pumped into the system, and eventually the heart rate increases and the heart muscles constrict."

McCoy nodded.

Frowning, Rosenhaus asked, "Have there been any other causes of death besides heart failure?"

"Cause of death is the virus, not—"

He waved a hand. "I realize that, but there are other side effects of pumping epi and norepi into the system. I mean, lipolysis and pupil dilation isn't usually fatal, but what about constricting of blood vessels? Just from a purely mathematical standpoint, some of these people should have died from a burst blood vessel rather than their heart giving out."

"I see what you're saying," McCoy said with another nod. "Some people do have stronger hearts but weaker blood vessels." He rubbed his chin. "Computer, call up the autopsy reports from Kurkjian Memorial Hospital and Sierra City Medical Center."

"Working."

"Are any of the specific causes of death *not* heart failure?"

A brief pause, then: *"Negative."*

Rosenhaus snorted. "The odds of that are *real* slim."

McCoy gave him an annoyed look. "Thank you, Doctor, for stating the obvious. Computer, were any of the people autopsied checked into the medical facility prior to dying?"

"Affirmative."

"How many?"

"Two."

"Put their records on screen at this station."

Rosenhaus moved his chair over so McCoy could stand next to him and they both could see the monitor screen.

"Look at this," McCoy said, pointing to one part of the screen. "The norepi count is fifteen percent lower

than the epi count. That accounts for why it's always been heart problems—epi is what contracts the heart muscles and increases the rate. Norepi constricts blood vessels, but that isn't in as high a concentration."

"The virus probably only consumes norepi, then." Rosenhaus leaned back in his chair. "Can we inject norepi directly into the virus itself, maybe?"

McCoy shook his head. "That's already been tried. Do me a favor, son—read over *all* the reports before giving me diagnoses?"

That was the third time McCoy had snapped at Rosenhaus, and he wasn't even apologizing anymore. *Maybe working with a Starfleet veteran isn't all it's cracked up to be,* he thought sourly.

Over the course of the next several hours, they continued to pore over the data. On several occasions, Rosenhaus had a breakthrough, only to have McCoy shoot it down—either as something already tried on Proxima or as not practical.

"I *still* think that a kerylene solution would do the trick," he insisted.

McCoy closed his eyes. "Kerylene turns dopamine toxic—"

"In only five percent of the cases. It's an acceptable—"

Slamming his hand on the desk, McCoy shouted, "There is no such thing as an acceptable loss—not in *my* sickbay! Is that understood?"

"What if the alternative is death?"

"My God, man, we've barely scratched the surface!

Maybe—*maybe*—I'd accept kerylene as a last resort, but we're nowhere *near* that yet!"

Rosenhaus took a deep breath. He tried to keep his voice as calm as McCoy's was hysterical. "Fine, but I think we may want to consider synthesizing some just in case it becomes a last-resort situation. If you won't, I'll have the *Constellation* lab do it."

"You want to waste your people's time, be my guest." He got up.

"Where are you going?"

Before McCoy could answer, the computer beeped. Rosenhaus turned to see a status display on the monitor. "Finally! We've now got *all* the medical records from the planet. Their computer must be at least three or four decades old to take this long."

"I'm sure they'll be heartbroken at your disapproval," McCoy muttered. "To answer your question, I'm heading down to the planet. I need to take a look at some of the current patients—maybe see if one of 'em can be brought up here."

"Are any of them stable enough for transport?" Rosenhaus asked.

"Even if they were, I wouldn't go scrambling a sick person's molecules all over creation. But that's what shuttles are for."

"That'll take *hours*. Doctor, we've got all the reports, and we can do simulations here without disturbing a live patient."

"What the hell're they teaching you at Starfleet Medical these days, boy, medicine or computer programming?"

"They teach us medicine," Rosenhaus said, standing up, "and I'm really getting tired of your attitude, Dr. McCoy. I'm a certified physician, just like you. I'm a chief medical officer on a starship, just like you. I'd appreciate being treated with something other than condescension. Or, at the very least, not being called 'boy.' I think I've earned *that* much at least."

McCoy's face did soften a bit. "I'm sorry—that was uncalled for, Doctor. Crises tend to bring out my unprofessional side. There's a commanding officer and a halfbreed Vulcan on this ship that can quote you chapter and verse on *that*." He took a breath. "As for the rest of it—the computer models we can build are based on guesses and hundred-year-old archaeological digs. Call me old-fashioned, but I prefer to work with the real thing. Besides, anything we *do* come up with will need to be tested on a live patient eventually, and I'd rather do that here, seeing as how down on Proxima they're having riots and all."

Rosenhaus found he couldn't argue with that.

After McCoy left, Rosenhaus went over every single patient, every single treatment that was tried (and failed). He was proud of the fact that everything that had been tried was something he had thought of independently. In addition, several things he *did* think of weren't tried at all, though McCoy had rejected each for a different reason.

The obvious solution was to "starve" the virus of norepi, but all the usual methods of suppressing the adrenal gland didn't work—the virus fought past them or prevented them. The one exception was the most gen-

eral method: sedation. Unfortunately, people couldn't just be kept sedated forever, and as each dose wore off, a higher dose of the sedative was required to achieve the same effect. Eventually, the patient would build up an immunity and sedative would be useless. Worse, the virus didn't "starve" as such. Even without norepi, it continued to live on in the adrenal gland, in as sedated a state as the rest of the host body.

What was more bizarre was that there was no obvious way to track how the virus got into the patients' systems. All indications were that it just materialized in the adrenal gland as if transported there.

Maybe it was, he thought. "Computer, call up all existing records of the Malkus Artifacts." Rosenhaus spent the next hour reading through the dryest scientific report he'd ever seen—*why do they let Vulcans write these things?* he wondered plaintively—and found that his analogy may have been apt. From studies of the Zalkat Union records found on Beta Aurigae a hundred years previous, beaming a virus right into a person was definitely within the realm of possibility for one of the Malkus Artifacts.

They need to find whoever's doing this, and fast. Then he sighed. *That's Masada's problem. Mine is to figure out how to stop this.*

Another possible solution was to poison the norepi in such a way that consuming it would be fatal to the virus. The problem was that every known method of doing so was equally fatal to the person hosting the virus.

Then it hit him. *Vrathev. I'm such an idiot.*

He dug through the notes he'd brought over from

the *Constellation. C'mon, c'mon,* he thought as he riffled through the not-as-organized-as-he-wanted-it-to-be pile, *I know you're in here somewhere—aha!*

Reading through the notes he now had called up on the screen, he smiled. *Damn, you're good, Lew.*

Back at the Academy, in his final year, Rosenhaus had aided in the treatment of an Andorian cadet named Vrathev zh'Ethre. She had been suffering from psychotic berserker fits that had no discernible cause. It turned out that her own adrenal gland equivalent—what the Andorians called their *parafra*—was being hypercharged in a similar way to what this virus did to humans.

"Computer," he said, excited for the first time since he came on board the *Enterprise,* "create a new program." He immediately had the computer run a simulation to see how the treatment used on Vrathev would work on the virus. When he was done, he asked, "Time necessary to run program?"

"Two hours, fourteen minutes."

For some reason, that prompted a yawn in Rosenhaus. That, in turn, prompted the realization that he hadn't gotten a good night's sleep the previous night, having been awakened by the Proximan distress call. *Might not be a bad idea to take a nap.*

He checked the time, and saw that it had been four hours since McCoy left. Shrugging, he called out to Chapel.

"Yes, Doctor?" she said with an air of both demureness and professionalism for which Rosenhaus was grateful, since it meant she wasn't holding his dopey comments from earlier against him.

"I've got a program running that's going to take two-and-a-quarter hours. I'm gonna grab a quick nap. Wake me if Dr. McCoy comes back, okay?"

"Of course, Doctor."

Rosenhaus hesitated as he got up from the chair. "Uh, is there any word from McCoy?"

"He reached the surface safely, but he hasn't checked in with me since. I can double-check with Lieutenant Uhura on the bridge, if you like."

Shaking his head, he said, "No, don't bother. I'm sure he's fine. Is there a free bed in sickbay I can sack out on?"

"Of course, Doctor. Help yourself."

Nodding, Rosenhaus exited the lab and went two rooms over to the exam room. He lay down on one of the two beds.

The biomonitor immediately fired up. Sighing, Rosenhaus said, "Computer, discontinue bioreadings."

"Disabling of medical functions requires authorization by chief medical officer."

"Authorization Rosenhaus-426-Gamma."

"Authorization not recognized."

Again, he sighed. *You're not on the* Constellation, *Lew. Computer doesn't know you from Schweitzer.*

This was a quandary. The only bed that didn't show bioreadings was the exercise bed across the room, but that was too small to lie down on. "Computer, can you at least mute the noise?"

"Negative."

A third sigh. "Nurse!" he called out.

After a moment, Chapel came into the exam room. "Yes, Doctor?"

"I'm going to beam back to the *Constellation* until the program's run. I need some familiarity for a bit."

Chapel actually smiled at that. "I understand completely, Doctor. I'll have Lieutenant Uhura contact you if Dr. McCoy comes back before the program finishes running."

Viewing that smile as a good sign, Rosenhaus returned it. "That's very good of you, Nurse Chapel. Thanks."

As he walked through the sickbay doors, he had a mild spring in his step. *I'm willing to bet that the Andorian treatment will do the trick. And then, once I've saved the day, maybe I can convince the lovely nurse to let me make up for my gaffe with dinner. . . .*

"I can assure you that we are doing everything we can to ensure that a cure is found quickly, and that your lives can return to normal operation. I repeat, this is a temporary measure. For now, we ask that people stay in their homes unless they have sanctioned duties. A list of those duties is readily available on the information net. Please carry identification with you at all times."

She stared at the image of the young man in the golden Starfleet uniform in something like shock.

They've declared martial law. Amazing.

She hadn't thought that her oh-so-esteemed former colleagues would do such a thing.

But then, maybe they didn't. Maybe Starfleet just waltzed in and took over.

Not that it mattered. They could impose curfews, restrict movement, quell riots—none of it could possibly have made the tiniest difference.

Because she had the power.

She walked over to her gift. It sat on her kitchen table, pulsating with the green glow that she first saw on Pirenne's Peak.

She still didn't know where the gift came from or who built it. Images had flooded her mind of strange alien beings who died in odd ways, thanks to this gift, but ultimately the images had no meaning to her, no context.

It didn't matter. It provided her with deliverance. It provided her with vengeance.

She loved the irony. Not only did it instantly make people fatally ill, but the illness also had hard-to-identify symptoms. Nobody would even know there was anything wrong until they were dead.

Dead by her hand.

The only drawback was that it could only do so much at once. She had hoped to destroy everyone on Proxima in one shot, as it were, but that had proven beyond the gift's capabilities. Only a few hundred had contracted the virus before the green glow dimmed.

At first, she had been furious. Killing a random group of people in Sierra City hardly satiated her need for revenge. *Everyone* had to die. More to the point, everyone had to *suffer.*

Then the green glow had come back. By that time, people had started to die, their hearts exploding like photon torpedoes in people's ribcages. Her only regret was that she had been unable to stand over their bodies

as they expired. She wanted everyone's last sight to be of her. She wanted them to know why they were dead.

When the glow returned, she used it again, this time on everyone occupying the Government Center, which had called an emergency session.

Now it was glowing again.

Who shall I destroy next?

The voice on the newsfeed droned on. *"Medical scanners are being distributed to all residents of Proxima. Distribution schedules are posted on the nets as well. Please use these scanners regularly, but do not tamper with them. They have been specifically calibrated to seek out the virus. If a scan turns up positive, report to the nearest hospital* immediately *for treatment."*

She turned in anger. They had identified the virus? They were treating it? Worse, they were now giving people the means to find it?

Damn them!

She had originally considered targeting police headquarters. *With Starfleet involved, that won't work anymore. So who—?*

Then she realized what she had to do. *Oh, this is too perfect.*

The annoying Starfleet face went away, to be replaced by the usual newscaster. *"That was Captain James T. Kirk of the* U.S.S. Enterprise, *one of the two starships that has declared martial law on Proxima. It should be added that the first decree made by Kirk and the* U.S.S. Constellation's *Commodore Matthew Decker was that the news sources would be allowed to*

continue uncensored. To repeat, medical scanners are being handed ou—"

She turned off the feed. Infecting both ships with the virus wasn't possible—at least not at once. But she could take down one of them . . .

The computer diligently woke Lewis Rosenhaus up two hours after he'd hit the pillow in his quarters. As usual, he was wide awake in an instant. First Rosenhaus checked in with the lab, where Technician Shickele assured him that the synthesizing of kerylene was proceeding apace. *McCoy may not want to be prepared for every eventuality, but I'm not going to make the same mistake.*

He then contacted the bridge and asked the communications officer to put him through to Nurse Chapel on the *Enterprise.*

"Yes, Doctor, what is it?"

Rosenhaus blinked. Gone were the demure tones of the woman whom Rosenhaus had embarrassed with his verbal blundering about Roger Korby. Now she sounded as excitable as a Klingon. "Uh, I wanted to make sure my program—"

"Yes, your program's all done, and no, Dr. McCoy hasn't come back on board yet. I would've told you that, Doctor, I did promise you that. I can assure you, I'm the type that—"

A fist of ice clenching his heart, Rosenhaus said, "Nurse, do you have a medical tricorder on you?"

"What the hell kind of ridiculous question is that? Of course I do, but I hardly—"

"Scan yourself, please."

"Why should I—?"

"Nurse, *please,* run a scan on yourself."

Even as Chapel spoke, Rosenhaus could hear the telltale sound of the Feinberger running over Chapel's form as it read her biological data. *"Dammit, Doctor, I really don't have time for—Oh my God."*

"You have the virus, right?"

"Yes, I—"

Rosenhaus got up from his bed and put a fresh shirt on. "Where are you?"

"Sickbay. Doctor, I'm so sorry, I—"

"Never mind that. Run a scan on some other people—pick crew members at random, then report back to me."

"Yes, Doctor."

She signed off, then he contacted the bridge. "This is Dr. Rosenhaus again. Put me through to Dr. McCoy, Priority One."

After a few moments, a familiar, cranky voice came on the line. *"This better be damned—"*

"Doctor, I believe the *Enterprise* has been infected."

A pause. *"What!?"*

"I'm back on the *Constellation.* I left your ship two hours ago while I had a program running and took a quick nap. And before you bite my head off, I only got an hour's sleep before the distress call from Proxima came."

"That's one hour more than I got," McCoy grumbled, *"but that doesn't matter. What happened?"*

"I contacted your Nurse Chapel, and she sounded more excitable than usual. I asked her to scan herself,

and she had the virus. I asked her to scan some random crew members to be sure, but—"

"But whoever's doing this probably targeted the whole ship. Damn." McCoy sighed. *"Jim's gone and declared martial law, so I'd better let him know, too. At least he's safe down here, and Spock's on the* Constellation *with your pal Masada."*

Running a hand through his shaggy red hair, Rosenhaus said, "We'll need to declare a quarantine on the *Enterprise*. We can't let anyone on or off."

"Don't be an idiot! First thing we verified is that this isn't contractible unless you're targeted by that blessed artifact."

Rosenhaus cursed his own stupidity. "Sorry. Force of habit. Not used to a disease that doesn't wipe out the whole room."

"None of us are, son," McCoy said in a surprisingly conciliatory voice. *"I sent up a woman on a shuttlecraft to the* Enterprise. *She volunteered to be our guinea pig. I'll have it divert to the* Constellation. *You'll need to go over to the* Enterprise, *verify this and retrieve all the data, then—"*

Another voice interrupted. *"Bridge to Dr. Rosenhaus."*

"Rosenhaus here."

"Doctor, I have Nurse Chapel on the Enterprise."

"Put her through, please." Rosenhaus took a very deep breath. *Here it comes . . .*

"Chapel here."

"Nurse, I have Dr. McCoy on the line, also. What's the verdict?"

"The ship's been completely infected. I've got Lieutenant Sulu here as well—he's in charge of the bridge, with the captain and Mr. Spock both off-ship. I've informed him as well."

Another voice, this one deep and male, said, *"You know more about this disease than I do, Doc. What do you recommend?"*

McCoy's voice was surprisingly gentle. *"I hate to do this, Hikaru, but the only treatment we've been able to come up with is sedation. At that, it's only a temporary measure."*

"Not only that," Rosenhaus said, scratching his cheek, "it'll take forever to administer the sedative."

"That's not an issue," Sulu said. *"We can flood all decks with anaesthezine gas."*

"You can do that?" Rosenhaus asked, incredulous.

"Of course," Sulu said, as if it were the most natural thing in the galaxy. *"How long do we have, Doc?"*

"What do you mean?"

"Well, before we implement any kind of mass sedation, I'd like to check with the captain, and Mr. Scott will need to put the ship on automatic so we don't fall into the atmosphere when we're all asleep."

"You don't need to do that," Rosenhaus said. "Some relief crew can come over from the *Constellation*."

"Won't they get the disease?" Sulu asked.

"Of course not. The disease isn't contractible." Rosenhaus tried not to sound quite so haughty, but he still felt foolish after his previous blunder.

"All right, I'll have to coordinate with Commander Takeshewada," Sulu said with surprising calm, consid-

ering that he had a virus that was pumping adrenaline into his body at a great rate. *"I'll need at least an hour to get everyone to report to their quarters and set things up for the replacements. Our best bet is to keep the relief crew on the bridge—as long as they don't have to do anything too complicated, they can run the ship from there. And then we'll flood every other deck."*

"Sounds like it should work," McCoy said.

"I agree."

"I wasn't asking your approval!" McCoy then took a deep breath. *"Sorry, Doctor. Just goes against the grain to put your crewmates to sleep."*

"As long as the sleep isn't permanent," Rosenhaus said. He was starting to understand why McCoy was so snappish. He hated the idea of being helpless. *I guess we all deal with that in our own way. Me, I prefer to let it drive me to greater heights.*

Within the hour predicted by Lieutenant Sulu, the entire *Enterprise* staff had reported to their quarters, prepared for a very deep sleep. The chief engineer—an obscenely excitable man, though Rosenhaus supposed the virus could have been responsible for that—had routed all functions to the bridge. Takeshewada had roused the *Constellation*'s gamma-shift bridge crew out of their beds and they had taken their bleary-eyed places at the different-yet-familiar consoles. Rosenhaus had also brought his junior physician over to keep an eye on things, since the *Enterprise*'s medical staff was going to be just as incapacitated as everyone else.

Then, finally, the entire *Enterprise,* save the bridge, was put to sleep.

Rosenhaus had, of course, beamed off the *Enterprise* at that point, after verifying that neither he nor the relief crew had contracted the virus. Captain Kirk had, he understood, made some sort of speech to his people telling them something no doubt inspirational and encouraging and downright tiresome, but Rosenhaus hadn't bothered to listen. He was too busy gathering his notes.

When he returned to the *Constellation,* he saw that a woman under sedation had been placed on a biobed.

He summoned Emil Jazayerli, his head nurse. "Who is that woman, Nurse?"

Jazayerli squinted at the biobed, a habit in the older man that Rosenhaus found almost as annoying as the nurse's tendency to run his index finger and thumb over his thick black mustache. "That's the woman that arrived with the *Galileo,* Doctor."

Blinking, Rosenhaus said, "The *Galileo?* There's *another* ship in orbit?"

"No, Doctor, the *Galileo* is an *Enterprise* shuttlecraft." He walked over and picked up the woman's chart, then held it out for Rosenhaus. "I believe she's a Proximan volunteer with the disease."

"Oh, right," Rosenhaus said, taking the chart, "Dr. McCoy's guinea pig." He peered at the chart, which showed that her name was Mya Braker, she served as the Representative for the Ninth District, and she'd gotten the disease at the same time as everyone else in the Government Center. "All right," he said, handing the chart back to Jazayerli, "keep an eye on her EEG

and her epi and norepi count. If any of them change in even the slightest degree, let me know immediately."

"Of course, Doctor."

It irked Rosenhaus that Jazayerli never called him, "sir." It probably wouldn't have bothered him all that much, except that he always called him "Doctor" in a tone of voice that indicated that the nurse didn't think much of the title. *Hardly the right attitude for a subordinate.*

Sighing, he went into the lab. *Maybe I can convince Decker to let me transfer him off when this is all over.*

As he sat down at the desk, he called up the results of his test—which, in all the hugger-mugger on the *Enterprise,* he hadn't had the chance to thoroughly look over.

After reading over the results, his pale face broke into a huge grin. *I think we've done it!*

He contacted the bridge. "Is Dr. McCoy still on the surface?"

The communications officer—a friendly young lieutenant named George Howard—nodded. *"He's meeting with the commodore and Captain Kirk right now. You need to raise him?"*

He was about to say yes, then changed his mind. "No, he can find out when everyone else does," he said with a smile.

Frowning, Howard asked, *"Find out what?"*

"I've got a good line on a cure. I'm going to test it now."

The communications officer's face split into a grin. *"Lew, if that's true, it'll be the first good news all day."*

Rosenhaus belatedly realized that gossiping with

the communications officer was probably not such a hot idea. "Well, keep it to yourself, George. I still haven't tested it yet."

"No problem, Lew. My hailing frequencies are closed till you say otherwise."

"Good," Rosenhaus said with a smile. "Sickbay out."

Howard's face faded, to be replaced by the computer simulation. Rosenhaus looked it all over one more time. Briefly, he contemplated waiting until he could have a second set of eyes look them over, then decided that wasn't practical. His junior physician was back on the *Enterprise,* and McCoy was still on Proxima. *Besides, he'll probably just come up with sixteen reasons why it won't work,* he thought sourly.

He went over to the synthesizing lab, where the stout form of Norma Shickele sat hunched over a computer terminal. "Get off my back, L.R.," she said in her booming voice, "you'll have your damn kerylene soon enough."

"Hold off on that for a minute," he said, forcing his voice to remain calm. He *hated* being called "L.R.," which was, of course, why Shickele insisted on doing so. Rosenhaus also knew he couldn't afford to antagonize the lab techs because he relied on them in situations—well, much like this one, so he had to be on his best behavior in her presence. She knew that, too, and so always did everything she could to goad him. So far, he hadn't risen to the bait.

Maybe I can get Decker to transfer her along with Jazayerli, he thought wistfully.

He continued. "I've got a serum. I need you to prepare a test batch."

"You said the kerylene was priority."

Patiently, Rosenhaus said, "This is *higher* priority. The kerylene has the potential to be a last-resort cure. This could be the actual cure." Shickele, he had learned, preferred to have things explained in detail. Just giving an order and expecting her to do as she was told was never sufficient.

She reached out one pudgy hand. "Fine. You're the doctor, after all."

Sighing with relief, Rosenhaus handed her the data. The words, "you're the doctor," said in that snide tone that Shickele had probably spent most of her adult life perfecting, usually signified the end of the conversation.

Grateful, Rosenhaus headed back into the main part of sickbay, and once again looked over Braker's chart. Everything seemed to be in order—but for the presence of the virus, she'd be in perfect health.

The doors opened to reveal Commander Takeshewada, holding a hand to her forehead. "Got anything for a headache, Doc?"

Smiling at the small woman, Rosenhaus said, "Of course. Follow me." As he led her into the dispensary, he asked, "Rough day?"

"Rough *hour.* First I had to rearrange the shift schedule, since our third shift is now off on the *Enterprise,* then I spent twenty minutes going at it hammer and tongs with Matt."

"The commodore?" Rosenhaus asked, surprised, as he fetched an analgesic from the cabinet.

"No," Takeshewada snapped, "Matt the quartermaster. Of *course* the commodore." She sighed. "Damned stubborn ass of a man, he is."

He handed her the pills. "What was the argument about?"

"Martial law, pros and cons. Thank you," she added as she took the pills. She swallowed them quickly. "I understand the rationale behind it, but I've always been leery of outside authorities waltzing in and taking over. Besides, Kirk lived on Tarsus IV."

Takeshewada spoke as if that planet should mean something, but Rosenhaus hadn't a clue to its significance. "Okay," he said, hoping not to sound too foolish.

Chuckling, Takeshewada said, "I keep forgetting how young you are." Quickly, the first officer told a story about a colony world, a poisoned food supply, and an insane governor.

"My God," Rosenhaus said. He had had no idea that something like that could even happen in the Federation. "And Kirk was there for that?"

"As a teenager, yes. And *he* was the one who suggested declaring martial law today. According to Matt, he wants to 'do it right,' so to speak. Still, I can't help but think of the old saying about abused children growing up to become abusers." She took a very deep breath.

"Well, wouldn't the commodore keep him in line?"

Takeshewada pursed her lips. Rosenhaus didn't like the expression it formed on her face. It was a bizarre combination of frightened and concerned. "Between you and me, Doc? The problem with Matt Decker is

that he's impulsive. Once he gets an idea in his head, he tends to jump into it feet first and figure out the consequences later. He's made it work for him so far through a combination of stubbornness and dumb luck. I just hope today isn't the day his luck runs out."

Grinning, Rosenhaus said, "Not likely. After all, *I'm* on the job, and I think I've got us something."

Eyes widening, Takeshewada said, "Oh?"

"I've got the lab synthesizing a serum based on a project I was involved with at Starfleet Medical. Computer sims show that it should work. Dr. McCoy sent up a volunteer from the surface, so as soon as it's ready, I can test it on her."

Smiling a small smile, the commander said, "Best news I've heard all day, Doc. Hell, wish you'd told me sooner, it probably would've taken the headache away and saved you a couple of pills."

"Lab to Rosenhaus. Your magic potion is ready, L.R."

Thumbing the intercom, Rosenhaus said, "Thank you, Shickele," in what he hoped wasn't a cranky voice. "I'll be right there."

Now Takeshewada's smile was wider. "'L.R.'?"

"Don't ask." Rosenhaus shuddered. The last thing he wanted to do was get into the sickbay politics he'd been dropped into the middle of. *Then again, she is the first officer* . . . "Or rather, don't ask now. I'd actually like to sit down with you and talk about some—issues I have regarding sickbay."

"Fine by me," she said with a nod. "We'll set something up—after you perform your miracle."

Rosenhaus's Miracle. I like that. "That's fine, Commander."

Heading for the door, she said, "Thanks for the pills—and keep me posted."

"I will."

With a spring in his step, Rosenhaus headed back to the lab. Even the dark look Shickele gave him couldn't spoil his mood.

"Can I get back to the kerylene now, L.R.?"

He considered telling her not to bother—the serum was bound to work—but one didn't wish to take chances. "Yes, please do."

"You're the doctor."

Damn right I am, he thought triumphantly as he took the hypo that Shickele had prepared, and went to Braker's bedside. He checked to make sure the dosage on the hypo was set properly, took a deep breath, and applied the hypo to Braker's neck.

Then he let out the breath he was holding.

Over the course of the next hour, he and Jazayerli monitored Braker's progress, watching as the virus's attempts to produce epi and norepi were frustrated by the serum. *Yes!* he thought triumphantly. Where sedation simply put the virus to "sleep" in the same way it retarded all other bodily functions, this serum actively inhibited the virus without doing any damage to the patient.

It works!

The doors opened to Dr. McCoy. "What's this I hear about a cure?"

Rosenhaus blinked. "How'd you find out? I only

just tested it an hour ago." He indicated the medical scanner. "Take a look."

"The transporter chief mentioned it when I came on board," McCoy said as he approached the scanner.

Sighing, Rosenhaus made a mental note to keep his damn mouth shut next time he talked to George Howard.

Peering at the readout, McCoy said, "Seems to be working. What'd you use?"

"It's a serum that was developed at Starfleet HQ about five years ago to treat an Andorian who was sufferi—"

McCoy looked up sharply. "What!? Dr. Derubbio's treatment? On a *human?*"

"Yes," Rosenhaus said with a smile. "I interned under him when—"

"Doctor!" Jazayerli said in a voice of warning.

Just after the nurse spoke, an alarm went off on the biobed scanner. Rosenhaus looked up to see that Braker was going into cardiac arrest.

"What the hell—? That shouldn't be happening!" Rosenhaus said.

Then both he and McCoy cried, "Cordrazine, two milliliters!" in perfect unison.

Well, Rosenhaus thought dryly, *at least we agree on something.*

Jazayerli prepared a hypo and, to Rosenhaus's annoyance, handed it to McCoy, who applied it to Braker's neck.

Within a moment, her heart started up again. "We've got to flush this damn serum out of her system, now!" McCoy said.

"We don't know that the serum is causing this," Rosenhaus said. "It could be—"

McCoy interrupted. "Nurse, get me eighty CC's of dicloripin." Then he turned to Rosenhaus. "Dave Derubbio's serum is fatal to humans—when it interacts with human blood, it creates xelaxine."

Rosenhaus's face fell. "What?" Xelaxine was toxic to humans. For that matter, it was toxic to Andorians, but it didn't—

Then he thought about the differences between Andorian and human blood, and saw the possible connections.

"Here you go, Doctor," Jazayerli said, handing McCoy the hypo.

As he applied the hypo to Braker, McCoy said, "Didn't you run one of those damned computer simulations you were going on about before?"

"Of *course* I did." Rosenhaus was offended that McCoy would even consider the possibility that he didn't do so. "I tested it on the virus and the gland and it showed—"

McCoy looked up. *"Just* the virus and the gland?"

"What do you mean?" Rosenhaus asked, looking up to see that Braker's vitals were returning to normal.

"They may call 'em artificial intelligence, son, but trust me, they ain't that bright. You tell 'em to test the virus and the gland, that's *all* they'll check! You didn't check how this might affect the blood cells or any of the organs it came into contact with!"

Rosenhaus closed his eyes. "You're right. I didn't— I mean, I—" He sighed. "I'm sorry, Doctor, I—"

"You don't need to apologize to me, you need to

apologize to this woman here," he said, pointing to Braker. "Assuming she lives through this." He sighed. "Assuming we all do, and don't go off half-cocked." McCoy took one last look at Braker's vitals, then ran a Feinberger over her. "Times like this, Doctor, we have to be extra careful—both with what we do and who we say it to. Ships're like small towns. Word spreads like wildfire." He looked up. "And another thing—you don't need to prove anything. You said before that I should treat you with the respect you deserve, and that's fine, but you gotta *earn* the respect." Turning the Feinberger off, he picked up Braker's chart and handed it to Jazayerli. "The virus is still in the gland. Update the chart, please, Nurse."

"Of course, sir."

Rosenhaus sighed. That was the first time he'd ever heard Jazayerli use the word "sir" to refer to a doctor.

"Now then," McCoy said, "let's take a look at this serum. Obviously it made some headway—we just have to figure out how to make it work without killing the patient."

Stunned, Rosenhaus said, "Uh, right."

"Something wrong, Doctor?"

"You're being nice to me. I just almost killed a woman. You spent half the day chewing my head off when I didn't do anything, but now—when you actually have cause to scream at me—you're being calm and reasonable."

Smiling, McCoy said, "Son, all the titles in the world don't mean a damn thing. Yeah, we're both chief medical officers, but at heart, we're just human. Me,

I'm an old country doctor who let his temper get the better of him. You, you're a young kid who made a mistake. Luckily, that mistake wasn't fatal." He put an encouraging hand on the younger man's shoulder. "So let's see what we can do to make the mistake work for us, all right?"

Rosenhuas nodded. "Let's get to work, Doctor."

Chapter Five

"COMMODORE, you're not being reasonable."

Matt Decker rubbed the bridge of his nose between his thumb and forefinger in a futile attempt to stave off the pounding headache he was developing. Normally, he'd call sickbay for a remedy, but his own sickbay staff was presently occupied with the search for a cure, and the local hospitals and dispensaries had much bigger problems right now.

Dealing with the infinite demands of running a colony under siege by disease and terror, however, was combining with his lack of sleep to create a phaser on overload in his sinuses.

Now, topping it all off, he had to deal with a tiresome bureaucrat.

He stared at that bureaucrat's face on the small

viewscreen embedded in the desk he'd taken over. It sat opposite another like desk, which Kirk had taken over, in the small office in the Government Center. The office normally belonged to some government functionary or other. Neither Decker nor the young captain had felt comfortable taking over the office of the late Chief Representative. Besides, they could do the job as easily from here as anywhere else. Indeed, they could have adminstered from orbit, but both of them saw that as precisely the wrong kind of symbolism. They needed to be among the Proximan people if this was to work.

"Mr. Malruse," Decker said, "I'm under no obligation to be reasonable. Proxima is currently in a state of martial law. That means what I say goes. It also gives me broad discretionary powers as to who to say it to and where to put them when they don't do what I say. Am I making myself clear?"

The face on the viewscreen in front of Decker scrunched into a frown. *"Commodore, I have several contracts I need to fulfill. While the current situation is regrettable, I can't just—"*

Decker leaned forward and put on his intimidating look, the one he'd used to good effect on subordinates and his son alike. "I see I'm *not* making myself clear. As of now, you don't have any contracts to fulfill. You don't have a business. All you've got is a mandate from the person running things to take over the supervision of food distribution to the counties of Arafel, New Punjab, and Rivershore. What you've also got is my promise that your not fulfilling this mandate would

be a bad career move. *Now* am I making myself clear?"

Malruse's frown somehow grew deeper, something Decker wouldn't have credited it capable of. *"I don't appreciate threats, Commodore."*

"Oh, this isn't a threat. It's an explanation. So what's it going to be, Mr. Malruse?"

Decker watched as Malruse's face flashed several facial expressions over the course of about three seconds, ranging from anger to annoyance and finally to resignation. *"Very well, Commodore. My people will start taking charge of the food distribution within the hour."*

"Glad to hear it. The person you'll be coordinating with is Ensign Litwack—she's my assistant chief of security. She'll be there to make sure everything goes smoothly." Decker assumed the implication was obvious.

"Of course, Commodore," Malruse said with a sigh, then signed off.

As soon as the screen went dark, the phaser in his sinuses did go on overload. *If I had known that this was going to entail forcing private-sector nincompoops to do public-works projects, I'd've told Kirk to go hang himself.*

That wasn't entirely fair, Decker knew. Most of the slack of public jobs had been taken up by private enterprise with remarkable ease. In some cases, the work was more efficient. But, given the situation, Decker or Kirk had to deal with it only if something went wrong, so he was hyperaware of the few problems and needed

to remind himself of how much was actually going smoothly.

He was about to get some coffee when his communicator beeped twice. *Oh great, now what?* He pulled it out of his belt as he headed for the food slot embedded in the wall. "Decker here."

"Takeshewada here. A ship's just pulled into orbit and you need to talk to the pilot."

"Uh, why ca—?"

"I tried to handle it," Takeshewada said, as usual anticipating him. *"I explained about the quarantine and the dangers and the fact that every second she spends in orbit she risks contracting a fatal disease that we don't have a cure for. I told her about the martial law. I, in fact, went on at great length on the subject of why she needs to beat a hasty retreat out of orbit, if not out of the entire star system. You know what her reply was? 'Let me speak to whoever's in charge.' "*

Decker sighed as he entered the command for coffee into the food slot's panel. "That's me, isn't it?"

"Unless you want to fob this off on Kirk."

"Fob what off on Kirk?" came a voice from the doorway. It was Kirk, returning from his latest state-of-the-colony address to the people. They had agreed early on that Kirk—younger, better looking, and generally less intimidating than Decker—would be the voice of the temporary government to the people of Proxima, and he had been giving those every couple of hours or so. Decker had admired the strategy. It reassured the Proximans that there was somebody in charge—especially since Kirk had made an effort to

put substance in the addresses, specifying what was being done.

To answer the question, Decker said, "Someone in orbit who won't take 'get the hell out of here' for an answer." Back to the communicator, he said, "Have Howard pipe it down here, Number One."

"Have fun."

Decker could picture Takeshewada's not-quite-a-smile in his mind's eye. *I get the feeling I'm in for another fun conversation,* he thought with a sigh.

He went back to his desk, coffee in hand. Kirk came around to stand behind him. Decker was silently grateful for Kirk's presence, as the younger man would likely be a calming influence. Kirk had a certain charisma about him that he used to good effect on people he dealt with. Takeshewada had a similar quality—Decker himself had never had the patience for such things.

The screen lit up to show the face of the most beautiful woman Matt Decker had ever seen in his life.

"You must be Commodore Decker," she said in a voice that sounded like the songs of angels.

"Yes," Kirk said before Decker could reply, "and I'm James T. Kirk. How can we help you?"

"I'm Aidulac, captain of the Sun," she said with a bright smile that seemed to light up the viewscreen. *"I have this problem that I'm sure you two could easily solve."*

"We'll be happy to do anything at all that we can to help you," Kirk said, again cutting Decker off before he could say anything. Not that he minded that

much—he was just happy to be looking into Aidulac's beautiful black eyes.

"I have this cargo that needs to be brought down immediately. That commander on the Constellation *gave me some song and dance about a virus, but I—"*

"It's not a song and dance, I'm afraid," Decker said. "The virus is quite real, and very dangerous. Honestly, you should probably leave orbit as soon as you can for your own safety." He spoke in an urgent tone, as he was actually frightened of the possibility that Aidulac might be harmed by the virus. "Surely your cargo—"

"The items are perishable," Aidulac said, and she pouted in a manner that melted Decker's heart. *"Surely you can at least let me land one shuttle?"*

Kirk asked, "Why not transport it down?"

"It can't be transported. So can you help me, please?"

Decker pried his eyes away from the vision of gloriousness on the screen and turned to look at Kirk. "What do you say, Captain, can we—"

Then he blinked. He realized that he suddenly couldn't recall what Aidulac looked like, even though he'd been looking at her for the past minute. More to the point, his head cleared and he realized just what he'd been thinking during that minute. And then he remembered the *Constellation*'s trip to Pegasus Major.

"Computer, disengage video transmission, now!"

Kirk was aghast as the screen went dark. "Commodore, why did you do that? That poor woman needs our help."

"Commodore, I don't understand, why have you—"

"Don't even think about it, Captain Aidulac. You are hereby instructed to leave orbit, or I will order the *Constellation* to fire on you. Do I make myself clear?"

Kirk grabbed Decker's shoulder. "Commodore, what are you doing? This woman has a simple—"

" 'This woman,' Kirk, is a Siren."

A blank expression came over Kirk's face. "A what?"

"Can I assume," Decker said, addressing himself to the darkened viewscreen, "that the *Sun*'s registry is to the Peladon Affiliation, Captain Aidulac?"

The silence that met the question spoke volumes.

"As I expected. Captain Kirk, maybe you're familiar with the world of Pegasus Major IV. A humanoid race evolved there known as the Peladons, who eventually founded an Affiliation that encompasses the entire solar system. On that planet, there's a sect of specially trained women who can exert great influence on the male of the species—as well as the males of several other species. Vulcan men have proven to be able to overcome it, and Andorians are immune for some reason, but every other species they've encountered that has men in it have succumbed. The first Federation captain to deal with one called them 'Sirens.' "

"Commodore, you're being horribly unfair. I just want—"

"Still there, Aidulac? I'd have thought you'd have obeyed my instructions by now." He took out his communicator. "Decker to *Constellation*. Has the *Sun* left orbit yet?"

"Takeshewada here. Not yet. Orders?"

"Give her two more minutes, Number One, then blast her out of the sky."

Aidulac's voice—now sounding rather petulant, though Decker suspected it was the same tone of voice she used when pouting earlier, he simply was interpreting it differently now—came through the desk's speakers. *"There'll be no need for violence, Commodore. But I can assure you, I have friends at Starfleet—"*

"All men, I'm sure," Decker muttered.

"—and they're going to hear about this. Trust me, these aren't men you want to have as enemies."

"They'll have to get in line, Captain," Decker said with a snort, thinking back on all the people he'd pissed off in his decades of service. "Proxima out."

As he cut off the connection, Takeshewada said, *"She's leaving orbit now, Commodore. She was a Siren, wasn't she?"*

Decker blinked. "You knew?"

"It was a guess. I wasn't entirely sure. Best way to be sure was to gauge your response. If you gave in, I'd know for sure."

Sighing, Decker said, "Remind me to yell at you for that later."

"Of course, sir." Again, Decker could envision his first officer's not-a-smile. *"Constellation out."*

Closing his communicator and directing several unkind thoughts in Takeshewada's direction, Decker turned to look at Kirk. The captain had an angry look on his face.

"I'm sorry, Commodore. I can't believe I fell for such a—a cheap parlor trick."

"Easy, Kirk, it's no parlor trick. The Peladons have been breeding and training Sirens for centuries. Hell, I *knew* about 'em, and I almost gave in."

Kirk shook his head. "Still, it's not a weakness a commanding officer can afford."

Shrugging, Decker said, "Maybe. But the good COs figure out how to pay it off anyhow." Decker leaned back in his chair. "So, how'd the address go?"

"Well enough," Kirk said after a hesitation. The captain obviously didn't want to change the subject, but Decker had always thought of recriminations as being generally useless, self-recrimination even more so. His mindset was more toward solving the problem than apportioning blame.

Before Kirk could elaborate, Decker's communicator beeped.

Sighing, Decker muttered, "Does it ever end?"

"Never soon enough," Kirk replied with a smile.

With a snort, Decker opened the communicator. "Decker here."

A cacophany of noise erupted from the communicator—people shouting, mostly, and the occasional sound of soft impacts. *"Vascogne here, Commodore,"* said Decker's security chief. *"We've got a situation."*

"You still at SCMC?"

"Yes, sir." Vascogne had just reported everything being quiet at the Sierra City Medical Center a mere hour earlier.

What have they done this *time?* Decker wondered. "What kind of situation?"

"Somebody started a rumor that they found a cure

up on the Constellation. *Now everyone's trying to get into the hospital to get it. Request permission to pacify the crowd, Commodore."*

Decker's eyes grew wide. Vascogne wouldn't have made the request if he thought there was a better alternative. For a security chief, the middle-aged lieutenant was remarkably nonaggressive. "Is that your recommendation, Lieutenant?"

There was a pause, and an "oof" sound could be heard through the speaker amidst the growing crowd noise. *"It's my opinion, sir, that no other option is viable."*

"Commodore, wait," Kirk said before Decker could give the order. "I'd like to try something else."

I really hate my job, Lieutenant Etienne Vascogne thought as he pulled the large Proximan off his leg.

"Keep these people back!" he screamed at his people, who were mixed in with some local police.

Should've joined the police force back home on Gammac like Uncle Claude wanted me to, he thought as he awaited the arrival of his commanding officer.

Vascogne was glad that Captain Kirk had apparently come up with some kind of alternative to shooting these poor people down. He hadn't been able to come up with a better plan of his own, and stunning a large crowd was infinitely preferable, to his mind, to said large crowd stomping all over him. The people were pressing up against the cordon with such force, Vascogne couldn't tell whether it was his own sweat he smelled or that of the person shouting epithets into his face.

Most of the cries of the people in that crowd were so much white noise, but certain phrases kept cropping up: "We want the cure!" "Give us the cure!" "Stop holding out on us!" "Cure *now!*" Some held signs with similar sentiments. Despite himself, Vascogne was impressed with how quickly the signs had been put together, given that the rumors had started less than an hour earlier.

Suddenly, an amplified voice blared out over the crowd. "Please, ladies and gentlemen, there *is no cure!*"

Vascogne allowed himself an instant to turn around, and he saw both Decker and Captain Kirk standing at the hospital entrance. He wondered briefly how the hell they got there, and then realized that they must have transported. *That's quite the loud crowd,* he thought, *if they can drown out a transporter. Either that or I'm just getting old . . .*

The crowd noise abated slightly at Kirk's utterance, but not much. "Don't gimme that!" "We *know* there's a cure!" "They told us you had it!" "We need it!"

"I can assure you that people are working around the clock to find a cure for this plague—but whatever you've heard, it's just not true!" Kirk raised his hands as if he were trying to push the crowd back. "Now please, return to your homes—your families. I promise you, the *minute* we find a cure, we will be distributing it to everyone as fast as we can, but until then—"

"Liar!" "We want it *now!*" "You're never gonna give it to us!"

"If you want, I can have the doctors working on the problem give you an update themselves. But right now they're working diligently—both the medical staffs of

the *Enterprise* and the *Constellation, and* the acting surgeon general of Proxima."

"You want to kill us all!" "I bet you're not even working on it!" "Liar!"

Kirk looked directly at the person who called him a liar. "I'm not lying to you! I have no *reason* to lie to you! All I have to do is give one simple order, and these security guards and Proximan police will fire their weapons and leave you all lying stunned in the street. Or one of our ships can do the same thing from orbit. But I don't want to do that to you—because *you don't deserve that.* You *deserve* the truth—you *deserve* to not have to live in fear that you may be the next one to contract the disease—you *deserve* not to be treated like criminals in your own home. That's why we've been keeping you all updated—so you *know* that we're doing *everything we can* to help you! We *will* get through this crisis—I *know* we will. All it will take is patience on your part. Give us a chance to *prove* ourselves."

He looked out over the crowd, seeming as if he was trying to look each person in the eye, even though that wasn't really possible. Despite himself, Vascogne admired the rhetorical technique. *Guess they're teaching public speaking at Captain School these days,* he thought wryly.

"Whoever's doing this to you *wants* this. Whoever's doing this *wants* you all at each other's throats—fighting each other like animals, rioting like maniacs. This virus is being used as a weapon of terror—and the best way for you to fight back is *not* to let it change anything! The best way to fight this battle is to *let us do*

our jobs—and to go on doing yours. Show whoever's attacking you that you *won't* let this stop you—*won't* let their cowardly attack turn you into savages."

Now he seemed to be looking at all of them. There was a pleading look in his eyes—and, at the same time, a very tired one.

"Please—go home. We *will* inform you the *minute* there's a cure."

As Kirk's speech had gone on, the crowd had slowly quieted down, and had just as slowly calmed. Shouters had shut up; people gesturing and holding up signs had let their arms fall, the signs lowered or dropped to the ground; those rushing the cordon of security and police had ceased their forward motion.

Then what had been a furious, amorphous blob of humanity gradually became a group of individuals slumping their dispirited way home. The captain's words had broken the mob spirit.

Vascogne just hoped it was replaced with something—well, *calmer.* His cynical side was quite sure that said replacement would not be permanent unless a cure was found, and damn soon.

As his people and the Proximan police kept an eye on the erstwhile mob and guided them away from the SCMC, Vascogne approached the captain, standing next to Decker. "Nice speech."

Kirk blew out a sharp breath. "Thank you."

Smiling, Decker said, "I especially liked all the dramatic pauses."

"Just fumbling for words, Commodore," Kirk said with a smile.

"I gotta say," Vascogne said, running a hand over his bald head, "I didn't think anything short of phaser fire would stop that crowd."

"It was certainly *my* first choice," Decker said.

Kirk took a breath. "No offense, Commodore, but—well, weapons fire is what Kodos would have done. For years I thought of martial law as inherently evil because of what Kodos did. But don't you see?" He clenched his fists. "This is our chance to show that it *can* be a source of good if it's used properly."

"Yeah, well, from your mouth to these people's ears," Vascogne muttered. "What I want to know is how that rumor got started in the first place."

Decker shook his head. "Situation like this, rumors are flying all over the damn place. I'm sure half the people on the planet are convinced that Starfleet made this up so we could declare martial law and take over."

Taking out his communicator, Kirk said, "We'll just have to prove them wrong, won't we, Commodore? Kirk to *Constellation*."

"Constellation *here*."

"Put me through to Dr. McCoy, please."

After a moment, another voice came through the communicator's tinny speaker. *"McCoy here. What is it, Jim?"*

"Progress report, Doctor. How goes the search for a cure?"

"Slower the more I talk to you."

"Sorry, Bones," Kirk said with a small smile. "I'm going to need one of you to give an address to the people down here—fill them in on your progress."

"I don't have time to be giving press conferences. Besides, that's how rumors get started, and we've got enough of that going on here."

Frowning, Kirk asked, "What do you mean?"

"Ah, it's nothing. Rosenhaus thought he found a cure and made the mistake of telling someone before he tested it."

Vascogne almost groaned out loud. He knew how fast the rumor mill on the *Constellation* could function. Within two-and-a-half seconds of Rosenhaus saying he found the cure—and knowing the young doctor, he probably sounded supremely confident as he said it—the whole ship probably knew about it. That could just as easily have spread to the planet through one of Vascogne's own people.

"Bones, does that mean—?"

"It means we're on a track, Jim, but I don't have any idea whether it's the right track, or how far we have to go on it. I'll keep you posted. McCoy out."

Decker regarded Kirk with a quizzical look. "Kirk, I can't help noticing that that doctor of yours didn't actually agree to give a statement."

"He thinks it'll distract from his work. All things considered, it's probably best to let him proceed as he sees fit. Perhaps your Dr. Rosenhaus can speak at our next state-of-the-planet address?"

Vascogne rolled his eyes. "Like the doc needs a reason to feed his ego."

Chuckling, Decker said, "Don't worry, Vascogne, I'm sure we'll all work to make sure he doesn't live it down."

Chapter Six

GUILLERMO MASADA blinked as he entered the sensor room and saw Lt. Commander Spock sitting at one of the consoles. "What're you doing here?"

Spock's right eyebrow climbed up his forehead. "I assume that is a rhetorical outburst and not an actual request for information?"

Chuckling, Masada said, "Yeah, something like that. Sorry, but when I said we should take a break for twenty minutes, I thought that meant that you'd, y'know, be out of the room for twenty minutes."

Turning back to the readings he was getting from the sensors, Spock said, "Your exact words, Lieutenant, were an expression of exhaustion, followed by the words, 'I could use a break. What do you say, Spock, twenty minutes?'"

Smiling as he sat at the console next to Spock, Masada said, "Yeah, well, when you agreed and left with me, I thought that meant you were going to take the full twenty."

"Your assumption was made on a faulty premise. I don't require large amounts of 'break-time.' "

"Really?" Masada said with a smile. "And that's because you're a Vulcan."

"Correct."

"Except you're not—entirely. You're half-human." He grinned. "That explains two things, actually. One, you're half-human, so you only needed half the break time."

The eyebrow shot up again. "Oh?"

Masada turned to face Spock directly. "I do love that trick. Ensign Sontor does it, too."

"Trick?"

"The eyebrow thing. My theory is that's the Vulcans' secret for repressing their emotions—they channel them all into that one eyebrow. That's why you guys raise them so often—it's the focal point of all those emotions you're suppressing."

Spock turned back to the sensor display. "Your reasoning could charitably be referred to as 'specious,' Lieutenant. Barring the unlikely happenstance that you have scientific data to back it up, it is a hypothesis, not a theory. In addition, it's equivalent to hypothesizing that you cull information from your hair."

Masada frowned. "Excuse me?"

"The small gathering of hair at the back of your head. You have a tendency to grab it before providing information."

Straightening in his chair, Masada said, "I do not!"

Again, the eyebrow shot up.

"Fine, whatever. And it's called a ponytail."

"A misnomer, given that ponies actually have much longer tails."

Masada laughed. "That's the second thing that you being half-human explains. You, Commander Spock, are a laugh riot."

To Masada's great joy, that earned him a sharp look from the *Enterprise* first officer. "I fail to see how my conversations are akin to the behavior of the people on Proxima."

"No, no, not that kind of riot. It's an old expression—it just means you're funny. One of my staff is a Vulcan—that Ensign Sontor I mentioned. I've worked with a bunch of other Vulcans, and you're the only one of 'em that's cracked me up."

"Fascinating," Spock said dryly as he turned back to the console. "However, I can assure you that any humor you might perceive is solely a construct of your own interpretation."

Masada said, "Don't you see, though, that's exactly what makes it funny? The literal-mindedness, that dry tone of yours—by being *so* serious, you become humorous."

"That is a contradiction in terms, Mr. Masada. If one is serious, one cannot be humorous."

"Sure you can. It's the inherent contradiction of human existence. The difference between the interpreter and the interpreted, the—" He cut himself off.

"Sorry, I guess I'm still tired. I only get philosophical when I'm tired. Feel free to ignore me."

"I had already decided on just such a course of action," Spock said.

Laughing, Masada said, "See? There you go again. You just crack me up."

Turning his gaze back to Masada, Spock said, "I do not discern any ruptures in your skin, Lieutenant."

"It's another expression," Masada said with a sigh.

"Another contradiction of human existence?"

"Sort of. More like a metaphor. You make me laugh so hard, I'm in danger—well, metaphorical danger, anyhow—of shaking myself to pieces. Hence, 'crack me up.' "

"That is less a metaphor than a simile, Lieutenant, and it is also rather imprecise. It would be better if— should something amuse you in the future—to simply say that it amuses you. It would save you from having to make lengthy explanations of things you find to be patently obvious."

Again, Masada laughed. "You're too much, Commander."

"Too much what?"

He started to answer, then said, "Never mind." Turning to his console, which showed him the lateral sensor array—presently detecting many things, with the irritating exception of the precise location of the Malkus Artifact—Masada then asked, "How's our search coming?"

"Thus far, sensors have been unable to localize the energy signature." Spock, Masada noticed, had no difficulty changing the subject back to business.

They had started their search on the bridge, but soon realized that they would need the more widespread capabilities of the sensor room to work with. Masada had dismissed Soo and most of the rest of the science staff, telling them to work on collating the data from the neutron star. There was no chance they'd get back to it anytime soon—even if they solved the problem here in Alpha Proxima within the next hour, there was no way they'd be able to return to Beta Proxima to do any significant work on the star before they'd have to go off to that silly conference at Crellis.

And at the rate we're going, he thought, *it's gonna take a helluva lot longer than an hour to find that damn artifact.* Plus, the *Constellation* was probably going to stick around for at least another day after the crisis was past—*if* the crisis came to a satisfying conclusion, which was, of course, no guarantee. Masada had therefore resigned himself to the fact that they'd done all they could with the star, so there was no reason not to have Soo and the others start on the final report.

The only member of the science staff he held back was Sontor, who was presently monitoring the data upload from Vulcan with everything they had on the Zalkat Union in general and the Malkus Artifacts in particular. Masada assumed that the Vulcan records were more complete than the Starfleet ones, which didn't have much beyond the existence of the energy signature. But then, Beta Aurigae was first explored by an Earth ship, pre-Federation, and prior to the duotronic revolution in computer storage. Not every record survived that particular transition. *Thank God that old*

ship had a Vulcan observer on board to take good notes.

Masada ran his hand over his head, then tugged on his ponytail. *My God,* he thought, *I do tug my ponytail! Gotta watch that . . .* He looked over their records—which he'd been looking at steadily for many hours—and for the first time realized that the pattern they were using was a bit of a time waster. *Funny how you don't notice something until you've stepped away from it for twenty minutes.*

"Why don't we narrow the field to the northern hemisphere—better yet, to just where there are sentient lifesigns? I mean, those are the only places where there are people, so the artifact has to be there."

"It is unlikely that the Zalkatians took human comfort into consideration when hiding the artifact."

"Yeah, but there's an intelligence behind this. You yourself pointed out that this has to be directed by a person or persons with malice aforethought."

Spock made an adjustment to the console as he spoke. "That does not require that the artifact be where there is sentient life. Whoever is controlling the artifact could easily have access to a transporter, and could leave the artifact anywhere on the planet."

Stopping himself from reaching back to pull on his ponytail again, Masada said, "Oh come on, that's taking possibilities to an extreme. Besides, we've got a deadline here—we've got to narrow the search. *Logically,* we should eliminate less likely avenues of exploration."

For several seconds, Spock didn't move. Masada

was about to ask if something was wrong, when he finally spoke. "Your point is well taken. I will narrow the search."

Just then, Sontor entered the sensor room. "Sirs, the download from the Vulcan archaeological database is complete."

"About time," Masada said, blowing out a breath. "Anything interesting?"

Sontor's right eyebrow was far thicker than Spock's, but it crawled up his forehead in a disturbingly similar way. "I would be willing to debate at some length that all of it is interesting, Lieutenant. However, I assume that you are referring to data relevant to our current search."

"See what I mean?" Masada said, turning to Spock. "He's nowhere near as funny as you."

"I beg your pardon, sir?" Sontor asked, both his tone and his eyebrow arched.

Spock added, "I detect no significant difference in timbre, pitch, or verbal delivery between Ensign Sontor and myself to account for your perceptions, Lieutenant." Before Masada could reply to that, Spock said, "Then again, as you yourself pointed out, your fatigue may be having an effect on your perceptions."

Masada started to say something to Spock, stopped, started again, stopped again, then finally said, "Never mind." He turned back to Sontor. "What'd you find?"

Sontor leaned down into one of the consoles and punched up a record. "According to T'Ramir, who has been the primary specialist in Zalkatian matters for the last ninety-seven years and seven months, the Malkus

Artifacts might be more easily traced by using a low-band sensor sweep. The lower bands are closer to what is believed to be the primary form of electronic detection during Malkus's reign. Logically, the artifact's distinctive emissions would be more readily found with a method similar to that used by the creators of said artifact."

"Unnecessarily complicatedly put, Sontor." *As was that sentence,* Masada rebuked himself, but didn't say aloud. *I really am tired.* "But that follows. Changing bandwith of main sensor array." He suited action to words as his fingers played about the console.

"Unfortunately," Sontor said, "the lower band means that the readings will take considerably longer to obtain. A full sweep will take up to four-point-two-three hours."

"Give or take point-three hours," Masada said with a small smile.

"Negative. 'Give,' perhaps, as the search may take a shorter interval due to the possibility of finding the artifact before the search is complete, but it will not take any longer than that."

Pointing at Sontor but looking at Spock, Masada said, "See, now if *you'd* said that, it would've been *much* funnier."

Spock, however, was looking at the sensor readouts. In fact, he looked to Masada as if he were studiously ignoring both Masada and Sontor.

Grinning, Masada said, "Let's start the scan at Sierra City and work our way outwards."

"Logical," Spock said.

"Glad you approve."

Sontor said, "A Vulcan would always approve of a logical course of action."

"Naturally," Spock said. "To do otherwise would be foolish."

Save me from all this self-congratulating, Masada thought with a wry smile.

"I think we've got something, Leonard," Lewis Rosenhaus said with a smile.

They had been working for hours, trying to find some way to modify Dr. Derubbio's serum so that it wouldn't produce xelaxine. Thus far, all the methods for doing so also eliminated the serum's effectiveness in actually removing the virus.

Still, for whatever reason, McCoy had become easier to work with. Instead of snapping at him, McCoy listened to all his questions and suggestions and had intelligent comments to make. He didn't denigrate, and his criticisms were bereft of the ire they had had earlier. *I never would've thought I could bond with a fellow doctor over almost killing a patient,* he thought with a happy smile.

McCoy rubbed his eyes as he came over to where Rosenhaus was sitting. "What've you got, Lew?"

That was the other good thing: Rosenhaus really liked the sound of McCoy calling him "Lew" instead of "boy" or "son." He hadn't even liked it when his own father called him "son," much less someone he'd only just met.

Rosenhaus looked at McCoy's lined face. The older

man's blue eyes were bloodshot, and they had good-sized bags under them. "You should probably take a break, Leonard—or take a stimulant."

"I'm fine," McCoy said, waving him off. "Answer the damn question."

Great, he's getting crotchety again. "I was checking the pH readings. Xelaxine is basic. If we lower the pH value, make it neutral, it'll go inert. Now, Derubbio's serum is neutral, and the acidity is irrelevant to its effectiveness. What if we try adding an acid compound to the serum?"

"You want to introduce an acid into the human bloodstream?"

Rosenhaus sighed. "It was just a thought. If we can find an acid that's relatively harmless—ascorbic, maybe, or citric."

McCoy looked at the computer model Rosenhaus had called up, and shook his head. "Won't work. The only acid strong enough to bring xelaxine's pH down to seven would have to be a lot nastier than the human body can take. It'd eat the blood vessels alive."

"Dammit." Rosenhaus pounded a fist on the table.

Putting a hand on Rosenhaus's shoulder, McCoy said, "Easy, Lew, we're not out of the woods yet. There's something—"

"What?" he asked, looking up at the older doctor.

"Computer, call up the molecular structure of Andronesian encephalitis."

Rosenhaus frowned. "What does—?"

"You ever heard of Capellan acid?"

"Uh, no."

114

"Not surprised. I was stationed on Capella IV for a few months before I reported here. The Capellans are warrior types—they had no interest in medicine or hospitals."

Rosenhaus blinked, then blinked again. "Okay, at this point I'm *completely* lost."

McCoy smiled. "Bear with me, Lew. Computer, call up molecular structure of Capellan acid."

As soon as Rosenhaus saw the second image pop up on the screen, he winced. *"That's* a naturally occurring acid on Capella? What do they use it for, sieges of the castle? You could do wonders pouring this over the battlements—wipe out your enemies in a microsecond."

"Believe it or not, it's in their drinking water," McCoy said with a smile. "They build 'em tough on Capella, but not *that* tough. One of the things I noticed when I was there was that they didn't suffer from Andronesian encephalitis, even though the conditions on the planet are ideal for it. Turns out, they *did* have it, and they also had this corrosive acid in their water."

Rosenhaus put it together and snapped his fingers. "The acid neutralizes the encephalitis."

"For starters, yes. It still leaves acid in the system, though, just nothing as nasty as the acid's raw form. The question is if it's enough to also neutralize the xelaxine."

"Only one way to find out."

McCoy nodded. "Computer, call up molecular structure of xelaxine." After it did so: "All right, now project what would happen if all three were combined in the human bloodstream."

Rosenhaus watched as the molecules rotated toward

each other on the screen. Atoms shifted, bonds broke and re-formed, shapes changed—first the xelaxine and the encephalitis each broke apart, then the Capellan acid did likewise, and then they all started to come together in new combinations. Finally, when they settled down, there were five molecules. One was a single oxygen atom bonded with two hydrogen atoms; three were carbon bonded with two oxygen atoms; the last was six carbon atoms, eight hydrogen atoms, and six oxygen atoms.

"Water, carbon dioxide, and ascorbic acid," Rosenhaus said. "I don't believe it." He laughed. "They go from dying of a nasty virus to the functional equivalent of eating a grapefruit."

Chuckling, McCoy said, "That and holding their breath too long. We'll have to monitor their CO_2 levels—probably need to flush it out of most people's systems before they can be safely discharged—and of course they'll all need to be re-inoculated for encephalitis."

Rosenhaus nodded. "We'll have to make sure everyone *is* inoculated first. If they haven't been, we'll have to give it to them."

"I want to run a few more tests before we try this on Ms. Braker over there, but I think we're on the right track here." He turned to Rosenhaus and smiled. "Nice work, Doctor."

"What nice work? I made a dumbass suggestion. You're the one who turned it into something workable."

Chuckling, McCoy said, "I tell you, I never thought anything good would come out of those months I spent on Capella."

Nurse Jazayerli—whose presence in the lab area Rosenhaus hadn't even registered—said, "I hate to interrupt this mutual admiration society, Doctors, but I have checked on Ms. Braker, and she has indeed received an inoculation against Andronesian encephalitis."

McCoy nodded. "Thank you, Nurse. C'mon, Lew, let's get to work."

Matt Decker swore he would never complain about the difficulties of running a starship ever again. As bad as it could sometimes get, it couldn't possibly be worse than co-running a planetary government for a day.

He and Kirk had been at it for almost twenty-four straight hours—and that was on top of a full day of neutron-stargazing. Decker was about as exhausted as he ever intended to be when there wasn't an actual war on.

Then again, he thought, *for all intents and purposes, we* are *fighting a war. We're just waiting on Guillermo and Spock to find the enemy for us.*

However, all the tasks that needed to be performed had been, and any others that were pending could wait until morning. There hadn't been any new outbursts of the virus since the *Enterprise* was targeted. Masada, Spock, McCoy, and Rosenhaus had all reported that they were making progress, but had nothing new to report. Bronstein had said that all had been quiet since Kirk's little speech at the SCMC. As the sun started setting on Proxima, things seemd to have quieted down.

Right now, Commodore Matthew Decker needed a good night's sleep more than anything.

Idly, he wondered how anyone on this planet did sleep. Proxima had a thirty-hour day. With the colony primarily in the northern hemisphere, at this time of year the sun was up for about twenty-six of those hours. He remembered Will's childhood joke about how it was always night in space—on Proxima, it was *never* night, it seemed.

Kirk had just gotten a couple hours' sleep—and he had also gotten some sleep prior to the mission, since his ship's time was at early morning rather than late night when they arrived at Proxima. The idea was that he would then stay up during the rest of the night in case of an emergency, leaving Decker to catch up on his desperately needed rest.

As he hauled himself up from his chair to head for the door, he said to Kirk, "So where are we supposed to sack out, anyhow?"

Before an irritatingly fresh-faced Kirk could answer, Decker's communicator beeped.

Shaking his head, he took it out of his belt. "I knew I should have phasered this thing when I had the chance. Could've just said the rioters did it." He opened the communicator. "Decker here."

"Wow, Commodore, you sound like hell," Takeshewada said.

"Number One, I'm going to sound like the ninth circle of hell if you don't give me a very good reason why you called me when I was on the way to bed."

"As it happens, I do, and it's good news, twice over. Our two doctors think they've nailed the virus. It's not

without small risks, but nothing as life-threatening as the virus itself."

Kirk stepped up. "How soon can they adminster it?"

If Takeshewada was bothered by being queried by a different CO, she didn't show it, and Decker himself was too tired to care. *"They have to verify that people have a particular inoculation—some kind of elephantitis or somesuch. Lew said it was a common vaccination, so it shouldn't be an issue. But they figure to have mass-produced the serum by morning."*

Decker smiled a happy smile for the first time since arriving at Proxima. "That's the best news I've heard since my son made commander, Number One. What's the other good news?"

"It's even better. Guillermo and Spock have localized the emissions from the artifact. Unfortunately, we can't get a transporter lock within fifty meters of the emissions—apparently this thing interferes with the beams."

"So much for pulling the beam-out-the-suspect trick," Decker muttered.

"Mhm. And we can't get any decent sensor readings in there. Best we can tell is that there may be some human lifesigns, possibly. Our only real option is to go in person. Permission to beam down and lead the security detail to apprehend the suspect."

"Denied. I'll take Bronstein, and—"

"Matt, with all due respect, you're exhausted. So's Bronstein. I've actually slept recently, and if we're dealing with the type of psychopath that would infect an entire colony and *a starship, you need a fresh hand*

*on deck, not a stubborn old commodore who's falling
asleep on his phaser."*

Decker sighed. Takeshewada had said all that without even taking a breath—she had obviously rehearsed
it ahead of time, knowing full well that he would insist
on leading the party himself.

"I'd like to go also, Commodore," Kirk said. "With
all due respect to the abilities of your first officer, I
think we owe it to the Proximans for one of the two of
us to be present when the person responsible for this
nightmare is taken in. And the commander's right—
you're in no shape to lead it. It should be me."

*"I'm perfectly capable of commanding the mission,
Captain,"* Takeshewada said in her most clipped tone.
*"And I think I've earned it after sitting on my rear end
since we got here."*

Decker sighed, as he feared he was going to have to
navigate some minefields here. He did not want to
have his first officer in a pissy mood.

"I'm not impugning your skills, Commander
Takeshewada," Kirk said tightly, "it's just that—"

"Both of you simmer down," Decker interrupted.
"Hiromi, you're right, I'm in no shape to deal with
this. But Kirk's right in that he should be in charge.
He knows the terrain better, and he's been the face
of the government all day—I think the Proximans
will appreciate his presence when we apprehend
whoever the hell this is. Where *is* this location, anyhow?"

*"A house in a residential section just outside Sierra
City."* She read off a series of coordinates. Decker

checked the wall map and saw that it was the Karsay's Point neighborhood, about half a kilometer outside the city. Takeshewada continued, *"We're still waiting on a profile of the occupant of that house. I've already talked to both ships' security chiefs. I've got a team of twenty set to meet up at Posada Circle."*

Kirk looked at the map. "I can be there in ten minutes."

"Fine," Takeshewada said, once again utilizing her we're-going-to-talk-about-this-later tone. *"Takeshewada out."*

Decker closed his communicator. *At this rate,* he thought, *Hiromi and I'll be talking for hours when this is done.*

"Don't worry, Commodore," Kirk said as he grabbed his phaser from out of the drawer of the desk where he'd been keeping it, "we'll have this taken care of by the time you wake up."

"Like there's a chance in hell I'm gonna be able to sleep," Decker said with a snort. "Hey, Jim."

Kirk stopped midway between the desk and the door and gave the commodore an expectant look.

"We don't know what we're dealing with—for all we know, there's an army down there. Even if it's just one nutcase, it's someone who's attempted mass murder. Be careful."

For one second, Jim Kirk looked just like Will did the day he got his commission—sober, calm, yet obviously ready to face whatever was coming. "Thanks, Matt. And don't worry."

As soon as he left, Decker let out a long breath that

sounded more like a snort. "Don't worry, he says. What'm I supposed to do, sleep?"

He fell more than sat into the chair behind his desk and called up a report from one of Bronstein's people. *May as well get some work done ...*

Hiromi Takeshewada took a moment to lean back against the statue of Captain Bernabe Posada, look up, and let the setting sun shine on her face. *It's been too damn long,* she thought.

Growing up in Tokyo on Earth and moving around to various cities all over the Sol system, Takeshewada had always considered herself a city person, never one for "the great outdoors." A career in Starfleet was a natural for her after living in tall buildings in the midst of cities.

But after spending so long indoors—whether on planets or in starships—she had grown to truly appreciate breathing fresh air, feeling the light of the sun on her face, and the unique tactile experience of standing on real ground. In her younger days, serving as an ensign aboard the *U.S.S. Mandela,* she never really appreciated what it was like to feel a planet under her feet instead of a constructed floor. Now, though, with age came wisdom, and she knew to appreciate when she stepped on a planet.

She never knew when it might be her last chance.

The *Mandela* had been destroyed less than a month after Takeshewada had transferred off the ship to take a post as a lieutenant aboard the *Potemkin.* She had lost a lot of good friends there. Right before she left, she had passed up the opportunity for shore leave on Starbase

13, which orbited a lush world. But she had had paperwork to catch up on, so she didn't bother, figuring she'd do so the next time.

If her promotion hadn't come through, there wouldn't have been a next time.

So she stood now in Posada Circle—like the statue that was its centerpiece, the circular road was in honor of the captain of the colony ship *S.S. Esperanza,* and also the first Chief Representative of Proxima's government—surrounded by a detail of *Constellation* and *Enterprise* security. As she waited for Kirk and Vascogne to arrive, she made sure she took a moment to bask in the sunlight. *Because the* Constellation *could be destroyed tomorrow—or the next day—or next year. And if it does happen, I will have done this. And it feels good.*

Then a government aircar landed six meters from the statue of Captain Posada, and Kirk stepped out of it. As the young captain walked toward Takeshewada, she noted that he was shorter than she had been expecting, though he was still taller than she was. Most people were, to her great irritation.

Kirk carried himself with a confident air. Takeshewada might almost have called it smug, though she admitted that she may have been overlaying her own annoyance at the way Kirk had muscled into this operation. Takeshewada had always been a hands-on type. She had bristled at spending so much of this mission on the bridge, and was looking forward to leading this party herself.

Rationally, of course, she knew that Kirk's reasons for being here made perfect sense. He had indeed been

the "face of the government" to the Proximans in these hard times, and putting him at the forefront of what they hoped was the arrest of the person responsible was good politics.

Takeshewada hated politics. She was good at playing the game—a blessing when serving as XO to Matt Decker, who was as anti-political as they came—but she still hated having to do it.

"Are we ready to move, Commander?" Kirk asked.

"We're just waiting on Vascogne. He's supposed to have the information on our suspect. Right now, we just know that her name is Tomasina Laubenthal. I've already had our people clear the streets between here and her house."

Just as Kirk nodded in acknowledgment, Takeshewada heard the whine of a transporter. Several of the security guards turned sharply, and one or two put their hands to their phaser holsters, just in case.

However, the two forms that coalesced in the beam were familiar ones: the bald head and compact form of Etienne Vascogne, and the taller, blonder, and slimmer form of his assistant chief of security, Helga Litwack.

"Sorry to beam in like this, Hiromi, but I was running late," Vascogne said as the transporter whine faded. "Captain!" he said upon sighting Kirk. "Didn't realize you were joining the party, sir. Or are you here to give another speech?"

"This time I'm hoping to commit some actions to speak louder than my words, Lieutenant," Kirk said with a disarming smile. Takeshewada hated to admit it, but it was a damn good smile. *No wonder he was the*

one doing the broadcasts. I love Matt, but he comes across as the irritating old uncle you could never stand. Kirk is much more personable.

"What've you got, Etienne?" Takeshewada asked.

"A doozy," Vascogne replied, running a hand over his smooth head as he looked down at his notes. "Our Ms. Laubenthal is a single caucasian female, fifty-three years old, born and raised here on Proxima. Graduated with a degree in political science from Yasmini University in '34, she's worked a variety of civil-service jobs since then, and then went into politics six years ago. Until about two months ago, she was the deputy assistant to the Proximan secretary of the interior."

Kirk frowned. "What happened two months ago?"

"The secretary's an appointed position," Vascogne said, glancing up from his notes. "When the old secretary retired, rather than promote from within, the Chief Representative decided to give it to someone new from outside. That new person also brought her own people in—Laubenthal was let go. According to some people Litwack and I talked to, she had been expecting to get promoted to assistant, with the assistant becoming secretary. Instead, they were both dismissed."

"Chikushou." Takeshewada muttered the curse.

With a wry smile, Vascogne said, "Yeah, I was thinking that sounded kind of motive-like."

"But why wait two months?" Kirk asked.

"That's the *real* fun part—she took a vacation to Pirenne's Peak. It's in a mountain range about a hundred kilometers south of here. It only recently became a popular spot because the weather's gotten milder in

that area over the last five years or so. Once I saw that, I got Litwack here to help me question some people about her. That's why we were late. Most of the people she worked with are under sedation or dead, but we found a friend of hers named Alvaro Santana who confirmed that she was bitter after being dismissed. He'd been bugging her to take the vacation, and she only did so recently—Santana said he was half-convinced she only went to shut him up about it." He looked at Takeshewada with a grave expression. "Nobody's seen her since she got back. And, according to the tourist bureau, she spent her entire time on the peak alone and unescorted—*and* she left sooner than planned. So if she *did* find the artifact . . ."

"I think we have a suspect," Kirk said dryly. "Time we apprehended her." Unholstering a phaser of his own, Kirk signalled to the security people. "Let's go!"

As a unit, they moved toward Laubenthal's house. Within minutes, they arrived at a nondescript three-story white house with a small lawn area in front. The first level was taken up with an aircar garage, with white stairs leading up to a door on the second level. The architecture was your basic prefabricated colonial standard—Takeshewada mused that it probably dated back to the colony's founding over seventy-five years earlier. Where most of the colony had, over time, developed its own architecture—varying from neighborhood to neighborhood—some still stuck with the functional original structures.

A sense of the practical outweighing the aesthetic,

Takeshewada thought. She wasn't sure what it meant, really, but she noted it anyhow.

One of the *Enterprise* guards—a woman named Leskanich—set up a comm system on Laubenthal's lawn. Vascogne handed Kirk an amplifier, which the captain attached to his uniform shirt. The rest of the guards moved into formation, surrounding the house, covering all the possible exits (the garage door, the front door, and a back door) and windows. Takeshewada tried to get a tricorder reading inside the house, but couldn't. Something was interfering with the scan—presumably the Malkus Artifact.

"Attention, Ms. Tomasina Laubenthal," Kirk said, his voice now loud enough to be heard for blocks around, "this is Captain James T. Kirk. I'm about to contact you directly—please answer." He then gave Leskanich an expectant look.

For her part, Leskanich had brushed aside a lock of curly brown hair to place an earpiece in. She seemed to be staring at nothing while her fingers played across the controls of her portable comm unit. Then she looked up and nodded just as Kirk's communicator beeped.

Kirk turned off his amplifier and flipped open his communicator. "This is Kirk. Am I speaking to Ms. Laubenthal?"

"I've got a hostage!"

For a second time, Takeshewada muttered, *"Chikushou."* This was a complication they didn't need.

Muting his communicator, Kirk asked Takeshewada, "Can you verify that?"

Takeshewada shook her head. "I can't even verify that *she's* in there right now."

Kirk set his jaw, then de-muted the communicator. "Ms. Laubenthal, I need you to listen to me. We don't want to hurt you. Please, let the hostage go, and we can talk thi—"

"There's nothing to 'talk' about, Kirk! They took it all away from me, don't you understand? Soon they'll all be dead and this will be over. Them and you and your precious starships."

"Ms. Laubenthal, you don't need to do this."

"Oh, I don't, don't I? What do you know about it, anyhow?"

"I know that you feel you were cheated out of your job, and I—"

"I feel?! You don't have the slightest idea how I feel, Kirk! They took everything from me! That job was mine, they had no business taking it away from me!"

Takeshewada sighed. She whispered to Vascogne, "She's hysterical. I don't think reasoning with her's gonna cut it."

"Maybe, maybe not," Vascogne said with a shrug. "We can't do anything else as long as she has a hostage. Besides, I've seen the captain in action before. Stopped a mob in its tracks. Damndest thing I ever saw. Give him a shot."

"I'd rather give Laubenthal a shot."

Vascogne grinned. "Well, we're working on that." He opened his communicator, which was set on a separate frequency from the one Kirk had Laubenthal on. "Talk to me, people."

Each member of the team reported in, but nobody could see anyone through the windows of the house.

Shaking his head, Vascogne said, "I can't believe this—how'm I supposed to work without tricorders? Who depends on line of sight, anyhow? It's like firing blindfolded."

"Life's full of little frustrations for you," Takeshe-wada said with a small smile.

Kirk, meanwhile, was continuing to try to talk Laubenthal down. "Ms. Laubenthal, I don't pretend to understand what you're going through—but I *do* know that we *can* work this out."

"Really?" Laubenthal let out a rather disturbing laugh. *"Why should I believe you? You really think anyone here is going to work anything out with me?"*

"You forget—Commodore Decker and I are in charge of the planet now. I can guarantee that you won't be harmed if you free the hostage and turn yourself and the artifact in now—before anyone else is hurt or killed."

"No—I can't take that chance! It won't be over until everyone is dead!"

"And then what?" Kirk said quickly. "Once everyone's dead, what will you do then? You'll be left with nothing but an empty planet. Starfleet knows what's happening here. When no one replies to any of their calls, they'll send someone else."

"Then I'll kill them, too. I'll kill everyone, if I have to!"

"Don't you understand, they'll *keep coming*—until they've stopped you, once and for all. In force if they have to, but they *will* come. If you end this now, we

can keep the damage to a minimum. *Please,* Ms. Laubenthal, end this now—*before* it gets beyond your control or mine."

Takeshewada heard only heavy breathing through the communicator for several seconds. *I don't like this,* she thought as she opened her own communicator, tuning it to the frequency the security guards were using. "Does anyone have a shot?"

Several choruses of "Negative" met her query.

Laubenthal's breaths got progressively slower. Takeshewada tried to convince herself that it was a good sign, but found herself unable to do so. The number of instances of psychotic episodes were many fewer than they were even fifty years ago, but Takeshewada had been present for one of them—when they established a mining outpost on Beta Argola six months ago. One of the miners had an episode and nearly killed both Vascogne and Takeshewada. After that she read up on the phenomenon.

Right now what she remembered most was that oftentimes psychotics were quite calm when they committed their most hideous acts.

"Maybe—maybe you're right."

Takeshewada held her breath. Laubenthal sounded *much* too calm for comfort.

"I *am* right, Ms. Laubenthal," Kirk said in a honeyed voice. "Please—*let* the hostage go."

"Maybe you're right, Captain," Laubenthal repeated in an even calmer voice. *"Maybe this does need to end. Maybe it needs to end now. Right now."*

Then they heard a phaser blast, followed by a scream.

Takeshewada didn't hesitate as she screamed into her communicator, "Move in! Everyone, *move in!*" *I can't believe she shot the hostage,* she thought angrily.

As fast as the commander and the security detail reacted, Kirk reacted even faster. The second the phaser blast sounded, Kirk was running full tilt toward the staircase that lead to the front door. By the time he reached the top of the stairs, his phaser was out. By the time *she* reached the top of the stairs, Kirk had tried and failed to get the door open. As Takeshewada was wondering if Vascogne had brought a P-38 with him, Kirk aimed his phaser at the door mechanism and fired.

The door opened a second later.

"Nothing like the direct approach," Takeshewada muttered as she and Kirk ran in, past the smoking remains of the door mechanism. She could hear Vascogne and several security guards running up the stairs behind them.

Dimly, Takeshewada registered the décor of the house's interior—several pictures of a woman at varying ages. A few trophies—a quick glance showed that they were for sports, and all dated from her time at Yasmini University. Several of the pictures of her in her younger days had her in climbing or hiking gear, which fit the profile of someone who'd take a vacation on a mountain.

Oddly enough, there were no pictures of anyone else. No family, no significant others, nothing. Just Laubenthal herself.

The furniture was fairly ugly to Takeshewada's eye—and she was no interior decorator—but the place definitely felt lived in. The gaudy flower-print couch

was piled with readers, and there were more on the shelves. Most of it was fiction, with titles Takeshewada didn't recognize.

The commander followed Kirk through a hallway and a sitting room—then he stopped short at a doorway. Kirk was, of course, taller than Takeshewada, so she couldn't see past him to determine what the room was, nor why he stopped.

"What is it?" she prompted.

That had the desired effect, and he moved out of the way, his head lowered.

What the hell—?

As Kirk walked back into the sitting room and Litwack and two others came into the room, Takeshewada looked into what turned out to be the dining room.

A white plastiform table sat in the middle of the room, surrounded by white plastiform chairs. A comm unit sat on the table.

Takeshewada registered that in her subconscious. Her conscious mind was taken up with the dead human female body on the floor next to the table with the very large hole in her chest.

The face on the body matched that of all the pictures.

Vascogne stuck his bald head into the room. "There's no one else in the house."

"Well, I was right," Takeshewada said with a heavy sigh. "She did shoot the hostage."

Chapter Seven

MATT DECKER found Jim Kirk sitting on the bench next to the statue in Posada Circle. It had been almost eighteen hours since Tomasina Laubenthal had killed herself. Decker, who had indeed been unable to sleep, had dealt with everything since then, as Kirk had left the scene and wandered back to this bronze likeness of Captain Bernabe Posada.

"You plan on spending the rest of your life here, Jim?"

Kirk looked up, his eyes bloodshot. "If you're here to reprimand me, Commodore—"

"What the hell would I want to do that for?"

"I failed," Kirk said, sounding surprised that Decker would ask such a foolish question. "I was supposed to take Laubenthal into custody, and I didn't do it."

133

Decker held up a small handheld computer. "Know what this is?"

Kirk shook his head.

"Laubenthal's diary. Vascogne found it when he and Bronstein went through her house. Most of it's pretty dry—until she lost her job. After that, she completely lost it. Jim, the woman was several crystals short of a warp core—there was *nothing* you could have said. She was completely insane. Those people you talked to at the SCMC were just scared, normal people. Words work on rational people. Crazy people, though, that's a no-win situation."

"I've never believed in the no-win situation."

Decker snorted. "Yeah, well, I don't like to lose, either. Doesn't mean it isn't gonna happen."

Kirk said nothing in response to that.

"Vascogne also recovered the Malkus Artifact. For all the trouble that thing caused, it's pretty dull. Just a square piece of metal with a slight green glow, and this weird marking on it. It can't be transported, so the *Enterprise* is sending a shuttle down."

That got Kirk's attention, and he looked up at Decker. "The *Enterprise?*"

Decker smiled. The last Kirk knew, his entire ship was under sedation. "That's right, Jim. You've got your ship back. Whatever Rosenhaus and McCoy came up with worked. They've been administering the antidote on your ship, and the hospitals have been handling it down here. It's not an instant cure, but your people should be ship-shape again in a few hours."

Kirk let out a long breath. "That's good news, Matt. Thanks."

"Not only that, but you and I can finally get out of here. The minister of state is going to be Acting Chief Representative until they can hold another election in a month or two. Once she's released by the hospital, she'll take over, and we can revoke martial law."

At last, Kirk smiled. "That's even better news." The smile then fell. "What was the final death toll?"

"Four hundred and fifty-six. Well, technically, four hundred and fifty-eight, if you count Laubenthal herself and that other wrongful death Bronstein has had to deal with that was unrelated."

"That's more than the crew of either of our ships," Kirk said in a quiet voice.

"True," Decker said as he sat down next to the younger man on the bench. "On the other hand, over four hundred thousand were infected. That's a point-one-percent fatality rate." He sighed. "That doesn't change how much it stinks, but it could've been a lot worse."

Kirk stared straight ahead. "It could've been a lot better, too."

"Look, Jim, I know this wasn't easy. You sit in that chair on that bridge, and you know that everyone's relying on you—and when you don't come through, it's rough. But don't go beating yourself up over it. You did some damn good work here. Look what you did at the SCMC—hell, Vascogne and I were all set to stun 'em and sort it out later. Instead, you talked 'em out of it. That's a rare gift you've got there, my

friend. All right, so it didn't work on Laubenthal—but trust me, she was so far gone, I doubt that the entire Federation Diplomatic Corps could have talked her down."

Letting out a very long breath, Kirk said, "You're right, Matt—I *know* you're right in my head. But I've still got this sense of—of failure."

Decker stood up and put an encouraging hand on Kirk's shoulder. "Keep that sense of failure, Jim. But don't let it overwhelm you. Just make sure you try to do better next time. That's what separates the good captains from the great ones."

Kirk stood up and chuckled. "I'm hardly a 'great' anything, Commodore."

"Maybe not yet. Give it time. So, you done sulking? You've got a planet *and* a ship waiting for you."

"That I do, Commodore. Let's go."

As they walked toward the aircar Decker had arrived in, Kirk asked, "So what's next on the *Constellation*'s agenda?"

"Well, we have to spend the next few hours getting everything together for handing power back over. And there's a memorial service tonight that I think you and I should attend."

"Agreed."

"So, by the time that's all finished, we'll have just enough time to get to the Crellis Cluster."

"The diplomatic conference?" Kirk asked, wincing. "I was wondering who got saddled with that."

Decker shuddered. "Yeah, lucky us. Hiromi's handling most of it, but I still need to at least be visible.

I'm barely gonna have time to shave," he added with a rueful rub of his stubble-filled cheek. "As it is, I haven't slept in two days."

"Actually, Matt, I've found that half-asleep is the best way to deal with diplomats."

Decker considered that. "Good point. Have to remember that." As he climbed into the aircar, he asked, "Don't believe in no-win situations, huh? You must've just *loved* the *Kobayashi Maru* test back at the Academy."

"Oh, it was a challenge," Kirk deadpanned.

Frowning, Decker asked, "What's that supposed to mean?"

"The night before, I reprogrammed the simulation so I could rescue the *Maru* and got away from the Klingons." He smiled. "You're not the only one who doesn't like to lose, Matt."

Decker didn't know whether to be outraged or amused. The bark of laughter that exploded from his mouth settled the debate. "You're a piece of work, you know that?" he said as the aircar took off.

"That's what the instructor said when she gave me the commendation for original thinking."

"You got off easy—and I'll bet that wasn't all she said, either." Decker shook his head, then offered his hand. "It's been a pleasure ruling the world with you, Captain Kirk."

Kirk returned the handshake. "Likewise, Commodore Decker, likewise."

"So this is it, huh?"

Guillermo Masada stood outside the Shuttlecraft

Galileo with Spock and Leonard McCoy. They were preparing to bring the Malkus Artifact—currently cradled in Masada's arms—into orbit. The *Enterprise*'s next port of call was Starbase 10, whereas the *Constellation* was going straight to the Crellis Cluster, so the former ship would drop the artifact off at the starbase, for its ultimate transfer to the Rector Institute on Earth. Spock and Masada had contacted the institute directly, and the director was champing at the bit to get his hands on it, as was a team of human and Vulcan anthropologists. T'Ramir herself was catching the next shuttle from Vulcan to Earth.

Meanwhile, a day and a half after Tomasina Laubenthal took her own life, most of the infected population had been given the serum to cure them of the virus, the senior staffs of both ships had attended a general memorial service led by Chief Bronstein and the new Acting Chief Representative, and life on Proxima was starting to return to a semblance of normal.

And all this because of a ninety-thousand-year-old artifact. Masada wondered if the folks at the Rector Institute would react the same way McCoy did upon seeing the thing.

The doctor continued: "It's just a box."

Spock did his eyebrow thing again. "I believe, Dr. McCoy, that there is a human saying about judging a book by its cover. Sometimes the outer form gives no indication of inner capabilities."

"Oh, I don't know, Mr. Spock. Looking at you, one would expect a cold, emotionless Vulcan—and they'd be absolutely right."

"And looking at you, they would see an overly emotional human," Spock said, "which is why I used the adverb 'sometimes.' "

Masada chuckled. "There you go again. You really do crack me up."

Before either *Enterprise* officer could reply to that, the artifact—which had been glowing a slightly greenish color—suddenly let loose a quick burst of bright green light.

So surprised by this action was Masada, that he dropped the box—right onto his right foot. "Yeow!" he screamed as the metal corner of the artifact slammed into his boot.

As he pulled his foot out from under it, he noticed that the artifact's green glow had disappeared altogether.

Both Masada and Spock took out their tricorders. To Masada's surprise, he was now getting a reading from the thing—whatever interference it had been running before was gone—though the reading he got was, in essence, nothing.

"The artifact has gone inert," Spock said, his words matching what Masada's own tricorder was telling him. "Fascinating."

"Maybe it's shutting down," Masada said. "According to the records, it was attuned to Malkus. If it became similarly attuned to that Laubenthal woman, her death may have caused it to go inactive again."

McCoy said, "She died almost two days ago." He had taken out his Feinberger, and was now running it over the three of them.

Masada shrugged. "So it's not a perfect hypothesis."

"Well," McCoy said, "that discharge doesn't seem to've done any harm. Low-level radiation, only about half a rad. No damage to any of us that I can find." He smiled. "Well, except for that foot."

"The artifact was a tool of an absolute monarch," Spock said. "It is logical to assume that any displays it is programmed for would be ostentatious—much like the lieutenant's histrionics."

"Histrionics?" Masada asked angrily as he knelt down to massage his hurt foot.

"Yes. Although, I do admire your continued quest for knowledge. Having already exhausted the possibilities inherent in deconstructing Vulcan speech patterns in order to extract a nonexistent humorous intent, you have now moved on to the much simpler examination of the form of humor known as slapstick."

Having satisfied himself that nothing was broken, Masada stood up. "I have *not* been studying slapstick, all I did was drop the artifact when it surprised me. For that matter, I haven't 'exhausted' anything, I was just pointing out what I observed and you know all of this already, don't you?" He shook his head, and also noticed that McCoy was trying, and failing, to keep a straight face. "You've been pulling my leg all along, haven't you?"

"I can assure you, Lieutenant," Spock said gravely, "that I would never assume such an undignified position. I leave that to you, as you have just proven yourself quite adept at it."

McCoy abandoned all pretense of the straight face,

and was now grinning. Holding up his hands, Masada joined McCoy in his grin and said, "Fine, fine, I surrender." He indicated the artifact. "Anyhow, that thing's all yours. I need to head back up to the *Constellation*. Commander Spock, it was a pleasure working with you." He held his hand up in the Vulcan salute. "Peace and long life."

If Spock was surprised at Masada's knowledge of Vulcan ritual greetings, he didn't show it. Instead, he simply returned the gesture and said, "Live long and prosper, Lieutenant Masada."

To McCoy, he offered his hand. "And Doctor, congratulations on surviving the experience of working with Lew. I don't know whether to offer condolences on having to work with him or give you a medal for not killing him."

"Ah, he's not that bad," McCoy said, returning the handshake. "He's got good instincts, he just needs a little more experience. Give him a couple years, he'll make a damn good physician."

"Tell you what, in two years, I'll let you know if he's gotten tolerable."

"Fair enough," McCoy said with a smile. "For now, I'd just settle for him slowing down a little. When we were on the *Enterprise,* he jostled my arm while we were preparing some of the antidote. Spilled some Capellan acid on my lab table. I'll never get that damn spot out."

"Really?" Masada grinned. Rosenhaus had twice been involved in incidents in the mess hall that resulted in food and drink on the floor—once with a par-

ticularly aggressive Tellarite security guard. Vascogne and Takeshewada had managed to defuse both situations, but they had quickly become part of the *Constellation*'s gossip network. Masada was looking forward to adding this to it, as well.

The two *Enterprise* officers boarded the shuttle, Spock now carrying the artifact. Masada took out his communicator. "Masada to *Constellation*. One to beam up."

As the transporter returned him to his ship, he wondered if he'd get a chance to work with them again.

He hoped so. If ever anyone needed a practical joke played on him, it was Lieutenant Commander Spock . . .

The third planet in the Narendra system was Class-M. Located in territory proximate to Klingon space, the empire had been eyeing the planet as a possible base for some time.

Buried deep under the ground of the smallest of Narendra III's twelve landmasses lay a metal box, emblazoned with the name of its former owner on one side. The slight green glow it gave off was lost in the rock and dirt that encased it.

Within the box, a telepathic voice screamed. Unencumbered by the limitations of a larynx, it had continued this scream for over ninety thousand years. That mind had lived alone in the box for all that time.

The first chance for freedom had finally come after so long—but she turned out to be weak and foolish. A nobody with insignificant dreams of a pointless vengeance.

Suddenly, and only for a moment, the artifact glowed brighter. When the glow dimmed back to normal, three brain patterns had imprinted themselves on the box.

Now the telepathic voice had company, after a fashion. Three minds that could be controlled.

When the time was right, in any case . . .

FIRST INTERLUDE

Captain's personal log, *U.S.S. Enterprise,* Captain James T. Kirk, Stardate 4208.5.

In my official log, I noted that Matt Decker died in the line of duty when he piloted the *Enterprise* shuttlecraft into the so-called planet-killer. Though his actions were tragic, it did lead us to the solution to stopping the planet-killer before it reached the Rigel Colonies.

In this personal log I wish only to add that I regret that the commodore was unable to take the advice he had given me on Proxima over a year ago: not to let my sense of failure overwhelm me. Ultimately, Matt was unable to get past the deaths of the crew of the *Constellation,* whom he had beamed down to the third planet of System L-374 only to watch helplessly as that world was destroyed.

Keith R.A. DeCandido

I also wish to express my regret for the loss of the *Constellation* crew—Commander Takeshewada, Lieutenant Masada, Dr. Rosenhaus, Lieutenant Vascogne, and the rest of the men and women who served on that fine vessel. I only hope that the *Enterprise* can live up to their example of courage and bravery.

®

Part 2: The Second Artifact

2370

This portion of the story takes place shortly before the
Star Trek: Deep Space Nine second-season episode
"The Jem'Hadar."

Part 2: The Second Artifact

2175

The Keyhole of Sky, guarded by the sacred Mandala, fell into the hands of those who wished to use it for their own ends.

Chapter Eight

"WELCOME TO THE *ODYSSEY*, Commander Sisko. I'm Joseph Shabalala, first officer."

Joe Shabalala offered his right hand to Benjamin Sisko as he stepped off the transporter platform. The *U.S.S. Odyssey* had just arrived at Station Deep Space 9, a Bajoran station administrated by Starfleet and commanded by Sisko. Shabalala knew of the tall man—as tall as Shabalala himself, in fact, not a common occurrence—only by reputation, mainly due to the sudden prominence both Bajor and DS9 had gained almost two years earlier when Sisko had discovered a stable wormhole in the Denorios Belt. That wormhole linked the Alpha Quadrant to the Gamma Quadrant and turned the station from an insignificant backwater to the most important port of call in the sector.

The handshake Sisko gave in return was firm, the smile that accompanied it friendly. "A pleasure to meet you, Commander. I was sorry to hear about Captain Simon."

Shabalala blinked in surprise. "You knew the captain?"

"She was two years ahead of me at the Academy—and," Sisko added with a grin, "captain of the wrestling team when I joined."

Chuckling, Shabalala said, "Ah yes, what she called her 'misspent youth.'"

Sisko looked around the transporter room. "You seem to have done well for yourself. First officer of a *Galaxy*-class ship."

Thinking about the disastrous final mission of the *U.S.S. Fearless* at Patnira, Shabalala said gravely, "Perhaps. But I'd rather have the captain back. We'd been together on three different ships, you know—going back to when she was a full lieutenant and I was an ensign on the *Bonaventure.* And then she chose me to be her first on the *Fearless* when they gave it to her. It's—very odd to be serving under someone else." Banishing thoughts of the past out of his head, he forced a smile onto his face and indicated the door to the transporter room. "Speaking of which, we shouldn't keep Captain Keogh waiting. Shall we?"

"After you, Commander."

They walked in companionable silence to the captain's quarters. Sisko suddenly seemed a bit skittish. As they approached Keogh's quarters on deck

nine, Shabalala asked, "Is everything all right, Commander?"

Sisko shook his head as if trying to shoo away a fly. "It's nothing. Just—some odd memories of my last trip aboard a *Galaxy*-class ship."

Nothing more was forthcoming, so Shabalala shrugged it off and touched the doorchime for Keogh's quarters. "Come," came the captain's deep voice from behind the doors, and they obligingly opened.

Keogh was standing near his desk, ramrod straight, his hands behind his back, as if he were conducting an inspection. When he had first reported to the *Odyssey* three months earlier, Shabalala had thought that Keogh was just an on-duty pain, but he'd since seen the older man in a variety of situations, both on and off duty, ranging from a meeting with the admiralty to drinks in Ten-Forward to a pitched fistfight against members of his own crew that had been mutated by spores. No matter what, he always stood perfectly straight, always maintained a hard, cold expression on his face, and—if at all possible—had his hands behind his back. It had been a difficult style for Shabalala to get used to after so many years of Captain Simon's easygoing manner.

Still, he'd lasted three months—he was halfway to tying the *Odyssey*'s record for tenure by a first officer. The ship had left Utopia Planitia's shipyards five years previous and had never had a first officer last more than half a year. One only lasted a week.

"Greetings, Commander Sisko," Keogh said with as small a smile as it was possible for his face to engage

in and still be recognizable as such. "I'm Declan Keogh. Welcome to my ship."

"Thank you, Captain."

Walking toward the replicator, Keogh asked, "Can I get you a drink?"

"A *raktajino* would be nice," Sisko said after a moment's consideration.

Keogh looked expectantly at Shabalala, who shook his head. He could have asked for what he wanted—a syntheholic Saurian brandy. But if he did, he would have had to endure yet another tirade about how he should try a *real* drink like whiskey, not "this Saurian swill." It had only taken the first officer a week to determine that sharing drinks with the captain wasn't worth the trouble. *As it is,* he thought, *Sisko's probably going to get an earful about his choice of beverage.*

"A *raktajino* and a black coffee," Keogh instructed the computer, which obligingly provided two mugs with same. As he handed the former to Sisko, Keogh said, "Klingon coffee, eh? Can't abide the stuff. Never could see how a human could handle it. Like drinking an oil slick."

Unable to resist, Shabalala added, "Only without the tangy aftertaste."

Sisko laughed. Keogh didn't. Shabalala shrugged, having expected precisely that reaction.

"Curzon Dax introduced me to it when I served under him as an ensign. I'm afraid it's become something of an addiction." Sisko took a seat on the couch against the outer bulkhead of the quarters.

Through the window over Sisko's head, Shabalala could see the spires of Deep Space 9 from the *Odyssey*'s vantage point at one of the station's upper pylons. Looking like a hollowed-out crab, the station had the aesthetic sense that Shabalala would have expected from the Cardassian Union, who built it as the seat of their occupation of Bajor decades before: hideous. Shabalala preferred the sleeker, rounded designs of Starfleet.

"You knew Dax?" Keogh said, taking a seat on the chair perpendicular to the couch. "Good lord, I haven't heard from the old man in years. How is he doing?"

"He isn't—exactly," Sisko said with a smile. "Curzon died three years ago. Dax is now in Jadzia, a lieutenant in Starfleet, and my chief science officer."

"Jadzia? You mean to say that Curzon Dax is a *woman* now?"

Sisko nodded.

"Some would call that ironic. Others would call it poetic justice."

Again, Sisko smiled. "I call it lucky enough to get a damn fine science officer."

Diplomatically put, Shabalala thought, but was wise enough not to say aloud.

Keogh tilted his head. "Perhaps. In any event, Commander, we didn't come to your station to talk about mutual acquaintances. What's this assignment you need my ship for?"

Sisko took a sip of *raktajino,* then set the mug down on the coffee table and leaned back on the sofa. "It's

several assignments, actually, Captain. Admiral Toddman said you'd be detached to the Bajoran sector for the next two weeks."

Shabalala smiled. "Those are the precise words he used with us. They were also the only words he used."

"We were told you would elaborate," Keogh added.

"Bajor is still trying to rebuild after the Occupation. Unfortunately, Cardassian mining operations have ruined some of their most arable lands. My first officer, Major Kira, has come up with a plan to convert a part of Bajor's second moon to farmland. She and Lieutenant Dax wrote a proposal that both the provisional government and Starfleet approved."

Keogh nodded. "And you want the *Odyssey* to set up the farm?"

"Eventually, yes," Sisko said with a small smile. "There's something you need to do first."

"Oh?"

Shabalala had to stop himself from grinning. Keogh only said "Oh?" like that when he expected to hear something he wouldn't like.

"Well, what's a farm without farmers? You need to pick up a group that has volunteered to toil in the fields. They're presently in the Valo system on the Cardassian border—specifically on the ninth planet. The *Enterprise* relocated them there two years ago."

This rings a bell, Shabalala thought. "Isn't that where many Bajorans set up resettlement camps?"

Nodding, Sisko added, "And also the base for some of their offworld terrorist activity against the Cardassians. One terrorist in particular has stayed away from

Bajor even as all the other refugees were welcomed home after the withdrawal."

Keogh's eyes smoldered. "You're talking about Orta, aren't you?"

"That's the one," Sisko said with a grin.

Standing, Keogh said, "Commander, you can't possibly be serious. Orta's a terrorist of the worst kind. He was never interested in Bajor's freedom, he just wanted revenge against the Cardassians for maiming him."

"I see you're familiar with Orta's file," Sisko said dryly.

"I've had my share of run-ins with the Cardassians over the years, Commander Sisko. I've made it my business to know as much as I can about them—and their enemies. In any case, assuming Orta's desire to come home and be a farmer is genuine—which I very much doubt—why on Earth do you need my ship to get him back?"

"Orta refused to be escorted by a Bajoran ship. He asked for the *Enterprise,* but they're unavailable, so he said another Starfleet ship would do. Since you're in the area . . ." Sisko shrugged.

"Wonderful," Keogh said, sitting back down. "I've been reduced to Picard's understudy."

Shabalala kept his best poker face on and asked, "After we've delivered Orta and his followers to their new home, Commander, what then?"

"Then," Sisko said, picking up his *raktajino,* "it's a matter of getting the farming colony started. There's some material you'll need that's on Bajor right now, plus part of the plan calls for use of a starship's phasers to change the composition of the land."

Keogh actually looked intrigued by that. "Really?"

"The moon's surface is primarily rock, but the top layers are cooled lava. Dax has come up with a way to use a ship's phasers to convert that to soil. We'll provide you with all the specifics," Sisko added quickly as Keogh opened his mouth to ask another question. Again, Shabalala kept his poker face intact.

Sisko went on: "Once that's done, we'll have some supplies for the New Bajor colony that you'll need to bring through the wormhole to them, and then Admiral Toddman wants you to patrol the Cardassian border for a few days. Things have been a bit tense in the DMZ lately, and Starfleet wants a top-of-the-line ship to do border patrol—remind the Cardassians that we're taking things seriously."

"And perhaps remind our own people of what we stand for," Keogh said irritably.

On this, Shabalala could get behind his captain. Many Starfleet personnel had been joining the Maquis lately. A recent treaty ceded several Federation colonies near the Cardassian border to the Cardassian Union and vice versa, and also declared a Demilitarized Zone between Cardassian and Federation space. It probably seemed reasonable to the politicians who negotiated it, secure in the knowledge that it would have no direct bearing on their lives.

Meanwhile, Federation citizens who refused to give up their homes, even though those homes were no longer in Federation space, found themselves harassed by the Cardassian military. The situation deteriorated quickly, and a group of terrorists formed, naming

themselves after the Maquis, resistance fighters from a twentieth-century war on Earth. Indeed, one of the Maquis founders was a former Starfleet lieutenant commander named Cal Hudson, and several Starfleet personnel had "defected" to the Maquis since then.

Keogh stared at Sisko. "Orta's really interested in becoming a farmer?"

"I've spoken with Major Kira on the subject. She knows Orta better than anyone else on the station, though she's only met him once. From the sounds of it, he doesn't want to fight anymore, but he doesn't trust the provisional government, either—and he has no interest in setting foot on Bajor again."

"Why not?" Shabalala asked, confused.

"He was tortured on Bajor," Sisko said quietly. "It's not always easy to put aside those associations."

Shabalala thought about how he would react if he ever had to return to Patnira. "I see your point."

Again, Keogh stood up. "Well, if that's what Starfleet wants us to do, it's what we'll do. But I don't see any good reason to like it. Mark my words, Commander— Orta is a killer. I've studied many freedom fighters in my time, including your own Major Kira, and he does not fit the bill. He's a killer who happened to find a semi-legitimate outlet for his need for vengeance. Bringing him to Bajor in anything other than a prison transport is a mistake. I just hope we all live to regret it."

Sisko and Shabalala also stood up, Sisko finishing his *raktajino* as he did so. "I hope so, too, Captain. I'll have Lieutenant Dax forward the specifications of the farm's setup to you so you can study it on your way to Valo."

Again, the just-barely-a-smile. "Thank you, Commander. Mr. Shabalala will show you to the transporter room."

"We'll see you back here tomorrow, then."

"Barring complications, yes." Keogh shook the tall commander's hand. The captain looked even more sour than usual as he looked at Sisko's smiling face. He was definitely expecting those complications.

After they left, Sisko said to Shabalala, "You were awfully quiet in there."

"Had nothing to say."

Sisko shot him a look.

Smiling, Shabalala added, "Well, nothing that was worth trying to get a word in to say, anyhow. I've found that Captain Keogh's monologues are best left uninterrupted. He always finishes them anyhow; it just takes longer if he has to start over."

Sisko laughed at that, and Shabalala joined in the laugh.

As they entered the turbolift, Sisko said, "Keogh may be right about one thing—Orta's record isn't exactly spotless. He's not the only former resistance member who's stayed away from Bajor, but he is the most vocal."

"I know, I've seen some of his speeches." At Sisko's surprised look, Shabalala shrugged. "Captain Keogh isn't the only one who's studied Cardassia's enemies. Orta's a borderline anarchist. He makes those *Kohn-Ma* fellows you put down last year look positively calm by comparison. I just don't see him as the farming type."

The turbolift stopped and its doors opened. As Shabalala led Sisko out, the latter said, "I tend to agree,

but this is what the chamber of ministers wanted—and they wouldn't approve the farming plan if Orta wasn't part of it."

"I thought Bajor needed this farm. Why would they jeopardize it just to please someone like Orta?"

Sisko smiled. "They're politicians."

Snorting, Shabalala said, "An excellent point."

"Seriously, they need to pull all the old factions in. If Bajor's going to get back on its feet, it needs *all* of Bajor—even the anarchists. They can't afford another internal squabble like that mess earlier this year."

"The Circle?" Shabalala remembered reading about the Alliance for Global Unity—or, simply, the Circle—that had attempted a coup d'état, leading to Starfleet temporarily abandoning Bajor and Deep Space 9. Sisko and his crew had exposed the Circle as being supplied by Cardassia—something even the Circle themselves did not know—and the coup died aborning. But that kind of unrest was not uncommon on Bajor even now, and Shabalala saw the wisdom in the provisional government attempting to unify the factions in order to avoid another such civil conflict.

"We'll keep you apprised of our progress, Commander," Shabalala said as they entered the transporter room.

Nodding as he stepped onto the platform, Sisko said, "Energize."

It had all been going too smoothly—Orta knew that now. Not a single military ship had even come close, despite their going through one of the more densely

populated shipping lines, and when they landed on the planetoid, they had met no resistance until they reached the rendezvous in the caves.

Cardassians loved their theatrical trials, after all, and it would be a much better show if they had footage of Orta actually purchasing the weapons from the Yridian.

Once the transaction was completed, it was as if the Cardassian soldiers grew out of the rock. It was ironic, since Orta himself had been the one to insist on meeting in the caves. Orta had always preferred dark spaces far underground. Sensors didn't work as well under-ground, and the darkness was better for Orta's guerilla tactics than Central Command's more overt ones.

But this time they used that predilection against him. They got the Yridian to make the deal, and made the weapons—stolen Starfleet phaser rifles—impossible for Orta to resist. It was the perfect setup, and Orta fell for it.

They brought him to Bajor, of course. It was the first time he'd set foot on his homeworld since he stowed away in the cargo hold of a Ferengi trader at the age of ten. His foster parents—Orta had been orphaned as an infant—had just died. They were collaborators who had made the mistake of betraying the Cardassians to help a group of Bajoran refugees. They tried to play both ends, and wound up disintegrated for their trouble.

Orta had no great love for his foster parents, but he had less for the Cardassians who rewarded their com-passion with death. He swore he would show them death.

He showed them plenty. For twenty years, "Orta" went from being the name of a forgotten runaway or-

phan to that of the scourge of the Cardassians. He made dozens of strikes against Bajor's oppressors, gaining a deserved reputation for brutality. It got to the point where every off-Bajor terrorist act was credited to Orta whether he was involved or not.

And now they had captured him. He had brought only one compatriot to the rendezvous, and she had died in the firefight. Central Command knew he had dozens of followers. The trial would be much more effective if it ended with a score of executions instead of one. But Orta would not yield, not to the glinn who ruined his face on the transport, nor to the Obsidian Order agent who carved out his vocal cords on Bajor.

When even the vaunted Obsidian Order proved unable to pry the information out of Orta, they—in a rare show of cooperation with Central Command—agreed to transfer Orta to a gul named Madred. Orta knew of many who had been sent to Madred. None returned unbroken.

That was when he struck back.

The Cardassians' mistake was in thinking that burning off half his face and allowing him to speak only through the benefit of an electronic vocoder attached to his neck had softened him up, with Madred prepared to deliver the killing blow.

It only increased his determination.

Orta never found out the name of the Obsidian Order agent who ruined his larynx. But as Orta carved the man to pieces with the very kitchen knife the agent had used to cut his food while eating in front of a starving Orta for days on end, the Bajoran pretended that it was his foster mother he was killing, that it was

his foster father who screamed in agony, that it was the Cardassian who'd killed them who begged for his life.

His people rescued him at great risk to themselves. A team of fifteen had mounted the rescue mission, and only four of them—counting Orta himself—made it back to the Valo system.

Within an hour of his return, he had already planned an assault on Central Command's listening post at Chin'toka.

Each Cardassian he killed was that Obsidian Order agent, that glinn, Madred, his foster parents—it didn't matter. None of it mattered, as long as Cardassians continued to die. It would never end.

Orta woke up suddenly. He did not scream—he could not even if he felt the urge to. His vocoder lay on the ground next to his pallet. Without it, he could not utter any sounds. With it, he spoke clearly and eloquently, albeit with a slight artificial timbre. With the damage done to his face, his mouth could not properly form words in any case. In many ways, the Obsidian Order agent had done him a favor. Had he left his vocal cords intact, Orta's speaking voice would have been slurred, distorted, foolish. Forced to rely on technology, he could still rally his people to his cause with the same eloquence he'd had before his temporary capture.

At least for a while. After a time, the terrorists' equipment started breaking down. Weapons ceased to function, warp drives went inert, and Orta's reputation had grown to such epic proportions that everyone was scared to even do business with him. The Cardassians

made it clear that anyone caught dealing with Orta would receive the strictest punishment possible. His activities became curtailed, limited to strikes on the border at the Valo system. It got to the point that the Cardassians' attempt to frame Orta for the attack on the Federation colony at Solarion IV failed because the terrorist's own resources had dwindled to the point that such an attack was no longer physically possible for him to achieve.

Two years ago came the final insult: the cause no longer existed. The Cardassians had withdrawn from Bajor. His homeworld was free. Orta had thought it too good to be true—a trick to lull the refugees, the terrorists, the freedom fighters out of hiding and then have them all killed.

Instead, he soon realized, the Cardassians had played the ultimate joke on Bajor: they now had to govern themselves. They proved as inept as Orta had feared. A "provisional" government formed. At the first opportunity, they begged the cowards of the Federation for help; they fell victim to internecine politics and attempted coups. The only leader on the planet worth a damn was Kai Opaka, and she died within months of the withdrawal.

Bajor was still helpless. Orta had been helpless twice in his life. He saw no good reason to repeat the experience.

So he had resisted all attempts to bring him "home." The caves of Valo IX were more of a home than Bajor ever would be, as long as Bajorans remained weak and foolish.

But his followers grew restless. The Cardassians

had gone, and they were left with nothing. Without the Cardassians to rally against, they lost their fire, their motivation. In truth, so had Orta. True, he would always desire vengeance against the people who had destroyed his homeworld, destroyed his family, destroyed him—but that could only go so far with the others.

Then he found the prophecy.

Orta's gift had always been the ability to form plans in an instant. He had not been in Valo five minutes after being rescued from weeks of torture before he had come up with the scheme to destroy the base at Chin'toka. Likewise, as soon as he came across the prophecy in a derelict civilian vessel that his people had salvaged after it drifted into Valo, a new plan formed. He just needed to wait for the right moment— a moment that came when the provisional government came to him with an offer to go to Bajor's second moon.

"Ready to go through with it?"

Orta looked up to see Tova Syed, his most loyal lieutenant. They had first met as children on the refugee camp at Valo II. They had grown up together, suffered together, fought together. She had been the one to spearhead his rescue from the Cardassians, and she was one of the other three who survived the mission. However, in the last two years, she had also been the one urging him most strongly to return to Bajor. Like Orta, she did not trust Bajor's provisional government, nor the Federation—but she did believe that the time for violence was over. When the enemy was Car-

dassia, they had to fight. This war, though, needed to be fought in other, more peaceful ways.

But she also always deferred to Orta in the end.

After affixing the vocoder to his neck, Orta said, "No, I'm not ready. I don't think I'll ever truly be ready to become a farmer."

"Oh, I don't know," she said with a smirk that made the scar over her nose ridge curve in an odd manner. "I think after twenty years of destruction, working to create something will be a nice change. In any case, the *Odyssey*'s here to take us to the moon."

"How wonderful." Orta had been disappointed in Starfleet's choice of escort. He had no love for the Federation, but he had liked Jean-Luc Picard—mainly because the *Enterprise* captain had made his Federation superiors look like the fools they were for falling for the Cardassians' frame of Orta—and had been looking forward to seeing him again.

"Turns out that the *Odyssey* is of the same class as the *Enterprise*."

Orta made what would have been a snort when his larynx worked. "As if that mattered. It was Picard I wanted, not a ship that happens to look like his." He sighed, the one sound he could still make on his own. "Is everything in readiness?"

Tova nodded.

"Then let us prepare to depart."

He got up and headed toward the entryway to the alcove that Orta had taken over as his "bedroom." As he passed Tova, she put a hand on his shoulder. Orta stopped and looked down at her battle-scarred face—

and battle-weary eyes. Orta wondered if his own eyes would ever look like that, and was not at all disappointed to realize that they wouldn't. Full of battle, yes, but never weary of it.

"This is the right thing to do," she said.

"I wouldn't have agreed to it if I did not think so, Syed."

"You would if you had some other plan in mind. And you always have a plan. You have ever since we salvaged that derelict."

"My plan is to bring about peace, Syed. That has always been the plan."

Tova regarded Orta for several seconds before finally taking the hand off his shoulder. "I hope so," she finally said.

Then they went together to the beam-out sight.

It was time to leave Valo behind.

It was time to go home.

Chapter Nine

"ENTERING BAJORAN SYSTEM."

Declan Keogh nodded at his first officer after that report from the conn. Shabalala returned the nod and said, "Go to impulse and set course for the second moon."

"Aye, sir."

The pickup had gone well enough, Keogh mused. He had been worried that Orta and his people would cause a scene, but—though they could hardly have been described as docile—they came on board with a minimum of fuss. They had spent their time in their quarters, with some of them venturing to Ten-Forward. The latter group—which did not include Orta—took to sitting in a corner, not mixing in with the rest of the crew. *Hardly an auspicious omen for a group that's supposed to be involved in a cooperative effort,* Keogh

thought disdainfully. He knew this mission was going to end badly.

"Commander, take a look at this," said the second officer, Maritza Gonzalez, from the ops position.

In reply, Shabalala went over to the ops console and peered at the readouts therein. "What am I looking at?" he asked.

"Bajor's moons," Gonzalez said. "I just compared their orbital paths—in a few days, almost all of them will be perfectly aligned for about half an hour. The funny thing is, the only one that won't be is the second one."

"Put it on screen, Lieutenant."

Keogh looked at the display—to the naked eye, the moons seemed scattered in various orbits as usual, but when Gonzalez overlaid indications of their orbital pathways, he saw that all but the second would indeed line up soon. "Fascinating," Keogh said with a nod. Then he frowned as he looked at the fifth moon. "Lieutenant Gonzalez, the fifth moon—that *is* Jeraddo, isn't it?"

"Yes, sir."

As displayed now, Jeraddo was a fiery red, looking about as uninhabitable as a ball of flame, when Keogh was sure that it was supposed to be Class-M. "So what in blazes happened to it?"

Gonzalez turned, gazing upon her captain with almond eyes. "Sir, Jeraddo's core is being tapped as part of an energy-retrieval project begun by the Bajoran government a year and a half ago."

Keogh nodded. "Very well. Thank you, Lieutenant." Silently, the captain chastised himself. He had tried to

familiarize himself with all aspects of this mission, but that particular fact had eluded him.

"Sir," Shabalala said, "another ship is coming into orbit of the second moon."

"It's a *Danube*-class runabout," Gonzalez added. "Registry reads as the *Rio Grande*."

From behind him at the tactical station, Lieutenant Talltree said, "We're being hailed by a Major Kira Nerys on the runabout."

Shabalala moved back to the command section and took his seat next to Keogh while saying, "On screen, Mr. Talltree."

The display of Bajoran moons was replaced with the image of a Bajoran woman in a red uniform of that planet's Militia. Next to her was a Trill in a blue Starfleet uniform.

"This is Captain Keogh of the *Odyssey*," he said. "You must be Major Kira."

"Yes," she said simply. *"Welcome back, Captain. This is DS9's science officer, Lieutenant Dax."*

Keogh blinked. It had been one thing to be told that Curzon Dax was now a woman named Jadzia, but being confronted with the rather attractive reality was still jarring. He recovered quickly, however, and said, "A pleasure, Lieutenant. It's been a long time."

Dax frowned. *"Excuse me?"*

"We, ah, met on the *Lexington* about twenty-five years ago."

"I'm sorry, Captain, I'm afraid—oh, wait," she added, her face brightening. *"Deco Keogh?"*

Shifting uncomfortably in his chair, Keogh said in a

hard voice, "It's been quite some time since anyone called me that, Lieutenant."

"Of course, Captain. I just didn't recognize you with so much less hair. My apologies. It's good to see you again, too."

Damn the woman, he thought angrily, *she has that same smile Curzon had whenever he said something guaranteed to embarrass you.*

To Keogh's relief, neither Shabalala nor Gonzalez nor Talltree visibly reacted to Dax's comment. He did notice Ensign Doyle at conn was trying to hide a snicker, and he was quite sure that the other junior personnel at the aft stations were doing likewise. *I'll deal with that later,* he thought angrily. "We're preparing the required modifications to our phasers, and we have a full team standing by to help set the colony up on the surface, along with your farmers from the Valo system."

"So Orta did come," Kira said with a nod. *"I wasn't sure he would."*

"Honestly, Major, neither was I. I still doubt his intentions. But he's here, as are his followers."

"Good." Next to her, the Trill started manipulating controls. *"Lieutenant Dax is transmitting beam-down coordinates for both Orta's people and your team."*

"Excellent. We'll meet you there, Major. *Odyssey* out." As the screen went blank, Keogh stood up, Shabalala doing likewise next to him. "Mr. Talltree, have Orta and his people gather in Transporter Room 3 and have them beamed to the major's first set of coordinates. Have the scientific team meet Mr. Shabalala and myself in Transporter Room 1."

"Yes, sir," the large security chief said from the tactical station.

"You have the conn, Lieutenant," he said to Gonzalez, who nodded and moved to the command chair.

Shabalala let Keogh enter the turbolift first, then followed him in and said, "Transporter Room 1."

Keogh nodded to his first officer. He liked Shabalala. After the string of incompetents that Starfleet had saddled him with over the years, he was grateful to have someone who properly served as an interface between him and his crew, and who kept his ship operating at peak efficiency—in other words, what a first officer was *supposed* to do.

As soon as the doors closed, Shabalala said, " 'Deco,' sir?"

"Commander, let me be perfectly clear: I don't ever expect hear that word again."

"Of course, Captain," Shabalala said with an emphatic nod.

"And I want Ensign Doyle reprimanded for her behavior."

"Naturally, sir."

Keogh nodded, confident that this would truly be the end of it. Shabalala had served under Captain Simon on the *Fearless*—a good commander whom Keogh had been sorry to see lost, especially under such horrendous circumstances. Simon and Shabalala both were the kind who understood the need to run a tight ship.

Within minutes, they had beamed down to the moon, along with a team of both science and engineer-

ing personnel led by Keogh's chief engineer, Commander Rodzinski.

Keogh was not encouraged by what he saw. The moon was a dark, desolate place. Long stretches of barren ground to his left were broken only by small markers. In the distance was a single mountain—which, he recalled from his reading of Kira's proposal, was an inactive volcano, one of several on the moon

The moon also had an underground network of rivers. One of the teams from the *Odyssey* had been assigned to set up the irrigation system that would tap those rivers. Meantime, those markers were placeholders for the Starfleet-issue prefabricated housing structures that would serve as the farmers' homes.

To Keogh's right was a large expanse of equally barren land, but without the markers. Most of this would be the actual farmland, once the *Odyssey*'s soon-to-be-modified phasers did their work to turn the rock into arable soil.

Worse, it was *cold*. Part of that was because the sun had set. For approximately six months of the year—a period that would end in a month's time—the sun was "up" only four of every fourteen hours. That was why this was the optimum time to start this project—by the time the seeds they planted were ready to sprout in a month's time, the moon's rotation would take it out of the shadow of the third moon, and the sun would be up for twelve of those fourteen hours.

The sound of a Starfleet transporter beam heralded the arrival of Kira and Dax.

Kira smiled as she looked at Keogh. "Doesn't look like much, does it?"

Keogh actually returned the smile. "I was just thinking that, Major. But then, that's what you need me and my ship for. So, let's get to work, shall we? I looked over your proposal while we went to pick up Orta and his people, and I put together a plan of attack, as it were. We should start—"

"Uh, Captain?" Dax said in a voice that sounded like she was talking to a child, a tone Keogh rather resented. "We already *have* a plan."

"Lieutenant, you're using my staff, my equipment, my ship—I think, therefore, that I've earned the right to implement their deployment."

"Captain—"

"Why don't you two talk this out," Kira said quickly, stepping between the two of them. "I'm willing to bet that there's a common ground the two of you can find."

"Major," Keogh said, "I see no reason—"

Kira now stood right in front of Keogh. She was shorter than Keogh by half a head, but no less impressive for that. "Captain, this is *my* project. I'm the one who conceived it, I'm the one who practically shoved it down the chamber of ministers' throats. The Bajoran government has also put me in charge of the project."

"Are you giving me an order, Major?" Keogh had to admit that he liked this woman's aggressiveness, but there were chain-of-command issues to be settled here. Kira was subordinate to Deep Space 9's commander— whom Keogh outranked. He wanted there to be no question of who gave orders to whom on this mission.

Kira's smile grew wider—and it was the smile of a predator swooping down on prey. "Starfleet is a guest of Bajor, Captain. As your host, I'm asking you to work *with* Lieutenant Dax. She helped me write the proposal, including developing all the technical aspects of it. Her presentation of those aspects is a lot of what sold this to the provisional government. You've only *known* about this project for a day. I would think you'd want the input of someone with more experience."

Nodding, Keogh said, "An excellent point. Very well, Lieutenant, let's see what you have in mind."

Smiling much more sweetly than Kira was, Dax said, "Happy to, Deco."

Keogh winced.

As Joe Shabalala led Kira to where Orta and his people had beamed down, she asked, "How, exactly, do you put up with him?"

Smiling, Shabalala said, "I grind my teeth a great deal."

Kira laughed. "That's usually how I deal with the chamber of ministers. It's the main reason why they sent me up to DS9. I'm far enough away that they can only hear me shouting when I contact them on subspace, and even then, they can always cut me off. They like . . ." She trailed off. Her eye was caught by something on the horizon. Shabalala followed her gaze.

Bajor was starting to rise.

Shabalala had seen an Earthrise from Luna once—the sight of the huge blue ball slowly coming into view over Armstrong City had left him in open-

mouthed amazement for a good fifteen minutes. His wife had told him he was going to catch flies if he wasn't careful. He pointed out that there were no flies on the moon, but that sort of logic never deterred Aleta.

As glorious as that sight had been, Bajor's rise was even more spectacular. Whether it was because the green-tinged planet took up more room in the moon's sky than Earth did in Luna's, Shabalala couldn't say— and right now, he didn't care that much.

"When I was younger," Kira said, "I came up to the fifth moon with my resistance cell. Prylar Istani used to make me stop and watch every time there was a Bajor-rise. I used to think it was a waste of time, but she *was* a prylar, so I watched, waited for it to be over, and got back to work. After a while, though, I started to appreciate it. Once I started watching them without her, she said she was glad. *'That's* what we're fighting for, Nerys,' she used to say. 'Don't ever forget that.' "

"Wise woman," Shabalala said.

Kira nodded. "I haven't forgotten, I can tell you that." She smiled sheepishly. "Sorry, Commander."

"That's quite all right," Shabalala said. "This project obviously means a lot to you."

"Bajor means a lot to me," Kira said with a quiet vehemence that impressed Shabalala, and frightened him a bit. "This project will help Bajor, so yeah, you could say it's important. And I don't want it messed up because a Starfleet captain's ego is larger than the quadrant."

Shabalala laughed. "Don't worry, Major. Part of my

job description is to keep Captain Keogh's ego at least planet-sized. We'll get this done."

"So there's Bajor."

Starting in surprise, Shabalala whirled around to see a Bajoran wearing a scarf around his head. The scarf obscured most of his face. The voice with which he had spoken so suddenly was mechanical and cold.

Orta.

The odd voice continued. "It's good to see you again, Nerys—though I'm surprised to see you in that uniform."

"I'm doing what I can to help our home, Orta. Now, so are you. And if you ask me, it's about damn time."

"Are you questioning my loyalty, Nerys?" Despite his computerized voice, Orta managed to imbue his question with a fair amount of menace. Shabalala suddenly wished he'd thought to bring a phaser.

Kira smiled sweetly—a smile that scared Shabalala even more than her earlier vehemence—and looked Orta right in the eye. Though Orta was not as tall as Keogh, he was still taller than the major, but she managed to look bigger even as she gazed up at him. "I'm not questioning anything, Orta—except for what took you so long to come home."

"I'm here now. And I'm eager to serve. So tell us what we are to do, and we shall do it." He pointed at the rising planet. "For the greater glory of Bajor."

Kira pointed to a security detail about a quarter-kilometer away. Lieutenant Talltree had sent most of his staff down to aid in the preparations. Shabalala also

noticed some Bajoran Militia security amongst them, no doubt lent by Deep Space 9.

"Good," Kira said. "You can start by helping those Starfleet people set up the processors. The ground needs to be properly prepared before the *Odyssey* can start the operation. It'll go faster if you help them out."

Orta stared down at Kira, then looked over at the security people. "Two years ago, Cardassians trembled at my name. Now I'm preparing ground for farming. Some would call that tragic."

"Really?" Shabalala said. "I'd call it progress."

"I'm sure you would, Commander. I'd think that you have never had to fight for your very survival."

Unbidden, images from the final mission of the *Fearless* entered Shabalala's head. He banished them quickly. "You'd think incorrectly. It's true that I've never had to live in caves, or wonder where my next meal was coming from. I've never been physically tortured or mutilated. But don't think I've never had to fight, and don't think I don't know what it means to fight *for* something. The question for you is, were you fighting for Bajor or against the Cardassians? If it was the former, then now you've got a chance to make that fight mean something."

Orta stared at Shabalala for several seconds before turning and heading toward the security detail without another word.

"Nicely put," Kira said, giving her fellow first officer an appreciative look.

Shrugging, Shabalala said, "I simply said what I believed—as you did, Major. We shall see soon enough if

it actually *meant* anything. What was that?" he added, hearing some shouting in the distance.

"What was what?" Kira asked.

Closing his eyes, Shabalala listened closer. Then he sighed. "Captain Keogh is yelling at Lieutenant Dax. If you'll excuse me, Major, I'll leave you to make sure Orta and his people prepare the ground. I need to go save my captain."

"Good luck," Kira said with a chuckle.

For Shabalala's part, he winced at his own phrasing. *Save my captain indeed,* he thought. *You aren't exactly overburdened with a good track record in that regard, are you, Joe?*

As he got closer, the shouting coalesced from Keogh-sounding noise to coherent words from the captain's mouth: "—and *then* we can fire away."

"That's ridiculous!" Dax's voice was not quite as loud as Keogh's, but she, too, had raised her voice.

"No, Lieutenant, what's ridiculous is wasting the time it will take to prepare the ground."

Shabalala put on his best smile and asked, "Is something wrong?"

"Nothing is 'wrong,' Commander—" Keogh started.

"Except," Dax interrupted, "that your captain's not thinking things through." Keogh was about to say something else, but Dax overlaid him. "With *all* due respect, sir," she said with no respect in her tone whatsoever, "there's too much risk in what you're proposing."

"It will take time to prepare the ground *and* modify the phasers to the right heat and magnitude *and* get the irrigation system up and running before we're ready to

178

begin," Keogh said. "While that's going on, we can have the housing entirely constructed—it'll shave a good twelve hours off the start time."

"Except," Dax said, "that the housing then comes under the risk of being hit by a stray phaser blast. Orbital blasting isn't exactly what you'd call an exact science."

"We can protect the houses with force fields."

"Or we can protect them by *not building them at all* until after there's weapons fire nearby."

"My ship is capable of precision firing, Lieutenant," Keogh said tartly.

Shabalala sighed. This was typical Keogh: once he got an idea into his head, you couldn't get it out with a phaser rifle. Even though Dax was obviously right, Keogh would not easily give in on this point.

"Captain," Shabalala said before Dax could say another word, "our timetable is such that we don't need to rush this. Yes, we'd save twelve hours—but that would be twelve hours we'd spend sitting on our hands. We can't go to New Bajor for another three days in any case, as the supplies won't be at DS9 until then. Why take the chance—admittedly, a small one, but still a chance—that something will go wrong with the phasering?"

Keogh glanced at his first officer. "I suppose you're right, Commander, but I still feel like we're wasting time."

With that, he turned and walked away.

Dax looked at Shabalala and said, "Thank you. Is he always this—this—"

"Single-minded?" Shabalala asked with a smile.

Chuckling, Dax said, "I was going to say arrogant,

but that works, too." She turned toward the small mess area that had been set up a few meters away. "Join me for a cup of *raktajino?*"

"Gladly," Shabalala said, following the intriguing lieutenant toward the circular array of benches and tables, in the center of which sat a replicator. About a dozen blue- and gold-shirted individuals sat at assorted benches—mostly noncommissioned engineers and science personnel who were taking a break from either irrigation or ground-preparation duty. Shabalala was proud to realize that he knew the names of each of them—and after being on board this ship with its complement of a thousand only for three months. "In any case, with the captain it's mostly a matter of managing him. He *is* a good CO."

Dax snorted. "Never thought I'd hear *that* about Deco Keogh." They arrived at the replicator. "Two *raktajinos.*"

Shabalala smiled as the two Klingon coffees materialized. Dax had just given him a handy opening. "All right, Lieutenant, I *have* to ask—why do you keep calling him that?" It had, in fact, been the real reason why he agreed to join her in the *raktajino.*

"Because that's what he asked me to call him." Dax's smile was very small and very mischievious looking—in fact, to Shabalala's amusement, she looked exactly like his eleven-year-old daughter when she did something she wasn't supposed to do. She handed him his mug, and they both sat down at an empty table. "He was a brash young lieutenant when I met him—and I was a cranky old male ambassador

named Curzon who didn't suffer brash young officers gladly."

"That can't be all there is to it?"

The smile widened. "No." She took a sip of *rakta-jino*. Shabalala did likewise, and was instantly reminded why he mostly avoided this particular drink. Gamely, he swallowed the bitter liquid anyhow.

"So what's the rest of it?" Shabalala asked, realizing that Dax wasn't about to volunteer it.

"There was this woman."

Unable to help himself, Shabalala laughed. "Why is it that every embarrassing story about a human male in his youth starts with the phrase, 'There was this woman'?"

"Not sure," Dax said thoughtfully, "but you're right, it *is* a universal constant. In any event, I was on the *Lexington* for a diplomatic assignment—they were hosting a conference with the Antedeans. Young Lieutenant Keogh was chief of security, so he and I interacted quite a bit, since the Antedeans are prickly."

"I thought they hated travelling through space."

Nodding, Dax said, "They do. But as long as we didn't hit the warp drive, we were fine. Anyway, remember this was two-and-a-half decades ago. So your esteemed captain looked—well, a bit different."

"Different how?"

"Full head of lustrous brown hair down to his middle back, which he kept tied back in a ponytail."

Shabalala blinked. He suddenly wished he'd ordered a Saurian brandy—a real one—instead of *rakta-jino*. "Captain Keogh? In a *ponytail?*"

Dax nodded. "And you know, looking back, he wasn't at all bad looking. Not really my type, but I can see why several women on the ship vied for his attention."

Grinning, Shabalala said, "Really?"

"*Oh* yes. Now the opening reception was supposed to happen on the rec deck. The night before the Antedeans were supposed to beam on board, I went down there to make sure all the preparations and such were in order.

"Unfortunately," and here Dax's smile grew deeper without growing wider somehow, "somebody was using the room, and had forgotten to engage the privacy seal."

Shuddering, Shabalala said, "Captain Keogh?"

"Ol' Deco himself, with a female crewmate in a *very* compromising position."

Now I really *wish this was a Saurian brandy,* Shabalala thought with a plaintive look at his beverage. "I believe, Lieutenant, that that mental image will haunt me until my dying day."

"How do you think I feel? I'm stuck with that image for dozens of lifetimes."

He raised his mug. "My sympathies."

"You *did* ask, Commander."

"Yes. Yes, I did." He drained the bitter brew, hoping it would wash the taste of the image in his head out. At that, it failed rather spectacularly. He shook his head. "It's funny, these days, he wouldn't be out of place on a Vulcan ship. I wonder what happened to change him."

"He got older—it happens to all of us. Well, most of us. Some of us get to do it all over again."

"Lucky you." Shabalala rose. "If you'll excuse me, I'm going to go wash my mind out with soap. Thank you for the drink."

Dax's face never lost that little smile of hers. "You're welcome."

Chapter Ten

"*WE'RE READY TO BEGIN on your signal, Captain.*"

From the command center that they had set up ten kilometers from the farm site, Keogh said, "Thank you, Mr. Talltree," to the image of his security chief on the small viewscreen. "Stand by."

The command center included a large portable science console from which they could monitor the phasering of the future farmland. Keogh turned to look at Dax. "Are we ready, Lieutenant?"

The science officer frowned as she peered down at the readings she was getting. "Give me a minute," she said distractedly.

The past eighteen hours had been a nightmare for Keogh. The new Dax managed to be even more irritating than the old one, and her arrogance had to be seen

to be believed. She simply *had* to do things her way. Pulling rank was a lost cause, as she seemed to be much more the centuries-old Trill than the twenty-nine-year-old Starfleet lieutenant she appeared.

Just because she knew me when I was young and foolish is no reason—

He cut the thought off as unworthy of him.

She was a talented scientist, he gave her that much at least. But how Sisko put up with her on a daily basis was beyond him.

The operation itself was, Keogh had to admit, rather elegant. The moon was, basically, a big rock made up of solidified lava and extinct volcanoes. Talltree had modified the phasers to vary temperatures so that it would pulverize the surface layer of scoria and pumice into component minerals. Phase one would have the mineral grains heat and cool, expand and contract—the functional equivalent of several decades of seasonal weathering without having to actually wait several decades. The scoria and pumice would turn into fine-grained dust, which would then be inundated with water from the irrigation system. After that, phase two would consist of more phasering to simulate more decades of seasonal weathering, resulting in a mixture of clay, sand, and mineral grains. After that, phase three would be the simple mixing of organic matter—presently in an *Odyssey* cargo bay, fresh from Bajor—with the transformed lava via the transporter and, as Dax had said, "Presto-change-o-*poof!* We have arable land."

Kira and Shabalala were on the runabout, monitoring the operation from there. It was one of the few rec-

ommendations Keogh had made that Kira and Dax had actually listened to. The likelihood of something going wrong on either the moon or on the *Odyssey* was minimal, but it was worth having the *Rio Grande* in reserve, both as a monitoring station, and as an armed vessel.

"Okay, we're ready," Dax said. "I thought there was an anomalous reading, but it was just a higher concentration of minerals. Nothing to worry about."

"If you say so," Keogh muttered. Then he turned to the viewer. He was about to instruct Talltree to prepare to fire, but the security chief's image had been replaced by the standby screen. "What the hell?"

Then Gonzalez's round face appeared. *"Captain, we have a bit of a problem. There's a civilian ship entering orbit, and her captain wants to speak to you."*

"We're a little busy down here, Commander. Tell her—"

"I've already told her, sir. She insists on speaking to 'the person in charge.' "

Dax smiled. "I say, sic Major Kira on her."

"Very funny."

"Sir, she's threatening to fire on us and the Rio Grande. *It's crazy—she couldn't put a dent in our shields, and even the runabout would probably give her a run for her money—but it would be a nuisance."*

"Firing on a lesser vessel is hardly a 'nuisance,' Lieutenant," Keogh snapped.

"Of course, sir, I'm sorry, it's just—"

"Never mind. Let's just get this over with so we can move on. Put the captain on the viewer down here."

"Switching."

Gonzalez's face was replaced by the most amazing sight Declan Keogh had seen since he first met his now-ex-wife twenty years ago.

"I'm Aidulac, captain of the Sun," the woman said with a bright smile that seemed to light up the viewer. *"I have this problem that I'm sure you could easily solve."*

"Of course, Captain," Keogh said happily. "Anything you want."

"Captain—" Dax started, but Keogh ignored her.

"I'm afraid you'll have to wait a while. We're in the midst of an operation that requires phasering the surface of the moon we're on. As soon as that's done, I promise to do whatever I can to solve your problem."

"Captain—" Dax started again, but Keogh waved her off.

"That's very kind of you, Captain, I'm extremely grateful to you for your help—but I'm afraid I'm in a bit of a rush. Do you think I could land on the moon before you start your operation?"

"I suppose it's possible," Keogh said without even considering it. All he wanted was to make sure that Aidulac was happy.

This time, Dax pulled him away from the viewer as she bellowed, "Captain!"

"Dammit, Lieutenant, I don't see—"

Then his head cleared.

He tried to reconstruct the last minute or so, and found that he couldn't. "What just happened?"

"Captain Keogh, please, you must believe me, I

need to come down there." Keogh heard Aidulac's words, but refused to look at the viewer.

"Lieutenant, what the *hell* is going on?" he whispered.

"She's a Siren, Deco, and she's trying to trick you into letting her land."

Keogh had heard stories about the women of Pegasus Major IV who had been specially trained by the Peladon Affiliation to be irresistible to men, but he had always dismissed them as tall tales told at bars by older officers to junior officers or by junior officers to cadets.

As a Starfleet captain, Keogh had had his share of experiences with telepathy and mind control, including one rather nasty occasion last year when he'd been possessed by an energy creature that was trying to blow up a planet as a practical joke. He did not take kindly to it then, and he was out-and-out furious about it now.

"Keogh to *Odyssey*. Tactical specifications of the *Sun*, Mr. Talltree?"

"*Ah, standard shields, one phaser bank, no torpedoes of any kind.*"

"So in your professional opinion—"

"*We could take her out with one shot, sir. Maybe two.*"

"Did you copy that, Captain Aidulac? You have one minute to leave the Bajoran system, or we test to see which of Mr. Talltree's guesses is accurate."

"*Very well, Captain. I'll leave.*" Aidulac's tone was petulant. "*But you'll regret this, I promise you that.*"

Keogh heard the viewer switch off. Only then did he trust himself to look at it. The weakness he'd shown irritated him—more so for having it happen in front of Dax, of all people.

"Gonzalez to Keogh. The Sun *is leaving orbit, sir, and is now on a course for the Federation border."*

"Good," Keogh said. "Mr. Talltree, ready phasers."

"Kira to Dax. Is everything okay down there, Jadzia?"

Dax was about to answer when Keogh interrupted. "A slight delay, Major. Nothing to worry about. We'll begin the operation momentarily."

"If you say so, Captain. Rio Grande *out."*

Smiling sweetly at Keogh, Dax said, "Don't worry, Deco. It could've happened to anyone. If your Commander Shabalala had been on the *Odyssey* instead of Gonzalez, she might have talked him into it."

"Still and all, Lieutenant, I would appreciate it if you didn't bring up the details of what just happened."

Dax looked down at her console, still with that damned smile of Curzon's. "As I recall, *Captain,* those were the exact words you said to me on the *Lexington* twenty-five years ago." She then looked at him. "Besides, from what Ensign Pérez told me a few weeks later, it wasn't really worth mentioning."

Keogh closed his eyes. *I knew she was going to bring something up sooner or later, either the holodeck or Curzon's liaison with Rosita. So naturally, she mentions both in two sentences.*

Then he opened them and, pointedly not looking at Dax, said, "Mr. Talltree, you may commence firing when ready."

And feel free to aim a shot at Dax's head.

* * *

Aidulac set a course out of the Bajoran system. Once she was safely out of range of either the *Odyssey* or the *Rio Grande,* she pounded a console out of frustration.

Damn, she thought, *now I've got a bruised hand to go with my bruised ego.*

She had hoped that her failure with Decker and Kirk was a fluke, that when the next Instrument was revealed she would be able to convince whoever was in charge to turn the Instrument over to her.

But it was time she faced facts. Her skills had atrophied.

Of course they've atrophied, she admonished herself. *It's been how long?* She couldn't even remember how to keep track of the passage of time in Zalkatian terms anymore—it had been that long—but by Federation timekeeping, it had been ninety thousand years.

A long time to wait for someone to stumble across where those fool rebels had hidden the Instruments.

Things would have been so different if Malkus had never come to me. If he had never forced me to oversee the construction of the Instruments.

Of course, it wasn't as if she had a choice. Malkus was the supreme ruler of the entire Zalkat Union. Aidulac was a mere scientist working on a world as distant from the Homeworld as it was possible to be and still fall within the Union's borders. She had spent her life working in relative obscurity, developing new technologies, figuring out new ways to use existing technologies, and trying to stay out of the way of other people. Aidulac had always preferred solitude. Once something was finished, she sold the patent to some-

one else who would develop it and make it available to the general public.

She had set up shop on a small planetoid in a star system that she couldn't even remember the name of now. In the intervening millennia the sun had gone nova, the planetoid long since consumed by the star's death throes, but back then it was just another dying stellar body that nobody cared about except as a scientific curiosity.

Which was how Aidulac liked it.

The only company she had were robot servants, who only spoke when spoken to, the occasional supply ship that would stop by, and the agents she employed to auction off the rights to anything she invented that might have practical mass-market use. Even then, she limited the contact as much as she could. She was only truly happy when she sat in her lab, trying to unlock the secrets of the universe. Since the universe was miserly with those secrets, the challenge had never lost its luster.

Then the strange ship arrived.

It had all the necessary authorization codes to enter orbit without being shot out of the sky by her automated defenses, which meant that they had been able to bribe that information out of one of her agents. At that moment, she sent out messages informing all her agents that their contracts were terminated, effective immediately, and she made a note to begin searching for new ones the next day.

The ship identified itself as the flagship of Malkus the Mighty. Aidulac was skeptical, obviously, but Malkus's flagship was identifiable through a variety of

unique and secure identifiers—most of which were based on Aidulac's own designs.

"Very well," she told the obsequious young man who contacted her. "I will grant The Mighty One an audience."

That left the young man nonplussed, but he signed off, and within minutes, Malkus had shifted down to the surface—specifically, to the atrium where Aidulac received her few visitors.

She had seen images of The Mighty One, of course—they were impossible to avoid—and she had expected the reality to be disappointing. After all, it was extremely easy to make oneself better looking, more charismatic, and larger than life on a viewing surface, but, in Aidulac's experience, few accomplished it in real life.

Malkus, however, was one of those few. He stood half a head taller than Aidulac—who was unusually tall herself—and had a bearing that could only be described as regal. Even though the atrium had directed lighting that emphasized the potted plants and sculptures that she had placed to make the room more relaxing, it seemed that every light in the room shone on him.

She knew the rituals of her people. She bowed from the waist and said, "Mighty One."

When he spoke, it was in honeyed tones that practically begged to have every word hung on to in the hopes of gaining great pearls of wisdom.

"I am told that *you* were granting *me* an audience. I rather thought it was the other way around." The smile that accompanied this statement took the threatening edge off his words, though Aidulac now noted that his

four bodyguards—whose presence she hadn't even registered—had moved their hands to their rather large (if still holstered) sidearms.

"It is you who came to me, Mighty One."

He laughed, then, a relaxing, pleasant sound. The bodyguards' hands went back to their sides. "Quite correct, quite correct. You are Aidulac of the Girons, yes?"

"It has been some time since I identified myself as belonging to the Girons, Mighty One, but yes, that is I."

"Excellent. I am told that you are the greatest inventor of our age."

She shrugged. "Perhaps."

"I hope so," he said with another smile. "I would hate to think that I was lied to. In any event, Aidulac of the Girons, I am the greatest leader of our age. It seems only fitting that we work together."

With those words, Aidulac knew that her life would irrevocably change. People in the scientific community knew of her, of course, and some did indeed revere her to a degree she found frankly embarrassing. But she had shunned public acclaim because it got in the way of her work.

Now, however, she had come to the attention of not just the public but the leader of them all. Her days of solitude, she thought, were over.

She was both absolutely right and completely wrong.

"How, Mighty One?" she asked, resigned to the inevitable.

"It will take some time. Will you dine with me aboard my flagship, so I may detail my plan?"

The question was a formality. To decline would be

as good as telling one of the bodyguards to shoot her down where she stood. She agreed.

Soon, she had shifted to the flagship. She had not changed her clothes, as all she owned to wear were single-piece jumpsuits that were functional and easy to put protective gear on over when she needed it. The Mighty One allowed the breach of protocol.

They did not speak of his plan during dinner, which was a feast unparalleled with anything in Aidulac's experience. She had lived most of her adult life on a steady diet of processed food, brought regularly by the supply ships and stored until they were eaten. The Mighty One, however, dined on fresh game, vegetables, and drinks that had obviously been prepared specifically for this meal. Aidulac had no idea how it was transported on the ship, but considering the huge amount of space wasted on the vessel—which was a hundred times larger than actually necessary to serve its function—Aidulac was sure that they managed to find somewhere to store live animals, grow plants, and harvest flavored liquids. She herself had pioneered the technology for ship-based hydroponics gardens, though she never imagined anything that could produce such bright yellow *clamdas*. They ate at a large table made from actual tree pulp, using utensils of the finest tin.

Much from that era had blurred in Aidulac's mind with the passage of ninety thousand years, including the specifics of the conversation during the meal. Aidulac was sure that The Mighty One spoke at great length about his own accomplishments, or perhaps

about the food, or maybe his family's history—the only thing she knew for sure was that it was ultimately inconsequential. After the final course was served, he said, "And now, to business. I wish you to create four Instruments of Power. I do not know how they may be created, but I wish them to allow me absolute control over all my subjects. I wish them to be portable and responsive only to me."

Aidulac waited for more details. "What are the specifications of these Instruments, Mighty One?"

Again, he laughed. "How should I know? If I knew how to construct such items, Aidulac of the Girons, I would not need you. The Instruments must grant me power."

"What kind of power?"

"Absolute power."

"Your pardon, Mighty One, but I'm afraid I will need instructions a tad more specific than that."

Malkus gazed upon Aidulac from across the table. He seemed to be studying her the way Aidulac herself would have studied a one-celled organism or a piece of plant life in her laboratory.

"Very well," he finally said, and Aidulac found herself letting out a breath she hadn't even realized she was holding. "I wish to have power over the elements. Power over the mind. Power over life and death. And most of all, the power to overcome my enemies."

For quite some time, she continued to ask questions. However, Malkus never got any more specific than that.

Finally, she said, "Mighty One, I am but a single person. I cannot possibly—"

Malkus laughed, then. "I do not expect you to achieve this by yourself. While it is true that you have accomplished many great things, you are, as you point out, but a single person. I have already assembled some of the finest minds in the Union. What they require is someone to direct them, to lead them, to mold them—and thus allow them to see my vision through to fruition. That someone, Aidulac of the Girons, is you."

When the meal ended, Aidulac was permitted to shift back to the planet to sleep.

By the time she woke up, all of her equipment had been packed by her own robots, which had been instructed by Executive Order—the one way that a robot could be overridden by its rightful owner, an override that was required to go into every robot constructed within the Union's borders. Aidulac had done so to secure hers (erroneously, as it turned out) in the knowledge that it would never be used, but not wanting to find herself subject to an inspection and failing it. As with all of The Mighty One's laws, those who enforced them took them *very* seriously, and surprise inspections from The Robotics Authority were not unheard of.

Aidulac would never see the planetoid again.

She no longer remembered how long she and her team—which, as promised, included most of the finest minds in the Zalkat Union, including many with whom Aidulac had studied or corresponded, many more whom she had never heard of—spent laboring over the Instruments. All she remembered was that it consumed

her very existence—and that Malkus spared no expense on their behalf.

Eventually, at a time when several outer worlds were fomenting rebellion and The Mighty One's armies were stretched thin to keep order, Aidulac presented him with his Instruments. She had prepared a properly ostentatious speech to make the presentation, having learned how much The Mighty One liked his spectacles.

"You asked me, Mighty One," she said when she approached him in his Place of Governing, "to give you power over the elements, power over the mind, power over life and death, and power to overcome your enemies." She indicated the simple black boxes, which she had adorned with Malkus's name. "Behold, the Instruments of Malkus. With this one," she said, pointing at the first of them, "you may control the weather on any world with a natural atmosphere, and control the environment of any place with an artificial atmosphere—power over the elements. With this," she continued, pointing to the second, "you may manipulate the thoughts of any sentient being within its range—power over the mind." She moved on to the third one. "With this, you may infect up to five hundred living beings with a virus that will kill them by making their hearts explode—power over life and death. And finally, with this," she pointed to the last of them, "you have a weapon of tremendous power that can disintegrate matter in less than an instant—power to overcome *any* enemy."

Malkus did not laugh. But he did smile.

For ninety thousand years, Aidulac remembered that smile.

Aidulac had hoped that Malkus would not use the Instruments, had hoped that the threat of their existence would be enough. But no one understood the power behind a simple black box without a demonstration.

And Malkus the Mighty was only too happy to provide such a demonstration.

The rebellions were all put down by having their ships disintegrated, their hideouts wiped out by hurricanes, their soldiers killed by the virus, and their leaders confessing to their crimes and repenting while under mental manipulation. The borders of the Union expanded by solar system after solar system, as Malkus used his Instruments to gain more and more territory.

Aidulac had hoped that her own obligations would end, and she and her team would be permitted to go back to their own work—work that might help the people of the Union rather than its leader. How many inventions had fallen by the wayside, how many more secrets of the universe might they all have pried loose had they not wasted so much time giving The Mighty One his toys of conquest?

But Malkus was not done with them. He wanted immortality.

They developed a genetic therapy that would prevent Malkus from aging. Then The Mighty One made sure all evidence that it ever existed was destroyed.

That evidence extended to the people who created it.

One by one, the members of Aidulac's team were killed.

The only one to escape the executioner's pistol was Aidulac herself. She had half expected this kind of treachery, and had laid the groundwork for an escape. As an added bonus, she also had the only copy of the genetic therapy for immortality left—and so, when she made her escape from the Homeworld, she also gave herself the therapy. After all, even The Mighty One would be overthrown eventually. When that happened, then, perhaps, she could return to her work.

How naïve she was.

The Mighty One did fall, of course. He had thought himself invulnerable because he was "immortal," but all that truly meant was that he could not die *naturally*. The universe's worst-kept secret was that it was far easier to destroy a thing than to sustain it. His body was devastated, and the Instruments confiscated.

She herself was tracked down and arrested. Aidulac was inextricably associated with The Mighty One as the primary inventor of his Instruments—and also the only one of that team still alive. While Malkus was in power and had a use for her, that meant that her life would always be comfortable and she would be treated with reverence. With Malkus overthrown and her own usefulness at an end, she became an object of disdain at best—an accessory to genocide at worst.

Until the rebellion succeeded, Aidulac had never thought about the cost of her inventions to living beings. For that matter, she had never thought about the benefits of her early ones. She had always viewed it as a scientific puzzle to be worked out, the latest in a se-

ries of dialogues with the universe to try and trick it out of another nugget of information.

Members of the rebellion—now the Zalkatian government—took her to some of the worlds that had been ravaged by her inventions. She saw the mass graves of people who'd died by disease or by destructive weather. She saw the cities ravaged by the energy weapon she had invented.

She saw death by her hand.

The rebels had tried to destroy the Instruments, but Aidulac had built them too well. Instead, they spread them to the corners of the Union—but did not inform Aidulac of the location of those corners. Having seen the death they caused, Aidulac understood the rationale, but she would have preferred to take custody of the Instruments herself—she knew that, eventually, she would find a way to destroy them.

But nobody trusted her to do that. Instead, she was put in prison.

What they did not know was the process she had perfected just as the rebellion started to succeed: the ability to convince anyone to do her bidding. It was an ability that would (so she thought) improve with use as her brain took to the genetic changes she had introduced.

It was, therefore, easy to escape her incarceration by simply convincing the guards to free her. She stole a ship called the *Sun* and made her escape, convincing everyone who followed her to give up the pursuit.

They never found her, but they also stopped looking, as they had problems of their own. The universe hadn't

made it any easier to sustain something than destroy it, and running the Zalkat Union proved a task far beyond the capabilities of those who had removed Malkus from power. Different factions fought amongst themselves, and the Union was plunged into civil war.

Aidulac began her search. The Instruments gave off a distinctive wave pattern. They would not stay hidden forever, and Aidulac herself was immortal. She would wait in solitude.

It was how she had always preferred it.

She set a course to continue her search.

The phasering went off without a hitch.

Orta had watched from a safe distance along with the others as the Federation starship's powerful weaponry sliced through the atmosphere like a dagger, transforming a section of the moon's surface from hard rock to dust. *Oh, if only I'd had such weapons at my disposal,* he thought with envy. *The Cardassians would never have stood a chance.*

Soon the water was added, a process that was surprisingly loud. Orta had expected to be nearly deafened by the phasers—which were, after all, noisy instruments even in their handheld version, and a *Galaxy*-class ship's array was several orders of magnitude more powerful, and fired at a concomitantly greater volume—but the controlled rushing of water had been a massive cacophony as well.

Then the phasering began again. It was a very small-scale version of what humans ethnocentrically referred to as "terraforming," and remarkably effective. One

ship was, in essence, changing the face of the planet—
or at least a part of its face. Again, Orta marvelled at
the sheer power at work here.

Admittedly, Orta saw many tactical problems with a
ship the *Odyssey*'s size—it presented a huge, easy-to-
hit target, and was impossible to hide. But it would have
been worth it, Orta thought, to have those weapons.

Once the procedure was finished, which took most
of the day, Orta and the others were put to work con-
structing the dwellings they were to live in. The Federation captain carried on for some time about how if
they had followed his plan, that would have been done
already, but no one paid attention to him.

Certainly Orta didn't. He was far too busy depress-
ing himself by thinking about what his life had in store
for him. *Seeding the fields. Living in a Starfleet-pre-
fabricated home. Waiting for crops to grow.*

He mentioned this to Tova who only snorted. "And
what's the alternative? Living in a cave, eating whatever we can scavenge, waiting for the Cardassians to
find us and bomb us into oblivion? No thank you. At
least now we're accomplishing something."

Orta said nothing in reply.

"Excuse me?"

Turning, Orta saw an old man holding a welding
tool. "Yes?" he prompted.

"You're Orta, aren't you?"

It was so ridiculous a question that Orta was
tempted to say no just to gauge the old man's response.
Then Orta looked more closely and saw the awe in the
man's face. "Yes, I'm Orta."

"I thought so. Well, honestly, who else would you be?" The old man chuckled. "I just wanted to meet you—and to say thank you. My daughter worked in the mines at Amrahan. After you liberated that camp, she was free—she joined the Resistance, and fought till the day she died."

"How did she die?" Orta asked, out of morbid curiosity.

"The fumes from that damned mine—she'd have died anyhow, but at least she spent her last days fighting the spoon-heads instead of working for them. And we have you to thank." He reached up and grabbed Orta's malformed ear, as if the old man were a vedek or something. It took all of Orta's willpower not to break the man's neck. "May the Prophets walk with you, Orta."

"And you also," Orta said by rote. He stopped believing in the Prophets when the Obsidian Order agent sliced his vocal cords in twain. He only continued to wear an earring so they could identify his body.

The old man walked away. Orta watched him for several seconds. Many of the farmers had been culled from Orta's own people, but others, like the old man, were volunteers—people who had lost their own farms, or who just wanted to do some good for Bajor.

He remembered Amrahan. It was one of the last attacks they had made outside Valo before the last of their warp drives had failed. The odd thing was, they had had no idea that there was a mining operation there, nor that there were Bajorans on the planet. Orta had wanted to hit it because the gul who ran it was the brother of the glinn who had first tortured him. That he

liberated a brutal mining camp with a death rate of seventy-five percent had been purest coincidence—but one Orta happily exploited for his own purposes. After all, anyone could assassinate a gul, but liberating a mining camp was the stuff of legends.

That night, before he went to sleep, he took out the padd he'd taken from that derelict and read the prophecy again. Then he went to the window of his new, Starfleet-created home and stared at the sky.

He saw many moons. Most were less than a day away from perfect alignment.

All he needed now was the right weapon.

A plan started to form in Orta's head. A plan for taking over the *Odyssey*.

Chapter Eleven

IT'S GOING WELL, Shabalala thought as he looked out over the land.

Three days ago, he'd stood on virtually the exact same spot and saw barren nothingness. Now he saw a row of houses, a twenty-square-meter construction with multiple protrusions that went underground to harvest the subterranean water systems for irrigation purposes, and small robots that were tilling the newly created soil under the watchful eyes of a group of Bajorans, most of whom were former terrorists.

"Looking good, isn't it, Commander?"

Shabalala turned to see Dax walking up next to him. "I was just thinking that very thing, Lieutenant. Well done."

"I'm sure Captain Keogh would disagree." In a sur-

prisingly good impersonation of his commanding officer's tone, Dax said, " 'If we'd followed *my* plan, Lieutenant, we'd have been at this stage yesterday.' "

Laughing, Shabalala said, "Perhaps." He considered. "Well, no, not 'perhaps,' at all, I'm sure that is what he'd say. But that is his way. I also can't help but notice that you called him 'Captain Keogh' rather than 'Deco.' "

Once again, Dax put on the smile that mirrored his daughter's. "Well, he's not here for my use of the name to annoy, so why bother?"

"Good point."

Just then, Keogh and Kira approached from the west. The first officer waved to them.

"Commander," Keogh said to Shabalala as he approached in as jovial a tone as he ever had. Then he glanced at Dax and added, "Lieutenant," with somewhat less joviality.

"It's going well," Kira said, looking out at the workers.

Chuckling, Shabalala said, "That seems to be the general consensus, yes."

"With good reason, Commander," Keogh said. "Of course, if we'd followed *my* plan, we'd have been at this stage yesterday."

Shabalala and Dax exchanged a knowing look.

"*Odyssey to Keogh.*" It was the voice of Maritza Gonzalez.

Keogh tapped his combadge. "Keogh. Go ahead."

"*We've gotten word from DS9 that the supplies for New Bajor have arrived.*"

"Good to hear, Commander. Set course for the station and stand by to engage at full impulse."

"We'll be ready to go as soon as you and Commander Shabalala beam on board, sir."

"Negative on half of that. Mr. Shabalala will be returning, but I'm staying behind with the scientific team."

"Yes, sir. Odyssey out."

Keogh turned to a confused Shabalala. "You're in charge of the *Odyssey.*" Next to him, the first officer saw Dax frown and Kira's eyes widen in surprise, both reasonable reactions to Keogh's surprising announcement.

"Sir, I'm sure that—"

"You're not questioning my orders, are you, Mr. Shabalala?"

"Of course not, sir, but—"

"Good. I'll accompany Major Kira and Lieutenant Dax back to Deep Space 9 when they report back there in two days. I assume you'll be done by then?"

"That is the plan, sir, yes," Shabalala said with a sigh.

Keogh nodded. "Excellent."

Kira smiled, but Shabalala recognized it as the polite smile one used on people one didn't like but didn't wish to annoy, either. "Captain, it *really* isn't necessary for you to stay."

"The commander here is perfectly capable of handling the *Odyssey,* Major. And I want to keep an eye on things here."

"Captain—" Kira started.

"I'm not doubting your abilities—or even yours, Lieutenant," he added to Dax. "It's not the project I'm concerned about." He pointed to the scarved indi-

vidual presently inspecting one of the hoeing machines, which appeared to have some kind of fault. "It's *him*."

Kira pursed her lips. "I can't stop you from staying, Captain, but I'm perfectly capable of keeping an eye on Orta."

"Of that, Major, I have no doubt. Still, and all—"

"Fine," she said, throwing up her hands. "Do what you want." With that, she walked off.

Keogh regarded Dax, who was giving him a disdainful look. "Is something wrong, Lieutenant?"

"Just wondering how much this has to do with Orta and how much this has to do with Aidulac."

"Nothing whatsoever," Keogh said in a tight voice. "I've had these concerns about Orta since the mission started, as your Commander Sisko can attest. Since they are my concerns, I feel it's only appropriate that I address them."

"If you say so." Then she turned and followed Kira.

As the women retreated, Keogh let out a breath.

"Sir?" Shabalala prompted.

"I can understand Kira's reaction. This *is* her project, and she's never been a hundred percent happy with the Federation's involvement in Bajor. Hell, from all accounts, she views Starfleet as little more than a necessary evil. She's the type who hates the idea of relying on someone else to keep the freedom that she spent all her life fighting for."

"I agree," Shabalala said.

"Dax, though—her behavior is inexcusable. All right, she saved me from doing something stupid with

that Siren woman, but I fully intend to note her comportment in my log."

"Of course, sir. If there's nothing else, I'll be returning to the *Odyssey*."

Keogh nodded. "Carry on, Commander."

As Shabalala requested transport back to the ship, he thought back on Dax's words, and wondered how the life of the party became the man he now served under.

After Shabalala dematerialized, Keogh turned his gaze back toward Orta, who was still struggling with the hoeing machine. Several others were now gathered around the device with him. Keogh tapped his combadge as he started walking toward the tableau. "Keogh to Rodzinski."

"Go ahead," said his chief engineer, who was also staying behind to make sure all the machinery worked properly.

Keogh gave the coordinates of Orta's location. "Report there immediately—there seems to be some trouble with the hoeing equipment."

"Yessir."

"Keogh out." He tapped his combadge to close the connection just as he reached the crowd. Orta; a woman named Tova Syed, who had been Orta's chief lieutenant for years; and two other Bajorans whose names Keogh did not know were now poking at the machine, which lay inert in the soil. Tova ran a diagnostic tool over it.

"What seems to be the difficulty?" Keogh asked.

"It's broken," Tova snapped in an annoyed tone. To

punctuate that annoyance, she threw her tool into the dirt.

"I've contacted Commander Rodzinski—he'll be here any moment."

Pointedly picking up the diagnostic tool, Orta said, "That won't be necessary, Captain. We don't need to run to Starfleet every time a machine breaks down. We will fend for ourselves—as we always have."

"You're not living in a cave anymore, Orta. You're part of a team now—and that means that you work with other people, and you make use of the resources available to you. Right now, you have a Starfleet engineering team at your beck and call. A terrorist works on his own and solves his own problems. A member of a team asks for help from other team members."

"But, Captain," Orta said in what may or may not have been a smug tone of voice—it was hard to tell with his vocoder—"I am no longer a terrorist."

"Then act like it."

Rodzinski showed up a moment later. "What's wrong with it?" he asked.

"It's broken," Tova said again. "Maybe you can tell us why. The diagnostics all say it's working fine, but it's not moving forward like it's supposed to."

Giving Rodzinski a nod, Keogh said, "I'll leave you to it."

"We appreciate your help, Captain," Orta said.

The hairs on the back of Keogh's neck stood up. Something was very wrong here, but he couldn't put his finger on what. Orta being nice was just so damned out of character. He was even more convinced that he

needed to stay here to keep an eye on him. Kira was too similar to Orta, and would probably excuse any odd behavior out of loyalty to a fellow Resistance fighter.

As for Dax, he wouldn't trust her with command decisions under any circumstances. When he was younger, he had looked up to Curzon, even emulated him in many ways. But after Altair VI . . .

No, he thought, *it needs to be me. I'll get to the bottom of what you're up to, Orta. That's a promise.*

Orta shook his head as he watched Keogh walk away. *Idiot,* he thought. *Like all Starfleet. Well, most,* he amended, remembering Ro Laren and Jean-Luc Picard. But they were the exceptions. *It will be a pleasure to take command of his ship when it returns.* In fact, the captain's idiotic insistence on remaining behind would be a key to Orta's plan. He would make a fine hostage . . .

The Starfleet engineer, Rodzinski—a diminutive human with gray-and-black hair—stared at his tricorder. "There's nothing wrong with the machine," he said.

"That's what we told you," Tova said in a tight voice.

"But it's not moving," Rodzinski said. "Which can only mean one thing."

"What's that?" Orta asked.

Rodzinski looked up and regarded Orta with a grave expression. "If the cause isn't internal, it must be external." He held the tricorder display-out toward Orta and Tova. "What's wrong with this picture?"

Orta peered at the display, which showed a schematic version of the hoeing machine—based on

the words over the image, it was the results of the scan of the hoeing machine that Rodzinski had just done. "It looks normal."

"Look again."

Tova snarled. "Can't I just kill him? Don't worry, they'll *never* find the body."

"Very funny," Rodzinski said. "Can't you see what's wrong here?"

Orta was coming around to Tova's view of Rodzinski's prospects for mortality, but calmed himself. "Obviously, Commander, we cannot. We would like you to enlighten us."

He pointed to a protrusion on the bottom of the machine—which was presently under the soil. "See that?"

Rolling her eyes, Tova said, "That's the—" Then she frowned. "No, wait, it isn't. What is that?"

"An excellent question," Rodzinski said, "to which I don't really have an adequate answer. We'll need to see what's under there. Which, given the fact that it can't move, is a *bit* of a problem. I'll get some antigravs over here."

As Rodzinski's hand moved toward his combadge, Orta said, "That won't be necessary." He looked at the other Bajorans, who all nodded.

The four of them positioned themselves at equidistant points around the front, back, and left side of the machine and each grabbed a handhold. Orta himself stood at the front of the machine and grabbed it at one of the diggers, and crouched.

"Everyone ready?" Tova said. "And—*heave!*"

Orta straightened his knees, his back straining with

the weight of the machine as he lifted it upwards. The vocoder rendered his grunt as an odd kind of metallic whining, which annoyed him.

At the back, Tova did likewise, while the three at the side not only lifted up, but also pushed it to the right, overturning the machine.

Rodzinski's mouth hung open. "Okay, I'm impressed."

Tova smiled. "What, you Starfleet types don't do heavy lifting?"

"Not if we can avoid it."

Orta almost snorted. *Typical Starfleet weakness,* he thought derisively.

"Look at this," Tova said, kneeling down by the depressed spot of soil where the hoeing machine had been. The repeated attempts to move the machine without success had resulted in a hoeing-machine-sized divot in the ground.

Sitting in the middle of that divot was a rather nondescript black box, which gave off a mild green glow. Orta also noticed a marking in some kind of script. He was no linguist, but he was fairly certain it wasn't Bajoran.

"Okay, this is *very* odd," Rodzinski said. "Don't touch it!" he added quickly as Tova reached for it.

"Why not?" Tova asked, sounding irritated.

"Because I really don't like the readings I'm getting."

Orta walked over toward Rodzinski. "And what readings are those, Commander?"

Rodzinski frowned. "I'm honestly not sure. I'm getting odd energy emissions—but I also can't get a solid

213

reading on the object itself. *Don't touch it!"* This time he yelled at Tova as she reached for it again.

"I'm not one of your stupid engineers, Commander," Tova said, standing up.

I can give you what you want.

"What?" Orta asked.

"I said I'm not one of his stupid engineers. It's just some box. Let's get rid of it so we can get on with the work."

"Not you," Orta said, waving his arm. "Something—"

I can give you what you want.

Images suddenly flooded Orta's mind: Strange alien beings of a type he'd never seen before. One of them hoisting this very box over his head. A beam of pure force emitting from the box as he did so. The other aliens being vaporized by it.

With this device, all that you desire will be accomplished.

He did not recognize the world, the beings, none of it—but he recognized the box for what it was.

It was the final piece to the puzzle. When he found the prophecy, he knew what he had to do. He just needed the right weapon to implement the plan. At first, he thought the *Odyssey* would be that weapon, but he no longer needed to take over an entire *Galaxy*-class ship and its crew of a thousand for the sole purpose of making use of its powerful weapons.

Because now he had the ultimate weapon. Something that he now knew—just *knew*—was stronger than even the *Odyssey*'s phasers. And he could hold it in his hands.

I can give you what you want.

"Oh, no," Rodzinski said.

"What?" Tova asked.

"According to the tricorder's database, this energy emission is flagged as belonging to a very dangerous artifact. General Order 16 specifically states that I have to take this thing into custody right now."

"I'm afraid that will not be possible, Commander Rodzinski." As Orta spoke, he knelt down and took the box—the artifact—the *weapon*—in his hands.

"Put that down! You have to—"

Rodzinski never finished the sentence. As soon as the weapon was firmly in Orta's grasp, a bolt of green energy lanced out from it and struck Rodzinski square in the chest. He was vaporized instantly—Orta was quite sure that the engineer never even knew what hit him. Unlike, say, a phaser, the beam made no noise as it fired. It simply destroyed the engineer without a sound.

That silence continued for several seconds, as the others were too stunned to say anything—except for one, who muttered a quick oath to the Prophets.

"You were right, Syed," Orta finally said, turning to Tova. "No one will find the body."

Tova looked outraged. "I was *kidding,* Orta! You didn't have to kill him!"

"Oh, but I did. You see, he was going to take this away from us—and we cannot let him do that." Cradling the box under one arm, he adjusted the volume on his vocoder. He wanted to make sure he was heard. "Most of you know of the prophecy we unearthed back at Valo. It is a prophecy that, in the natural course of things, won't be fulfilled for many hundreds of years.

"But, in the natural course of things, we would never have been conquered by Cardassia. In the natural course of things, Cardassia would never have withdrawn. In the natural course of things, I would have died under interrogation by Gul Madred. Destiny is not what the Prophets write out for us, destiny is what we *make* it. The prophecy will be fulfilled, my friends. And this—" he held up the weapon "—is the means by which we will make it be done!"

Over the years, he had made many speeches just like this one. He waited for the inevitable cheer that would go up in reply. They *always* cheered. It was how Orta knew the speech had gone over well. He couldn't remember the last time a speech didn't.

No cheers were forthcoming.

"You *killed* him," Tova said.

Her eyes reflected shock and disgust. The same woman who had stood by his side as he sliced open Cardassians along their neckridges, the same woman who had gleefully detonated a series of bombs on a fleet of *Galor*-class warships, the same woman who chased a Cardassian scout ship into an asteroid belt just to make sure that the glinn who piloted it was dead—that same woman was now appalled because he'd killed a weak human in an imbecile's uniform.

Next to her, the other two looked frightened.

As well they should. You are a man of power now. Use it.

He gazed down upon his lieutenant, his childhood friend, the woman he'd trusted for most of his adult life. "Do you doubt, Syed?"

Tova's eyes smoldered. "Yes! Orta, the war is *over.* We can't—"

"The war is not over until Bajor achieves *true* peace—*true* prosperity. Sacrifices must sometimes be made if we are to forge our own destiny. Good people have died for our cause before, and they will do so again. Commander Rodzinski has died today. He may not be the last. But when we are finished, all will be well, because the prophecy will be fulfilled, and Bajor will at last have its true, ordained place!"

"No, it won't, Orta. I can't let you do this."

Orta gazed into the eyes of his oldest friend. Tova Syed, who always came through for him, who spearheaded his rescue, who never doubted, was opposing him.

What's more, he knew he would never convince her otherwise.

A green beam of force lanced out from the device. Tova disintegrated in an instant.

Orta had killed many enemies over the years. This was the first time he had killed a friend. He thought it would be harder.

Almost as an afterthought, he destroyed the other two. They would be of no use.

Besides, he didn't *need* anybody. He had the device. Soon, he would have everything he needed.

I will give you what you want.

"Kovac to Keogh."

Keogh had been inspecting the houses with Dax and Kira when the call came from Assistant Chief Engi-

neer Kovac. Neither woman had kept her irritation at Keogh's presence much of a secret, but Keogh didn't care. As far as he was concerned, he was in charge of this project, at least from Starfleet's perspective. If anything went wrong, he would be held responsible. At present they were at the back of one of the houses, making sure that the feed from the generator worked properly.

"Go ahead."

"Sir, Commander Rodzinski hasn't reported back yet."

Keogh frowned. "That's odd. Can you locate him?"

"That's just it, sir—the tricorder isn't picking up his combadge."

Dax and Kira exchanged glances. Dax took out her own tricorder.

Tapping his combadge again, the captain said, "Keogh to Rodzinski, come in."

Silence greeted his request.

Looking up at Keogh, Dax said, "I'm not picking it up, either. Where was he last?"

Keogh gave the precise coordinates. "It's only about half a kilometer from here. He was assisting Orta and some of his people with a problem with one of the hoeing machines."

"I'm not reading any lifesigns in that area," she said grimly.

"Mr. Kovac, set up a search party," Keogh said.

"Yes, sir."

An alarm went off on Dax's tricorder. "What the—"

Kira asked, "What is it?"

Dax tapped her combadge. "Dax to *Rio Grande*. Computer, this is Lieutenant Dax. Link with my tricorder and verify readings."

After a moment, the familiar vocal interface that all Starfleet computers used replied. *"Energy emissions correspond to those described in Starfleet General Order 16. Recommended protocol: locate Malkus Artifact and confiscate immediately."*

"What's a Malkus Artifact?" Kira asked at the exact same time that Keogh repeated, "General Order 16?"

Dax looked up from the tricorder. "Have either of you heard of the Zalkat Union?"

Both Kira and Keogh shook their heads. Keogh knew that General Order 16 required any Starfleet personnel encountering an item with a particular energy signature—presumably this Malkus Artifact the computer mentioned—to confiscate said item, but he didn't recall any specific details beyond that.

Dax, however, filled them in quickly, ending by saying, "The artifacts give off a distinct energy signature when they go active."

"You're picking up that signature now?" Kira asked.

"Mhm."

Frowning, Kira said, "So you know about this because of Emony, right? Two hundred years, that's about her time, right?"

"Actually, no," Dax said with a small smile. "Neither Emony, Audrid, nor Curzon knew about the Zalkat Union. I came across them in the Academy—fascinating stuff."

Keogh rolled his eyes. "This is no time for a stroll

down memory lane, Lieutenant. We need to find that artifact. Can you pinpoint it?"

Shaking her head, Dax said, "Not yet, but—" Again, she tapped her combadge. "Computer, access data files on the Malkus Artifacts. How many of the artifacts have been discovered?"

"One of the artifacts was discovered on Stardate 1699 by the Starships Constellation *and* Enterprise *on the planet Alpha Proxima II."*

"Which artifact was it?"

"Artifact Gamma, which transports a deadly disease into target."

"Is there a way to recalibrate my tricorder so it can pinpoint a Malkus Artifact?"

"Affirmative."

"Do so, please."

"Working."

Keogh spoke up. "Computer, what are the characteristics of the remaining three artifacts?"

"Artifact Alpha grants the user mental control over other sentient life forms. Artifact Beta manipulates weather patterns. Artifact Delta can project energy beams of great force."

"None of those are particularly appealing," Keogh muttered.

"Tools of tyrants never are, Captain," Kira said.

"Tricorder calibrated."

Dax gazed over her tricorder, then looked up and smiled. "Hopefully we can find this while we're looking for your chief engineer, Captain."

Keogh blinked. That was the first time Dax had ac-

tually addressed him in a manner consistent with a lieutenant addressing a captain since the mission started.

Before he could revel in this, a mechanical voice said, "That will not be necessary. I have the weapon you are looking for right here. And Commander Rodzinski is quite dead."

Turning, Keogh saw Orta standing holding what looked like a simple black box with a slight greenish glow. The Bajoran had come from around the other side of the house that the trio had been inspecting.

As Keogh reached for his phaser, Orta said, "I would advise against that, Captain—unless, of course, you intend to hand your phaser over to me. Any other course of action will result in you following Commander Rodzinski into oblivion."

"You killed him?" Kira said angrily.

Orta shrugged. "It was necessary. Just as it's necessary now for you to drop your weapons."

"I'd do it if I were you," Dax said quickly, throwing her own phaser to the ground. Pointing at the box in Orta's hands, she added, "That's one of the artifacts."

"The Trill speaks the truth," Orta said. "Commander Rodzinski didn't even have time to scream before he was annihilated."

Keogh hesitated. Whatever these things were, they were powerful enough to warrant a Starfleet General Order, which meant they weren't to be sneezed at. On the other hand, it was just a black box. It hardly seemed like a threat. Further, Orta could have been lying about Rodzinski—or, if the engineer *was* dead, it

could have been by phaser. The farmers were supposed to be unarmed, but he hardly expected those regulations to stop a terrorist like Orta from smuggling a few weapons in.

"Very well," Orta said, "if you refuse to believe me, a demonstration."

Orta held up the artifact in the direction of the house they had been inspecting. A green beam shot out from it. Eerily, the beam made no noise whatsoever. In fact, the only noise Keogh heard was the rush of air to take up the space that was suddenly vacated when the home was vaporized. That, and the gasp that escaped his own mouth.

"My God," Keogh muttered. The captain knew that there weren't any people in the house, but he was also quite sure that Orta didn't know that. Worse, Orta obviously didn't care.

Keogh wanted nothing more than to wipe the smug look off of Orta's face—preferably with a phaser. Instead he threw his phaser to the ground. Next to him, Kira did the same.

"You're making a mistake, Orta," Kira said.

Orta laughed—it was a most unpleasant sound, filtered as it was through the vocoder. "You may not think so when I tell you what I am going to do with this wondrous discovery of mine, Nerys. Are you familiar with Akwar's Ninth Prophecy?"

Based on the way Kira's eyes widened, Keogh suspected that she was indeed familiar with it—which put her one up on Keogh. He had never paid attention to Bajoran spirituality.

"You can't be serious," Kira said.

"I am always serious. You should remember that about me most of all. Now then, I need you to take me to your runabout."

"Never," Keogh said.

"It's all right, Captain," Kira said. "I think we should do as he says."

Orta looked at Keogh and smiled—if one could call the odd shape that was all his mutilated lips a smile. "Kira is right, Captain. Unless, of course, you wish to end up like your Commander Rodzinski."

Keogh took a deep breath. "I knew you couldn't be trusted, Orta. Of course, I never expected anything like this. But you can rest assured, whatever you have planned, you won't get away with it. I'll stop you if it's the last thing I do."

The foul rictus masquerading as a smile grew wider. "I'm certain it will be, Captain."

Chapter Twelve

"ODYSSEY *TO* SHABALALA! *Sir, we need you back on board immediately!*"

Joe Shabalala had to blink several times and shake his head before he could even acknowledge Lieutenant Talltree's frantic message. That it was so frantic by itself was worrisome—Jason Talltree's reaction to a Borg attack would be to shrug his massive shoulders and say, "Oh, well." When they had looked over the specifications for how the phasers would need to be modified in order to transform the lava layer into soil, Rodzinski had practically pitched a fit at all that would need to be done, but Talltree had simply said, "No problem," and made the modifications in under an hour.

The *Odyssey* first officer had been exploring the monk's retreat that had just been completed on New

Bajor. The Gamma Quadrant colony had been up and running for a couple of months, and already felt like it had been inhabited for years. Shabalala had been expecting something more unformed—more like the farming colony, truth be told. But where Bajor's second moon was functional—primarily meant to provide a service to Bajor—New Bajor was to be these people's homes for a long time to come.

Centuries ago, the Bajorans had been known for their spectacular architecture, and their influence could still be seen all across the sector. Now, thanks to New Bajor, that influence extended to the Gamma Quadrant, as the monk's retreat where Shabalala was standing had been designed in the Jarrovian style from some three centuries previous. Shabalala's amateur eye recognized elements from three different substyles with the Jarrovian method that combined into a elegant whole.

So lost had he been in his observations that Talltree's communiqué had caught him off-guard, and it took several seconds for him to say, "Report."

"We just heard from DS9, sir. Captain Keogh and Commander Rodzinski are missing."

Shabalala blinked. "What happened?"

"Not sure, sir. Commander Sisko has asked us to go through the wormhole and report to DS9 immediately."

Making his way to the exit—the monks did not allow transporter beams within the sanctuary—Shabalala said, "Get all hands back on board and have Doyle set course for the wormhole. As soon as everyone's back, engage at warp five."

"Yes, sir."

It took five minutes to get everyone on board, ten minutes to arrive at the wormhole, and another two to arrive at DS9. Shabalala didn't even bother docking.

Within three more minutes, Sisko and two other members of the station's senior staff—the Bajoran security chief, actually a shapeshifter named Odo, and the chief of operations, Miles O'Brien—had beamed on board, and met with him and Gonzalez in the observation lounge.

O'Brien started. "This is the communication we got from your Lieutenant Kovac." He pressed a control, and the image of Mislav Kovac came on the screen.

"Deep Space 9, this is Lieutenant Kovac on the farming colony. We have a situation here—Commander Rodzinski has gone missing, and shortly after I alerted Captain Keogh to his disappearance, he too disappeared, along with Lieutenant Dax and Major Kira. We're conducting a search right now. In addition, we cannot raise the Rio Grande, *though indications are that it is still in orbit."*

Sisko leaned forward. "Both of our other runabouts are off-station, so we'll need to take the *Odyssey* to the moon and investigate."

"Bridge to observation lounge."

"Go ahead, Mr. Talltree," Shabalala said.

"Sir, Mr. Kovac is checking in."

"Put it through," he said, turning to the viewscreen.

The recording of Kovac's previous transmission was replace by a live image of the black-haired man. *"Commander, we still haven't turned up any of our people, but there are conspicuous absences among the*

*farmers. Orta and three of his followers—Tova Syed,
Pin Terim, and Hasa Jol—are also missing. The site
where Rodzinski was last known to be presently has an
overturned hoeing machine and no people anywhere
nearby."*

"Any signs of a struggle?" Shabalala asked.

*"No. But I can't see any good reason why they'd
leave an overturned hoeing machine right in the middle of a farming operation in the field like this, either.
There are also energy traces that my tricorder is flag-
ging as relating to General Order 16."*

That got Gonzalez's attention. "You're kidding."

"No, ma'am."

Shabalala said, "Keep up the search, Mislav. Report
in every twenty minutes, please."

"Yes, sir. Kovac out."

O'Brien shifted uncomfortably in his chair. "I'm
afraid I'm not familiar with General Order 16."

"Neither am I," Odo said.

At Shabalala's nod, Gonzalez quickly filled them in
on the Zalkat Union and the Malkus Artifacts. "Assuming that the one found on Proxima a century back
is still in the Rector Institute where it belongs," she finished, "someone on that moon has managed to find either a weather controller, a mind controller, or a very
big ray gun."

Sisko fidgeted, as if his hands needed something to
hold. "I think we can rule out the weather device—if
someone had it, we'd know."

"So far, the evidence points to the mind controller,"
Odo said in his gruff voice. "It's possible that Orta

227

took possession of Major Kira and the others and is using them for his own ends."

"Assuming that it *is* Orta," Shabalala said. "We don't have any proof at all. And I'm not eager to wait to find out." He tapped his combadge. "Bridge, set a course for Bajor's second moon, full impulse." Turning to the three from DS9, he added, "I hope you gentlemen don't mind taking a little trip."

"We want our people back as much as you do, Commander," Sisko said. Then he turned to Odo. "Constable, you mentioned Orta's 'own ends'—what might those be?"

Odo, already sitting as ramrod straight as Keogh normally did, somehow managed to sit even straighter as he gave his report. Shabalala wondered if that was an aspect of his shapeshifting ability. "Orta is the only name he goes by. There are records of a ten-year-old orphan named Gan Orta, who disappeared after his foster parents, Gan Marta and Gan Treo, were arrested and executed for treason. The boy's description matches what Orta looked like as an adult when he became involved in the Resistance. He primarily operated out of the resettlement camps in the Valo system, but he made strikes all throughout Cardassian territory. He was only captured once, and later escaped—during his capture he was mutilated. His attacks became even more brutal after that. Following the Cardassian withdrawal, he refused numerous entreaties to come home by the provisional government. He finally gave in when the opportunity to work on this farming colony came through." Folding his arms, Odo said, "Person-

ally, I've never met him, but he strikes me as the type who would have difficulty assimilating to a peaceful Bajor. If he gets his hands on one of these artifacts, he might well use it to wreak some form of havoc."

"Why would he do that?" O'Brien asked. "He won. I'd think he'd want to keep the peace."

"I'm not convinced he was fighting for peace," Odo said. "Many of the Resistance fighters were indeed struggling for Bajor's independence, but plenty of them just wanted revenge against the Cardassians."

Shabalala nodded. "Revenge can be a great motivator."

"I suppose you're right," O'Brien said quietly. "I remember poor Captain Maxwell, and—" He shook his head. "Well, never mind."

Turning to the second officer, Shabalala asked, "Maritza, can we pinpoint the Malkus Artifact?"

She nodded. "I can try."

"Please do. I suspect that wherever it is, that's where we'll find Captain Keogh and the others."

He dismissed the meeting and they adjourned to the bridge. Sisko took Shabalala's usual seat next to the command chair, while Odo and O'Brien went to the aft of the bridge.

As he sat in the command chair, Shabalala thought, *I'll find you, Captain. I'm not losing another captain. That I swear.*

Declan Keogh had to admit that Orta tied a good knot.

He, Kira, and Dax were presently sitting in the aft

section of the *Rio Grande,* each seated at a chair around the mess table. Using some rather coarse rope that Orta had brought with him from the surface, the terrorist had secured each of them to the chair with an exceptionally good knot. Orta had tied the ropes around their arms, legs, and necks in such a way that any attempt to struggle resulted in the rope tightening around the neck.

After they had beamed aboard the runabout, Orta immediately set about securing his prisoners. Keogh grudgingly admired the technique—Orta never put the weapon down, so he tied them up as best he could with one hand. Only after they were all sufficiently encumbered was he willing to put the weapon down and do a proper job with the knots—and even then, he made sure that the other two were in plain view and that he was between them and the weapon.

Orta had, of course, left their combadges on the moon.

Very professional, Keogh thought. *But then, I'd expect no less.*

Orta then went to the fore compartment. As soon as he was gone, Keogh looked across the mess table at Kira, who had a pensive expression on her face. "What is this prophecy he was talking about?"

Kira looked up. "Akwar's Ninth Prophecy states that when Bajor's moons align, then peace will reign. The thing is, the moons aren't supposed to align for another two hundred years."

Remembering what Gonzalez had said a few days ago, Keogh said, "Most of them will be. I think it's today, now that I think on it."

Dax, who looked more grim than usual, nodded. "In about half an hour, actually. Every moon except this one will be aligned."

"But that's not what the prophecy says," Kira said. "So I don't see how—"

"The artifact," Dax said simply.

Kira's eyes widened. "No."

Keogh frowned, then realized what Dax was implying. "Lieutenant, do you expect me to believe that that weapon is powerful enough to knock the moon out of its orbit?"

"No, Captain, I don't expect *you* to believe it," Dax said snippily. "But what you believe doesn't matter a whole lot. The point is, *Orta* believes it, and I'm willing to bet half a dozen bars of latinum that his plan is to mount that box onto the *Rio Grande* and try to bring the moon in line with the others."

"Brava, Lieutenant," came Orta's mechanized voice from the hatch to the fore section. "That is, in fact, my precise plan."

"There's no way that thing of yours can accomplish this," Keogh said.

"Oh, you're wrong, Captain," Orta said in a surprisingly quiet voice. "In fact, it is the least of what this wondrous device can do."

Dax snorted. "You really think you can change the moon's orbit just by firing a big gun at it?"

"I know I can—especially with this runabout to plot a precise course. I have no love for Starfleet, Lieutenant, but I will concede one thing: you build excellent machines. I'm quite sure that this ship's computer

can aid me in bringing *all* the moons into alignment. This will bring about *true* peace."

"Bajor *is* at peace, Orta," Keogh said. "The only one preventing that right now is you."

"I'd pretend to be shocked at your naïveté, Captain, but you *are* Starfleet, after all. Bajor is at the very antithesis of peace. When the Cardassians left, Bajor would have lasted less than a year before the squabbling tore it apart. The only reason it didn't was the fortuitous discovery of the wormhole. And even with that, the Circle's attempted coup almost brought Bajor down less than a year after the withdrawal. The Federation and the Cardassians still fight with each other and with us. Then there's the deplorable situation with the Maquis, and Bajor has been drawn into that, as well. The government still calls itself 'provisional.' Bajor is not at peace, Captain. Bajor will never be at peace, until Akwar's Prophecy is fulfilled."

"The prophecies aren't there for you to make happen, Orta," Kira said.

"Nonsense. If the Prophets have shown us anything, Nerys, it's that we make our own destiny. *We* threw the Cardassians out, not the Prophets." Orta then smiled again, as revolting a sight as Keogh had ever seen. "Besides, the prophecy only says that peace will come when the moons align—it says nothing about them aligning naturally."

"There's something I don't understand," Keogh said.

The sound that came out of Orta's vocoder was probably a laugh. "I daresay there are several, Captain."

Keogh ignored the barb. "You don't strike me as the kind of person who gloats over his victims. You're telling us all of this for a reason. I'm not a very patient man, Orta—I'd prefer you simply tell us what you want from us instead of boring us to tears with rhetoric."

"My intent is not to bore you, Captain," Orta said, moving closer to Keogh. "I wish you to understand the scope of what I'm trying to achieve. The prophecy is very clear."

"Prophecies are *never* clear," Keogh said angrily, "and you can't seriously expect me to believe that a freak astonomical phenomenon is capable of bringing about peace."

"You doubt the prophecies, Captain?"

"Of course."

"So you have no intention of aiding me in my quest to bring about peace on Bajor?"

"I can't see any good reason why I should."

Orta nodded. "Understandable. So I'm sure I can't count on you to provide me with the access codes to this runabout?"

"You haven't tried to access any of the runabout's systems?" Kira asked.

Laughing a mechanical laugh, Orta said, "I didn't survive as long as I did by being a fool, Nerys. I know how well Starfleet likes to secure its secrets. If I even attempt to touch a control panel, I have every faith that the runabout will totally shut down. So you will provide me with the access codes."

"And if I don't?" Kira asked.

Orta held the box proximate to Keogh's head. "Then the captain dies."

"Don't do it, Major!" Keogh shouted. "That's an order!"

"You *do* have a death wish, don't you, Captain?"

Keogh turned and looked up at Orta, who was trying to loom menacingly over the captain. But Keogh refused to be so menaced. "Ten years ago, Orta, I was captured by a Tzenkethi raider. While I cannot say that I endured anything on the level of what you went through in Cardassian hands, I fully expected to die. In my time, I've seen combat against Romulans, Tzenkethi, Cardassians, Tholians, and alien races that I'm quite sure you've never heard of. Each time, I was ready to die—because I swore an oath to—"

"Tell me, Captain," Orta said, "does this speech have a point? Or an end? Or perhaps you *do* have a death wish, and are hoping I'll vaporize you rather than listen to a pretentious Starfleet diatribe." He leaned in close. Keogh noted that the man had malodorous breath. "You know *nothing* about suffering or dying for a cause, Captain—or about believing in it. *Nothing.* You took an *oath?* Words are meaningless without action, without *passion*—without faith."

Keogh snorted. "Honestly? My speech was more interesting."

Again the awful smile. "Perhaps." Orta stood upright and looked at Kira. "But you understand my point, don't you, Nerys? You know what the Prophets are capable of—if we just seize the moment. They gave us the prophecies for a *reason*. And we can make

it work for us—transform Bajor into the place it was *meant* to be."

Intellectually, Keogh was impressed by Orta's skill with oratory, especially when handicapped with a vocoder. Philosophically, of course, he found the man infuriating. He was exactly the kind of fanatic Keogh had feared he would be, and the trouble he was causing now was as bad as anything he might have predicted to Sisko days ago on the *Odyssey*. If he pulled off this lunatic plan to fire his weapon at the moon, the damage it would do would be incalculable. Tide shifts, gravitational fluxes, weather disruptions—not to mention the likely loss of life, particularly on the farms below.

But much more infuriating was that Kira appeared to be buying his line.

"Don't kill him," Kira said in a small voice. "I'll give you the codes."

Furious, Keogh started, "Major, I gave you a direct—"

"I don't report to you, Captain," Kira said sharply. Then she turned to Orta and rattled off a series of numbers and Greek letters. Keogh held out some hope that the codes she gave were gibberish and Orta would enter them, be seen by the computer to be a fraud, and lock down.

"You have done the greatest service you can for your home, Nerys," Orta said. "Believe me, you won't regret this."

Orta turned and headed back to the fore chamber. Within seconds, Keogh could feel the thrum of the run-

about's impulse engines, though the ship did not yet move, based on his glance at the viewport.

"You actually did it." Keogh shook his head in dismay. "Major, I can't believe you'd be so stupid! He's a terrorist—Starfleet doesn't deal with terrorists."

"I used to *be* a terrorist," Kira said in a tight voice. "I know how they think, I know how they operate—and I can assure you, Captain, that this is the only way. You have to trust me."

Keogh couldn't believe what he was hearing. *"Trust* you? Major, you just handed over a Starfleet runabout to a lunatic! And why? Because he's quoting some nonsense?"

To Keogh's surprise, it was Dax who spoke. "It isn't nonsense, Captain. Don't forget, I've *met* the Prophets. I was with Benjamin when he discovered the wormhole, and I've had an Orb experience."

Eyes wide, Keogh said, "Since when, Lieutenant, do you subscribe to the Bajoran faith?"

"I don't," Dax said in a tone Keogh found to be unconscionably smug, "I'm a scientist. And I don't let narrow-minded prejudices get in the way of empirical evidence."

With a snort, Keogh said, "I'm not the one who just handed a weapon of mass destruction to a madman."

Kira sighed. "I don't expect you to understand, Captain. But you will. Trust in the Prophets."

Easily keeping his temper under control by dint of years of long practice—besides, he could hardly get a proper mad-on while tied to a chair—Keogh nonetheless was furious as he said, "Right now, Major, the

only thing I can trust is my own officers—Lieutenant Kovac should have discovered our disappearance by now. I can only hope that he's alerted DS9 and they've alerted the *Odyssey*. And when this is over, assuming we survive, I can assure both of you that you'll face the full disciplinary wrath of Starfleet for what you've done today."

Chapter Thirteen

"JOE, WE'LL BE AT BAJOR in ten minutes," Gonzalez said. "Coming into range now."

Shabalala hadn't realized he was gripping the sides of the command chair until he let go and realized how cramped his long fingers were becoming. "Full scan," he said.

"The *Rio Grande* is still in orbit. Can't get a solid fix on it—there's interference," Gonzalez said, shaking her head in annoyance. "I can tell you that there are four humanoid life-forms on the runabout, but I'm not picking up any combadges."

"What's causing the interference?"

Gonzalez turned toward the command center and half-smiled. "Well, since the readings got clearer after I compensated for the interference generated by the

Malkus Artifact, I'd say that. It's not perfect resolution, unfortunately, but I'd say whoever's on that runabout must have the artifact."

"What about on the surface?"

The second officer gazed back down at her readings. "Plenty of lifesigns—mostly Bajoran and human. I'm reading combadges for everyone who should be there except for Captain Keogh, Commander Rodzinski, Lieutenant Dax, and Major Kira."

"*Odyssey* to Kovac," Shabalala said, reopening the channel to the surface. "Anything, Mislav?"

"*No, sir. We haven't turned up a trace of them, or Orta's people.*"

Shabalala muttered a favorite curse of his mother's.

Odo, standing next to Talltree at tactical, said, "We have to assume that they're dead, and the four people on the *Rio Grande* are Orta and his followers—and they obviously have the artifact. We may need to destroy the runabout."

"General Order 16 is very specific, Constable," Talltree said. "We have to retrieve the artifact, not destroy it."

"You may not have that luxury, Lieutenant," Odo said in a belligerent tone.

Shabalala said nothing. He still was thinking about Odo's words.

The captain may be dead.

He shook his head. *We don't know that yet. We can't assume it's happened again. Even if it has, it isn't my fault this time.*

Unbidden, images came to him of the strange, mutated *thing* that Captain Simon had been transformed

into by the Patniran weapon, of Shabalala raising his phaser and destroying her before she could kill him, and then being helpless while other crew members who had been similarly mutated destroyed the *Fearless*.

Not again, dammit, not again . . .

Gonzalez interrupted his reverie. "Joe, the *Rio Grande* is powering up."

Talltree said, "That means whoever's on board has the access codes. It could mean that either Kira or Dax gave the codes away before they were killed."

"That is exceedingly unlikely," Odo said. "Besides, it could have been Captain Keogh."

"He didn't know them," Sisko said. "But I agree with the constable. We need to find out what's going on on that runabout." Sisko looked expectantly at Shabalala.

I need to make a decision. He forced away the image of Captain Simon, his dear friend, his commanding officer, dying at his hand, and focused on the situation at hand. "Hail the runabout, Mr. Talltree."

"Yes, sir." After a moment: "No reply."

"Joe, I've managed to refine the scan," Gonzalez said. "At least one of the people on that ship is giving off a bio-signature that matches that of a joined Trill."

Sisko broke into a grin. "Dax."

"She may have betrayed us, sir," Talltree said.

"We don't know anything, Lieutenant," Sisko snapped. "And I'd advise you to be careful of who you accuse of betraying the uniform."

"That's enough!" Shabalala said. He was so busy wallowing in the past, he was losing control of the

bridge. "Mr. Talltree, lock phasers on the *Rio Grande,* and open a channel."

Talltree manipulated his console. "Phasers locked, channel open."

Shabalala stood up, for no other reason than that he needed to stand alone—to be in command, not to sit uselessly next to Sisko. "This is Commander Joseph Shabalala of the *U.S.S. Odyssey.* If you do not respond to our hails, we will be forced to open fire."

Several tense seconds went by. "Nothing, sir," Talltree said.

"Joe, I don't like this," Gonzalez said.

Shabalala walked over to her console and stood next to her. "Don't like what, Maritza?"

"I'm picking up some modifications to the weapons systems."

"What kind of modifications?"

Grimly, she said, "Well, that's the fun part—the interference is strongest there. To my mind, that says that they're hooking the artifact up to the weapons array."

"If they have the energy weapon," Odo said, "then they could be attaching it to the runabout's systems."

"That's my guess, too," Gonzalez said.

Again, Shabalala muttered his mother's curse. "Prepare to fire, Mr. Talltree."

From one of the aft science consoles, O'Brien said, "Excuse me, Commander, but I'm picking up fluctuations in the *Rio Grande*'s power signature."

Both Sisko and Odo shot O'Brien looks, then moved as one to the back of the bridge. "Is that what I think it is, Chief?" Sisko asked.

"Probably, sir."

Frowning, Gonzalez said, "It's just a minor power fluctuation."

"That's all it's supposed to be," Sisko said. "Commander, don't fire on the *Rio Grande.*"

"What?"

"Trust me—let them power up the weapon."

Less than a year ago, a Patniran doctor he didn't know asked Joe Shabalala to trust her when she said that Captain Simon would suffer no ill effects. That bit of trust led to Shabalala having to murder his captain and watch as their ship was destroyed.

Sisko stepped down the horseshoe and stood eye to eye with Shabalala. "Give them one minute. If Dax has done what I think she has, this will be over then. *Please,* Commander."

(*"Kill me, Joe.* Please *kill me."*)

Shaking off the memory of Captain Simon's last words to him, Shabalala stared at Sisko's intense brown eyes.

"Stand by, Mr. Talltree," he finally said.

Talltree didn't sound happy as he said, "Yes, sir."

In Declan Keogh's mind, the court martial was already in session.

Jadzia Dax and Kira Nerys stood before a tribunal. Keogh had chosen the three admirals he knew to be the toughest around—Brand, Haden, and Satie. No, wait, Satie had resigned in disgrace. *Maybe Nechayev. Alynna's always been a major pain in the neck.* Besides, she was in charge of the Maquis mess

in the DMZ, so she knew the players. *Yes, she'll be perfect.*

Keogh imagined some useless JAG officer defending the major and lieutenant. He remembered some lieutenant commander or other who'd defended Keogh's old Academy classmate during a court martial several years previous. He was an incompetent boob, as Keogh recalled, so he defended. The prosecution, of course, was handled by Keogh himself. So what if he wasn't trained? This was his fantasy, after all.

"And so, sirs," he said in a loud, clear voice, "it is my recommendation that Lieutenant Dax and Major Kira receive the full penalty for disobeying a direct order and aiding and abetting a known terrorist."

Haden handed down the verdict: guilty. They didn't even need to meet to discuss it. The three admirals just glanced at each other and nodded. Keogh's case was, after all, airtight.

Then Keogh amended the situation. After all, they were entitled to *some* defense. Kira pointed out that she wasn't in Keogh's chain of command, as she had done on the runabout only minutes earlier, but Keogh blew holes in that theory quickly. She was subordinate to a Starfleet officer, Benjamin Sisko, and Sisko was subordinate to Keogh. Therefore, simple logic dictated that she was beholden to his orders.

Hm. Maybe I should have Admiral T'Nira on the tribunal instead of Brand.

Dax, naturally, went on at great length about all the Dax symbiont had accomplished, in her usual arrogant tone. Of course, Keogh was able to dash that argument

as well. After all, Jadzia Dax was a different person—that was why she had to go through the Academy, achieve the rank of lieutenant. The accomplishments of the other hosts of the Dax symbiont were not relevant to the proceedings.

Keogh took special pleasure in the mental image of Dax returning forlornly to her seat from the witness stand after that, carrying the same look on her face that he himself had had two-and-a-half decades ago when Curzon Dax barged in on him in the rec deck.

The verdict came down: guilty.

Then he saw it through the viewport: the *Odyssey*.

At last, Keogh thought. *Now maybe something will get accomplished.*

"So, Orta, when are you going to tell the truth?"

Keogh blinked. This was Kira talking. The captain noted that she, too, had spied the *Galaxy*-class ship's presence nearby and, as soon as she did, she smiled. *What is going on here?*

"What makes you think I haven't told the truth, Nerys?" Orta asked.

Dax spoke up before Kira could. "Because we've seen your type before. You think the Federation is as bad as Cardassia, and you're trying to get rid of us by blowing up a Bajoran moon with a Federation runabout. You figure that'll be enough to get the Federation out of Bajor."

"Is that what you think?" Orta said with a sneer.

"It won't work," Dax said. "With the wormhole there, the Federation won't pull out easily."

Orta's laugh was chillingly sterile. "They already did once, when the Circle threatened your precious

space station. I'm quite sure they could be convinced to do so again, given the right circumstances. But you're wrong. You're forgetting the prophecy."

Then Kira did something that shocked Keogh: *she* laughed.

She laughed very long and very hard.

Keogh, Orta, and Dax all looked at her as if she was slightly demented—certainly Keogh was starting to believe that.

"Something amuses you, Nerys?" Orta asked. That got Keogh's attention, because the smug, supercilious tone was gone. Now Orta sounded angry.

Keogh wasn't sure if that was good or bad.

"When are you going to tell us the truth, Orta? The *real* truth. Not what you wanted me to believe, and not what Dax thinks you're doing."

Dax blinked. "Excuse me?"

Keogh took a certain satisfaction out of the hurt look on Dax's face.

Kira, though, ignored her. "Come on, Orta, I know you. Hell, I used to *be* you. You don't want peace. If you did, you'd have been the first person to come back home, not the last. You've been sitting in that cave on Valo IX waiting for the war to start up again—hoping and praying to gods you don't even *believe* in that the Cardassians were kidding. That they'd come back so you could blow up more of their ships and depots and outposts. And, after two years, when that didn't happen, you figured you'd manufacture your own war."

Keogh looked aghast at Kira. "He wants to start a *war* with the Federation? That's insane."

In a low voice, Orta said, "That's what they told us about fighting the Cardassians, Captain."

It took Keogh a moment to find his voice. "Is she right? Is this what you plan?"

"I have obtained a weapon of mass destruction, Captain. Its purpose is to destroy—not to *push*." Again, the smile. "Except, perhaps in a metaphoric sense."

"So that nonsense about the prophecy was—?" He let the question hang.

Orta shrugged. "A way to convince you that my motives were pure. I knew that Nerys was one of the devout, so she was likely to believe me—and having the lieutenant support me was an added bonus."

Kira laughed again. "You're an idiot, Orta. You always were."

"You think so?"

Keogh said, "You damn well sound like one. Do you have any idea of the consequences of your actions? Shifting the moon's orbit was deadly enough—to actually destroy it will cause uncounted changes to Bajor, none of them for the good. The planet's entire ecosystem will be thrown off-kilter. The planet's barely recovered from the Cardassians. You won't be starting a war, you'll be committing genocide."

"Bajor survived Cardassia's occupation, Captain," Orta said. "I survived having my throat cut. For that matter, Qo'noS survived Praxis's destruction eighty years ago. Your attempts to frighten me are fruitless."

"Don't even bother, Captain," Kira said with disdain. "You'll never convince him. Go ahead, Orta, fire up your weapon. See how much good it does you."

"Major!" Keogh barked. He couldn't believe this fool woman was *encouraging* him to destroy the moon. *And why the hell is the* Odyssey *just sitting out there? Why don't they* do *something?*

"Computer," Orta said slowly. "Fire the weapon."

Then the entire runabout went dark.

"All systems on the *Rio Grande* read dead, Joe," Gonzalez said from the ops station. Then she turned and looked at the command center, smiling. To Sisko, she said, "Looks like you were right, Commander."

Jason Talltree couldn't believe his eyes. He had been sure that the whole thing was a waste of time, that they needed to disable the runabout and then beam a team on board. He didn't expect some Bajoran Militia thug like this Odo person to understand the niceties of Starfleet General Orders, but Talltree knew that they had to *capture* the artifact. And that was what he'd do.

He had not expected things to be this easy.

Turning to Odo, he asked, "What, exactly, just happened?"

The Deep Space 9 security chief turned his disquieting gaze upon his *Odyssey* counterpart. The constable had what looked like an unfinished face—it was almost uncomfortable to look at. Odo was a shapechanger, and Talltree wondered if he chose so bizarre a facial structure as an intimidation tactic. If so, he found himself admiring it.

"Security, Mr. Talltree," Odo said. "I don't know if you've kept abreast of activity in the DMZ, but the ranks of the Maquis are growing—particularly with

Starfleet personnel," he added with a disdain that Talltree thought unfair. "On DS9, we devised a security protocol to keep our runabouts out of Maquis hands. The security codes were changed, but the old codes still work—after a fashion. A coded message is sent, embedded in the power signature so the saboteurs won't detect it. Normal operation of the runabout proceeds unless the library computer is accessed, or any defensive systems or the warp drive go online."

Talltree nodded. "If they do, the runabout shuts down."

O'Brien put in, "The idea's to keep any thieves in place until a Starfleet vessel can pick 'em up."

"An excellent idea," Shabalala said, "but you might want to inform people of this next time." The commander spoke in his usual pleasant tone, but Talltree noticed an undercurrent of annoyance.

"We, uh, only just installed it in the *Rio Grande*," O'Brien added hesitantly.

Sisko smiled toothily. "We hadn't tested it—until now, that is."

"Fair enough," Shabalala said, though he did not return Sisko's smile. "Mr. Talltree, get over there with a security team—Mr. O'Brien, go with them."

Talltree nodded. "Yes, sir." They still didn't know the captain's fate, after all—this wasn't over yet. He tapped his combadge as he headed toward the turbolift, O'Brien walking alongside. "DeNoux, Hyzy, report to Transporter Room 3."

He then heard Odo's voice from behind him. "Request permission to accompany the away team, Commander."

After only a brief hesitation, the first officer said, "Granted." Talltree almost objected, then decided he'd rather have Odo's experience with Bajoran terrorists on his side.

The trio rode the turbolift in silence. Within minutes, they arrived at the transporter room, DeNoux and Hyzy already present and armed and ready to go. The transporter chief handed out wristlamps, since there'd be no other light source until O'Brien could re-establish power on the runabout.

"On stun, people," Talltree said as the five of them stepped on the platform. As his people and O'Brien set their phasers, Talltree noted that Odo wasn't armed. To the transporter chief, he said, "Get the constable a phaser."

"No need. I don't carry weapons."

"You don't?" The idea of a security chief who went about unarmed was incomprehensible to Talltree.

"Trust me," O'Brien said with a smile, "he doesn't need one."

Shrugging, Talltree said, "Suit yourself."

"I always do," Odo muttered.

"Energize."

Although he had anticipated having to adjust from the brightness of the *Odyssey* transporter room to the darkness of the runabout, it still took Talltree's eyes several seconds to adjust. Those seconds were, he knew, crucial given that they had no idea what to expect. Even with the runabout powered down, the artifact was interfering with sensors. They still only knew

for sure that Lieutenant Dax and three other humanoids were on the runabout.

It quickly became apparent that none of them were in the fore compartment, where they had beamed in.

"What the hell is that?" O'Brien asked.

Talltree followed the path of O'Brien's wristlamp to one of the side consoles. Talltree wasn't completely familiar with runabout design, but he was fairly certain that a small black box attached to one of the consoles wasn't standard.

"That's probably the artifact," he said. "I assume you want to disconnect it?"

"Definitely," O'Brien said emphatically.

Smiling, Talltree said, "Get to work, then. De-Noux, stay with him. The rest of you, let's check the aft—"

The security chief's instructions were interrupted by a grunt of pain from the aft compartment.

"That sounded like Major Kira," Odo said.

He had no idea how Odo could tell that from a muffled grunt, but Talltree wasn't about to argue, either. "C'mon," he said, and dashed toward the aft compartment, Odo and Hyzy right behind him.

Orta had not screamed when he watched his foster parents eliminated by Cardassian soldiers. He had not screamed when he was tortured on Cardassia. After that Obsidian Order agent cut his vocal cords, he couldn't scream.

But when the *Rio Grande* went dark, mutilated throat notwithstanding, Orta screamed.

This can't be. It was all in my grasp. It can't *go wrong now!*

"It's over, Orta," came the hated voice of Kira Nerys.

Orta blinked several times, trying to clear his vision, to adjust to the darkness that the runabout had been plunged into. *What could've gone wrong?*

He reached out with his mind to the glorious weapon that had made all this possible. *Why have you betrayed me?*

Before he could get an answer, a fist collided with his jaw.

As he fell to the deck, he instinctively kicked with his left leg, and felt its impact against something soft. A female voice let out an "Oof!" in response.

"Damn you!" Orta said. Somehow he just knew the woman who attacked was Kira. The Trill didn't have the skill to untie Orta's knots. "You have ruined everything! You have betrayed Bajor!"

"I'm trying to *help* Bajor—help our people," Kira said, sounding winded.

Orta clambered to his feet. "Then you'll die for Bajor," he said, running for the sound of her voice.

To his surprise, he was tackled from behind. "Not today," Kira said.

As he and Kira fell to the deck once again, Orta cursed himself. Kira had deliberately spoken and then moved so he would go for the sound of her voice. He had then fallen for a similar trick—she had jumped him after locating him via his voice.

They rolled on the floor for a moment. Orta tried to

land a punch, but failed. Kira, though, got a grip on his vocoder and ripped it off.

The pain was unimaginable. A small control would release the mechanism's grip on the mutilated skin of his throat, but by simply tearing it off, Kira also removed a layer of that skin.

Again, Orta screamed, but this time no sounds emerged. Blood seeped from his neck.

You betrayed me! his mind screamed, both at Kira and at the device that should have been his salvation. *You're like all of them! Mother, Father, Syed, Starfleet, the provisional government—betrayers, all of them!*

In his now-silent rage, Orta kicked at Kira, who was knocked off him by the impact.

The device's oh-so-compelling voice sounded in his head. *I can still give you what you want. You must kill this woman. It is the only way to accomplish your goals.*

Orta stood, put a hand to his throat to stanch the bleeding, and smiled. He would kill Kira as he killed Syed and the Obsidian Order agent and so many others who stood in his way. They all had to die.

It was the only way . . .

As Jason Talltree entered the aft compartment, he shined his wristlamp inside. The first thing the beam fell on was the pleasant sight of Keogh in a chair. His arms were behind his back in such a way to lead Talltree to believe that they were tied together—but that was comparatively irrelevant. Talltree was just relieved to see him alive. "Captain!"

"Over there, Lieutenant!" Keogh said, just as Odo bellowed, "Kira!"

Before Talltree could turn to see what they were talking about, his attention was drawn by the thud of bodies crashing into a bulkhead. He shined his lamp to see two Bajoran figures struggling—one in a red Militia uniform, the other in civilian clothes.

"Stand back!" Odo said as Talltree drew his phaser. Talltree planned to just stun both of them and sort it out later, but Odo seemed to have something else in mind.

The shapeshifter made as if to throw something with his right hand, though that hand was empty. As his arm came around, it seemed to dissolve—in fact, it turned into a golden liquid and extended toward the scuffle. By the time the protrusion reached the non-Militia Bajoran, it looked like a length of rope tied into a lasso, which wrapped around the Bajoran's left wrist.

Odo pulled his now-rather-long right arm downward, which yanked the Bajoran off the Militia woman. Talltree then fired his phaser at the Bajoran. He missed, as the Bajoran ducked—

—right into Hyzy's shot, which stunned him.

Just as the Bajoran—whom Talltree realized had to be Orta—hit the deck, the lights came on. "Thank you, Chief," Talltree muttered.

Talltree looked around and saw the Bajoran Militia woman—Major Kira—rubbing her wrists, and Keogh and Dax tied to chairs.

"Hyzy, take care of the captain and lieutenant, will you?" Talltree said.

Keogh was looking at Kira. "Major, how the hell did you get out of your bonds?"

She smiled. "Orta always tied a lousy knot."

Talltree wasn't sure, but he thought that Keogh got an unusually sour look—even by his high standards—at that.

"It's good to see you alive, sir," Talltree said to Keogh as Hyzy finished undoing his hands.

The security guard moved over to Dax while Keogh undid his feet. "It's good to be seen," the captain said. He undid his feet and stood up. "Major, would you mind explaining to me what the hell happened here?"

Before the major could reply, Shabalala's voice sounded over the comm channel. *Shabalala to runabout. Report.*

Keogh went to an intercom on the wall and tapped it, his own combadge having gone missing. "This is Keogh. We're all fine, Commander."

"It's very *good to hear your voice, Captain. We were worried that you'd been killed."*

"Negative, Commander, though Mr. Rodzinski wasn't so lucky. I'll tell you all about it back on the ship. Tell the transporter room to prepare to beam us over."

Chapter Fourteen

A FEW HOURS LATER, Keogh stood with Sisko, Kira, and Shabalala in the shuttlebay of the *Odyssey,* the *Galaxy*-class ship's own shuttles having been moved out of the way to make room for the larger *Rio Grande.* O'Brien had gone over the runabout to make sure that no further damage was done by Orta before being done in by the counter-Maquis program. The *Odyssey* was preparing to return its various passengers (including Orta, presently in the brig) and the artifact to Deep Space 9, then proceed to its scheduled patrol of the Cardassian border.

"I wish you'd told me about that little security program of yours, Commander," Keogh said to Sisko, who held the Malkus Artifact, which had been recovered from the runabout. With a glance at Kira, he added, "It might've saved us all some embarrassment."

"I *am* sorry about that, Captain," Kira said, "but I couldn't very well let Orta run loose, and I couldn't clue you in without cluing him in as well."

"Besides," Sisko added with a smile, "I'm sure your bickering helped keep Orta in the dark—so to speak."

Keogh grudgingly conceded the point. "Perhaps."

"I'm sorry for the loss of your chief engineer, Captain," Sisko said in a quiet voice.

"Thank you," Keogh said formally. He had already gone through the onerous duty of informing Rodzinski's wife and daughter—both also Starfleet officers, presently serving on Starbase 12 and the *U.S.S. Sugihara,* respectively—of his death, and the bittersweet duty of promoting Kovac to lieutenant commander and giving him Rodzinski's job.

"In any case," Kira said, turning toward the runabout hatch, "I need to get back down to the moon and try to put things back together. I'll see you all back at the station in a few days."

Just as she started to walk toward the runabout, the artifact in Sisko's hands—which had been glowing a slightly greenish color—suddenly let loose a quick burst of bright green light.

Then the glow disappeared altogether.

Keogh reacted immediately. "Computer, scan the shuttlebay for any anomalous readings and report."

After a moment, the computer's voice calmly said, *"No anomalous readings."*

Shabalala had taken out a tricorder. "The artifact is reading as inert, sir."

Sisko shrugged. "Probably shutting down now that it isn't being used."

"I hope that's all it is," Keogh said.

After Kira departed, Sisko, Keogh, and Shabalala went to a turbolift.

"Would you like to join us in Ten-Forward, Commander?" Keogh asked Sisko.

"Perhaps later. I want to bring this thing to Dax for safekeeping. Someone from the Rector Institute on Earth is scheduled to come to DS9 and pick it up in a month or two."

"I have to say, Commander," Keogh said to Sisko, "I was less than impressed with your science officer. She's a bit on the—well, arrogant side. I know she's a friend of yours, but—"

"It's hard not to be arrogant after three hundred years, Captain." With a small half-smile, he said, "I'll be sure to let her know of your assessment."

Keogh and Shabalala got off at deck ten, leaving Sisko to continue up to deck eight and the guest quarters.

After a hesitation, Shabalala said, "It's—good to have you back, Captain. You had us worried."

"I'm afraid the center chair is going to remain occupied for a while longer, Commander," Keogh said, allowing himself a smile.

"And you're welcome to it, sir. I'm just glad I didn't have to lose another CO so soon."

Keogh frowned. He knew the details of Patnira, of course, but had thought Shabalala recovered from it. Now, he wasn't so sure.

As they entered Ten-Forward, he said, "I suppose you'll want that Saurian swill of yours."

"Actually, sir—I think I'd like to share a whiskey with you." Shabalala broke into a grin.

After blinking in surprise, Keogh then smiled again. "I'd be honored, Commander."

Within minutes, they sat at a table, sharing a bottle of syntheholic whiskey.

"Captain, if you don't mind my asking—what happened?"

Again, Keogh frowned. "What happened when, Commander?"

"What happened to make you decide not to let anyone call you 'Deco'—or even say the name in your presence?"

Instinctively, Keogh started to shoot down this line of conversation, but then stopped. *If he isn't as over Patnira as I thought, maybe my story will do him some good.*

"You may find this hard to believe, Commander, but I had something of a reputation in my younger days as a—well, a wild man."

"Really, sir?" Shabalala said, sounding surprised.

"Yes, really. I insisted everyone call me 'Deco,' and that informality stretched to—many things. Mostly to women and drinking." He held up his glass. "Usually liquids far stronger and less syntheholic than this." He took a sip from the glass, then set it down, staring at the amber liquid, imagining he could see his younger self. "One night, twenty-two years ago, I was security chief on the *Lexington*. I indulged in both pursuits rather aggressively the night before we arrived at Al-

tair VI to attend a presidential inauguration. It was someone's birthday—I don't even remember whose—and we had a very loud party on the rec deck. I woke up the next morning with an overloading phaser in my head, cotton in my mouth, and a sudden desire to not attend a dull ceremony. So I changed the duty roster—perfectly within my rights as chief of security, mind you—and stayed on the ship at tactical while sending down my assistant chief in my place, along with the five other security guards that had been requested to attend the inauguration."

Shabalala gave Keogh a look. "Wait a moment—twenty-two years ago? Wasn't that when—"

Keogh nodded. "The coup, yes. All five of my people down there died when the *an-Jirok* attacked—including Ensign Manojlovich, who should've been safe back on the bridge. But, because I was young and stupid, he died."

Shabalala took a sip of his whiskey, then gave Keogh as serious a look as the captain had ever seen from his first officer. "Sir, you can't blame yourself for that. Every two years since the founding of the Federation, Starfleet has sent three ships to attend the inauguration at Altair VI. The only time they didn't was during the time the *an-Jirok* ruled, and that only lasted three years. Starship crews live in dread of getting the assignment. There was no reason for you to attend as chief of security for an event that had, until that point, had the same level of security concerns as walking to the bridge from your quarters."

"That's not the point," Keogh said angrily. "I *was*

going to attend, and the only reason I didn't was because I thought a party was more important than being ready to do my duty."

"Maybe." Shabalala hesitated, then put a hand on Keogh's shoulder—a familiar gesture that surprised Keogh, and angered him slightly. "And certainly you're not going to change your ways now. But you still can't blame yourself. Every day, I think about what happened on Patnira. Every time I close my eyes, I see the horrendous *thing* that Captain Simon became. Every time I'm in a quiet room, I can hear her voice begging me to kill her. And yet, no matter how much that day haunts me—I don't regret what I did. It needed to be done, I did it, and if I had to go through it again, the only thing I'd do differently is that I wouldn't have hesitated before firing the phaser. Life is far too short to waste on might-have-beens, Captain."

Keogh then heard a sound he hadn't heard in quite some time: his own laughter.

Several heads in Ten-Forward turned in surprise, as their captain laughing was a unique experience.

Shabalala himself was grinning. "I hadn't realized that what I said was so amusing, Captain."

"It's not that, Commander, it's just—one of the reasons why I told you about the *Lexington* was that I wasn't sure if *you* had gotten over what happened on Patnira. Looks like I was the one who needed the therapy."

"Well, if I were you, sir, I wouldn't go signing up for sessions with Counselor Zumsteg *just* yet." Another

hesitation. "But I'm glad we had this conversation, nonetheless."

"As am I, Commander, as am I." Keogh raised his glass. "To many years of serving together, Mr. Shabalala."

"I'll definitely drink to that—Deco."

Over the years, the Klingon Empire had built a large base on Narendra III. Proximate to both the Romulan and Federation borders, it was the site of a treacherous attack by several Romulan warbirds. Only the sacrifice of the Starship Enterprise, *commanded by Rachel Garrett, enabled the base to survive.*

In all the years that the Klingons occupied the world, though, they never managed to disturb—or even discover the existence of—the metal box with the green glow.

The screams had continued all but uninterrupted. Their only pause had been a century ago. There had been hope then, but it was fleeting.

That hope revived itself with a second chance for freedom. This one was much better suited to the task—he was a fighter, a warrior, and, best of all, a warmonger. The signs were much better than they were the last time.

But he too failed.

And the screaming continued.

However, now four more minds joined the three that had imprinted themselves before.

Now there were potentially seven to fight on behalf of Malkus the Mighty.

When the time was right . . .

SECOND INTERLUDE

Station log, Deep Space 9, Commander Benjamin Sisko, Stardate 47999.2

The *U.S.S. Yorktown* and *Venture* are on their way to the station, the former to transport the survivors of the *Odyssey,* the latter to begin the cleanup work on what's left of the New Bajor colony.

To say that the existence of this new threat from the Gamma Quadrant troubles me would be a vast understatement. The Dominion has made its hostile intentions clear with the destruction of New Bajor and the kamikaze attack on the *Odyssey* that resulted in the deaths of Captain Keogh, Commander Shabalala, and the rest of their fine crew. Captain Keogh at least offloaded all civilians and nonessential personnel before their mission to the Gamma Quadrant, but that

still leaves the death toll in the hundreds of thousands—merely to prove a point.

I have requested that Starfleet assign additional forces to the station. The deaths of the good people of New Bajor and the valiant crew of the *Odyssey* will *not* go unavenged.

TO BE CONTINUED . . .

About the Author

After a trip to the galactic barrier in order to save an injured Klingon, **Keith R.A. DeCandido** found himself seventy thousand light years from home and put on trial for the crimes of humanity, after which he was declared Emissary. Eventually, after switching bodies with an insane woman, he was able to become one with the Prophets, stop an anti-time wave from destroying the multiverse, and get home with the help of his alternate future self. These days, he writes in a variety of milieus. His other *Star Trek* work ranges from the *Star Trek: The Next Generation* novel *Diplomatic Implausibility* to the *Star Trek: Deep Space Nine* novel *Demons of Air and Darkness* to the *TNG* comic book *Perchance to Dream* to the *DS9* novella "Horn and Ivory." In addition, he is the co-developer of the *Star*

ABOUT THE AUTHOR

Trek: S.C.E. line, and has written or cowritten over half a dozen eBooks in this series of adventures featuring the Starfleet Corps of Engineers (some reprinted in the volumes *Have Tech, Will Travel* and *Miracle Workers* in early 2002). The year 2003 will see the debut of *Star Trek: I.K.S. Gorkon,* books starring Captain Klag and his Klingon crew—the first time Pocket Books has published a series focusing on *Star Trek*'s most popular aliens. To say Keith is thrilled at this opportunity would be the gravest of understatements. He will also be contributing to the *Star Trek: The Lost Era* miniseries.

In addition to all this *Trek*kin', Keith has written novels, short stories, and nonfiction books in the worlds of *Andromeda, Buffy the Vampire Slayer, Doctor Who, Farscape, Magic: The Gathering,* Marvel Comics, and *Xena.* He is also the editor of the upcoming anthology of original science fiction *Imaginings.*

Keith lives in the Bronx with his girlfriend and the world's two goofiest cats. Find out even more useless information about him at his official Web site at the easy-to-remember URL of DeCandido.net, or just e-mail him directly at keith@decandido.net and tell him *just* what you think of him.

Look for STAR TREK fiction from Pocket Books

Star Trek®

Star Trek®: The Original Series

Star Trek: The Next Generation®

Novelizations

Enterprise®

Star Trek®: New Frontier

#5 • *Martyr* • Peter David

#6 • *Fire on High* • Peter David

The Captain's Table #5 • *Once Burned* • Peter David

Double Helix #5 • *Double or Nothing* • Peter David

#7 • *The Quiet Place* • Peter David

#8 • *Dark Allies* • Peter David

#9-11 • *Excalibur* • Peter David

   #9 • *Requiem*

  #10 • *Renaissance*

  #11 • *Restoration*

Gateways #6: *Cold Wars* • Peter David

Gateways #7: *What Lay Beyond:* "Death After Life" • Peter David

#12 • *Being Human* • Peter David

Star Trek®: Stargazer

The Valiant • Michael Jan Friedman

Double Helix #6: *The First Virtue* • Michael Jan Friedman and Christie
  Golden

Gauntlet • Michael Jan Friedman

Progenitor • Michael Jan Friedman

Star Trek®: Starfleet Corps of Engineers (eBooks)

Have Tech, Will Travel (paperback) • various

   #1 • *The Belly of the Beast* • Dean Wesley Smith

   #2 • *Fatal Error* • Keith R.A. DeCandido

   #3 • *Hard Crash* • Christie Golden

   #4 • *Interphase, Book One* • Dayton Ward & Kevin Dilmore

Miracle Workers (paperback) • various

   #5 • *Interphase, Book Two* • Dayton Ward & Kevin Dilmore

   #6 • *Cold Fusion* • Keith R.A. DeCandido

   #7 • *Invincible, Book One* • David Mack & Keith R.A. DeCandido

   #8 • *Invincible, Book Two* • David Mack & Keith R.A. DeCandido

  #9 • *The Riddled Post* • Aaron Rosenberg

#10 • *Gateways Epilogue: Here There Be Monsters* • Keith
   R.A. DeCandido

#11 • *Ambush* • Dave Galanter & Greg Brodeur

#12 • *Some Assembly Required* • Scott Ciencin & Dan Jolley

#13 • *No Surrender* • Jeff Mariotte

#14 • *Caveat Emptor* • Ian Edginton & Michael Collins

#15 • *Past Life* • Robert Greenberger

#16 • *Oaths* • Glenn Hauman

#17 • *Foundations, Book One* • Dayton Ward & Kevin Dilmore

#18 • *Foundations, Book Two* • Dayton Ward & Kevin Dilmore

Star Trek®: Gateways

#1 • *One Small Step* • Susan Wright
#2 • *Chainmail* • Diane Carey
#3 • *Doors Into Chaos* • Robert Greenberger
#4 • *Demons of Air and Darkness* • Keith R.A. DeCandido
#5 • *No Man's Land* • Christie Golden
#6 • *Cold Wars* • Peter David
#7 • *What Lay Beyond* • various
Epilogue: Here There Be Monsters • Keith R.A. DeCandido

Star Trek®: The Badlands

#1 • Susan Wright
#2 • Susan Wright

Star Trek®: Dark Passions

#1 • Susan Wright
#2 • Susan Wright

Star Trek®: The Brave and the Bold

#1 • Keith R.A. DeCandido
#2 • Keith R.A. DeCandido

Star Trek® Omnibus Editions

Invasion! Omnibus • various
Day of Honor Omnibus • various
The Captain's Table Omnibus • various
Star Trek: Odyssey • William Shatner with Judith and Garfield Reeves-Stevens
Millennium Omnibus • Judith and Garfield Reeves-Stevens
Starfleet: Year One • Michael Jan Friedman

Other Star Trek® Fiction

Legends of the Ferengi • Ira Steven Behr & Robert Hewitt Wolfe
Strange New Worlds, vol. I, II, III, IV, and V • Dean Wesley Smith, ed.
Adventures in Time and Space • Mary P. Taylor, ed.
Captain Proton: Defender of the Earth • D.W. "Prof" Smith
New Worlds, New Civilizations • Michael Jan Friedman
The Lives of Dax • Marco Palmieri, ed.
The Klingon Hamlet • Wil'yam Shex'pir
Enterprise Logs • Carol Greenburg, ed.
The Amazing Stories • various